A REALM OF HEALING

A REALM OF HEALING

C.A. CAMPBELL

A Realm of Healing
By C.A. Campbell

First Paperback Edition March 2026

Copyright © 2026 by Chris A Campbell
All rights reserved. No part of this book may be reproduced, stored in a retrieval system, or transmitted in any form or by any means—electronic, mechanical, photocopying, recording, or otherwise—without prior written permission from the publisher or author, except in the case of brief quotations embodied in critical reviews and certain other noncommercial uses permitted by copyright law.

This is a work of fiction. Names, characters, places, and incidents are either products of the author's imagination or used fictitiously. Any resemblance to actual persons, living or dead, or actual events is purely coincidental.

Cover Design and Interior Formatting by Chris Campbell
Illustrations by Amelie Butkus
Map Design by Melissa Nash

Printed in the United States of America

Harcover ISBN: 979-8-9925607-3-2
Paperback ISBN: 979-8-9925607-4-9
Ebook ISBN: 979-8-9925607-1-8

https://cacampbellbooks.com/

For my parents.

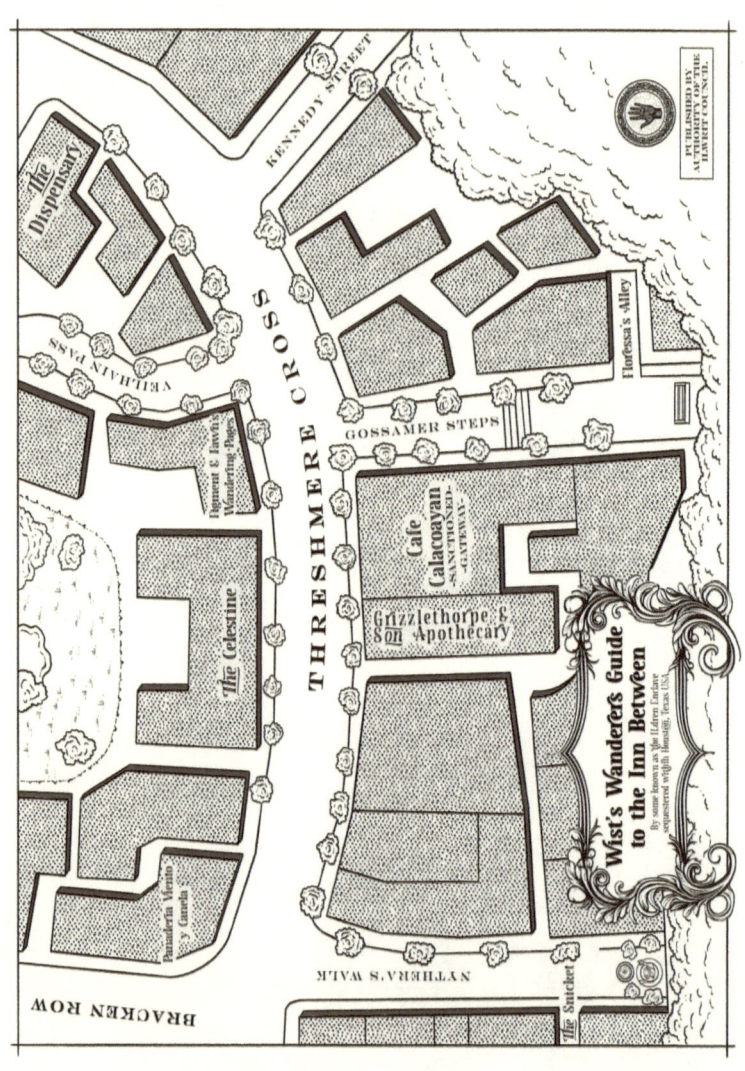

"It's no use going back to yesterday, because I was a different person then."

– *Alice in Wonderland*

CHAPTER 1

"It's all your fault…"

Lizzy Luna just lost a patient, but all she could focus on was the final words of her best friend, Vic. He died in her arms a week ago today. While everyone else on the team took a moment to honor the patient's passing, Lizzy stared blankly through the body. She didn't see a heart attack victim; she saw Vic's body sprawled on the pavement. His limbs splayed unnaturally while blood pooled around his head. She had accidentally put her hand in it. The thick stickiness stuck in her head, and she rubbed her fingers together. She could still feel it.

"Liz," a voice from the present whispered. She blinked herself free from the replay. Her fellow nurse, Galloway, who had come up with her through school, leaned in close to get her attention. Galloway briefly dated Vic and was crushed by his loss, but didn't see his head smash against the pavement.

"Liz!" Galloway said again, her eyes darting over Lizzy's face, sharp with alarm. Galloway's perpetually dimpled cheeks looked out of place anytime she wasn't smiling. Like now. Usually, all they did was laugh, even during the hard times, but this was different. Over the past week, Lizzy had hidden behind quips, but the mistakes, missed steps, and delayed reactions were a giveaway. She was struggling.

"Yeah, sorry, must have been off in Wonderland again," Lizzy said, forcing a silly face as she prepped the bay for the next patient. Galloway scoffed and snatched something from Lizzy's hand. She motioned for Lizzy to wait until the other nurse left the bay and then pulled her to the corner.

"What is this?" Galloway said, holding up a syringe of Epinephrine.

"Shit! Shit. Did I not administer it?" Lizzy said. Panic tightened her chest. "Was this my fault?" She looked at the patient on the gurney, and a crushing weight made her shoulders ache. Since she was a little girl, caring for her stuffed animals, her lifelong dream had been to heal others. Vic's too, though she often wondered if he was only doing it to follow her. The thought that she may have just cost someone their life sent her mind spiraling.

"Shhh," Galloway said, checking to make sure no one heard them. "No, you weren't supposed to. I administered it already. But I think you were also going to." Lizzy stared at her blankly as the panic subsided. She still messed up, though.

"I don't even remember picking it up from the crash cart," Lizzy said, frowning. She couldn't even remember reaching for the syringe. There was nothing. The last thing she did remember was hearing the patient's name: Victor.

"Maybe you should think about taking some time off," Galloway said, quickly slipping the syringe back into its package on the cart.

"I don't want to," Lizzy said. It had been a week, but she was sure that throwing herself into work would fill the hollow void consuming her. Staying home would only push her into it. "I need to keep busy. You're sure this wasn't my fault, though?"

"No, of course not," Galloway said, putting a hand on Lizzy's arm. She gave it a loving squeeze. "This was just one of those things. He couldn't be saved. But you need to get your head in the game. You're gonna lose that nurse of the month award." Lizzy mustered up another fake smile. She was getting better at it. "Come on," Galloway continued, winking at her. "I'm sure the rest of the morning'll be fine. Besides, the new guy was trying to check out your butt again."

"It's so big, I don't know how he could miss it," Lizzy said, snickering at her friend's attempt to distract her.

"Right?" Galloway responded and smacked Lizzy's butt cheek as they went back to work.

Lizzy was walking out of the room when a stabbing pain cut through the inside of her forearm. She examined it but only found the scar left by a dog attack when she was young. She had trauma about that day for years. The large black dog haunted her nightmares and lurked in reality's shadows. She would gladly welcome it back if it would replace the image of his head on the sidewalk. She would endure anything if it could bring him back.

She massaged the pair of faint circular marks until the pain subsided. It wasn't unusual for her to feel it during times of high stress. More often than not, when there was a difficult case like the one they just lost.

"Luna!" Dr. Lewis said, motioning for her to join him at the nurses' station, freshly painted gray. He was their new attending and didn't appreciate the nurses' playfulness. Or anything for that matter.

"Girl," Galloway said under breath. "Don't let him blame you. Game face."

Lizzy nodded and did her best Galloway impression. Though another doctor called Dr. Lewis away for a quick consult, his stiff pointer finger commanded her to wait. She imagined replying with her middle finger, but instead stared at the framed Nurse of the Month photo.

It *was* her. The girl in the picture, with wavy brown hair, freckles, thick eyebrows, and a carefree grin, felt like a stranger to her now. That girl was living the dream—loving life, helping others. Her world now was fracturing, and she couldn't hold the pieces together.

Lizzy really just needed to sit down and talk to Tita, her 115-year-old great-grandmother. She was the only other person in her life she could really open up to. And she always had all the answers. She wanted to go by and see her earlier in the week, but Tita had been under the weather. They could have at least talked on the phone, except that Tita was deaf.

"Luna!" Lewis said, towering over her. He wasn't a very tall man, but her height made it easy for him to feel like it. Lizzy took a step back. "This *zoning out*. This is exactly what I'm talking about."

"Sorry, boss," Lizzy said, rubbing her eyes. "It's been a long night."

"No, that's not what this is. You want to tell me what's going on?"

"I'm just struggling a little, my best friend was hurt…,"

"Dr. Vasquez?" Dr. Lewis said, nodding. "No neurological

response, right?"

"Yeah, I mean, the family is still holding out for hope."

"You too?"

"No, I mean I know the chances are pretty much zero—

"No, they *are* zero," Dr. Lewis said, glancing at a notification on his matte black smartwatch. "Don't get your hopes up believing otherwise. That'll only make it worse for you. You have an advantage that others don't. Science. Use it. Don't get caught up in all the woo-woo."

"I get it. I know. It's just hit me hard—I'm good though."

"Look, I'm not heartless," Dr. Lewis said, trying to soften his voice. It only came out stiff and rehearsed. "The loss of a friend is tough, but we have a job to do. We can't have mistakes like what occurred in there."

Lizzy stared at him, wide-eyed.

"Yeah," Dr. Lewis said, with parental glare. "You thought I didn't see you prep a second dose of epi? You know what would have happened, right?"

"I'm…," Lizzy started to apologize, but caught Galloway watching. "I didn't give it to him. I picked it up before I saw Nurse Galloway administer it, but I never used it. It didn't affect the outcome. There's nothing we could have done to save him."

"I concur, but what if it had. Hesitation and 'zoning out' are unacceptable. I can't have this in my ER."

"I won't let it happen again," Lizzy said, setting her face with determination. He studied her. They had only worked together for a month, but even he could see the change.

"You can finish out your shift," Dr. Lewis pronounced, checking his smartwatch again. "But then you're taking a week off."

"No, but…," Lizzy said, but Dr. Lewis had already walked off, shaking his head.

"And Galloway will take the lead the rest of the morning," he called over his shoulder.

Lizzy balled her hands into fists and closed her eyes. This time, Vic's intubated body was there to greet her. She could see his mom and sisters gathered around his bed, praying for a miracle. Guilt dug its fingers into her head and twisted her stomach.

The family had invited her to stay, but she had seen the accusations in their eyes. Galloway assured her they weren't real. It didn't matter one way or the other—Lizzy knew it was her fault. He had said so. She should have been paying attention. Or she should have been the one hit by the car. Not him.

"Maybe this is a good thing," Galloway said, suddenly beside her.

Lizzy jumped, wiping at her eyes. She'd lost time again. The same thoughts and images she tried to contain, saving them for moments when she could breathe, had broken loose and flooded her.

"No, we're short-handed," Lizzy said. "And now, because of me, we are going to be shorter."

"Even with you, we're short," Galloway said with a raised eyebrow and measuring her height with her hand. Lizzy mimicked a sneer in response and then laughed.

"Maybe you're right," Lizzy said. "It's a good thing. I probably just need to get some sleep. I think that's all it is, really."

"You do look tired. Take something and then sleep for a few days. If you want, I'll come by and check on you."

"I'm just worried about missing…it. You and I both know he's gone, but his family is holding out hope. I don't know how long that'll last, though. What if they decide to let him go tonight, or tomorrow? I have to stay awake in case they text. I should be there."

"Listen, I still have his sister's number. I'll text her and ask her to let me know when they decide. I'll come get you when they do."

Lizzy nodded at Galloway, but before she could thank her, the ambulance bay doors slammed open.

"Vitals: BP 92 over 58...," the EMS driver said, as they wheeled a patient in. He continued in a drone of information, but Lizzy recognized the skinny young Indian woman who accompanied the patient. She had gotten to know Mykayla, who was deaf like Tita, over the past year. She moved in as one of Tita's tenants in the halfway home she ran out of her own house. Mykayla looked through the bangs of her short boy cut to lock eyes with her, and Lizzy knew. Tita was on that gurney.

Lizzy rushed to meet them as they slid into the trauma bay.

"I don't know what happened," Mykayla signed to Lizzy. "I found her lying on the kitchen floor." Lizzy ignored her and went to Tita's side.

"Ma'am, can you hear us?" Galloway said as she worked on the IV drip.

"She's deaf," Lizzy said as she shook Tita's shoulder and then massaged her chest. Galloway paused and looked at her patient. It dawned on her as Dr. Lewis entered the bay.

"Your great-grandmother?"

"Yes," Lizzy said, chin trembling.

"Luna, outside," Dr. Lewis said in a stern tone.

"No, but it's..." Lizzy blurted out, tears already choking her.

"Listen to me, I've already sidelined you," Dr Lewis said,

stepping between Tita and Lizzy. "This being your relative is even more reason why you need to leave—now!"

Lizzy stumbled back, only able to focus on Tita. She was her favorite. More so than even her dad. Lizzy's childhood summers were spent either at Tita's creaky house just outside of downtown Houston or at the cozy beach house in Galveston. Either way, the days were full of adventures, exploring the world around them, and the evenings full of fairy tales. Tita elaborately signed the most amazing stories of a far-off land and its fantastic inhabitants.

"Once in a realm of wonder…," Tita always started the story. Lizzy would lose track of the story, distracted by her great-grandmother's expressions. She could have sworn Tita had experienced every castle and mountain. She knew she had to have met the fairy queen and the great magicians of the Realm. Tita would clap her hands to get Lizzy to refocus on them. Afterwards, she would pull out a weathered leather sketchbook she claimed was 100 years old, and illustrate a scene from the story. The book was full of the people, places, and wondrous items that appeared in those stories.

"Get her out of here," Dr. Lewis barked. She barely felt Galloway's hands on her shoulders as she guided her out. She was so numb. So helpless. It didn't feel right.

"It's gonna be ok, Lizzy," Galloway assured her, as she lowered her into a chair. "I got you."

Lizzy nodded absently as Galloway slipped in and closed the curtain. Lizzy gripped the arms of the chair; the world was collapsing in on her. Her heart pounded, and her breath came in short gasps. A tap on her shoulder made Lizzy jump, breaking the free fall into a panic attack.

"Will she be ok?" Mykayla signed. Lizzy might have been

able to hold it together, but even Mykayla, usually tough, looked like the world was ending. Lizzy sputtered and buried her face in her hands. Mykayla awkwardly patted Lizzy's head.

Lizzy jerked her head up at the clatter of a metal tray, gasps, and a hiss from the other side of the curtain.

"Shit!"

"Look out!"

"Where the hell did that come from?"

Lizzy spun in the chair in time to see a snow white cat shoot out from between the curtains. In an instant, it leaped into her lap and pushed up against her chest.

"Fresita!" Lizzy exclaimed as she hugged the cat. The white cat, with a pink heart-shaped tuft of fur on her chest, was a new "friend" of Tita's. She had told Lizzy that Fresita had wandered into her life one afternoon. Tita and Fresita had been best friends ever since. Lizzy expected a garnish to the story, like a princess trapped in a cat's body, a dog cursed to be a cat, or a spirit cast out of the Fae realm, but there was nothing more. It had seemed odd to Lizzy at the time, but she assumed later that Tita would have the time to make up a story about her. Now she was afraid there were no more stories to look forward to.

Fresita rubbed her head against Lizzy and then suddenly turned towards Mykayla, as if realizing she was there for the first time. Fresita hissed. She leapt from Lizzy's lap and sprinted out of the ambulance bay doors as the paramedics left.

"Shit. I'll get her," Mykayla signed. "You'll be OK by yourself?"

Lizzy nodded, and Mykayla gave her an awkward chuck on the shoulder before jogging after the cat.

Lizzy sat heavily in the chair and hugged herself. A cold

settled into the ER, feeling unnatural. She hugged herself tighter, but could not warm up. She tried to recall the last story Tita had shared with her. She couldn't remember anything.

"Hey," Galloway said, startling Lizzy back to reality. Her friend knelt beside her and squeezed her knee.

"Is she...," Lizzy struggled to speak.

"They got her back," Galloway said. Lizzy tried to jump up, but Galloway held on to her knee. "Wait."

"What is it?"

"Sweetheart, listen," Galloway said in the tone she reserved for delivering bad news to patients. She pushed some papers into Lizzy's hands and looked up at her with teary eyes. "She had this in her hands, but we didn't look at them until we revived her."

"I need to see her," Lizzy insisted.

"Lizzy, it's a DNR."

"What?" Lizzy was astounded. Her attention turned fully to Galloway. Tita had never mentioned having one; in fact, she had a defiant aversion to any legal or rule-setting paperwork. She grabbed the papers out of Galloway's hands, trying to read through teary eyes, but Tita's signature was unmistakable. It was true.

"I don't understand," Lizzy mumbled.

"I'm so sorry," Galloway said. "She's asking for you."

Lizzy dropped the paperwork and jumped up. She stepped in as the others filed out of the room. Tita was slightly propped up in the hospital bed, a thin grey blanket swallowing her body, and doing her best to smile at Lizzy.

"Oh, Tita," Lizzy said, smiling, though the tears streaming down her cheeks betrayed her.

Tita shook her head and weakly tried to sign.

"Don't, it's ok," Lizzy insisted, taking Tita's timeworn hand into hers. She had always been warm, never frail. Now she was cold and weak. "Save your strength. We're going to get you into a room and make you all better."

Tita responded with a firm shake of her head. She nodded to one of the DNR papers that had slid under the curtain when Lizzy dropped them.

"Why?" Lizzy pleaded with her.

"It's time," Tita signed slowly.

"No," Lizzy said, tears rolling down her face. "No, I need you. The women in your house need you."

"It's theirs now," Tita responded with a smile. "They need it more than me." She closed her eyes and seemed to be gathering her strength to continue. "And soon you will have what you need."

"No, I don't. I need you. What am I going to do without your stories? Your drawings?"

"Sweetest cupcake, they were never just stories. They were real. History. Lessons for your future."

"Well, I didn't learn anything," Lizzy signed, sobbing through a brave smile. "So you are going to have to stick around to keep teaching me."

"My time is over. It's time to start your own adventure. Realize your dream."

"I already am," Lizzy said, rubbing tears from her face. "I've got this amazing job. I've got you. That's all I need."

"There's more for you. You will heal the world."

"Maybe someday, but for now, let's start with you. Please?"

Tita responded with a slow shake of her head. She closed her eyes and gathered a last bit of strength before she continued.

"Do something for me."

"Anything."

"Take my Dragonscale ring," Tita said, barely able to lift her hand from her side. Light glimmered on a patinaed bronze ring cast to resemble overlapping scales. Lizzy blinked through her tears and obediently slipped the ring from Tita's frail finger. "It will reveal what was hidden. Betela's Blossom will heal…"

Tita smiled, patted Lizzy's teary face, and then fell limp.

"Tita!" Lizzy said, cupping her great-grandmother's face. "Please."

Tita refocused on Lizzy and offered a sad smile. She cleared her throat and then did something Lizzy rarely heard her do. She spoke.

"Look at the end of the story," Tita said, so soft Lizzy moved her ear closer. With her final words, she closed her eyes. Her face relaxed. Her chest rose one final time, and then with a slow exhale, Tita was gone.

"NO!" Lizzy cried. "It's not the end of your story." She sobbed and buried her face in Tita's perfumed neck. She clung to her body, but it felt empty.

"Galloway!" Lizzy suddenly sat up and started chest compressions. "Get in here!"

"Lizzy, what are you doing?" Galloway exclaimed as she came into the room.

"Help me!"

"You can't do this," Galloway said. She grabbed her friend's wrist and pulled her away. "It's not what she wanted."

"She can't go," Lizzy cried.

"I'm so sorry, honey," Galloway said, wrapping her arms around her friend. Lizzy clung to her, fighting the urge to fall apart. If she started crying now, she wouldn't be able to stop, so she turned it into anger. She shoved Galloway back and spun around to look through the medicines on a nearby tray. "Hey, Lizzy, please stop."

"Where's the epi?" Lizzy said, trying to read the bottles through teary eyes.

"Babe, she's gone. Let her rest."

"I should have been in here," Lizzy shouted and tossed the bottles to the floor. "Why did I just stand there?"

"It was a shock," Galloway assured her. "You didn't do anything wrong. Besides, I was here with her. We did everything we could. We got her back."

Lizzy shook her head. The pressure of the loss surged in her temples and stabbed like knives through her wrists. Galloway went to her and wrapped her arms around her again. Lizzy relaxed for a moment into the embrace, then stiffened.

"Let me sit with her for a little bit," Lizzy said, pulling away.

"Of course," Galloway said, but gave her a doubtful look. She pulled a chair to the bedside and sat Lizzy in it. "I'll be right outside." Galloway slipped outside but stood just outside the curtain, turning her ear so she could hear.

Lizzy caressed Tita's arm as she fidgeted with the Dragonscale ring in her hand. She had always admired the beautiful ring. Tita once told the story of a Goblin prince who gifted it to her. He had wanted to impress her with a gift of great power. He claimed it could hide or reveal great secrets. Lizzy had always wanted to try it on, but Tita said it was important that she never take it off.

Lizzy kissed Tita's hand gently; her skin was still warm and smelled of sweet pine. She rested her cheek against her belly. Lizzy couldn't imagine a world without her in it. The urge to sob threatened to overwhelm her, but she couldn't let herself start now. She'd be useless, and she still needed to make sure Tita's body was taken care of.

She had closed her eyes to imagine Tita's smile, but a bright light pushed at the darkness of her eyelids. Lizzy jerked up, ready to murder with her eyes, but she was still alone. She rested her head back on Tita's stomach and closed her eyes again. The light returned, but before she could respond, she winced at a sharp jab in her arm.

She sucked in a sharp breath and stared wide-eyed at her arm. There was a tattoo on her arm, and it was glowing.

A soft purple illuminated a beautiful yet strange design on the inside of her forearm. It was not there before. She had never even had a tattoo, despite her sister's relentless begging when they were younger. The image stretched from her wrist nearly to the crook of her elbow: a flowing, Nouveau-esque pattern framing a pair of exotic flowers. They looked alien, wrong, and yet something in her chest tightened with recognition.

Her breath came fast. *There is no way it was real.*

She reached over and touched it. Waves of pain dug into her skin, cresting in a blinding rush, of the memory of a dog's teeth sinking into the same spot decades earlier.

Lizzy cried out and instinctively looked to Tita for help. Her body was so still. She whimpered as she looked back at her arm. The glow and pain faded, leaving behind only the tattoo-like image on her skin. It was a shade lighter than her light brown skin and almost looked as if Lizzy had fallen asleep on rumpled sheets. Cautious of triggering the pain again, she lightly brushed her finger across the image. Slightly raised lines formed the flowers and vines that grew from them. It was real.

Will we match?

Lizzy suddenly remembered asking the morning after the dog attack. Tita always had a rectangular scar on the inside of her arm that she claimed was from a misadventure early in her life. Lizzy reached for her great-grandmother's arm but paused. It was as if she were taking an afternoon nap, and little Lizzy was afraid to wake her. Gingerly, Lizzy turned Tita's arm over and laid her own alongside it. Lizzy gasped.

They were remarkably similar. The size and shape were the same; even the curly scarred ripples in Tita's skin seemed to mirror the flow of the vines and leaves now adorning Lizzy's arm. She shook her head, struggling to make sense of it. There were medical…scientific explanations for a scar to reactivate, but not like this. Nothing could explain the vivid design or the glow. It was unearthly. Magical.

The design glowed brighter, and Lizzy felt warmth seep from her arm to Tita's. She jerked back and watched as the Tita's scar smoothed out and faded until only unadulterated skin remained. Lizzy shot up, sending her chair scooting noisily across the floor. Galloway rushed in.

"Liz, are you ok?" Galloway said, studying Lizzy's bewildered expression. "Lizzy?"

"Look at this," Lizzy said, shoving her arm in front of the nurse.

The nurse stared at her arm for a moment, then back at Lizzy, confused.

"The tattoo…it just appeared there…and then her scar disappeared." Lizzy shook her arm in front of the nurse and then pointed to where Tita's scar had been. "I've never had a tattoo before. You know that, right? You've seen my arm before."

"I don't understand," Galloway said with a concerned look.

"What tattoo?" She looked again at Lizzy's arm and then spotted the faint marks from the dog attack. "Do you mean those? The scar from the dog attack?"

"What? No! The design…the flowers."

Lizzy shoved her arm closer to her friend's face and scowled at her.

"Dr. Lewis, could you come in here…," Galloway said, turning her head slightly to one side but keeping worried eyes on Lizzy. "Lizzy, sit down. You're going to need some time to recover; you're just overwhelmed right now."

"What are you talking about?" Lizzy said as Galloway tried to make her sit back down. "Being overwhelmed doesn't make this happen. Tattoos just don't magically appear, Galloway. What's happening to me?"

"I just think that emotional trauma can affect us in strange ways. You know, make us see things that aren't there."

"What are you saying?" Lizzy stammered. "You can't see it? How can you not see it? Here touch it." Lizzy grabbed her friend's fingers and ran them over her arm. Galloway shook her head apologetically.

"Yeah…," Dr. Lewis mumbled as he stuck his head in.

"Give me a second," Galloway said softly to Lizzy and stepped outside with Dr. Lewis. Lizzy could hear them whispering, but was intently focused on her arm. She ran her fingers over the design, feeling the raised lines, and shook her head.

"It can't be a hallucination," Lizzy mumbled. She was still staring at her arm when Dr. Lewis came in. He gave her a sympathetic glance and then examined her arm, turning it over and running his hand over the skin. It was apparent he couldn't find any trace of the supposed tattoo.

"Hey, so why don't we get you some water and maybe a snack. Something sweet?" Dr. Lewis looked over his shoulder at Galloway, and she nodded.

Lizzy started to protest, but thought better of it.

"I'm sorry," Lizzy said, trying to prevent Psyche from being called. She just wanted to go home. Figure things out. "I'm really overwhelmed."

"It's ok to feel that way," Dr Lewis said. He never spoke this way to them, only to a patient's family members. It felt so fake. "You're just going to need some time, ok?"

Lizzy nodded, still focused on her arm. He placed his hand over the area, and she refocused on him.

"Is there someone we can call to come be with you?"

"No, I'll let my family know soon," Lizzy said.

Galloway returned with a paper cup of water and a small cake. The doctor motioned for her to leave the trauma bay, and Lizzy gave Tita's arm a final touch before following her co-workers to the break room.

Lizzy guzzled the water and took a bite of the cake.

"What can I do for you?" Galloway said. Lizzy shrugged in response.

"We got a couple of buses coming in," another nurse said, poking her head quickly.

"I've gotta go," Galloway said, trying to meet Lizzy's eyes. "Are you going to be ok?"

Lizzy nodded. Galloway gave her arm a quick squeeze before hurrying out.

Lizzy was alone. She felt empty but not numb. A noisy buzz filled her ears and prickled across her skin. There was one part of her that was calm now—her arm. She stared at it. The tattoo didn't make sense. It looked as if it had always been there, always a part of her. She rested her palm on it; warmth radiated into her hand. It comforted her, reaching into her soul like a hug from Tita.

Her eyes burned. She closed them, reluctantly, afraid of what memory would be waiting for her. Instead, there was only a peaceful darkness. Outside of the break room, a chaotic buzz of urgent voices relayed information and treatments. For years, this had been her home, her dream. Now it was stained by two nightmares. It hurt to be here.

Long ago, she had sat in this very break room after her first shift, exhausted but happy. She had finally made it. Back then, she had closed her eyes and thought back to the moment she decided to *heal the world*. It was on the beach with Vic and her sister.

The ocean breeze whipped away the afternoon heat as the Gulf swallowed up the sun. Dry grass whipped around them atop the small dune they sat on. A few years earlier, the dog attack had taken place not far from there, but she felt safe with Ashley and Vic by her side.

They chatted about the day. It was almost tragic. They had been eating chips on the beach when Vic began choking. A passing nurse jumped into action and saved his life. As kids do, he laughed it off, but it stuck with Lizzy.

"I've decided I'm going to be a nurse," Lizzy declared, as she examined a blue pebble they found in the sand.

"That's a whole lot of studying," her sister had scoffed. "You hate reading."

"Yeah, but think of all the people I could save just like that nurse

today. I'll study a lot and then save everybody! The whole world!" Lizzy beamed proudly.

"You can't just do that," Ashley said, staring at the ocean. Lizzy bent one corner of her mouth in an annoyed frown at Ashley's lack of enthusiasm.

"I'll help you study," Vic assured Lizzy.

"What? You're going to be a nurse too?" Ashley said, mocking him. "Nurse Vic! Nurse Vic."

"He can be a nurse if he wants," Lizzy said, passing the pebble to Vic. "Or even a doctor."

"Yeah," he said, passing the blue pebble back to Lizzy with a grin.

That grin. She so wanted to see it again.

She cupped the pebble in the palm of her hand. Tita had once told her the faerie queen whispered to colorful stones she came across in a meadow. They became her children. Lizzy hoped if she told this one her dream, it would one day turn into a fairy and grant her wish.

"I'm going to heal the world," she whispered into it. "We are going to heal the world," Lizzy said louder this time and then leaned forward to look at her sister. "Yeah?"

"Sure," Ashley said, and shrugged.

"Yes!" Vic said excitedly and hugged Lizzy. Ashley rolled her eyes at them, but then Lizzy saw something past her. She shivered. A large black dog was watching from a nearby dune.

A rough snort brought her back to reality. She looked up and found the memory had escaped from her mind. A massive black dog, almost pony-sized, stood in the doorway watching her.

Lizzy choked on a scream as she lurched backward, crashing into a cart behind her. With glowing purple eyes, the beast remained still, hunched forward slightly, an expectant guillotine waiting to be loosed. Fresh blood splattered onto the floor, dripping from thick, curling horns that crowned its head. There was nowhere to run to.

Her arm began to burn as if someone was pressing a hot iron against it. She cradled it as the tattoo glowed again, this time brighter than before. The monster took a step towards her and crouched, as if ready to pounce. She squeezed her eyes shut.

A touch on her elbow made her slam her head back against the cabinets, scream, and instinctively swipe her hand at her attacker. She didn't remember putting the Dragonscale ring on her finger, but it was there, and it tore against flesh. Lizzy opened her eyes, but it wasn't the monster.

"Fuck!" Galloway exclaimed, cradling her face. Blood dripped from a gash across her cheek. Lizzy's shoulders ached. She couldn't take anything more.

"What happened?" Dr. Lewis demanded as she stormed in.

"I'm fine," Galloway insisted, and grabbed some gauze from the table. "It was my fault." Lizzy could only stare wide-eyed at what she had done.

"That's it," Dr. Lewis said, "You need to leave. Immediately."

"Tita—

"You'll have to have another family member make arrangements for her. We will take care of her for you, but you can not stay here. You're a time bomb just waiting to go off."

Lizzy was at her breaking point. She had to be alone. She grabbed her things and ran out of the ER, shoving past Mykayla, who had just come in the door holding Fresita.

CHAPTER 2

Lizzy slammed her apartment door shut. She pressed her back against it, straining as if she could prevent reality from overtaking her by force alone.

She banged the back of her head against the metal surface of the door a couple of times. Her mind was a mess. Numb but overwhelmed; exhausted but racing. She opened her mouth in a silent scream and pounded her fists against the door.

They're both gone!

Her legs trembled violently until they finally gave out. She slid down, crumpled onto her side, and wailed. Lizzy needed, she *needed*, at least one of them in her life. She ached to feel their embrace or hear their voice.

His grin.

She clawed at the seams of the floor, pulling until the pain in her fingers was greater than what was inside her. Even then, it was only a flickering distraction. She curled in on herself and rocked. The gouged hollow expanding inside her was unbearable, a pain deeper than anything she'd ever known.

Lizzy lay there and wept for hours. When she could form coherent thoughts again, the conclusion came quickly: Tita's death was *her* fault as well. If she had been paying attention, Vic would still be there. If she hadn't been in a daze because of him, she would have been able to help save Tita. If nothing else, she might have seen the DNR papers and trashed them before anyone else noticed.

The realization made her stomach turn. She staggered to the bathroom and vomited until she was dry heaving. Too weak to even cling to the toilet, she crawled to her bed, pulled herself onto it, and passed out.

Her dreams were of the week before, when she and Vic had raced to the side of a heart attack victim, just collapsed off the sidewalk. Like the perfect team, they worked tirelessly until they got him back. She had held her arms up in victory and taken a step back. She didn't see the car; the driver didn't see her.

He did.

He swung her towards the safety of the sidewalk, but his momentum sent him straight at the car. Lizzy had turned to scold him for yanking her around and caught the moment his head bounced with a violent jerk onto the pavement.

In the dream, her perspective shifted; now she was watching herself from afar. She tried so hard to save him. Lizzy already knew the outcome but prayed it would be different this time. She pumped his chest until her arms were trembling, breathed into his mouth until her lungs burned, and then he came back—but only partially. Unable to open his eyes and barely breathing, he mumbled. Lizzy watched her past self lean in to listen, but clamped her hands over her own ears. Even so, his blame found its way in.

"It's all your fault…"

She spent night after night stuck in the nightmare, and every morning ruminating on his words. They tortured her, and Tita's words confused her. The tattoo only made things worse. It glared at her, a sacred mystery profaned by a painful reality. She even resorted to an attempt at scrubbing it away with bleach; it only turned her skin red and itchy. It was no figment of her imagination, and it was there to stay.

For the next few weeks, though it seemed like months, she confined herself to the crushed-eggshell-colored walls of her apartment, keeping her mind occupied with trash TV or doomscrolling. She kept her tattoo covered. It drove her crazy trying to figure out how it suddenly appeared, like magic. She barely ate and most days didn't even get out of bed. Sometimes she slept all day, and other times she stayed awake all night. At night, though, she kept all the lights on. Lizzy didn't want the monster to return, even if it was just in her head.

However, she was startled by an animal. A few times, she thought she saw a white cat peeking through the sliding glass door of her balcony. She wondered if somehow it was Fresita, though she had never even been to her apartment.

As the days dragged on, Lizzy sank further into her guilt and solitude. There was no returning to her job. Even if she had wanted to, Dr. Lewis had filed a report with hospital administration. She'd have to go through weeks of counseling and review before she was even considered to be fit to return to duty. Besides, she couldn't face Galloway; she'd hurt her. What if she hurt someone else? She couldn't risk it. She didn't want to heal the world anymore.

Lizzy hadn't heard anything about a funeral or any final word regarding *him*. She scrolled through her messages, there were so many, for any concerning either of them. On her way home that morning weeks ago, she had called her mother to let her know about Tita. Lizzy's mother sounded saddened enough to be polite. When she found out, however, that she would have to handle funeral arrangements herself, she was pissed. Her mother never got along with her dad's side of the family, and with Tita, things had always been especially frigid.

She archived friends' messages and scanned through Galloway's wall of texts, forgiving her, but found nothing about *him*. Finally, she found a message from his mom asking her to visit him. They were still praying for a miracle. Guilt sat like a stone in her stomach. She couldn't bring herself to respond.

There was nothing about Tita, though, not even from her mother. Reluctantly, she called her to ask about Tita's funeral.

"Well, I didn't think anybody would come," her mother explained, very plainly. "Your sister won't be back in the states until next week, and you haven't even asked or offered to help set anything up."

"Mom," Lizzy said, frustration sharpening her tone. "Are you serious right now?"

"And just who's going to come? Tell me."

Lizzy was silent, more dumbfounded than clueless.

Impatient, her mother snapped in that tone of hers. "Hurry up."

"The women at her house would," Lizzy finally said. "They

loved her."

"Yes, yes, they've already contacted me. They didn't offer to help either."

Lizzy breathed out sharply. "It's not their responsibility, it's ours, mother."

"Exactly. *Ours.*"

Lizzy ground her teeth, trying not to blow up. Tita had done so much for her mom when her dad passed away. Tita even loaned them money months later, when her mother fell behind on the mortgage.

After a moment of Lizzy's seething, her mother cleared her throat and continued.

"Besides, it doesn't matter now anyway. I had her buried next to your father a few days ago, AND before you hang up…" Her mother paused to make sure Lizzy was still there. "Those women are having a party for her next week. I'll forward you the e-vite. I just thought you'd like to know. I'm not going but—

Lizzy hung up. She forced herself not to throw her phone against the wall and grabbed a pillow instead. She screamed into it, then threw it against the wall. She fell into her love seat, balling her hands into fists so tight they shook, and her heart pounded against her throat. She shouldn't be surprised. Her mother always found a way to get revenge against anyone she thought had wronged her. This was her final chance to get back at Tita for whatever it was she thought she was owed. It was also her way of punishing Lizzy for leaving it up to her in the first place.

Lizzy let her frustration with her mom fill her headspace only for a little while. She didn't want to give her the satisfaction of being focused on her. For a moment, Lizzy considered skipping the party, but she owed it to Tita. She would make an appearance and leave as soon as possible.

The evening of the party, Lizzy shivered outside the fence of the old sun-bleached white three-story house near the Third Ward. It was late in the year, so the weather had finally begun to cool. The smell of grilled meat hung in the air, mixing with the hum of conversation and laughing. The place looked pretty much the same as it had for Lizzy's entire life. It was a solid building, in need of a little TLC. Loose boards. Flaking paint.

Even the decent-sized yard was overgrown in places, but there was no trash, just trees. Large ancient trees, somehow always lush with leaves. Even the Texas oven of a summer never seemed to brown them. When she was little, Lizzy would climb them, forever on the hunt for fairies. Stepping through the front gate always lifted her spirits and filled her with the anxious excitement of a new adventure.

Now, Lizzy backed away from the gate, massaging a tightness building in her chest. The only stories that remained here were painful reminders. And yet with swaying strands of lights looping from the second story to the trees, the house stubbornly retained its magical aura. A breeze danced across the leaves like a soft brush sweep under a melody. Somewhere in there, it was as if she could almost catch her name being whispered by Tita.

An overzealous burst of laughter broke the spell. Lizzy turned away and walked the length of the fence, her eyes sweeping the crowd. She was surprised by the number of people here. As she understood it, only five women had been staying at Tita's house. She didn't think Tita had been out much in her final years, or that she still had so many friends. She had outlived so many by decades. The few dozen faces here were unfamiliar to Lizzy.

While some were comfortable in jeans and t-shirts, others looked as if they had dressed anticipating a state dinner.

One woman in particular caught Lizzy's eye, an effortlessly regal figure in a black flared dress. She was about Lizzy's age, yet a relaxed maturity twice her age eased her face. Her dark hair swept back and up against her head in a stately French Twist, and a dusting of freckles sprinkled across her face. Her eyes danced across her surroundings, absorbing the world with curiosity. People around her noticed her, not because she demanded it but because they couldn't look away.

As the woman waved a greeting to another visitor, a dark Dragonscale ring was visible on her finger. Lizzy looked down at her own hand, realizing she had forgotten to put Tita's on.

"Hey," Mykayla signed, appearing beside her suddenly. Lizzy jumped and then frowned.

"Shit, you scared me," Lizzy replied outloud and then repeated it in sign.

"Sorry," Mykayla said, and then paused awkwardly. Mykayla, almost always in baggy jeans and a tank top, squirmed in her freshly pressed chinos and a button-down short-sleeve shirt. "I was hoping you'd come. We weren't sure whether your mom told you. She's kind of a bitch."

"Not kind of."

Mykayla smirked, but let it fade when Lizzy didn't smile. "So…are you coming in?"

"I don't know. Maybe not."

"That's cool. I can hang out with you out here if you want," Mykayla said, and started to take a drink of the beer bottle she was holding, but paused. "Want a beer?"

"No, I'm good. I was thinking about going back home

anyway," Lizzy said. She twisted the side of her mouth up anxiously. "I thought I could do this, but I don't think I'm ready yet."

"Oh yeah," Mykayla said, nodding and trying to hide her disappointment. "I understand. Losing two people so close together is shit. It's like your whole world is put through a meat grinder."

Lizzy flashed her a comforting look. "I remember you telling me about your parents…wait, how did you know about *him*?"

"Tita told me the night before she passed. She said she was worried about you because he was your best friend."

"But I never got to tell her," Lizzy said, frowning. "I was going to come over and talk to her, but she was sick the day I called."

"I don't know how she found out, but I do know she kept an eye on you. Especially lately."

"Kept an eye on me? Like she was having me followed or what?"

"Oh, I…," Mykayla said, studying her beer bottle. "I don't know. That's just what she said. I'm sure she wanted to make sure you were safe or something."

"Safe from what?" Lizzy asked, but Mykayla only shrugged and took a long drink.

"Huh," Lizzy said, and frowned. Nothing really made sense anymore anyway, so why should this? She stared up at the attic windows. Tita had made that space her room for the last few years of her life. She claimed it felt safer to be up high, where she looked out on the world. Maybe she was just paranoid in her old age.

"Also, the fairies love high places," Tita had told her once. *"It*

makes them feel taller."

As if reading her mind, out of the corner of her eye, Lizzy thought she caught a glimpse of glittering lights zipping around the yard. She snapped her head around, but there was nothing there.

"Did you see that?" Lizzy asked.

"See what?"

"Little lights flying around the yard. They looked like... fireflies or something."

"Nope," Mykayla responded, but acted nervous again. Lizzy shrugged, deciding it was more than likely just a passing car's lights. They were quiet for a while, watching the guests, and Mykayla drank her beer.

"Did Tita say anything?" Lizzy finally said. "That morning, did she say anything to you?"

"No, when I woke up and came downstairs, she was already unconscious on the kitchen floor."

"Ok."

"Did you..." Mykayla said, hesitantly afraid to upset Lizzy. "Were you able to talk to her before she passed?"

"Yeah," Lizzy said. That morning flashed in front of her. Her stomach twisted as if someone had wrapped their hand around it. Her chest rose in quick, unfulfilling breaths. Lizzy dug her nails into the fence as she tried not to slip into a panic attack.

Seeing her discomfort, Mykayla offered her beer. Lizzy grabbed it and guzzled what was left. She hated the taste of beer. Even the fancy craft beers *he* tried to get her into one time. This time, the bitter taste served as a welcome shock, derailing the coming attack. She shivered and handed the empty bottle back to Mykayla.

"Thanks," Lizzy said.

"I'm gonna grab another one. You sure you don't want one?"

"Actually, sure I'll take one," Lizzy said. She hoped that, if nothing else, it would help her through the evening.

While Mykayla was gone, Lizzy went back to people watching and found a pair of faces she recognized. Martin and his sister Imelda. While she was here, Tita had put them in charge of running the house. They were good to the women who stayed here, but eternally suspicious of visitors, including Lizzy. Martin waved, but his sister scowled. Lizzy quickly looked away, pretending not to see either one.

She locked eyes with a gentleman in business slacks and a thin wool sweater. He was bigger than almost everyone else here. Not just tall but muscular, though with a touch of a dad bod hiding many of the muscles. He had a weather-sculpted Nordic look and striking honey-colored eyes. More than anything, however, his face held her attention. It was an easy-going, happy face. It was the kind of face *he* had. However, this man had a bold but well-groomed beard. For a moment, he acted like he was going to head over, but an equally tall blonde woman approached him, and they began talking.

Lizzy was relieved. The man looked back over to her, but Lizzy had spotted Fresita. The white cat trotted over, pounced onto the fence, and sat in front of Lizzy. She tilted her head with an analytical gaze.

"Are you the one hanging out on my balcony?" Lizzy asked. She reached out to pet her, but Fresita leaned out of reach. "I was just trying to be nice." Lizzy stuck out her tongue at the cat, who responded with an annoyed swish of her tail.

"Hey, you found the cat," Mykayla said, as she hurried back

over to Lizzy. "She keeps running away, so I gave up going after her. She always comes back anyway."

"Maybe I'm crazy, but…," Lizzy said, trying to pet Fresita again. It didn't happen. "…I think she has been showing up at my apartment."

"Could be," Mykayla said, handing Lizzy a beer. "By the way, what does her name mean?"

"Tita called her that because of the shape of her pink hair."

"A heart."

"See," Lizzy said, her mouth hinting at a long forgotten smile. "That's exactly what I told Tita, but she insisted it looked like a strawberry to her. Fresita is 'little strawberry' in Spanish, but it can also mean something like 'posh' or 'stuck up.' And I think that fits the cat perfectly." Lizzy made a face at Fresita, who turned her back to the women and began grooming herself.

Lizzy took a long drink of beer and made a surprised face. It tasted really good. Slightly sweet, like honey. She examined the bottle but found no label. She assumed it was someone's homebrew. After a few more sips, though, Lizzy felt some of her tension ease.

A barking dog somewhere in the neighborhood startled Lizzy. Suddenly, she remembered they had been talking about Tita's last words, and it finally dawned on her where she had heard them before.

"Betela's Blossom," Lizzy said suddenly, surprising Mykayla. "Have you ever heard of that?"

"I don't think so," Mykayla answered. She glanced around, as if checking to see if anybody had heard Lizzy. "What is it?"

"They were Tita's last words," Lizzy said. "I just remembered where I heard them before. When I was little, I was attacked by this gigantic dog."

"Oh shit."

"Yeah, it bit me," Lizzy said, stopping short of showing Mykayla the scar, where the tattoo had now replaced it. Instead, she only patted her sleeve. "Anyway, when I was recovering, I asked her to tell me a story about my fairy doll, Maeve. Her adventures were my favorites. Instead, she said she had a new story to tell me. It was about an Elf girl who used a magic sword to heal people. I'm pretty sure her name was Betela, but I can't really remember. I wish I had Tita's old sketchbook. She always drew pictures to go with the stories. I'm sure there'd be more about it there."

"And this was a story Tita told you?"

"Yeah, Tita told me fairy tales all the time," Lizzy replied.

"A fairy tale!" A ruddy voice exclaimed from Mykayla's side of the fence. Startled, Lizzy peered over to find a rotund, bearded man about an inch shorter than the fence. He pointed and shook his beer at Lizzy as he continued. "Betela's Blossom? No. That is history, spoken and sworn. And it is not to be taken lightly."

Lizzy wasn't sure how to respond. Mykayla, however, kicked his foot and Fresita hissed. He looked at them angrily, but his eyes widened as Mykayla mouthed something to him. To Lizzy, it looked like she said 'Dull,' but she couldn't be sure.

"Crap!" the man bellowed.

"What's wrong?" Lizzy asked.

"It's nothing," the man said, but struggled as if trying to hold back. Finally, he added, "I was cursed always to speak the truth."

"Cursed?" Lizzy said, making a face. "What do you mean?"

"A goblin witch laid a curse on me for selling her produce past its time at the Night Camp," the man blurted out all at once before clapping his hand over his mouth. He gave the women a stiff bow, then hurried to the back of the house.

"What did he say?" Lizzy asked, her mouth twisting into a frown. Her stomach twisted. Had Tita been telling others her stories? She should have made an effort to visit her more often.

"I don't know, he was blabbering too fast for me to read his lips," Mykayla said. "Probably just some weirdo Tita knew. Have another drink."

Lizzy took a sip and leaned against the fence to people-watch. While most of the guests were on the younger side, closer to her age, more than a few looked much older. Several different languages were being spoken as well, most of which she had never heard before. She so wished she could sit here with Tita and listen to her tell stories of how she met each of them. She took a longer drink.

"So, we're drinking our sorrows away now, are we?" a familiar voice chided from the shadows down the sidewalk. The figure stepped into the light, revealing a frosted blonde-haired woman with impeccable makeup. Lizzy turned and immediately hurried to her. It was her sister, Ashley.

"They're gone!" Lizzy sobbed, throwing herself into Ashley's arms.

"It's ok," Ashley cooed, hugging and rocking her sister. "I'm so sorry."

Ashley took after their mother more than Lizzy did, but was never quite as harsh. She had kept her distance from Tita but was never cold towards her. Tita, on the other hand, always seemed to regard Ashley with pity, though Lizzy never understood why.

When they were young, the sisters were thick as thieves, exploring the world together, but something changed in Ashley.

She became obsessed with school, spending all her time studying, and later moving to England to attend university. She rarely visited.

"It's my fault," Lizzy whispered her confession to Ashley.

"What do you mean?"

"I wasn't looking. The car was supposed to hit me," Lizzy sobbed. "And then I was sooo wrapped up in him that I froze up when Tita came into the ER. I couldn't save her." Lizzy clung to her sister, afraid of being swept away by her own tears.

"Everything will be ok, Lizzy," Ashley said, hugging her tighter for a moment. She flashed Mykayla a sympathetic smile. Fresita hopped down from the fence and rubbed up against Lizzy's leg, but Ashley silently shooed her away. She was more of a dog person. After letting Lizzy cry for a bit, she pushed her back, and holding her shoulders made Lizzy compose herself.

"That's enough," Ashley said firmly. "You know that isn't true. None of this is on you. It's just life."

Lizzy didn't respond, but did wipe her tears away.

Ashley continued. "It's just life, and sometimes life is very unfair. But we do our best to carry on."

Lizzy noticed they had garnered a pity-faced audience and pulled herself together. She nodded and then chuckled.

"You sound like one of those signs where you live. 'Keep calm, and carry on.'"

Ashley let out an amused laugh as she looked down at her cream-colored wool coat. Lizzy had left a trail of tears along the lapel.

Reaching into her leather purse, Ashley pulled out a handkerchief. "Oh," she said as she unfolded it. "I brought this for you. I think you should have it."

From the folds of the cloth, she drew out a silver necklace set with a blue stone—the same one they had found on the beach years ago. Lizzy's eyes filled with tears all over again.

"No… are you sure?" Lizzy asked. Ashley stared at the necklace for a long moment. "He gave that to you."

"Yes," Ashley said softly. "But it has more meaning to you."

She stepped behind Lizzy and fastened the necklace around her neck. Lizzy touched the stone and took a steadying breath.

"Thank you, sister," she said, pulling Ashley into a hug.

Ashley laughed and gently pulled away, trying unsuccessfully to wipe Lizzy's tears on her coat.

Noticing Mykayla couldn't take her eyes off her sister, Lizzy waved her hand in front of her face.

"Stop gawking," Lizzy signed and then continued out loud. "Ashley, this is my friend Mykayla." Ashley offered a large smile as she extended her hand.

"It's a pleasure to meet you," Ashley said, as Mykayla readily took her hand and gave it a quick shake.

"The pleasure's mine," Mykayla said, her voice low and resonant, unmistakably feminine. Like Tita, she had lost her hearing as she grew older, so she could still speak aloud when she wanted to. Lizzy loved to hear it; its low richness was unique.

"Well," Ashley said, fluttering her eyelids at Mykayla. "If you'll excuse me, I'm going to clean your friend's snot off the front of my outfit." Ashley flashed Lizzy a faux mean look. "I'll be right back."

"She's freakin' gorgeous, Liz," Mykayla signed, watching Ashley stride towards the house.

"Uh-huh," Lizzy replied, with a laugh. She sniffled a few times and tried to clean the mess she had made of herself. She felt a little better, but at the same time, guilty. It wasn't right for her to be having fun after everything that had happened. She took another drink of her beer.

Mykayla motioned for her to come inside the fence, and Lizzy finally relented. They sat in a pair of metal lawn chairs in front of a small bonfire that Lizzy stared into. A couple of the women who lived in the house came over and offered their sympathies before drifting off again. The alcohol was cushioning Lizzy's system nicely. The guilt didn't feel quite as harsh.

"I'll have to come over and go through her stuff sometime," Lizzy said, turning in her chair to look up at the attic windows. "She kept everything. The sketchbook has to be up there somewhere."

"Yeah, but you'll have to take a few days off work, there's A LOT."

Lizzy shrugged. She already knew she wasn't going back to work, so that wouldn't be a problem. She suddenly wondered what she was going to do instead. She had at least a month or two of vacation time and sick leave, and after that, a good chunk of savings.

"Maybe I could be a coffee influencer," Lizzy mumbled, fiddling with the blue stone around her neck.

"A what?" Mykayla signed, motioning towards her mouth. Lizzy hadn't realized she had said anything out loud.

"Sorry, I was just trying to figure out what I'm going to do now. I was thinking how much I love coffee. I could make videos about coffee shops and roasteries. I'm not as *gorgeous* as my sister, but I'm pretty funny."

"But you're a nurse," Mykayla said, confused.

"Nah, not anymore. That part of my life is gone," Lizzy said, and then in a loud voice added: "The dream is over!" She took another long drink.

"Maybe you could just take a break for a while? Tita always said you were an amazing nurse. She said you had a big future ahead of you."

"Ha! If I'm such a good nurse, then why did I let her die?"

"Come on, she was over a hundred years old. It was just her time."

"Don't say that!" Lizzy shouted, bolting up from her chair and throwing her bottle in her friend's direction. The bottle thudded onto the ground, but Mykayla flinched as a bit of the beer splashed on her arm. "The next person that says that it 'was just her time' is going to…I'm going to…" Lizzy stopped.

Mykayla and the others nearby looked horrified.

"Liz…," Ashley said, as she hurried back from the house. "Come on, let's not make a scene." She tried to guide her back into the chair, but Lizzy jerked her arm away.

"Get off of me," Lizzy demanded. She looked at the group of people nearby staring at them. Their looks quickly melted into pity, making Lizzy even angrier.

"What are all of y'all even doing here? Did you even know Tita? Did she ever tell you stories or draw you pictures? No! She was my great-grandmother, not yours!" Lizzy kicked over her chair and then stormed off to the back of the house.

The backyard had the same string of lights running overhead, but the grass was a little wilder, so there were fewer guests. Further away from the house, a small clearing had been mowed down, and in it sat a shiny cherry red motorcycle with parts scattered around it. Mykayla repaired bikes for a living. Her own, a ratty brown Indian chief, leaned against the house. Tita had given it to keep if she could get it running. She swears she used to ride it everywhere.

Lizzy saw a stump; she hadn't even realized there had been a tree there, and plopped down beside it. The stump leaned to one side, revealing it wasn't a stump at all but the 'weirdo' from before. He looked at Lizzy wide-eyed.

"Shit, sorry, I thought you were something else," Lizzy said. The man nodded and tried to get up to leave, but Lizzy tugged on his arm. "Please don't go. I miss my great-grandmother."

"Oh," the man said and then gave her a warm smile. "You're Jules' family."

"Who?"

"Jules?" the man said. He looked genuinely confused. "This was her house."

"Her name was Tita. Well…at least to my family it was. It's from Julita," Lizzy rambled and then paused. "Oh! Julita…Jules. Got it."

The man chuckled and nodded.

"Yes, I'm sure that's what it was. Most of us knew her as Jules. Small in stature, she was great in spirit, and she lived a good life."

"Yep, I know," Lizzy nodded. "She told *me* the stories. Fairy tales to me, but maybe not to you. Hey, what's your name anyway?"

"Gairloch, but my friends just call me Gair."

"Ok, Gary it is," Lizzy said, clinking her bottle to his before taking another swig. "I'm Elizabeth, but my friends call me Lizzy. I had this one friend, my best friend…but he died. My fault. And when we were kids, he called me Liz-ard. Get it? Lizzy…Lizard? It was a joke between us. Between friends."

"And how many of those do you think your bones can still

carry?" he asked, pointing at her beer, amused.

"The drink?" Lizzy said, staring at the bottle. A warm, airy feeling completely masked the guilt now. "I don't know. Three?"

"Tread lightly. Honey mead holds old strength, and it does not spare the inexperienced."

"Oh, I'm definitely inexperienced. In-ex-perienced." Lizzy repeated herself a few times. The words sounded funny, and her tongue was numb. She suddenly remembered what he said before and leaned closer to him. "Your curse. You have to ALWAYS tell the truth?"

"Er...well, yes," Gairloch said, starting to stand up.

"Wait!" Lizzy demanded, with a tight squeeze to his arm.

"I really couldn't."

"Of course you can. My Tita would have wanted you to. Do it for her. For Jules."

Gairloch relented and settled back in. Lizzy smiled triumphantly and patted his arm.

"Thanks, you're the best, Gary."

"It won't matter much, I reckon," Gairloch said. "With that much honey mead in you, the words we've shared will likely drift off before dawn."

"Maybe," Lizzy said, putting her arm around his shoulder. "But I tell you what I remember now. You said Betela's Blossom wasn't a fairy tale."

"That I did."

"I only ever heard it as a story, but you claim it's not. Tell me what you know."

"It's a story for sure. Everything becomes a story once the sun sets on it," Gairloch said, and paused to look at Lizzy. She stared back, making her eyes exaggeratedly wide so he would be sure she was paying attention. He chuckled and continued. "This one took place many sunsets ago. There was a plague that swept across the once great race of the elves. A small elvish girl discovered a Bright Sword with healing magic. She used it to heal her people and became known as Lady Betela."

Lizzy narrowed her eyes. The story sounded so familiar.

"Wow...," Lizzy hummed and then snorted. "You're really not a great storyteller." Gairloch chuckled and took a long drink from his bottle. "So, what about Betela's Blossom? What is that?"

"It's a necklace, wrought from a shard of the sword," he said. "From what I've heard, the piece remembers the whole. Carry it long enough, and it will draw you to the blade. The sword itself was lost to time."

"Huh." Lizzy glanced up, but the stars had begun a slow, drunken spin. She closed her eyes, steadying herself before the nausea could catch up. "And with the sword... you could cure diseases?"

"It can heal anything. At least, that is what I was told."

Lizzy opened her eyes. "Anything?"

He hesitated. "I cannot say for certain. But... nearly anything."

Lizzy swallowed, the shape of a thought taking hold. "How severe an injury could it repair?"

"I'm sorry, I haven't a clue," Gairloch chuckled. "But I do know it is powerful. *Very* powerful."

"So, how do I find this blossom necklace thing?"

Gairloch shook his head slowly.

"People far smarter than me have spent lifetimes searching for it. I would not even know where to tell you to begin."

"But you have to," Lizzy said, her voice breaking as she began to cry. "You have to tell the truth, remember? And I have to heal the world. I have to fix what I've done because it's because of me that they're gone. I have to bring them back. I can't live without them." She fell into sobs and buried her face in her knees.

"Easy now," Gairloch murmured, patting her back. "I've no more truth to give you than that. It's old elven knowledge; few remain to remember it. Still, Café Calacoayan is a fair place to begin. Last I heard, they even keep a replica of what you're chasing."

"café Cala-what?" Lizzy said, popping back up, her face blotched and tear-streaked.

"Calacoayn."

"Where is that at?"

"I'm sorry, not even the curse can make me go against the rules of the Realms. If I had an invitation to give, I would gladly help you out."

"What does that even mean? How am I supposed to find this café?

Gairloch shook his head sadly and stood up.

"No!" Lizzy exclaimed, slammed her head onto her knees again, and cried.

"Ok, ok, listen…," Gairloch fidgeted with his hand a moment before he continued. "I can not believe I'm doing this."

"Please help me, Gary," Lizzy said, giving him the saddest eyes she could muster. It wasn't hard.

"The most I can tell you is to start looking in downtown Houston, just outside of Market Square Park. Now, you'll have to excuse me. I really have to go before I sink myself into any more trouble."

Gairloch turned and left, leaving Lizzy clueless. Downtown

was big. She let her head fall on her knees again. She felt horrible. The alcohol had numbed her guilt, but deepened the emptiness she felt inside. On top of everything else, the world began to spin and tumble.

She wiped her face on her sleeve and lay back in the tall grass, the blades prickling her cheeks as she stared at the stars. She thought of praying to them, of asking a magic sword to save her, but the sky spun too fast to focus on.

She closed her eyes and slipped into unconsciousness.

CHAPTER 3

An annoying sliver of sunlight landing on Lizzy's face woke her up the next morning. She sat up on her elbows and squinted. She was in her bed, wearing the same clothes as the evening before, but someone had covered her with a blanket. Tita had given her the multi-colored patchwork blanket a few years ago. She said it was made by a woman who lived in a village hidden deep within Central Park. It was so downy-soft, but Lizzy was careful about using it. She wanted it to last forever.

She remembered the party; how did she not have a hangover? In fact, she was surprised at how good she felt. She had slept the entire night through without waking up with 3 AM anxiety or enduring the usual nightmares. It was like waking up and breathing clearly after weeks of a chest cold. The only thing that bothered her was the warmth radiating from her new tattoo. She ignored it.

Lizzy squirmed; there was something under the small of her back. Twisted in the sheets, she found the Dragonscale ring and slipped it on.

She was startled to find Fresita sitting on her nightstand, bathing herself. She assumed Mykayla brought her and Fresita home after the party—her sister would never touch a cat. Lizzy flinched at how she had treated her friend the night before. Lizzy stared at Fresita, who blinked at her in silent judgment.

"I was a butt last night, huh?"

Fresita placed a paw on a plastic grocery bag sitting in front of her. Lizzy took it and blinked away the morning crud as she read the note attached to it.

"Sorry about last night. I hope this is what you were looking for. Myk."

Lizzy felt guilty but put the note aside and peered into the bag. Inside was a worn leather book. Excited, she shoved herself upright so suddenly that it startled Fresita, almost causing her to fall off the nightstand. Lizzy ignored her annoyed hiss and threw aside the bag as she fumbled with the leather cord that held the book shut. She threw it open and found Tita's drawings. It was the fairy tale sketchbook.

Tears filled Lizzy's eyes as she ran her finger across the textured off-white pages. Tita started it in her twenties, but even after so many years, it wasn't brittle. Lizzy brought the book close to her face and inhaled. The aroma of her perfume clung to the pages. Lizzy beamed.

Fresita pounced onto the bed beside Lizzy and nuzzled the book.

"You miss her, too?" Lizzy said, trying to hug the white cat. Fresita squirmed free of her arms but stayed beside her. "Ok, ok, I get it. You're not that kind of cat. Wanna see her drawings? They're really amazing."

Lizzy flipped through the thick pages, making sure Fresita could see too, and found all her favorite drawings. As a child, Lizzy was sure Tita was the greatest artist, but now, as an adult, she could appreciate how talented she truly was. Even quick sketches were far beyond anything Lizzy could produce. She marveled at Tita's wild imagination.

She paused at a self-portrait she either didn't remember or had never seen before. In fact, Lizzy couldn't get past the feeling that the sketchbook was much bigger, fuller than she remembered it being. She hoped that Tita had added more over the years.

Lizzy studied the portrait; a much younger version of Tita stared back at her. She looked to be in her mid-twenties, sporting a confident expression and a perplexing *Mona Lisa* smile. There was something so familiar about her. Her dad really didn't look like her, but maybe—

Lizzy grabbed her phone, turned on the front-facing camera, but immediately looked away. She barely recognized herself. She mustered up a half smile to match the sketch and looked again. The similarity was striking. The hair was different, and Tita did not have freckles, but otherwise they could have almost been twins. She admired the drawing for a while before flipping through more pages.

"She was so creative," Lizzy said to Fresita, who followed along with each page turn. "She told me stories about the pictures she had already drawn and created new drawings after she told me a new one. But they weren't the usual fantasy stories you've heard before. Let me see if I can find one that I remember." Lizzy flipped through the pages, remembering pieces of stories until she came across a fairy wearing a tubular glittery dress and a matching cloche. Lizzy almost grinned, but it felt wrong. The lithe creature struck a cute pose, with one leg kicked back, and blew a kiss. Fresita plopped a paw on the corner of the page, preventing Lizzy from turning to the next one.

"Maeve, the Flapper Fairy. She was my favorite," Lizzy said. Fresita stared at her intently.

Lizzy smoothed down the page and stared at the ceiling for a moment, searching for the memory of the story. Just as the Fresita turned to leave, Lizzy cleared her throat and began.

"There was once, in a realm of wonder," Lizzy said, and then stopped to look over at Fresita, who met her glance. "That's how Tita used to start the stories. You know, like 'once upon a time?'" Fresita seemed uninterested and looked back at the drawing before Lizzy finished explaining.

"Anyways, there was this unstoppable adventurous fairy. Though all of the Fae tended to be mischievous and bold as younglings, Maeve was the very most. What made things worse was that she didn't grow out of it. Even after five hundred years of childhood! When it came time for her to join their society, she was more interested in adventure and the human world."

Lizzy paused as memories of Tita weaving the story for her tugged at her grief. She cleared her throat and continued. "Her friends pleaded with her, and her elders scolded her. It didn't stop her, though, and she continued to visit the physical realms often. She loved clothes. She would study all the latest fashions and design her own outfits, with dreams of one day opening a clothing store for other fairies and magic creatures. When she was not studying fashion trends, she would meddle in the lives of humans in our world—"

Fresita stood up straight and twitched her whiskers as she glared at Lizzy. Lizzy looked at the cat for a moment, wondering

Maeve

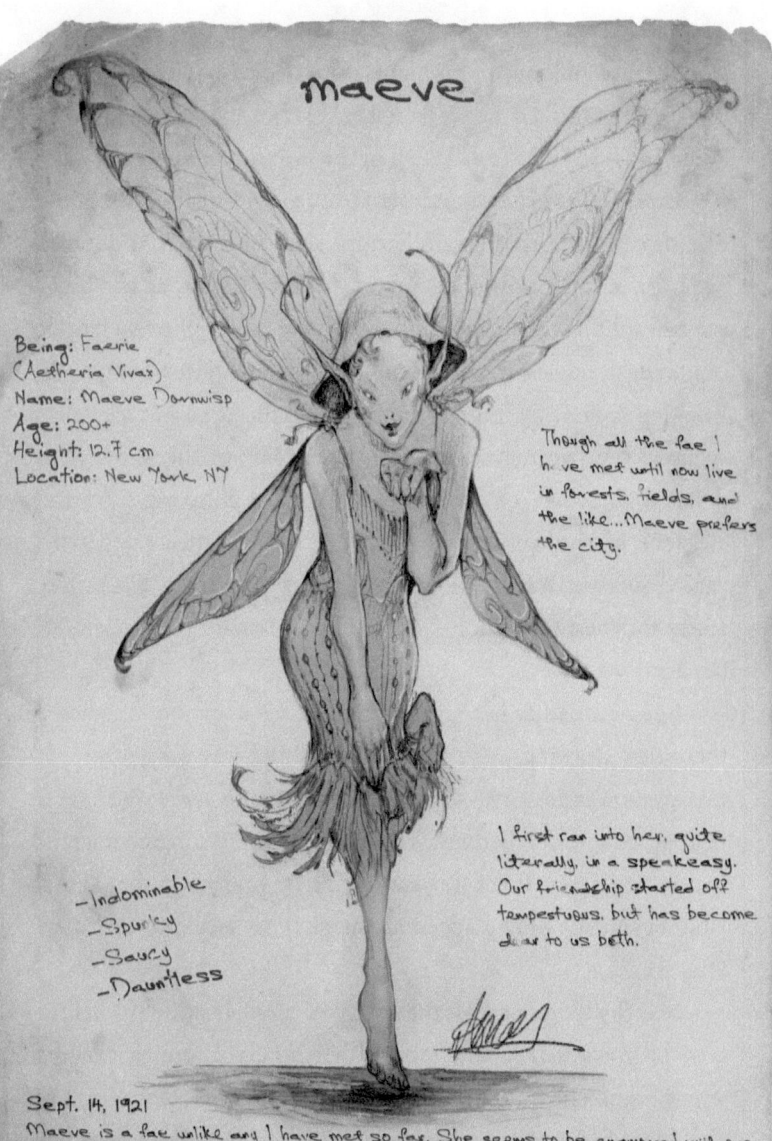

Being: Faerie
(Aetheria Vivax)
Name: Maeve Dawnwisp
Age: 200+
Height: 12.7 cm
Location: New York, NY

Though all the fae I have met until now live in forests, fields, and the like... Maeve prefers the city.

I first ran into her, quite literally, in a speakeasy. Our friendship started off tempestuous, but has become dear to us both.

- Indominable
- Spunky
- Saucy
- Dauntless

Sept. 14, 1921

Maeve is a fae unlike any I have met so far. She seems to be enamored with our world... it's fashion above all else. She dreams of one day running her own boutique and creating her own line of clothes for her kind. Though I have little interest in fashion trends, we actually have a lot in common. The words I use above to describe her have also been attributed to myself on more than one occasion.

what was going through her head, and then continued. "She would cause all kinds of problems until one day—,"

Fresita whisked her tail in Lizzy's face and prowled away. "Fine, it doesn't matter, that's all of the story I remember anyway."

Lizzy rolled her eyes and went back to investigating the book. She turned the pages carefully until she came across a double-page spread of a cloven mountain. It was massive, as if a great axe had split it wide open. In the valley created by the two halves, hundreds of houses rested among the branches of towering trees. Looking over it all, a great castle was built atop a bridge that spanned the two halves. Inset on either side of the pages were detailed drawings of the different homes. Tita captured the elegance of the wooden houses, their surfaces decorated with carved swirling leaves, vines, and flowers. Similar to her tattoo. Lizzy frowned but ignored the pull to compare the designs to her arm.

She returned to her investigation of the book; not only were there new drawings, but Tita's handwriting was everywhere. It was even on pages Lizzy was sure didn't have them before. Like a field notebook, detailed notes pointed out interesting characters, names, and facts. There was so much new to explore that, like a child again, she only glanced at the pictures as she turned page after page.

She finally paused on the image of a tall, beatific woman in a wispy gown. Lizzy remembered her beauty. Faint, cicada-like wings framed downy chiffon-colored hair that cascaded onto her shoulders. She was caught in the middle of a hearty laugh, as her delicate hand touched her chest. Underneath, carefully scribed letters read "Grace of the Fae Realm, Life-Giver, and Protector, Lady Floressa, The Faerie Queene."

Lizzy was about to recount the queen's story to Fresita, whether she wanted to listen or not, when she squinted and leaned close to the image. There was a faint mark on the queen's forehead; a leafy heart tattoo that almost looked like the front of a crown. She couldn't remember whether she had seen it before, but now it was obvious to her.

Lizzy was happy to be back in all these stories. She thought maybe she could hide here for a while and forget about the world. But she needed coffee.

For Lizzy, coffee was a necessity that she clung to. She wasn't an all-day drinker, but she made sure to have at least one good cup every day. Her friends lovingly called her 'our little coffee snob.' Since she began her self-imposed confinement, she had been making pour-overs, but today she was out of coffee beans. She had her usual spots she would have gone to before, but she couldn't spend the morning accepting people's condolences. She just wanted peace and coffee. She started searching online for a good coffee shop nearby, but remembered the strange conversation with Gairloch.

"Café Calacoayan," Lizzy said out loud, wondering if the place was even real. Fresita stood up and headed to the door as if she were ready to go as well. "Oh, do you think you are going with me?" Fresita sat by the door and waited patiently. "You're probably better off staying at home. I have no idea where I'm going."

For a brief moment, she was excited about heading out to the coffee shop until she instinctively picked up her phone. Before, she never once went without inviting Vic and vice versa. There were times when one or both were busy with work or school or had a significant other and couldn't go, but they always asked.

Her heart sank, and her legs felt weak. She leaned against the doorway to her closet and contemplated not going. However, the story of the magic healing sword tugged at her mind. She didn't understand why she even considered believing it, but something deep inside gave her a small flicker of hope.

She stood up straight and forced herself to go. She slipped into a pair of comfy jeans and a zip-up hoodie and tried to slip out the door without letting Fresita escape. She thought she was successful, but when she turned around, Fresita was innocently sitting in the corridor.

"Escape artist," Lizzy said, as she headed downstairs to catch the Metrorail.

Lizzy and Fresita journeyed to the downtown area Gairloch had suggested. The morning air hung gray and chilly, a silver weight bearing down on the city and on Lizzy's mood. The park took up an entire city block, boxed in by restaurants and bars that wouldn't really wake up for hours. As usual, Saturday mornings down here were quiet except for the dog park, which already sounded wide awake.

She scanned the businesses but didn't see any with a name that sounded like whatever Gairloch had said. But he'd also said it was near the park, not in it. Lizzy hoped it wouldn't take too long to find. She was getting close to the point where missing her morning coffee usually meant a caffeine headache was on the way.

She circled the park, then circled it again, each loop a little wider than the last, until frustration finally won. She only came across a few cafés, and none of them were what she was looking for. She even asked around, but no one had ever heard of such a place.

The thin spark of hope she'd brought with her flickered out. She wasn't even sure why she was doing this anymore. Like a fool, she was chasing a fairy tale.

Lizzy dropped onto a bench and let her head fall forward. At some point, even Fresita had given up, wandering off to do whatever it was that cats did when they were done humoring humans.

A shadow fell across her, and she looked up. A large man stood in the street as he leaned back to take a picture of the building above them. She almost ignored him, but just beyond his shoulder, a car was headed in his direction. The driver was staring at a woman walking on the opposite sidewalk, not where he was going.

Lizzy shot up and threw her entire body weight into the man to knock him out of the way. He was easily twice her size, so Lizzy bounced off of him and fell onto the pavement. Startled, he stepped forward and out of the way of the car to help her to her feet. The car swished by, and the man looked shaken as he realized what had just happened.

Lizzy looked up at him; it was the gentle-faced man she exchanged glances with at the party. He gave her a look of profound appreciation that faded into a grin. He recognized her as well. There was a long moment where they just stared at each other before Lizzy finally blinked and looked at her palms. They were scraped from landing on the street.

"Here," he said, offering his hand. "On your feet." His voice carried a deep Scottish lilt, warm and unhurried, complementing the gentleness of his face. "You were at the gathering last night, were you not?"

Lizzy got up on her own. "Yeah."

"Leonydas," the man said, extending his hand. His smile was friendly, hard to look away from. "It is a pleasure."

"Why in hell were you standing in the street?" Lizzy replied, ignoring his greeting with a frown.

"Just got the phone," he explained. "I was trying out the camera. Never had one before."

"You do realize you almost got run over?"

"I am sorry," Leonydas said quietly. "That was careless of me. Thank you for saving me." His gaze dropped to her hands, and his expression shifted. He reached for her without thinking. "You are hurt!"

"I'm fine," Lizzy said, frowning at the scrapes.

"This is my doing," he said. "Let me take you somewhere to be mended."

"To be mended?" Lizzy repeated, puzzled at first by his phrasing, but assumed it was just because he was foreign.

"Yes, Grizzlethorpe's?" he said, and reached for her hands again.

"Stop," Lizzy exclaimed. She shoved his hands aside, a little more forceful than necessary. "I said I'm fine— "

Before she could say anything more, Lizzy was shoved against a light pole and found herself back on the ground again. She shook her head and looked up. The tall woman she had seen Leonydas with the evening before loomed over her.

"Xel, no!" Leonydas knelt beside Lizzy, hands hovering, unsure where to touch. "I am so sorry. I did not mean for this. Are you ok?"

Lizzy stared at the glaring woman. She wore slightly oversized embroidered jeans and a loose blouse; however, it was evident she was muscular. Lizzy wasn't intimidated by her strength, though. A fierceness flashed in her icy blue eyes and was chiseled into her Norse-featured face.

Lizzy massaged her chest. The woman had barely touched her, but Lizzy felt like she had been wailed on.

"Leonydas, everything ok?" the woman said. She loomed over Lizzy, blending in with the skyscrapers around them.

"Yes, Xel, I am fine. Stand down, this woman just saved my life," Leonydas said as he awkwardly tried to help Lizzy to her feet without touching her. "I apologize deeply. Please, is there anything I can do to help you?" Lizzy looked at the odd couple with disbelief, one trying to help her, while the other was about to tear her to shreds.

"You both just need to stay back," Lizzy warned, pointing her finger at them as if it were a weapon.

"This is no longer your concern, little one," Xel said, her gaze steady and unkind. "You may take your leave."

"Gladly, Xena," Lizzy said.

"It is Xel," the woman corrected.

"Relax. It was a joke."

Xel looked Lizzy up and down, just once. "Yes," she said. "I see that."

Xel snapped her head around to peer down the street. "We should go." An instant after Xel spoke, a dog nearby barked a warning to anyone who would listen, and soon others in the area joined in. The hairs on the back of Lizzy's neck straightened at the sound of the dogs, but she pushed against the fear. Just a dream, she told herself.

Leonydas frowned but nodded as he gave Lizzy a final smile. "I sincerely apologize for...*all* of this. Is there anything I can do to make it up to you?"

Lizzy was about to insist that they just leave when she remembered they were at the party. Maybe they knew about this café.

"Café Calacoayan. Do you know it?"

"Of course," Leonydas said.

"How do I get there?"

Leonydas grinned and produced a small silver business card case from his pants pocket. "I can show you where it is."

"I'm not going anywhere with you," Lizzy huffed.

"He was not inviting you," Xel said with the hint of a laugh, her eyes only surveying the area.

"Xel, enough," Leonydas said with a touch of frustration. From the metal case, he produced a thick-cut amber-colored business card and held it close to his lips. He whispered to it: "Calacoayan."

He offered it to her.

"You will not find better coffee," he said. "The card will see you there."

Lizzy stared at the card suspiciously. There was a hole in the middle of it. Realizing she was not going to take it from him, he squatted down and placed it on the sidewalk.

"Please," Leonydas said, low and earnest. "It is the least I can offer you."

Xel seized his arm and pulled. He went with her, stepping backwards, eyes still on Lizzy.

"Next street," he said. "Two blocks up. Go quickly, the card will not last more than thirty minutes."

Leonydas and Xel crossed the street toward a motorcycle, much like the one Mykayla had been repairing, while Lizzy remained motionless, frowning at them.

"And beware of the alleys in that area, they can be tricky," Leonydas called out as Xel climbed on the bike and revved the engine. Xel gave Lizzy a sarcastic wave as he climbed on the bike behind her.

"Ok," Lizzy said to herself and shook her head as she watched the couple speed away. "Weirdos." Leonydas' eyes stayed on her until they turned the corner. It wasn't a creepy stare but hopeful and friendly. Lizzy realized her face had relaxed and frowned harder.

She turned her attention back to the card. She chewed on her lip for a second and then moved closer. At first glance, it seemed to be one of those old gimmicky business cards styled to stand out from the rest. But there was indeed something special about it. The hole in it was circled by glittery gold writing, tempting her. She picked it up for a closer look.

The card, made of a cardstock-thick parchment paper, held a sliver of grey rock that framed the quarter-sized hole. The stone was cool to the touch and seamlessly disappeared into the card itself, where the golden writing read, *Please turn and walk.* She turned the card over but found no contact information.

"How in the hell is this supposed to help me find anything?" she mumbled as she turned and took a few steps. She was still staring at the card when the words disappeared, a letter at a time as if someone had scrubbed a rubber eraser across them. She was startled at first, but it dawned on her that it must be some kind of new digital paper. "Cool."

Wrong direction, ma'am.

The writing reappeared, letter by letter. She wrinkled her face in doubt, wondering how it knew she was a woman. She tried turning in the opposite direction and took a few deliberate steps.

Onward!

Staring at the card, she headed down the block, bumping into poles and people as she went. She experimented by turning the card in different directions, but as long as *she* was headed in the same direction, the words did not change. She wondered how it was powered and where the circuitry was. It was barely as thick as a coin. When she arrived at the next corner, the words rewrote themselves.

Turn right and proceed.

She continued this way for a couple of blocks, with the card guiding her until she came to a street lined with apartments. At the card's request, she turned down the street. Halfway down the words on the card urgently changed.

A Thraewen, with the same destination, is nearby. Would you like to accompany?

"Thraewen?" Lizzy asked. She paused; the word sounded familiar.

The mysterious word was erased from the card, and after a pause, it was replaced with *Magic User*.

"Magic user?" Lizzy said, with amused exasperation. But then she remembered where she had heard the word before. Tita had used it in her stories. A Thraewen didn't just use magic but worked with it. They wove the world's hidden energies together to create, protect, and assist. She didn't think it was a real word, though, and had never seen it used anywhere else.

The words twisted into a small curly cue arrow that pointed behind her. Lizzy turned just as someone exited a nearby building.

The morning sun slipped through the clouds. It glinted off the rings on a young woman's fingers and the charms at her wrist as she tied a bespoke apron over rusty orange corduroy pants and a muted mauve turtleneck. She appeared to be in a hurry, but a content smile lingered on her lips, easing the tension in her face.

"Good morning," the woman sang with a wink as she passed by, leaving a trail of lavender and sweet Earl Grey tea in the air.

She has to be a barista, Lizzy thought. *Even without the apron, she just has that vibe.*

The golden-skinned Latina's hair bounced in a bun as she hurried down the sidewalk. She must have thrown it together on the fly because now strands of black hair stuck out here and there like pixies trying to escape. The entire thing was on the verge of collapse.

"Ok, I'll follow her," Lizzy said half to herself and half to the card. She looked back at it and waited for it to erase and then rewrite.

Hurry! The card scribbled.

Lizzy looked up. The barista was jogging. Lizzy quickly followed, trying to be as inconspicuous as possible, while still holding up the card to verify that it was the woman the card wanted her to follow.

She's running late.

"This is crazy," Lizzy mumbled. "How would it know that? How would it know anything?"

The barista reached the end of the street and darted around the corner, forcing Lizzy jog to keep from losing sight of her. She stretched her neck out and peered around the corner just in time to see the woman stop in front of an old abandoned three-story building framed by a pair of large trees inset in the sidewalk. Lizzy was sure she must have been by here before, but had never noticed this place. It was significantly older than the stark modern buildings that sandwiched it.

The barista stepped onto the first step of a short stairway and paused. She cocked her head and then looked around. Lizzy whipped towards the street and pretended to be waiting for a ride share. She felt the woman's gaze linger on her, so Lizzy waited. 'Magic user' conjured up memories of Tita's stories and a world of hope. She glanced at the card.

She's almost out of range...

Lizzy spun back; she was gone. Lizzy dashed diagonally across the street and stopped in front of the building, which stuck out a few feet from the others onto the sidewalk. The building, perhaps from the 30s, was constructed with smooth oversized white bricks for the first floor and a half. From there, rough-cut, ruddy-colored stones extended the building for a few more floors.

A row of unkempt holly bushes that stretched across the front stabbed Lizzy in the thigh as she tiptoed to look inside. Decades of dust, plus the absence of light inside, made the windows opaque. The bushes ran to the beginning of a short flight of cement steps leading up to a glass-and-metal door. Like the windows, there was no seeing through except for a vintage-looking 'For Lease' sign.

There was an odd electric buzz in the air, and as Lizzy tilted her head in thought, she caught a blinking light out of the corner of her eye. She looked up and at first didn't see anything, but the longer she stared at the upper corner of the building, the more she was sure something was there. The stone corner was subtly illuminated by an unknown source of neon light. It made Lizzy's head hurt to remain focused on it for too long.

She stepped back, checking up and down the street. Newer buildings sat on either side, but both had doors boarded over a decade ago. The barista was nowhere in sight, nor was there anywhere for her to go. The block was too long for her to have made it around the corner before Lizzy might have seen her.

Lizzy took a deep breath of the cool morning air, and her eyes lit up. The aroma of fresh-roasted coffee was coming from somewhere nearby. She looked around again; no stores, cafés, or even street signs. She scoured her memory of this street, and it was, as it is now, a block of perpetually empty nondescript buildings. She looked back at the card for help.

The magic user is still nearby, as is your destination: Café Calacoayan.

"Is she inside?" Lizzy murmured.

Use the hagstone.

The card displayed cute curly cue arrows towards the stone-framed opening. Lizzy's head bobbed back in doubt as she stared at the card. A vivid memory of Tita taking her on an 'adventure' through a creek came to mind.

"What are we looking for?" Lizzy had signed, as she stomped playfully through the water. Tita smiled as she looked back at her great-granddaughter and joined her in with own splashing.

"A hagstone!" Tita replied.

"What is that?" Lizzy asked, scanning through all the rocks in the water. "What color stone is it?"

"Brown, black, grey, green," Tita responded. "Purple, pink, red, rust. It can be any color, cupcake! But! But…it must have a hole through it."

"A hole? What for?"

"For seeing things… It's a seeing stone."

"What kind of things?"

"Fairies…Magic…and more! It allows non-magical people to see the things in our world that they normally wouldn't."

Young Lizzy's eyes had been wide with wonder and excitement, but now they narrowed with doubt. She turned the card over in her hand a few times.

"A seeing stone?" Lizzy asked.

There was no further response from the card. She sighed and looked around. Seeing no one else, she reluctantly held the card up and peeked through the hole. Self-conscious, she immediately lowered it, but in that glimpse, something amazing appeared.

Lizzy immediately snapped the card back up and gawked into the little hole. Just above the third floor, a neon sign hung with glowing letters that read "Café Calacoayn." Underneath, an image of a hand with a floating coffee pot above it, poured animated coffee. From the side, an arrow curved down and directed her eyes to the front windows of the previously abandoned building. Flabbergasted, she dropped the card.

"What is this?" Lizzy said, staring at the card on the ground. She quickly scooped up the card and looked through it again. The neon sign appeared again. She gaped, switching her view back and forth. "Is this a game?" She flipped the card over to examine it again and then poked her finger through the hole. There was no video screen.

Time limit approaching, the card warned. *It was an honor to serve you.* The card felt light in her fingers as little pieces around the edges tore away and evaporated like embers.

"No, wait! I want to see more!"

The golden writing that had been so bright on it before began to fade, then changed one last time.

Now the path is revealed, the ring will suffice, the card scribbled out quickly in letters that only lasted for a moment before disappearing with the rest of the card. Lizzy stood staring into the sky, confused as she fiddled with the Dragonscale ring on her finger. This was all just as strange as the tattoo magically appearing on her arm. But was it magic? Real magic?

Lizzy decided she had to press forward, no matter how much stranger things got. There had to be an explanation for all of it, and possibly hope? She had been standing still, thinking to herself for a minute, when a rustle in the leaves in the large tree near her drew her attention upwards. A creature hopped from one branch to another.

She expected a squirrel, but when she laid eyes on it, there was a grouping of odd wings. Clear and veiny like a cicada, these wings were much larger and attached to a strange, crouched body. The winged creature fluttered down from the branches, headed towards the coffee shop, and Lizzy gasped.

An untamed four-inch woman was the owner of the wings. This was not a drone or any toy; the little person was alive and unmistakably a fairy. Even if Tita had never told her dozens of tales about them, Lizzy would have no trouble realizing what this was.

Her little legs were tilted back, and a pair of dirty feet made a slight paddling motion as she butterflied along. As if to pass the time, she chewed on the fingernails of one hand while the other reached back and scratched her bottom through a skirt of Ash tree leaves.

"Hello?" Lizzy said. The fairy looked over her shoulder and froze when she realized she had been spotted. The generously curved creature hovered, bobbing up and down, in midair, but remained frozen, fingers in mouth, hand on cheek, as if hoping no one would notice her.

Lizzy grinned as she moved closer. While the creature wore leaves for a skirt, her breasts were covered in orangey green moss that seemed to grow in patches across her body. Tiny twigs were tangled in her hair along with a random flower petal or two. The fairy's wings glittered, and perhaps her skin might have too if she weren't so grubby. She looked like she had spent a few days playing in the countryside without being made to wash up.

The fairy followed her with her eyes until Lizzy reached up with an outstretched finger to touch her little feet. The Dragonscale ring gleamed, and the fairy's face pulled into a mocking pout.

"Mensongeux!" she spat, her small voice rough despite its pitch. She zipped forward, latched onto the ring, and with her tiny hands tugged at it. Amused Lizzy laughed and placed her thumb on the underside of the ring as the fairy's face turned dark pink. Unsuccessful, the fairy huffed, switched sides, and tried pushing the ring free, her bare bottom waggling through the leaves. Lizzy looked away.

Noticing Lizzy's thumb, the fairy let out a frustrated growl and flashed an evil smile.

"Vengelie!" The fairy exclaimed. An intense flash of pain made Lizzy yelp and look back. The fairy had sunk her teeth into the skin between Lizzy's fingers. It was as if someone had jabbed a shard of glass into a nerve.

Lizzy waggled her finger, but the fairy held fast. Lizzy blew on her like she was trying to put out a match. The fairy gagged as she flipped Lizzy the bird, but did not release her grip.

Lizzy was frustrated, and the pain crawled up her arm, so

she shook her hand hard. The fairy wrapped her legs around the finger in response and bit even harder.

"Little fucker," Lizzy growled. With a vicious flick to her attacker's backside, she sent the fairy tumbling through the air. The fairy quickly pulled herself out of the spin and turned to face Lizzy.

Lizzy flinched as the fairy, in a voice much too loud for her size, launched into a series of what surely were fae expletives. The fairy waved her fists and continued her tirade for so long that Lizzy's surprise wore off, and she began to laugh at her. Indignant, the angry fairy stuck out her tongue, turned around, and mooned Lizzy, intentionally—vulgarly this time. The fairy flipped her off with both hands as she waggled her bottom and then darted behind the bushes in front of the coffee shop. Lizzy could only stand there, finger throbbing, astounded.

If there was little hope of logically explaining away the tattoo and card, a fairy…a real-life flying fairy was impossible. She rubbed the bright red teethmarks between her fingers and wondered how clean fairy mouths were.

Did Tita know? The stories she had spun about fairies were spot on. Cartoons told everyone else that fairies were beautiful, fun, and wondrous. Lizzy, though, grew up hearing about a cabal of rude, mean-spirited, and tricky creatures. Though older and higher-ranking fairies, like the ones who often scolded Maeve, were more civilized, the young ones enjoyed their youth to the fullest. Lizzy's mind buzzed with something she hadn't felt in months. Excitement.

She turned her attention back to the front of the building and found that the spikey holly didn't run up against the front of the building. There was a three-foot gap where a set of stairs descended from an iron gate at the end of the building to another doorway to what must be the basement. Wary of the fairy, Lizzy did her best to peer into the stairwell, but it was doused in shadows.

Lizzy took a hesitant step down. She placed her hand against an ivy-covered wall for balance, but immediately yanked away. The vines moved, slithered around the spot where she had placed her hand. After a moment, they were still again, but with every movement she made, the leaves quivered. Lizzy kept an eye on them but continued down the middle of the stairs.

Near the bottom, tiny dots of amber light amongst the ivy flickered on, making it easier to see what she was getting into. While the steps were cemented, the landing at the bottom was made of large cobblestones. The ivy on the street side wall continued down and covered the wall in front of the stairway.

At waist level, an antique brass spigot with a rosewood handle stuck out of the ivy. Water dripped from it, creating a small puddle and saturating the area with the aroma of fresh rainwater. Lizzy glanced at it and then turned her attention to a large iron door to the right. This was not a modern commercial building door but an old industrial door held together with fist-sized round-head bolts. There was no handle.

Lizzy pushed against the door, but it was immovable. She pushed the tips of her fingers into a thin gap between the door and its frame. She pulled without result. Lizzy stepped back and looked for any evidence of a way in. Against her better judgment, she knocked on it. It didn't even sound like a door; there was only a solid thud as if she had knocked on the side of a mountain.

Lizzy sighed and sat on the steps to think. She looked over at the ivy and studied the little lights. They had a wavering glow like the sunken flame within the wax walls of a pillar candle. She leaned in close and found they were little cream-colored flower buds.

Lizzy was about to touch one when she realized there was a tiny pair of feet perched on top of the stem of the bud. She followed the legs up and found that damn fairy sneering down at her.

"Revoilà," the fairy murmured, annoyed. The little woman reared her fist back and clobbered Lizzy's nose with a haymaker.

Jerking back, Lizzy scrambled to her feet. Her nose felt like she had just walked face-first into that iron door. Charging Lizzy, the fairy let out a battle cry. Lizzy dodged out of the way and fell against the wall facing the door. It made a hollow wooden thud as she hit it.

Lizzy ducked and dodged repeated attacks but ended up tripping over her twisting feet and fell beside the spigot. The fairy zipped up the stairs and lined up an attack. Lizzy reached over and stuck her thumb against the opening of the spigot. As the fairy dived towards her, she spun the handle on and aimed a jet spray at the dirty fairy. The water pelted her square in the face, sending her tumbling backward. Lizzy removed her thumb from the spigot as the fairy crashed onto a cobblestone step.

Flashing Lizzy a look that could kill, the fairy coughed and choked up water. She fumed as she got up to inspect her now cleaner-than-before body.

"Ach! Non! Non! Non!" the fairy squawked, stamping her foot again and again.

"Sorry," Lizzy offered in a half-apology.

The fairy narrowed her eyes in response as she made her wings vibrate to shake off the remaining water. She pointed at

Lizzy in a silent threat and hovered into the air.

"Look, I'm new to all this," Lizzy said as she offered her hand to the fairy. "I've always wanted to meet a fairy. Could we please start over?"

The fairy tilted her head, giving Lizzy an inquisitive look as she floated closer. She drew her chin to her chest, cleared her throat, and spat an enormous ball of green phlegm into Lizzy's palm.

"Ugh," Lizzy exclaimed, shaking her hand and then her head in disbelief, again. The air filled with a squeaky belly laugh as the fairy zipped up the stairs and out of sight.

Lizzy turned the faucet handle to wash the fairy goo from her hands and jumped when the wall beside her began to slide aside. The water poured out of the faucet at first, but the more she turned the knob, the water eventually stopped flowing. Once the knob was fully turned, the wall completely retracted, revealing a door.

The door was arched and made of ancient-looking, thick wooden planks held together by elegant, flowing bands of decorative iron shaped like tree branches. The door could have been a hundred years old, but it was as solid as the iron one. She looked it over. This one *did* have a knob.

Lizzy stood up and, with her fingers, she turned the brass knob, also covered with decorative designs. It turned freely, but nothing happened. She pushed. She pulled. But the door did not budge. She knew there had to be some kind of trick or magic to get this door open. She searched for another faucet, a lever, or a loose stone to interact with, but found nothing. She wrinkled her nose at the gooey fairy juice still on her palm and turned to wash it off. But she remembered something Tita had once told her.

"Fairy magic," Tita said, "is some of the most powerful magic there is, cupcake."

"Where does their magic come from?" Lizzy had asked.

"The fae are full of a kind of magic called ilWunne. It is an old, raw magic that gives life to their Realm. That's why they are so chaotic when they're young. They have to flow through it and not let it flow through them. But even the younglings are powerful. I tell you this, if you have a fairy on your side, you can get through almost anything."

Lizzy looked down at her hand. Most of the green goo was still stuck to her palm and glittered from the glowing buds around her. She placed her palm on the door handle and tried again to turn it. There was a click from within the door. She felt more resistance this time as the knob rotated until it finally stopped with a louder click. She held her breath and then pushed the door in.

The door swung open to reveal a short hallway leading into a more expansive room. Further ahead, light poured in from a bank of large windows crowned with oval arches.

Lizzy blinked; not from the light but because she was confused. She was below street level. She should be looking at the sewer system or the basement of the buildings in front of her. She made sure the door wouldn't close, then ran up the stairs to look in that direction. There was the street, the sidewalk on the other side, and then another building.

She returned to the door and stuck her hand inside. It wasn't an illusion. The only thing she could think of was that this was part of Houston's tunnel system. It didn't look like it, though.

"Or it could just be magic," Lizzy said to herself. She stepped into the hallway and slowly walked towards the room. The robust aroma of coffee welcomed her in, and she smiled at the familiar clink of coffee mugs and chatter. She was sure she had found Café Calacoayan.

CHAPTER 4

The café was breathtaking. The room she walked into from the short hallway had a chevron-patterned wood parquet floor that met wainscoted paneling rising halfway up the walls. Above it was what Lizzy assumed to be sophisticated wallpaper: deep blue, topped with decorative vines stretching upward.

Then Lizzy's steps slowed. The pattern didn't quite repeat. She leaned in close. The vines were real. Thin stems climbed the walls, delicate leaves tracing the blue as if they'd grown there over time rather than been put in place. They reached all the way to the ceiling and across to a pitched skylight of green and gold Tiffany leaves, scattering light in soft hues across the tables and floor. Framing the glass garden, more living vines and leaves crept into the corners of the room like molding.

Amidst all this organic beauty lay a treasure trove of artifacts from a world that had, until now, existed only on the pages of Tita's sketchbook and in Lizzy's mind. On shelves, bookcases, and small tables sat paintings, statues, weapons, and a multitude of trinkets. It reminded Lizzy of Tita's house when she was younger, though more orderly—like an overcrowded museum.

Yet, it was still a café.

Customers sat at round tables chatting as they enjoyed coffee and pastries. The room bent around a corner, where the sound of an espresso machine steaming milk rang out. Lizzy was eager to get to the coffee, but she couldn't help taking her time, trying to absorb everything.

She wondered at a few paintings nearby: a majestic cliffside castle teetering over raging seas, an armored princess astride a unicorn, and a ragtag fray of fairies dancing before a golden-haired woman who looked just like Tita's fairy queen sketch.

The images seemed alive, with movement that would have made Van Gogh jealous. The curling strokes of the fairy's wings fluttered, the princess's hair waved, and the ocean below the castle roiled. Lizzy ran a finger across the cerulean sea, coating her finger in goopy paint, and sent waves crashing higher up the castle walls. She jerked her hand away, splatting paint onto the floor. Where it landed, a single tiny wave rose and crashed near her shoe.

"Shit!" Lizzy exclaimed as she stepped back.

"No worries, happens all the time," a young man said as he trotted over and knelt in front of her. He wore an apron similar to the one she had seen on the barista she was following earlier. "Wipes right up, see?" He swiped a towel over the paint and presented her with a cerulean stain.

"Yeah," Lizzy said, leaning closer to the painting of the princess. "But how does it move like that?"

She brushed her fingers over the golden-brown strokes spilling from beneath the helm. The paint wasn't smooth. Tiny hairs tickled her skin.

"It's part of the enchantment. I'm sort of an artist myself, but I can never get the movement part right. It ends up a little choppy. I signed up for some classes later this week. I hope it helps."

"Oh. What do you mean by enchantment?"

"You know, il'Thren," the young man said as if he were referring to something as familiar as a paintbrush. The clatter of a mug called him away for another clean-up, leaving Lizzy staring at the spotless floor. A door opened nearby. The hallway wasn't the only way to get into this place.

An arch-topped window bank ran until it reached a door painted chestnut-red, then continued on the other side. A wavy glass pane made up the top half of the door and had the café's name painted on it. She peeked between the caligraphed red-and-gold lettering. Outside, a cobblestone street ran past the café, and on the other side were more businesses in a style similar to the one she was in. The sky was visible, and past the businesses, Lizzy could see Houston's skyscrapers towering above them. Like trying to decipher an optical illusion, her mind did its best to place everything somewhere in downtown. However, it just wasn't possible.

I should be underground right now.

The street in front of her was moderately busy with people walking by and entering the neighboring businesses. From here, though, she couldn't tell what the businesses were. Lizzy's investigation was interrupted by someone in a purple velvet hood who opened the door in her face.

"Oh," a woman said, stepping inside. She lowered her hood to reveal a pair of protrusions, like stunted antler nubs, at her dark hairline. It was the regal-looking woman Lizzy had seen at the party. She was dressed more casually today in a brown wool skirt, an embroidered white shirt, and a golden band around her upper arm. She appeared modest; however, her carefully accessorized belts and gold jewelry hinted at her station in this world. She analyzed Lizzy thoughtfully as she preened her wavy hair.

"I'm late," the woman announced as she finished fixing her appearance and carefully scanned the café. "Have you been here long?"

The woman frowned when she caught Lizzy trying unsuccessfully not to stare at her nubs. She looked Lizzy up and down as if noticing her for the first time, and then raised an eyebrow as she concluded she was not who she was looking for.

"Oh, you're not…," the woman said.

"Sorry," Lizzy mumbled for being the wrong person, in her way, and staring all at the same time.

The woman only nodded in response and waited for Lizzy to move.

"Do you mind?" the woman finally said.

"Sorry… I'm sorry," Lizzy said, stepping aside to let the woman pass.

She pretended to search the room for an empty table while watching the woman join the short line at the counter. The woman checked the time on her smartwatch, and the Dragonstone ring on her finger caught Lizzy's attention. The woman slipped a book from a hidden pocket at her hip and began to read. When she looked up, her expression tightened as her gaze met Lizzy's. Lizzy turned away quickly.

Leaving the door behind, Lizzy wandered the café, gawking at the treasures displayed in its walls: statues of forgotten heroes, mighty swords, and fossils of fantastic creatures long dead. She laughed softly when a gray-furred "hat" on a cabinet flicked its tail and yawned, a long-lived cat. Everything seemed to be alive here. The walls themselves bloomed with orchid-shaped lamps casting a gentle, living glow.

Finally, Lizzy was about to head for the cashier when a painting of a deep blue mountain caught her attention. Like Tita's drawing, it was split in two with the majestic castle on the bridge in between them. The only significant difference was the vivid colors on display. The mountain was a deep blue, and the trees were earthy brownish-reds. The sky above faded from pale blue to dark grey, as the sun had long since set.

Tita must have seen this painting before, Lizzy thought. She was sure now that Tita had experienced all these things before. If that was true, and magic was real…was it possible the healing sword was as well? Maybe her once fanciful and now far-off dream could be real as well.

Lizzy was more excited than ever, but her head was starting to ache from not having her coffee yet. She forced herself to avoid further distractions and headed for the counter, stealing glances at customers as she passed. Most appeared normal, while others seemed like cosplayers trying to mix their costumes with modern clothes. Lizzy also noticed a small stack of books on each table. Some were old, some new, but every table had them.

She passed into another section of the café, where the bank of windows carried on, small tables lined beneath them, and the counter to order sat just off to one side. The first room had dazzled her with beauty and living magic; this one offered comfort instead. It was the sort of place meant for lingering—where a person could sink into a soft chair and lose hours inside a book.

Lizzy got in line behind the hooded woman, still reading her book, and made a point of not looking at her. The woman didn't seem to notice her anyway. The short line took its time as the cashier chatted with each customer, giving Lizzy a chance to explore from her place in line. A familiar slurping-sucking noise drew her attention to the counter and a unique espresso machine. The bronze contraption was a mash-up of levers, copper tubing, pressure gauges, and a round flask holding boiling water.

Coaxing a shot of espresso from the contraption was the barista she had followed earlier. Her bun still threatened to fall apart at any second, but somehow stayed together as she tilted her head to observe her work. She bit her tongue as perpetually smiling, honeyed eyes focused on her craft. Feeling that she was being watched, the corners of her thick lips turned up in a knowing smile. Her eyes met Lizzy's, who quickly turned away to find something else to be distracted by.

The twinkle from a framed glass box hanging from a nearby column saved her from feigning interest in something random.

"Oh my god," Lizzy said. "There's no way..." Inside the box mounted on a bed of crunchy velvet was a golden necklace with a silver pendant of star-shaped blossoms nestled in leaves. She peeked at her tattoo for comparison. The flowers were practically the same. She was sure this must be the replica of the necklace Gairloch had mentioned. The warmth around the tattoo returned, so she quickly tugged her sleeve over it.

A tapping on the counter, followed by an annoyed intentional clearing of the throat, pried Lizzy away. A young raven-haired Latina impatiently clacked her nails at the register to signal it was Lizzy's turn. The barista's dark brown skin peeked out between colorful tattoos; most were Mexica symbols, but there were plenty of contemporary designs as well. Lizzy wanted to like her, but a perfect eyebrow arched in contempt.

"Sorry, I'm new here," Lizzy said, as she searched for a menu.

"Yeah, you are," the barista said, judging her up and down. "You shouldn't be in here, Dullren." Her hoop earrings jigged as her head stressed each word. Lizzy opened her mouth to snap back at her when the other barista bumped up alongside her co-worker and pinched the back of her arm.

"Go, I'll take her order, Yarely," she said as the other yanked her arm free and strutted away.

"Hey, I'm Ruby," the barista said as she tilted her head slightly and flashed Lizzy the same knowing smile from earlier. "Nice to meet you." Ruby held her hand out confidently, but Lizzy only stared at her, thrown off by the stark difference between the two baristas. "Just ignore Yarely, she's an…acquired taste."

"Sure, ok, hi," Lizzy said as she gave Ruby's warm hand the smallest shake possible. Ruby let her ring-covered hand hold on to Lizzy's, a little too long for comfort, as she searched deep into her eyes.

At first, Lizzy thought she was being hit on, but realized this was something different. It was as if she was searching for something, flipping through her soul a page at a time. Ruby's expressive eyes roamed back and forth across her face, from one eye to the other and then down to her mouth, before starting again.

"Huh," Ruby said, coming to a smiling but confused conclusion.

"I'm Liz," Lizzy said, trying to reclaim her hand. Ruby glanced down with a little laugh and let her go.

"Cool, cool," Ruby said. "First time, Liz?" She spoke in a content and unhurried tone. Lizzy stepped closer to the bar just to hear her over the background hum of patrons.

"Yeah, someone gave me a card, and it led me here. Actually, it, uh, pointed you out on the way too."

"Oh yeah! Ok, the cute woman on the sidewalk. It all makes sense now. Well, welcome to Café Calacoayan. We've been around forever, in one form or another."

"How long is forever?" Lizzy asked, unconvinced.

"Couple hundred years…it could have been longer, but I've only worked here a little over a year," Ruby said and laughed. Sunlight sparkled in her eyes, turning the honey to gold and deepening her joyful aura. Lizzy frowned, unable to tell if she was joking. "So, this is your first time to the Inn?"

"Inn? I thought it was just a coffee shop."

"Um…" Ruby laughed. "No—sorry. It's just a coffee shop. I meant the Inn. As in, this whole area."

She gestured vaguely. "It's called the Inn Between, but everyone just says the Inn. I think there was only an inn here originally, back when it was just a stop for travelers. That was a long time ago, though. Might just be a legend."

"Ok, got it. Then yes, this is my first time at the Inn and the coffee shop. It's so…" Lizzy paused as she tried to come up with a word that would capture the vibe.

"Eclectic?" Ruby suggested.

"Well, I was going to say magical, but yes, absolutely eclectic." Lizzy nodded as she took in the shop again.

"Ok, let me ask you this," Ruby asked, leaning forward on her elbows. "What is your favorite piece here in the shop? Everyone's got one."

"That pendant over there," Lizzy said, glancing back at the necklace. "It's beautiful." Ruby cocked her head and then pointed at it.

"Betela's Blossom?" Ruby's smile faded into a curious expression.

"What is it?" Lizzy asked carefully.

"It's an ancient symbol of healing," Ruby explained. "But that one is just a reproduction."

"Oh, OK," Lizzy said as Ruby searched Lizzy's face again. She almost shared her tattoo with Ruby, but changed her mind at the last second.

"Lately," Ruby continued. "It has become a symbol of hope, what with the Hollowing and all."

"Right," Lizzy said as if she understood, but Ruby noticed her negative shake of the head.

"You know of the spread of the disease?"

"No," Lizzy replied, showing concern, but her gut twisted.

"It has been stripping Thraewen of their connection to magic."

"Mode of transmission?" Lizzy asked automatically and glanced around the café.

"You won't find it here, and it's passed by touch only. For whatever reason, it has been centered around close-knit Thraewen communities…families, usually low income. It's unfortunate, too, because if it were affecting the rich and powerful, then the search for a cure would be more of a priority." Ruby paused and studied Lizzy again with a hopeful look. "Are you a doctor?"

"No," Lizzy replied, quickly dropping her gaze to the floor.

"Well, it's too bad because a lot of people need help, and there aren't enough menders to go around. That's why there has been such a growing interest in the return of the Lady Betela. The original necklace is a relic lost to time. But there is hope that someone will find it again and heal the world."

"Do you believe that?" Lizzy asked, rubbing her arm through her hoodie.

"Of course, it's history," Ruby said, convinced. "Will she return? Who knows? But I think that if you expect good things to happen, they will…at just the right time. The Lady is a force for good. So, I'm hopeful she's out there somewhere."

A strange unease settled over Lizzy, the feeling that Ruby saw something in her she hadn't discovered yet. She frowned. After a brief, searching look, Ruby suddenly switched back into barista mode.

"So, you look like you could use a cup of coffee—stat," Ruby said, with a giggle. "A black coffee girl, single origin, right?"

"Yes," Lizzy said, pulling her thoughts away from the necklace. "What do you have?"

"Mostly Latin American: Chiapas, Costa Rica, Guatemala. We roast everything ourselves every week, but can I recommend our house blend? I prefer single origins too, but the blend we've come up with is literally the best coffee I've had. Like, ever."

"Sure, that's fine," Lizzy said. "Can I get it as a pour-over?"

"Mmm, I love a pour over too, but this'll taste just as good as a batch brew. Besides, you look like you need a cup ASAP."

Lizzy nodded her head empathetically.

"You feel…you look like you are having a bad day," Ruby said, her eyes offering concern.

"Yeah," Lizzy said. Strangely, she felt like she could open up to this person she barely met a moment ago. A few weeks ago, they could have been friends. "Most of my days are like that."

"Shit, I'm sorry to hear that. Well, I promise this will help," Ruby said. She hugged the full mug with both hands and set it on the counter. "If you don't love this, then please let me know, and I'll make whatever else you'd like. On me."

"Great, thanks." Lizzy managed half a smile as she reached for the drink, but Ruby held up a finger.

"Hot or extra hot?"

"I like it a little hotter than normal, but whatever is fine."

Ruby tapped a manicured but unpainted fingernail against the mug. A half second later, steam drifted up.

"Ok, then you should be good to go."

Lizzy raised her eyebrows, but then shrugged her shoulders as she turned to the tables. It was the least weird thing she had seen today.

"So...," Ruby said, as she touched Lizzy on the shoulder. "We have a lot of regulars that have their favorite spots, nothing's reserved, but I can point out one that should be free today." Ruby pointed towards a two-chair tabletop, under a lush hanging plant by the front windows. "And if you need someone to talk to, or listen to, I'd be more than happy." Lizzy was interested in learning more about the shop and *magic*. She opened her mouth to ask, but thanked Rubby instead and ducked out from under her touch.

She carefully navigated between chairs and tables as she headed for the window seat. She watched her coffee slosh. She knew she was going to spill it, somehow she always did, but even when it hit the rim of the cup, it never seemed to make it over. She set the cup down on the table, purposefully jarring it, and again the drink remained inside. She needed a cup like this for her place.

Lizzy slid into a wooden chair, beautifully adorned with carved, flowing vines, and found it much more comfortable than it appeared. The shop was chilly, but meadow sunflower rays warmed the table. She held her head over her cup and took a deep breath. Some of the day's stress eased away.

She took a cautious sip and smiled. It was bold with hints of dark chocolate, brown sugar, and cinnamon.

*Yessss. This **is** the best cup I've ever had,* Lizzy thought, and side-eyed the bar. Ruby wiped it down with her knowing smile. Lizzy sank into her seat and the comfort of the coffee.

As Lizzy enjoyed her drink, she watched others joke with friends or flirt with lovers. She was sure everyone knew each other's name here. With the allure of the delicious coffee, the beauty of the shop, and the fantastic things she encountered so far, Lizzy saw herself here for years to come.

A smile threatened to ease her face, but a twinge of guilt strangled it. She wished she could bring *Him* here and show him all the things. He would certainly enjoy the swords and fossils. He also would have loved the journey here. She played with the blue stone on her necklace as she pictured him sitting across from her, joking, and…his grin.

"It's all your fault…"

Her stomach tightened, and she held back an emotional groan. She did her best to shake off the weighted tug of emotion that threatened to pull her back into the hole. She knew she needed to stay focused if she was going to make things right.

She distracted herself by studying a postcard-sized painting hanging beside her table. She leaned in and squinted. A group of elves stood in front of a foamy gray creek. They looked formidable, dressed in lightweight armor, and had tattoos emblazoned on their foreheads. The symbol looked familiar, though Lizzy couldn't place it. It was probably something else she had seen in Tita's drawings. She turned her attention to the stack of three books on her table: *Alice in Wonderland, Wuthering Heights,* and *The Hobbit.* Everything here seemed perfect, but it also churned up so many questions.

Time slipped by unnoticed. When Ruby finally made her way toward Lizzy, she was wiping down a few tables as she went.

"So?" Ruby asked with a smile, touching Lizzy's arm. "How's the coffee?"

"Perfect. Honesty, I've never had a better cup. Thank you so much for recommending it."

"You're very welcome, honey. Is there anything I can get you? A refill? Pastry? Answers to your questions?"

Lizzy hesitated. She had so many, but she was afraid they might kick her out if they knew she didn't have anything to do with magic herself.

"It's ok. I can tell this is all new to you. You aren't the first."

"Does that happen a lot? Newbies?"

"On occasion. It's not a surprise for someone to wander in mistakenly, but usually, like you, they are invited."

"I wasn't really invited," Lizzy said, shrugging. "I saved this guy's life—"

"Oh wow! You *have* had quite a day," Ruby said, with an impressed expression. "Good for you. Every life is important."

"Yeah, I think so too. Anyway, he gave me this little card, and it led me here."

"That's what we refer to as *the invitation,*" Ruby said, punctuating her sentence with sparkle fingers and mock awe that gave way to a grin. Lizzy smiled despite herself. "It's near impossible to find this place just by looking. Invitation cards are only handed out to very special people. Even with your Dragonscale ring, it would be difficult to make your way here."

"I was told," Lizzy said, spinning the ring on her finger, "that Dragonscale rings were very powerful."

"Absolutely, but they are better at hiding things than revealing. It can be challenging to reveal something that does not want to be discovered."

"This place," Lizzy asked, "the Inn Between, doesn't want to be discovered?"

"You know, there used to be a time when it was much easier to visit the Inn and places like it. What you would call the magic Realm and yours were much closer. Nowadays, it's too dangerous."

"For who?"

Ruby's cheery face softened into a sad smile as she pondered Lizzy's question.

"Honestly, I think it's too dangerous for everyone. Overall, people are good, but the individuals in charge…that's another thing. Power and money tend to increase one's desire for more. Great wars have been sparked between those who have magic and those who do not. By remaining hidden, peace is maintained."

"That's sad," Lizzy said.

"Yes, maybe someday things will be different," Ruby mused and then brightened her smile. "But for now, we get to have beautiful moments like this when I get to meet amazing lifesavers. I'm going to bring you a pastry as a thank you for saving one of us."

Lizzy tried to turn her down, but Ruby had already turned away, moving back toward the counter with a light, almost dancing step.

Lizzy glanced over at the framed necklace and stared at it while she waited. Fragments of Tita's and Gairloch's stories flitted through her mind. She shook her head. Certainly, it all couldn't be true. Healing magic? It didn't seem likely, but neither did half the things she had seen that day. She pulled up her sleeve and stared at her tattoo until a shadow fell across her table.

A large salt and pepper mustachioed man with pointed ears loomed over her, sending icy pinpricks spidering down her neck. Had she seen him on the streets, she might have appreciated his long wool coat and turtle neck, but now she was afraid. Lizzy reached over to pull her sleeve down, but the man's heavy hand swallowed her small one.

"What are you doing?" Lizzy demanded, trying to pull back. The weight of his hand held it in place, and his fingers latched onto her sweater, pulling it further up.

"Impressive work. Who gave this to you?" The man's voice struggled to remain civil, but a searing anger rumbled just underneath it.

"A tattoo shop on Washington," Lizzy said, finally jerking free from his grip. She glanced over to the bar, but Ruby had just walked into the back room. She had wanted to stay longer and discover more, but this man was not safe. She slipped out of her chair and headed for the door. "I've gotta go."

She stepped outside and paused to look back. She didn't see him following her. She hurried a few steps down the street, looking for another shop to disappear into. She shivered. It was much colder wherever this place was, but it was also cleaner. There was a crispness to the air, and the smell of pine and cinnamon floated by with every tickle of the breeze.

Outside now, she could see the area, the Inn Between, more clearly. The buildings were beautiful and felt very out of place in Houston, Texas. They felt more like they belonged to turn of the 20th century Europe. As with the café, flowing organic designs could be found even in the smallest businesses. Lush trees lined the streets, and planters full of leafy plants were scattered everywhere. Lizzy was only able to enjoy her surroundings for a minute before the man with the mustache strode up beside her.

"I apologize," the man said. "That was very rude of me. I have not seen that symbol in many, many years, and it is very important. My name is Xeilan. I am the owner of the Celestine and a member of the Aurenthal." He looked at her as if she should be impressed, but she only frowned at him. "It is the hotel just over there. The big one." Lizzy looked where he was pointing. There was indeed a very big and impressive hotel.

"Look, I'm not interested in whatever it is that you want," Lizzy said and tried to turn away, but he placed a hand on her arm again.

"I only want to get to know you. I've never seen you here before. What is your name?"

"My name is *fuck off*," Lizzy said, angrily, trying to jerk free; however, he held her firmly. It started to hurt, but Xeilan only smiled.

"I will allow that kind behavior since I was rude to you first," Xeilan said, and then his smile faded. His brows dipped low as he continued. "But you will respect my authority. Now tell me your name." Lizzy's heart jolted, but she masked her fear with a feral flash of bared teeth. His eyes narrowed.

"Lord Xeilan," Ruby shouted, bursting through the café doors behind them. "Let her go!"

Surprised by Ruby's sudden arrival, he turned, loosening his grip. Lizzy wrenched her arm free, gave him a dirty look, and hurried down the street. Xeilan stared at her coldly, ignoring Ruby as she approached him. Lizzy didn't have a clue where to go, but a side street was the closest way to put some distance between her and that insane man.

"Liz, wait!" Ruby called out after her, but she was already around the corner. Lizzy needed some time to gather her thoughts. Ahead, she saw an alley and stepped into it. She leaned back against the wall, listening for footsteps. In the distance, she could hear arguing that quickly drifted away.

Lizzy frowned at her wrist. The pain was already subsiding, and a red thumbprint faded. She took a deep breath and pressed the back of her head against the wall. A warm, scented breeze coming from deeper inside the alley lured her to venture further into it. It was too dark from where she was to see how far back it reached.

"Cupcake?" a woman's voice whispered from within.

CHAPTER 5

Tita's affectionate term for her shocked Lizzy, but she instantly realized an unfamiliar voice uttered it. But still, she needed to know who else might know to call her that. She paused at the edge of the shadow until a sudden waft of Tita's flowery perfume encouraged her closer.

She cautiously stepped further in and was instantly blinded by the shadow. She stuck her hands out in front of her to find a wall, but froze; something moved in the darkness. Lizzy took a sharp breath and held it as still as her body. She only dared dart her eyes, but could not see anything yet. An intense temptation to run was smote by childhood nightmares of the dark creature pursuing her when she tried to escape.

Maybe whatever 'it' is can't see me either, Lizzy thought.

She didn't hear movement anymore, and as her eyes slowly adjusted, she discovered that she was alone in the alley. It was different from the others she had been in. She didn't make a habit of hanging out in the dark corners of the city, but she spent a few rotations doing EMT ride-alongs. What set this alley apart was how clean it was; it didn't smell of urine. The perfume's aroma had faded, leaving a humid, earthy atmosphere. It reminded her of the woods in spring.

She checked again for the source of the noise, then took a few steps forward. On one side of the alley, pieces of small furniture leaned against a wall. Lizzy shot her eyes toward a sudden purple glow from something sitting atop the furniture.

"Elizabeth," a feathery voice whispered. It was the same as the one she heard before. Lizzy spun around, but there was no one, only the soft light from the furniture.

"Who's there! How do you know my name?"

The silence was as deafening as the darkness had been blinding. Lizzy waited for another call until her chest began to hurt; without thinking, she had been holding her breath.

"Elizabeth."

The whisper came from the light and pulsed with each syllable of her name.

"Yes?" Lizzy said as she took a step closer.

She could see now that the purple pulse came from a flower bud sitting atop the peculiar shrine. Lizzy's face relaxed. When she was six, her dad bought her a purple light-up flower at a carnival. To her sister's annoyance, she would stare at it from her bed until she fell asleep. This was even more beautiful than that.

It grew out of a wooden pot atop the upside-down bookcase, balanced on the cupboard. It was a haphazard but cute shrine. The darkness of the alleyway and the increasing light of the flower made everything else around her fade away. As Lizzy came within reach of it, the bud unraveled to reveal a star-shaped purple flower. It had to be the Star Blossom.

Lizzy gasped, and tears ran down her face. Her new tattoo did not truly convey its beauty. Five pointy petals forming a star shape were embraced by another five, more rounded, beneath. It was cradled by large green leaves on either side. It captivated Lizzy. The purple petals framed and contrasted a chartreuse center that sprouted with tiny arms covered in pollen.

Lizzy drew in a deep breath, the soft scent of eucalyptus cooling her thoughts. Her shoulders eased, and whatever stress she'd been holding dissolved into something distant and unimportant.

From one of the flower's arms, a single dot of pollen floated free, drifting down between the petals. When it reached the soil, it had become liquid, its edges shimmering as it pooled and sloshed softly against the pot's narrow walls. The longer Lizzy watched, the larger the pool appeared to grow.

Or perhaps she was the one growing smaller.

Wait, what's happening? Lizzy thought, beginning to panic. *Is the flower hallucinogenic?*

She touched her wrist and checked her respiration, but the presentation of a hallucinogen could be identical to her panic attacks. She needed to leave before she succumbed to whatever this was. Lizzy stumbled backward, tripped over her own feet, and landed with a sharp splash in ankle-deep water.

The alleyway was gone. She scrambled onto her knees and twisted around searching for a way out. There was only a purple darkness around her, and peering down high above her was a single star. Its light pulsed her name.

Elizabeth.

A comforting calm soothed Lizzy's reeling mind. Tickling the cool water with her fingertips, she looked out across a serene ocean stretching out in front of her. In the distance, a fuzzy pink cloud hovered over the water and floated in her direction. It was like a lazy swarm of chartreuse fireflies pulsing, but as they neared, it became clear that it was the pollen.

Her own reflection caught her eye, and she gazed into it. It was not her own. A cold shock prickled across her skin, but then she recognized the eyes. It *was* her, but the Lizzy in the liquid looked elegant. Older.

No, not just older but wiser? Lizzy thought. *Confident?*

She put her hands on her knees and leaned down to study her face. Her skin was a little darker and her freckles more pronounced as if she spent a lot of time in the sun.

The other image obediently mirrored her as she widened her eyes, wrinkled her nose, and jutted her head forward as a playful threat. The corners of the other's lips started to form a smile, but faded back into seriousness.

Bullshit, this isn't me.

She narrowed her eyes, and the other appeared to have the same doubts. Lizzy turned her head; most of the other's ear was covered by her hair, but the lower half was decorated with gorgeous ear piercings. She touched her own lobe, but they were not there. The other's hair, longer than her own, and seasoned with streaks of silver. Ending their game, the other gave her a smile that reminded her of Tita's love.

"Who are you?" Lizzy interrogated the image, wondering if she was dreaming.

"This isn't a dream, Lizzy," the other said. Lizzy shivered at the eerie familiarity of her voice and put up her frown in defense. "You can't hide behind that frown with me."

"Fine then, who are you?" she asked again. "What is this?"

"The future," the other replied.

"The future?" Lizzy said. "I don't understand."

Lizzy recognized a stern look that flashed on the other's face. She gave it to *Him* when they were studying, and he asked questions without trying to figure things out on his own. "My future," Lizzy finally said. "You're me?" She wanted to hear the other one say it.

"Yes, but not yet."

"When then?"

"Maybe never," the other said and smiled, shaking her head. "Depending on how things go today."

"Sure, ok…," Lizzy sighed. "What is all this? Why do I feel like I'm having a bad acid trip?"

The other laughed and shook her head. Lizzy was jealous of her relaxed joy.

"If you're future me, or whatever, how long did it take to get like that?" Lizzy said. "How long until I am happy again?"

"That is up to you."

"What if I don't ever want to be happy again?"

"Why would you want that?" the other asked.

Lizzy started to answer, but narrowed her eyes instead.

"If you are really me," Lizzy said. "Then you should know exactly why."

"I do know. But I'm not sure that you know."

"Of course I do," Lizzy barked, poking herself harder in the chest. "I know because it's all my fault. I deserve this!"

"Why do you think it is your fault?"

"Why are you asking me questions that you obviously already know the answer to?

"As I said before, because you do not know the answer. In

fact, you have the wrong answers to the wrong questions."

"That doesn't make one bit of sense!" Lizzy lashed out, splashing the image, and stood up. She looked around for somewhere to run to, but there was only the endless sea of dark water.

"Why do you want to run from the truth?" the other asked.

"Which truth? That *he's* dead or Tita is?"

"That is not what I'm talking about. You already know those truths."

"Then what then?"

"Running away instead of walking through this is hurting more than just yourself."

"Who, my family?" Lizzy scoffed. "Friends? They are better off without me."

"No, someone else is being hurt by this…The people you could potentially heal."

"There are plenty of others to take care of them. One less nurse isn't going to make a difference."

"It would. Even if we weren't talking about something bigger, every single caregiver matters. Especially the ones that care with the love that you offered your patients. However, *you* have the opportunity to do even more—to help so many others. Follow the path, Elizabeth."

"What are you talking about? What path?"

The other leaned close to the water so that Lizzy could only see her eyes.

"The one that Tita started you on the day she passed. The tattoo. The necklace. You know what I'm referring to."

"Betela's Blossom? Is it even real?"

"You don't believe what you've already heard or the things

you've seen today?"

"I don't know what to believe."

Lizzy was quiet as she stared out across the water. A warm breeze, reminding her of Tita's beachhouse, caressed her face and played with her hair. The beachhouse reminded her of *his* grin.

"Can this healing magic bring him back?"

"Lizzy...," the other said, disappointment falling over her face.

"It was *my* fault. He's gone because of me. *I* stepped into the street, and he had to save me."

"That was his choice."

"He didn't choose that," Lizzy said, horrified. "He didn't choose to be flung down the street and land headfirst on the pavement. He didn't choose to have his beautiful, sweet mind destroyed as it bashed against his own skull."

As young Lizzy growled her reply, the older one struggled to maintain her composure until, in the end, both of them broke down and sobbed. The darkness around them flared, threatening to strangle the purple glow. After a moment, however, the glow became intense, and the older Lizzy wiped the tears from her face.

"He did choose that. Not because of you; for you."

Lizzy's face almost broke; instead, she hardened it.

"Same difference."

"Stop that," the other snapped in frustration. "You are taking the easy path."

"Easy?" Lizzy scoffed. "Do you really think I want to be like this? Do you think I don't want to help people anymore?"

"This is not about what I think."

"Isn't it, though?" Lizzy said, giving the other an accusing waggle of her head. "You *are* me."

"It is obvious, however, that we are of two different minds."

"Well, *I* am of the mind that if I keep to myself, then I can't hurt anybody else."

"Are you really protecting *everybody else*?" the other said with a raised eyebrow.

Lizzy grumbled. She was silent for a moment, letting the breeze cool the frustration from her face.

"You didn't answer my question. Is the healing magic real? Can I save everyone?"

"Not everyone can or even should be saved."

"I don't mean...I mean, can I heal *him*?"

"Healing comes with consequences, and as a healer, you will be the one to carry them. Sometimes those consequences will be more than you can imagine."

Lizzy's face contorted in anger, and she tightened her fists.

"So it's possible to save him, but I'll die?"

"That's not what I said," the other said. "Nor is it the most important consequence. Either way, you will have to live with what you decide to do."

"Why does healing have to cost something? Why can't it just help? Why can't I?"

The other suddenly looked exhausted and defeated, as if she had just competed in a marathon but stopped just short of the finish line. Lizzy noticed this and let her anger slip into the same feeling of defeat. She sat in the water and buried her face in her hands.

"It's not fair that I get to live and do what I love."

"Life is not fair...according to our individual desires. Our selfish desires."

"I am not selfish," Lizzy shouted, splashing the water again.

The other remained silent. Lizzy's own words became an accusation that echoed back at her. She turned away from the image of the other and squeezed her eyes tight as she cried.

For most of the day, she had found relief from the weeks of pain she had endured. But it returned, weighing even heavier than before. She had discovered a world full of magic and seen things that before would have excited her. But now she had no one to share it with. No one to go to for advice about what to do next. No one to spend hours over coffee discussing how any of it could be possible. No one to tell about the sights, smells, and sounds.

Now, someone, her future self, was hinting to her that there was a way to change that. The other was right. After everything she had experienced today, how could she doubt something equally as strange? Healing via magic sounded crazy, but if there was a chance it could save *Him*...

"Ok, where do I...," Lizzy said, but as she opened her eyes again, the water and darkness were gone. She was back in the alley, standing in front of the strange flower, but there was more. She rubbed the tears from her eyes to see more clearly. Dozens of other potted plants filled the little alley, converting it into an urban jungle.

She frowned at the new garden, but her mind was focused on one thing. There actually may be a chance to fix things. She would have scoffed had someone told her that the day before. She had seen the brain scans. It was impossible. But so was magic, and now it exists. She struggled with the consequences. She didn't care what happened to herself, but others...

"Lost?" a stern female voice said, yanking her from her

thoughts. Lizzy spun around with a yelp. At first, there was no one nearby. Lizzy studied the jungle carefully. Among the plants was an ancient woman holding a potted plant in her lap. Her white hair looked like a cat had gotten stuck in it and fought its way to freedom. She sat eerily still, in an old, worn bathrobe, until her mouth stretched into a wide, toothy smile.

"Oh, I didn't see you there," Lizzy stammered. She felt welcome, but as if she were trespassing at the same time. "I didn't mean to disturb your garden. I was just leaving." She sidestepped with a hop toward the opposite end of the alleyway. Like an owl, the old woman's eyes followed her without moving her head.

"Wait," the woman finally said, her voice was softer now, with age. Lizzy paused as the old woman stood and rushed towards her. She moved fast for her age; in a blink, the women were toe-to-toe.

She's shorter than I am! she thought. Then, Lizzy gasped. On the woman's forehead was a faint symbol: a heart surrounded by leaves. *Could this be the faerie queen?*

"You see my crown?" the woman demanded of Lizzy.

"I'm sorry…I didn't mean to stare." Lizzy apologized and stepped back.

"And the blooms?"

"Uh, the what?"

"The blooms…," the woman said with a frown. She reached for a nearby potted plant and wiggled her slender fingers in its leaves. "…the flowers! You see them as well?"

"Still? Yes. They weren't there before. Were they?"

The old woman frowned and leaned in too close. Lizzy withdrew as an age-bent finger reached out to poke her arm, but paused just before touching her.

"Wait," the woman said, as if suddenly realizing something.

"But I should just—"

"I said wait," the woman said. She stared at her wrist. There was no watch there, but she inaudibly counted five seconds before eying Lizzy again.

"How about now?" the woman said. She watched Lizzy carefully, like a doctor testing her reflexes. "The flowers human, the flowers…do you still see them?"

"Sure?" Lizzy said, glancing around the alley. There were flowers everywhere.

"Hmm, she has the look of a Dullren, but perhaps there is something distinctive about her," the woman said to herself. "You spent a time staring at the purple flower," the woman said. "What did you perceive?"

"Nothing," Lizzy answered. "I just have never seen anything like it. I was curious about it." The old woman shuffled to the flower. Lizzy considered taking off while her back was turned, but wanted to see what happened when she looked at it.

"Nothing?" She heckled. "You beheld yourself, yes? Hmmm. Let's discover what your face will be. Wrinkled like mine, I suppose." The woman hunched over the flower for a moment and moved her head back and forth, as if searching for something. "Mmm-hmmm, yes. I see." When the woman finally straightened, she laughed at herself, though Lizzy thought it was directed at her and frowned.

"I'm so sorry, cupcake," the woman said, her expression softening. "It's been so long, I hardly recognized you. I was beginning to wonder if you'd ever find this place."

"Cupcake?" Lizzy said, tilting her head. "My great-grandmother used to call me that."

"Did she?" the woman said innocently. "It is a sweet thing to say." She chuckled.

"Who are you? Have we met before?"

"Call me Flo," the woman said. "We have met before, though you were too young to remember it. This is one of my little gardens. I have them hidden here and there. It's a bit of respite for urban creatures."

"And you knew Tita?"

"Of course, we go waaay back. I was sorry to hear that she left this realm, but I'm excited to see what she'll do next."

"What she'll do next? She's…," Lizzy paused. Flo had a wild look in her eye. Maybe she wasn't entirely sane? "Ok, and what was that purple flower?" Lizzy nodded at the flower.

"It's called a Star Blossom, and it's extremely rare. It drinks from the same source as healing does."

"Magic?"

"Magic!" Flo said with a laugh. "Some call it that, but it is a special kind of magic. Healing magic. Aetherwilde."

"Healing magic, like Betela's Blossom? Can you tell me about it?"

"I could, but then how would you learn? If you start your journey, you will learn along the way."

Lizzy frowned. She was tired of her questions being answered with questions.

"This is ridiculous. All of it. This world. Magic. I mean, is any of this even real?"

The woman reached out and pinched the skin on Lizzy's upper arm between her fingernails.

"OW!" Lizzy yelped.

"Did that feel real, cupcake?" The woman chuckled as Lizzy

massaged her arm. The woman hooked her finger on Lizzy's sleeve and slid it up to reveal her tattoo. It was glowing. "Does this look real?"

"I don't know. No one else can see it."

"What does that matter?" the woman said. "You can see it. It's real to you."

She started toward the street. "Besides, now that Jules isn't hiding it, only a Dullren wouldn't be able to see it. You want answers?" She glanced back at Lizzy. "She's left hints for you."

Her steps slowed. "But you're running out of time."

She reached the edge of the street, the noise of the world returning to the alley. "Word is spreading that a new Lady Betela is at hand—and that's not a good thing. Not yet. Some would do anything to stop you from obtaining that power."

After a pause, she added quietly, "Even more dangerous are those who want you to obtain it for their own selfish ends."

With that, she stepped into the street and disappeared past the mouth of the alley.

"Wait," Lizzy said, and ran after her.

She rounded the corner, and the world changed. The woman was gone. The alley had opened into a city street, loud and ordinary. Lizzy jogged forward, breath shallow, until the familiar paths of the downtown park confirmed it. She was back downtown.

Lizzy sighed in frustration. She was tired; more tired than she felt she had ever been. It was time to head home.

CHAPTER 6

After a curious day that would have confounded even Alice, Lizzy finally made it back to her apartment. She needed a shower, but she had to rest first. Her mind raced with everything that happened as her gut somersaulted between excitement, fear, and back to the ever-present guilt. More than anything, though, the slim but insane possibility that she could bring Vic back ignited a flickering flame of hope.

The soft slide of the balcony door made Lizzy look up as it opened just enough for Fresita to wander inside. The door had always been loose, no matter how many times maintenance came to look at it. It wasn't a concern. She didn't care enough about anything she owned to worry about it being stolen.

"Where have you been? You took off just when things got interesting," Lizzy said. "You wouldn't believe the day I've had."

The sassy white cat hopped onto a side table and listened as Lizzy recounted everything since she last saw her. Lizzy paused here and there as she considered the things she had experienced.

A chirp from Fresita would snap her out of her thoughts and back into the story. Lizzy hopped on one leg as she struggled into her PJs, and ended her adventure with the strange old woman. Fresita seemed particularly interested in this part. By the time she was done, her exhaustion had been replaced with an excited energy.

"I have no idea what to do next," Lizzy said, flopping into her love seat. "I feel different, Fresita. I feel like someone swapped my mind with someone else's while I was out." Lizzy, who had been playing with the elastic of her pants, decided to make sure she wasn't in a dream. She yanked the elastic hard, letting it snap painfully against her skin.

"Ow...," she complained. Out of the corner of her eye, Lizzy could have sworn Fresita rolled her eyes and then turned away to take a bath.

Lizzy frowned, however, when she tried to decide what to do next. She had experienced things that her rational mind wanted desperately to explain, but just couldn't. She thought of herself as an educated woman who recognized a conspiracy theory; she had learned it from her mother. However, she also spent a lifetime hearing fantastic tales. She was always willing to consider the extraordinary at least.

She hopped up and made herself a peanut butter and jelly sandwich, a habit she got from Tita's afternoon snacks.

She sank back into the love seat and thumbed through her tablet searching for any mention of a café or an invitation business card. There were plenty of stories and movies about discovering magic in the real world, but nothing that had anything to do with what she had experienced. See tried "Café Calacoayan" and "The Inn Between" with no result. A search of 'socials' produced not even one grinning influencer in a perfect pose in the coffee shop. Impossible as it was, it had no online footprint.

Fresita pounced over to pester Lizzy. If she wasn't trying to snatch a piece of her sandwich, she was flicking her tail in her face as she walked along the back of the chair. Lizzy swatted her away numerous times before sliding the plate with the remaining quarter of her sandwich across the floor. Fresita side-eyed Lizzy incredulously before trotting over to eat it.

Unable to find real-world information, Lizzy grabbed Tita's sketchbook and looked through it again. This time, she took the time to examine each page carefully. Every image took on new meaning now that she thought it might all be real. It filled her with so many questions. She wanted to know how it all came about, how magic worked, and how it had all stayed hidden for all this time.

As she turned the pages, she came across a section about faeries. Among the copious notes about the lovely creatures, Tita had included an underlined section:

"Warning! Fairy bites can be a serious thing. They have dirty little mouths. If a nibble breaks your skin, you can be assured it will become infected. Treat with Ladybug Leaf and spring water."

Lizzy inspected her hand. There was no trace of the Faerie bite she received earlier. This wasn't the first time she had been surprised at a quick healing. Throughout her life, she had recovered quickly from any ailment. The strange woman in the alley had mentioned that Tita was hiding her tattoo. Was it possible it had always been there, helping her heal? Did that mean she already had healing powers? She needed to test it.

Lizzy stared at the knife block on her kitchen counter. A little cut wouldn't hurt. She got up, grabbed the biggest knife from it, and held it next to her skin. She stood there a moment, then paced her kitchenette, debating. If she didn't have the power, she would heal eventually, at normal speed. But if she did…

She pressed the knife harder into her palm and then sighed. She was being crazy. She headed back to the knife block, but tripped over a pair of pants strewn on the floor. The knife sliced across the back of her hand, sending blood splattering onto the floor.

"Shit!" Lizzy exclaimed, hurrying to her bathroom to treat her wound. Fresita trotted in behind her and perched on the back of the toilet to watch. "Yeah, yeah, I know that was stupid."

After wrapping her hand and cleaning up the mess, she sat back down with the sketchbook. She wiggled her hand, wondering how long it would take for her so-called powers to kick in. It ached in response. Lizzy rolled her eyes and returned to the book. After a few pages, she discovered several sketches of a beautiful short sword, its rose-gold hilt carved with flowers.

"IlBetela," Lizzy read the title out loud. "This is it." She traced the soft lines of engraved Star blossoms into it. Soft metallic leaves stretched up from the hilt, along the blade's center, their beauty betraying how dangerous the sword could be.

"Betela's Blossom," Lizzy read, after she turned the page and discovered a detailed drawing of the necklace. Alongside it was a close-up of the sword, the hilt missing the pair of flowers in the center. The necklace was almost identical to the one in the coffee shop. The one difference Lizzy noted was the size. The drawing showed the pendant resting in someone's hand. From the looks of it, the real pendant was almost twice as large as the replica.

Lizzy stared at the drawing. The necklace's chain hung between two fingers; on one of the fingers, there was a

Betela's Blossom

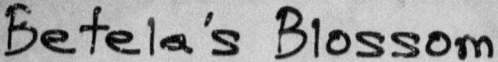

January 1922

I cannot say how I came upon this exquisite treasure, should my sketchbook one day fall into the wrong hands. However, its story and the power it holds within are extraordinary indeed. The wonders I have witnessed and accomplished with its assistance are the most astounding I have yet encountered.

I hesitate to confess it, but this necklace may well be the most important object in all the world!

il Thren, (what the citizens of the Realm refer to as magic) can do so many wondrous things but healing is not one of them. il Thren can only ease pain and assist the body in it's own natural healing processes.

This necklace is something else though. Maybe not even something of this world.

It is too much. I cannot. I should not...

Dragonscale ring. She looked at the ring on her finger. It looked similar, but it could be that all Dragonscale rings look alike, what with the scales and all. But what made more sense was if Tita were drawing it, she would hold it in her hand.

"Tita had the necklace!" Lizzy exclaimed, standing up so suddenly that Fresita jumped up and skittered across the room to hide under the bed. "If she had it, then she must have left it for me somewhere. Hidden." Fresita peeked out and then left the safety of the bed while Lizzy thought outloud as she paced through her apartment. "Unless…it is someone else's hand? She told me there were only a few rings, but I did recently see another one…I ran into the same woman from the party again at the café. Coincidence?"

Lizzy sighed, concluding that it probably was just a coincidence. She sat back down with the book and restudied the drawings. Not finding anything, she continued to search the rest of the book. There were creatures, relics, and lost cities, but no further mention of the sword or the necklace.

"What am I missing?" Lizzy asked Fresita. The white cat, however, was asleep, curled up in a ball in the far corner of the apartment.

"That's probably a good idea," Lizzy said, yawning. She curled up around the notebook and closed her eyes. "I want to head out early to the café." She had spent many nights sleeping in that chair, but she had never felt so comfortable in it. She pictured the other Lizzy, replaying their conversation until sleep tugged at her mind. Like a heating blanket, a relaxing warmth flowed from her arm and across her body. For the first time in forever, she felt the soft caress of peacefulness soothe her head. She hadn't felt like this since before the accident.

For once, she was free of the horrible nightmares of reality and instead dreamed of the story Tita told her after the dog attack. In the dream, however, Lizzy was the young elf girl. She walked through her village, holding the sword high, and healed her people. But there was one she could not save. He was lying on the ground at her feet. She took his body in her arms and looked into his face. It was Vic.

Lizzy gasped and sat up straight when the dream came to an end. Her neck was stiff from the position she had slept in. As she rolled it, she realized the sketchbook was no longer in her lap. It was bobbing about three feet in front of her.

Her first instinct was to reach out and grab it, but she kept still, afraid she might scare it.

Am I dreaming? Or is this more magic? she wondered. Lizzy scanned the apartment for Fresita, but she was nowhere to be found. It was quiet. Lizzy held her breath until she heard someone else breathe. Fear pricked her stomach; the sound was right in front of her.

"Who's there!" she shouted and jumped up to sit on the back of the love seat. The light from the hallway outside the open front door doubled her fear. "I know someone's here!" Her eyes scoured her place; she had mace in her backpack, but she froze again as the book began to move. Her heart was pounding so hard she was sure whoever was there could hear it, too.

"Thief!" a woman's voice hissed from the doorway. Lizzy spun around to see who had come to her rescue, but her weight flipped the chair over. She tumbled head over heels but popped back up in time to see a pink ball of light, crackling like lightning, whiz over her. The floating book dropped out of midair as the energy impacted against something invisible just behind it.

"Shit!" a young voice exclaimed. Out of thin air, a boy in a neon yellow hoodie appeared. He scooped the sketchbook up and was about to run when a second blast of light knocked him off his feet.

Lizzy turned and nearly forgot how to breathe. In the doorway, Fresita stood gracefully on two legs with a soft pink glow dancing in her paw like a miniature star. Her tail swished behind her, and sharp teeth glistened in a devilish grin as she aimed her paw at the boy.

"Fresita?" Lizzy gasped.

"Glisfarrr!" Fresita said, and the glow became a writhing tongue of flame. "Who sent you?"

"Fresita?" Lizzy mumbled again.

"Not now, Liz," Fresita said in an annoyed tone as she manipulated the flame in her paws.

"You can talk?"

"Yes, but there's a thief in your home! Which is morrre important?"

Remembering the boy, Lizzy turned back to him and mustered the angriest face she could.

"What the hell are you doing in my apartment!"

"Look, I'm really sorry, my Lady," the boy said in a sincere tone and offered a quick hint of a bow. "I had no idea who you were…what you could do, but I've got to take this book."

"You don't have to do anything except give me it back, or… or my cat will attack you again."

"I'm not *yourrr* cat," Fresita announced as she launched the ball of light at the boy.

In a swift motion, the boy ducked under the ball as he dashed for the sliding glass door. Fresita lept across the room towards the boy, but he snapped out of view. She stood up straight again and grimaced as she plucked a single strand of her fur from her tail. With a flick of her paw, the white strand floated in the air between her paws and then blazed to life as another pink ball of light. This time, however, she jerked her paws apart from each other, and the ball expanded until it filled the room with its light.

"There!" Lizzy pointed at the boy as he came into view again. Fresita dashed at him, but the boy pulled his hoodie over his head and flung it at her. She would have easily evaded it except that it had a life of its own; the sleeves shot out and wrapped around her body. She tumbled across the floor as she struggled to untangle herself from its embrace.

The boy, somehow in another hoodie, a black one, wasted no time in kicking open the door and bolting down the hallway. Lizzy looked from the escaping boy to Fresita, wrestling with the hoodie, and back again. Her face creased with anger as she scrambled to her feet and charged after the book.

"That's mine!" Lizzy shouted as the boy hesitated at an entrance to a stairwell at the end of the short hall. He shook his head in disbelief and then hurried inside when he saw her furious face.

She plowed herself into the door and almost went over the faulty stairway railing on the other side. Craning her neck, she looked up and down the shaft until she caught a glimpse of him heading up. She chased after him.

Lizzy didn't know what hurt worse, the strain in her leg muscles or the burning in her lungs. It had been years since she last exercised. She tripped and pain pelted her hands and knees, but she quickly got her feet back under her and shot forward. The door smacked open as she burst onto the rooftop. She desperately scanned the area.

The sun hovered just over the horizon, and she shivered at the chill of the evening on her sweaty arms. Lizzy panicked when she couldn't locate him. She needed that book; it was the brightest spot left in her past and a fleeting hope for her future. She felt like the answers to every question she had running around in her head were racing away from her.

"Damn it!" Her heart pounded in her chest, and her stomach pushed up against her throat. She bent over and put her hands on her knees as she tried to gulp air. The sound of rocks crunching made her look up. The boy was running towards the edge of the roof. Lizzy took off so fast that she had to force herself not to fall. She pushed herself harder than she ever had before, her body pleading with her to stop. It didn't matter, though; they were out of room. She had him.

The boy didn't stop; he hand-planted over the edge. Lizzy gawked, but in a split second, without thinking, decided that she was going to do the exact same thing. She pumped her legs, ignored the sharp pebbles digging into her soles, and built up whatever speed she could muster.

She was not athletic, nor had she ever taken gymnastics, so when the moment came to copy his hand plant, she had no idea how. So, she just jumped up on the little ledge and launched herself off the side. She figured, if he had just thrown himself over, then something had to be there for *her* to land on. She found herself, however, jumping into a twenty-foot gap sixty feet in the air.

She realized all her mistakes too late. She was exhausted, her legs wobbled, and there was no energy left to jump any kind of distance. Even if she had been well rested and fit, she could never have made the kind of leap the boy had. The boy barely made it across himself, struggling to stay on his feet, which he did, and quickly disappeared through the roof access door of the building he landed on.

Lizzy, however, sailed at best four feet through the air before she plummeted downwards. As the helpless rush of falling gripped her insides, random thoughts flipped through her head like a deck of cards.

Will He be there waiting for me?
This asshole is going to get away with Tita's book.
At least Mom will enjoy a nice little pity party at my funeral.

Suddenly, the waist of her PJs dug deep into her belly, and her body jerked upwards. A struggling grunt rang out above her as her fall slowed but didn't stop.

"Fledderrrbick! How are you so heavy?" Fresita's voice struggled. Lizzy had no idea what was happening. First, her cat can talk and now fly? Still, she was more concerned by the ground that rushed towards her. She shielded her face with her arms. "Not to worry. Going up!"

Lizzy's stomach lurched as her body was yanked upwards. She opened her eyes and gaped at the upside-down view of the world as they passed three, four, and then five floors. She twisted to look at her savior.

Fresita was suspended in the air by intangible fluttering dragonfly-like wings as she struggled to hang on to Lizzy with her front paws. Lizzy was beginning to calm down until she heard a ripping sound.

"My pants are ripping," Lizzy exclaimed, struggling to reach for a passing window ledge.

"For the love of the Grace, stop moving!" Fresita hissed, but Lizzy still tried to grab another ledge. As she touched it, the waistband in her pajamas tore, and she screamed as she felt herself fall. Luckily, they had just passed over the top of the building, and she smacked onto the rough rooftop.

Lizzy flipped over and watched as Fresita came to a running stop nearby. Her wings faded away as she stalked over to the door the boy had entered. She sniffed the air and then shook her head in frustration.

Lizzy gawked at Fresita. "So, you can talk AND fly?"

"Come, firrrst back to the apartment," Fresita said as she pounced up onto the ledge of the rooftop and scanned the area. "It's not safe."

"You're afraid of the boy?"

"Ha!" Fresita laughed and stood upright again. She placed her paws on her hips and gave Lizzy a defiant look. "I am Maeve, I fear no—

"Maeve! As in the fairy from Tita's stories?"

"Of courrrse," Fresita said in a hurt tone. She frowned at Lizzy before returning to all four paws. She walked the perimeter of the building, pausing to sniff the air every once in a while.

"I didn't know, I mean, how I could know," Lizzy said, following her. "You look like a cat."

"Not my choice," Fresita responded. She held up a paw and then sent fur flying when she shook it. "Look at this."

"I don't understand."

"Furrr everywhere! Annoying!"

"No, I mean, why are you a cat? Why are you here? Who was that boy? How are we going to get Tita's book back?"

Fresita blinked at a frazzled Lizzy.

"Too many questions."

"All I have are questions right now. Yesterday, fairy tales were the furthest thing from my mind, and now all of a sudden, every single story I heard as a little girl is reality. It's absurd. I'm talking to a cat right now, and I think that may be one of the least crazy things I've experienced today."

The hair along Fresita's back stood up. "Twenty questions once we arrre inside. It is not safe here, look." With a nod of her head, Fresita pointed out three dark individuals perched on a rooftop a few blocks away. Lizzy shivered.

"Who are they?"

"Not surrre yet," Fresita said, her eyes narrowing as she watched them. "They've been watching you in secret."

"I haven't seen them."

"In. Secret."

"Well, how did you see them then?" Lizzy said, giving her a sassy expression.

"Because I *am* a secret," Fresita said with a wink. "Let's get home, and we'll talk."

Lizzy and her furry companion headed downstairs, shrugging sheepishly at a maintenance man coming up, and returned to her apartment building. Inside her place, Fresita watched Lizzy sit on the floor and massage the soles of her feet, picking off a few tiny rocks that had stuck to them.

"How did all this happen?" Lizzy murmured as she paced her apartment, running a hand through her hair. At last, she stopped and looked at Fresita. "Why are you a cat?"

Fresita sighed. "I was going to do something Mother did not approve of. She trapped me in this form to stop me." She twisted, trying unsuccessfully to look at her back. "I miss my real wings."

Lizzy blinked. "Okay. Next question—how is magic real?"

Fresita meowed out a laugh. "How are you real? How is the

worrrld real? It's just life." She curled her tail neatly around her feet and studied Lizzy.

Lizzy hugged herself. "I just don't understand. Has it always been like this?"

"Yes."

"Magic has always been real?"

"Since the beginning of time."

Lizzy righted the loveseat and sat cross-legged. "Then how did Tita discover it?"

"Jules was an explorer," Fresita said. "Even more currrious than I."

"Then why didn't she ever tell me?"

Fresita scoffed. "She told you all the time. She drew it. She filled sketchbooks with it. She told you morrre than she should have." Her eyes narrowed. "Our world is best kept secret from people like you."

Lizzy stiffened. "People like me?"

"Dullren. Non-magic users."

Lizzy frowned. "That sounds offensive."

"Pffh." Fresita waved it away with a flick of her tail.

"Whatever," Lizzy huffed. "Then teach me about magic."

Fresita shook her head. "Magic, ilThren, cannot be explained. You must study the sketchbook. Learn through the people and places entwined with it."

Lizzy's stomach dropped. "But her sketchbook is gone."

"Do not worry. I will retrieve it."

Fresita padded to a neglected plant by the balcony and pawed through the dry soil, scattering dirt everywhere. From the pot, she tugged free a bundle of leaves.

"Hey! Stop that!" Lizzy groaned. "What is that?"

Fresita slipped her front legs through leather straps and slung the bundle over her back. "A Mosstragel."

Lizzy stared.

"A fairrry backpack."

"You're leaving?"

"I will not find the sketchbook here."

"Then I'm coming with you."

"No." Fresita's tone sharpened. She raised a paw. "You should never have gone to the Inn Between with the mark."

Lizzy looked down at her tattoo. "I've always had it, haven't I?"

"Since that morning on the beach."

Fresita stepped onto the balcony.

"Why do I have it?" Lizzy asked. "Why did Tita hide it from me?"

"Too many questions." Fresita leapt onto the railing. "Keep the mark hidden."

"Wait, look." Lizzy held out her arm. The bandage had fallen off during the chase. Only a pale scar remained, one that looked weeks old at most. She prodded it, fascinated. "If I can already heal, why do I need the necklace or the sword?"

"It is temporary," Fresita said, peering down at the street below. Her tail swished. "Just enough to assist you on your jourrrney to find the necklace."

"What if someone comes looking for me while you're gone?"

"They will not."

Fresita paused, then sighed. Reaching into the Mosstragel with her tail, she pulled out a small leather pouch tied with a thin vine.

"But if they do," Fresita said, tossing it to Lizzy, "throw this on the ground. Do not look at it."

Lizzy peered inside at the white, chalky powder. "What is it?"

"A distraction."

Fresita crouched, muscles coiling. "Be safe. I will returrrn."

Then she sprang from the railing and vanished into the night.

Fed up, Lizzy crashed onto her bed and stared at her hand. The more she interacted with this new world, the more questions it gave her. It made her head hurt. She rested her eyes until she had almost fallen asleep.

A skittering across the cement of her balcony made her sit up straight. She hurried to the glass door, expecting to see Fresita, but stepped back at the sight of a black figure hovering in the air in front of her balcony. As it floated into her home, Lizzy tripped backwards and ended up wedged between the coffee table and love seat.

"Hello Elizabeth," a woman's voice greeted her in a deep lilt from within a black hood. The woman slowly hovered downward until a tattooed barefoot touched the balcony. As the woman stepped inside, the lights in Lizzy's place turned off all at once.

Her clothes fit loosely, but did not reveal her identity. The hood, which cast a shadow that enveloped her face, became a cape as it draped over her shoulders and almost reached the ground. Though her clothes were all dark, muted greens and blacks, Lizzy noticed a raised velvet pattern of prickly holly-like leaves on her pants. She came to a stop in front of Lizzy.

"Who are you? What are you doing in my home?" Lizzy demanded. Her fear was tempered with the frustration that her place had suddenly become such a popular destination for strangers. She glanced at her bed, where she had stupidly left the powder Fresita gave her.

"I am Cendryn," the woman replied. "I'm someone who wants to help you achieve your dream." She loomed over Lizzy for a moment before finally offering a hand. Lizzy stared at it as if it were a loaded gun. Tattoed around her fingers were ornate gold rings.

Cendryn relaxed her hand and moved it closer. Lizzy relented and let the woman pull her off the floor. She nodded and then examined Lizzy's place, touching things as she slowly walked around.

"What dream?" Lizzy asked, keeping an eye on Cendryn while also watching the balcony for her dark companions.

"Don't worry, I came alone. My friends drew your cat companion away so we could have a private conversation."

"She's not a cat, she's a fairy," Lizzy corrected her.

"A fairy! Hmm, that would explain things," Cendryn said. She opened a closet and ran her fingers across the hanging clothes. She hummed a critical critique of Lizzy's fashion choices before continuing. "Maeve, no doubt."

"Uh…," Lizzy hesitated, suddenly realizing she should have kept that to herself.

"It's ok. I'm sure she thinks she is protecting you. But I know that unless you get out into the world, you will never find what you are looking for. And it is imperative that you do. Some would do anything to stop you." Cendryn finished her examination of Lizzy's things and stood in front of her. She wasn't that much taller, but her presence loomed over her.

"Who's trying to stop me?" Lizzy asked, subtly leaning in, trying to peer beneath Cendryn's hood.

"The Aurenthal," Cendryn said, stepping back out of reach. "They are the ones in power in our world. They make the rules, and they fear what you represent."

Lizzy frowned. "Me? What are they afraid I'll do?"

"Stop them," Cendryn replied without hesitation. "They fear the same thing all powerful people do: losing control. Losing wealth. Losing power."

"But I'm just healing people," Lizzy said. "What does that have to do with any of this?"

Cendryn's voice hardened. "The Aurenthal created the sickness."

Lizzy's breath caught.

"They saw an imbalance," Cendryn continued. "An increasing threat—the mixing of Realms. The disease progresses fastest in those weakly connected to ilThren. Most often, that means people who crossed over from your world."

"They created the Hollowing?" Lizzy gasped. "They're infecting their own people?"

"They released it in the lower class," Cendryn said. "That's where new magic users usually end up. It spread farther than intended, but to them, it's an acceptable loss."

Cendryn tilted her head, as if listening to something beyond the alley.

"I have to go," she said, turning back to Lizzy. "You don't have much time to find what you need."

"The necklace?" Lizzy asked. "Or the sword?"

At the word sword, Cendryn flinched as if struck. Pain rippled across her face before she forced herself upright.

"Both," she gasped.

Lizzy stepped closer to her, trying to appear unafraid. "Then give me back the sketchbook."

"That wasn't us," Cendryn said. "More likely Xeilan's people.

Tell your cat to check his hotel—she'll find it quickly enough."

Lizzy hesitated. "Then what do you want?"

Cendryn stepped closer. "Only that you heal me."

Lizzy recoiled. "You have the Hollowing?"

"Worse," Cendryn said. "I'll explain when we meet again. For now, I offer you hope."

"Hope?" Lizzy scoffed.

"That you can save your friend."

Lizzy's blood went cold. "How do you know about him?"

"I've been watching you," Cendryn said simply.

"Sure," Lizzy muttered. "But I've been warned not to heal anyone. That I'll lose my ability if I do."

"That's true," Cendryn said. "But I've found a way around it. You can heal your friend and still heal the world."

"How?"

"Find me tomorrow," Cendryn said, lifting from the ground with a flick of her wrist. "Outside the coffee shop in the Inn. We'll talk more. Tell no one of our meeting."

Lizzy squinted up at her. "Why should I keep this a secret?"

"Because I don't follow the Realm's rules," Cendryn said. "Others do, and that could cost them the cure."

"How do I know I can trust *you*?"

Cendryn paused, then shrugged.

"You can't," she said. "If you want to help people, that's a risk you'll have to take."

She drifted backward, rising past the edge of the balcony. Lizzy rushed to the railing, but there was nothing there. Only the distant hum of the city and a plane cutting across the night sky.

Lizzy slammed her fist against the railing. She was frustrated to the point of giving up, but the hope that *He* could be saved kept her from it. It was her fault that he was gone. If she could get the power to bring him back, to fix things, then she would stop at nothing to do just that.

CHAPTER 7

The next morning, Lizzy popped out of bed without completely waking up first. She stumbled through the room, blinking away crud as she searched for Fresita. Or was it Maeve now? She decided to stick with the cat's name since that's what she was used to. Either way, she had not returned from her hunt.

She glanced down at her hand. The wound was already fading, the scar little more than a pale mark.

Frowning, she stepped back inside, her thoughts fixed on Cendryn's visit. The encounter clung to her, impossible to shake. She needed answers—about the magic, about her ability to heal, and whether it could truly save Vic. Staying home wasn't going to get her those answers. And besides, her apartment didn't feel all that safe anymore.

Lizzy pulled on jeans and a pink hoodie with a plump unicorn on the front, shoved the pouch of powder into her pocket, and headed out in search of answers.

As soon as she stepped outside, Lizzy realized she didn't know how to get back to the café. She turned one way, then the other, grasping for a memory that refused to come. She could picture the building and the street it sat on with perfect clarity—but the path to get there was gone. She hadn't paid attention while following the card's directions. Now, she was lost.

"Shit," Lizzy said. She remembered being near the downtown park, so she headed that way. The sky was a cheery blue, but the sun was still low in the sky—the air nipped at her cheeks. She was glad to be free of the summer's oppression.

She came to a stop after only a few steps. Ruby the barista sat cross-legged on the sidewalk. Her head bobbed softly to the beat of a pair of headphones cradling her head as she made cute faces at a nearby squirrel.

Like a cartoon, the little creature *smiled* at her and offered a wet acorn from its mouth. Ruby politely refused with a giggle and a shake of her head. She showed the squirrel a paper cup of coffee she had been warming her hands with and took a sip. When Lizzy approached, the squirrel froze and stared at her. It gave her a slight bow before skittering off towards a tree.

"Hey, you," Ruby said, sliding the headphones to her neck and flashing her knowing smile. From her side, though seemingly from out of thin air, she produced another cup of coffee to hand to Lizzy.

"Hi,…uh, thanks," Lizzy said, trying to follow the squirrel with her eyes. She lost it in the leaves before taking the cup. "Did it just bow? Was it…," Lizzy paused and looked around before mouthing the word 'magical.'

"Squirrels, and most animals for that matter, are entwined with il'Thren. So I suppose the answer would be yes…but maybe not in the way you think."

"I don't know what to think."

"Understandable," Rubby laughed. "It was a very confusing answer. So, that was a regular squirrel; however, since I am 'magical,' it interacted with me."

"I guess that makes sense," Lizzy sighed and looked at Ruby expectantly. "So…"

"Oh! Maeve asked me to meet you this morning," Ruby replied, pulling out a small scroll from the pocket of her comfy-looking jean shorts. She was dressed far more informally than Lizzy recalled seeing her last, swallowed by a fuzzy orange sweater, but still with the same wispy knot of hair wobbling on her head.

Lizzy took the scroll, a rolled-up dogwood leaf, and stared at the illegible series of scribbles. She shook her head with a shrug and handed it back.

"Sorry! So sorry, I keep forgetting you're new. It says: 'Ruby, I need you to keep track of my girl today. I told her to stay put; she won't. I'll make it up to you. M…P.S. Look for my mark."

"Her mark?"

"Yeah, so I had no idea *who* she was talking about, so I just wandered around until I saw it."

"Saw what?"

Ruby glanced back towards the front of the apartment building. To the side of the front windows, a sparkling heart symbol pulsed. Lizzy walked over to find it was only a drawing.

"And only magic users…Thraewen?" Lizzy said, touching the image. It beat faster in response and then disappeared. "Only they could see it?"

"Yep, and I guess now you can too," Ruby said after taking a sip of her coffee. "Don't forget about your coffee."

"Oh yeah, is it from…?"

"Calacoayan?" Ruby responded. Lizzy nodded hopefully. "Of course!"

"You're amazing," Lizzy replied and took a sip. She closed her eyes for a moment as the warmth, flavor, and aroma comforted her. When she opened them again, Ruby wrinkled her nose and winked. Lizzy admired her carefree happiness. "Anyway…I think I can see your world because I've got this ring that my…," Lizzy's voice trailed off when she looked at her hand. She forgot to put the ring on before she left. She felt around in her pocket and found it there, but hesitated to slip it on.

"Once you start hanging around us," Ruby explained, "and spending time in the Inn, it gets easier to see it all. Especially if you've been hanging around a powerful fae like Maeve."

Lizzy looked around to see if she could find anything else that wasn't there before. The world did seem different this morning. It was like trying on a pair of prescription lenses for the first time. Everything was more defined. She slid the ring on and off there was no difference.

"So," Ruby said as she stood up and stretched. "Where are we off to?"

"Actually, I was headed back to the coffee shop. I was hoping to learn more about everything."

"Whew, that is a relief," Ruby replied with a genuine look of relief on her face. "I was concerned you wouldn't want to go back after your encounter with Xeilan yesterday."

"Ugh," Lizzy said, letting her shoulders slump. "With everything else, I honestly forgot about him."

"Don't worry. Calacoayan is meant to be a safe place for all. I made that very clear to him."

"So he won't be back?"

"Unfortunately," Ruby said, shaking her head apologetically. "I can't say that. In fact, I'm sure he will be back—often. General Xeilan is a very powerful, wealthy, and respected figure in the Inn. He owns the Celestine, a *fancy* hotel just down the street from the shop. But I won't let him bother you again." Ruby offered an apologetic smile.

"Ok," Lizzy said with a nod.

"You don't know why he acted like that towards you?"

"Uh-uh," Lizzy said, trying not to look at her arm.

Ruby shrugged and then smiled as if everything was right in the world. "Well, honey, I'm ready if you are."

"Sure," Lizzy said, and they began to walk. "You don't mind, do you? I hate to make you hang out there on your day off."

"I'm pretty much always on duty. But even if I weren't, I would still end up there when I'm not scheduled. I'll tell you a secret." Ruby feigned a whisper behind her hand to Lizzy with a giggle. "I love it there. The people are amazing, and there is always someone new crossing over or stopping in."

"I can imagine."

"So, did you have anything in particular you wanted to know more about?"

"First off…how does magic work?"

Ruby threw her head back in a loud laugh and put an arm around Lizzy.

"Oh, honey…," Ruby continued between laughs.

"I know it's a silly question," Lizzy said, trying not to react stiffly to Ruby's touch.

"No, no…I understand completely what you mean," Ruby

replied, releasing her hold on Lizzy. "I'm sorry, I shouldn't have laughed. To make up for it, the next time you order something at Calacoayan, it's on me."

"You really don't have to do that."

"I insist," Ruby said firmly. "Now, to answer your question…" Ruby tapped her chin as she stared off into the distance, seemingly pondering the meaning of life. Finally, her face lit up. "It's like sugar in coffee!"

"Ok…"

"Hear me out. We both are black coffee drinkers, right?"

"Yeah…"

"But you've had sugar in your coffee before."

"Sure," Lizzy said, with a slow nod.

"You can't see it!" Ruby said, excitedly.

"Right, it dissolves."

"And the coffee tastes sweet!"

Ruby watched with a hopeful smile as Lizzy silently worked through the logic.

"So magic is everywhere and makes life sweet?"

"I mean, sort of," Ruby squinted, now unsure of her analogy. "ilThren *is* everywhere. It permeates the living and inanimate; you can't see it, but you can experience it."

"Last night, Fresita…well, Maeve I guess, created these balls of magic energy and flung them at this guy."

"That's not ilThren," Ruby said, shaking her head. "She used it to create them, but it wasn't purely ilThren."

"What was it then?"

"Charged particles of matter, probably. Was it pink?"

Lizzy nodded.

"Ah," Ruby giggled. "Suckerwirl. It's a tuft of pink flowers…

like a dandelion, but if you touch it, it'll burn you. Fairies break them down and use them for attacks. They're usually only used in serious matters...what happened, if you don't mind me asking?"

Lizzy recounted the events of the previous evening, careful to leave out her tattoo. Ruby listened intently, her eyes wide, as Lizzy's former pet pulled off the mid-air rescue.

"Oh wow, that was quite an evening. I'm sorry your great-grandmother's book was stolen, but I'm sure that if anyone can get it back, it's Maeve. Do you have any idea why it was stolen?"

"No," Lizzy said, trying to look as honest as possible through a tight jaw.

"Huh," Ruby responded, studying Lizzy seriously for a moment before returning to her perpetual smile. "I know what will cheer you up. Today's the day señor Castañeda, the baker, delivers the weekly specials!"

"What's the weekly special?" Lizzy asked, letting Ruby's growing exuberance influence her own expression.

"Liz, you don't even know!" Ruby said, grabbing Lizzy's arm excitedly. "Each week, he creates something new and lets our customers be the first to try it out. If something hits, then he adds it to the bakery's seasonal menu."

"There's a bakery in the Inn Between?"

"Yep, Panadería Viento y Canela," Ruby said, rolling her eyes with a pleased sigh. "It's sooo good."

"If it's anything like the coffee, then I can't wait," Lizzy said, with a growing smile. It was getting easier to smile without forcing it, especially around Ruby. There was something about her. Something soothing. She felt like it was ok to feel something besides guilt when she was around her.

The two women chatted about pastries and coffee as they made their way to the café. Lizzy didn't even realize that they had crossed over into the Inn Between and were suddenly walking into the coffee shop. She relaxed as the familiar smells and ambiance washed over her.

"Grab a table, I'll get the goods," Ruby said over her shoulder, heading to the bar.

Lizzy glanced around for a table, but the framed necklace she had looked at the day before distracted her. She wanted to study it without being obvious, but it held her gaze. It was lovely.

Lizzy sighed and went back to finding a place to sit. Luckily, the table she was at the day before was free; it had a good view of the rest of the café.

Til now, the shop had a slow morning; most of the tables were empty, but a line was at the counter, and more customers were beginning to file in. Ruby headed back to the table with the biggest grin. She set down two fresh cups of coffee and a platter with a selection of the most delicious pastries Lizzy had ever seen.

"Wow!" Lizzy exclaimed.

"Which one do you want to try?" Ruby said.

"All of them?"

"Girl, I was hoping you'd say that," Ruby said and produced a knife from under a napkin. "I'll cut them in half."

Lizzy laughed as Ruby went to work dividing them. Some were soft and bouncy while others crunched as she cut through them. Ruby giggled mischievously as an octagonal-shaped croissant turned out to have a purple cream in the center. Beside it, a puffy sugar-coated bread shaped like a sleeping baby dragon magically snorted little puffs of smoke from its nostrils. Lizzy loved that one but raised an eyebrow at a donut that appeared to have a dew-covered moss topping. When Ruby finally finished, they laughed as each grabbed half of the purple-centered one to try first.

Lizzy imagined her eyes lit up at least half as much as Ruby's as she took a bite. Was it possible that the flavors themselves were enchanted, morphing as they drifted over her tongue? It began bright and juicy as a plucked grape, then relaxed into a mellow figgy-sweetness. Neither one talked but acknowledged the shared experience with a nod.

"Wow," Lizzy finally said after washing down a few more bites with coffee.

"You said it," Ruby agreed, before taking a bite of the donut and letting out a little moan of delight.

Not wanting to get too far off track with her fact-finding mission, Lizzy let her eyes wander around the room while she took another sip.

"What is the trick to finding this place?" Lizzy said after a moment. "I mean, if you don't have a guide to get here."

"No trick," Ruby said between bites. "You just have to have a little 'magic' in your spirit."

"So," Lizzy said, staring at an older man in a red vest at the counter. He looked like her, a Dullren— out of place but fascinated. "If someone has magic inside them, does that mean they can learn how to use it?"

"Not everyone who has a magical spirit can use magic," Ruby said thoughtfully. "Some only see it...others sense it. For some, it's just up to the magic to reveal itself. I think a lot of it has to do with appreciating it."

"Appreciating?" Lizzy frowned.

"Yeah, if you don't appreciate the gifts you've been given, you'll never be able to truly use them. You may never even know you have them."

"Not everybody can see all this?" Lizzy said. "Even if someone tries to show them?"

"If the magic is even the slightest bit hidden, yes. I could turn a boulder into a car in front of someone, and they may see the results but not the magic of it."

"So, trying to drag someone down here wouldn't work if they don't want to see it. It would just be confusing?"

"Uh-huh," Ruby said, picking at the dragon bread. "Not even all the people that get invited can remember how to get back." Lizzy nodded as she warmed her fingers with her mug. "Only the special ones return," Ruby added. Her eyes brightened when she noticed Lizzy's dragon scale ring. "Do you mind if I ask how you got your ring?"

"It was my great-grandmother's," Lizzy said, removing the ring and handing it to Ruby. "She recently passed and left it to me."

"Oh no! I'm so sorry. Were you close?"

Lizzy nodded, as tears burned the corners of her eyes. Ruby reached out and held Lizzy's hand. She looked like she might cry as well. Lizzy blinked back the tears and smiled at Ruby.

"Thank you."

"Of course," Ruby replied, and went back to admiring the ring. "I love rings." Ruby giggled, showing off her handful of rings. Delicate golden strands even connected one to a bracelet. "Yours is so beautiful and rare. Do you know the story of the Dragonscale rings?"

Lizzy shook her head in response. Ruby's eyes lit up, and she thought for a moment.

"How do they start the tale?" Ruby said, thinking out loud. "The older Thraewen always start their stories with this phrase—

"Once in a realm of wonder…?" Lizzy prompted.

"That's it!" Ruby said. "Once in a realm of wonder, there lived a dragon named Naram—the first of his kind. And he was very lonely."

She grabbed the dragon-shaped bread and turned it to face Lizzy, as if it were the hero of her tale.

"When he was young, Naram fell into a dark river that stripped him of his visibility. No one could see him. People would bump into him, literally, mutter a complaint, and keep walking. No one ever stopped to wonder what they'd stumbled into."

Ruby paused, digging through her charms until she found one shaped like a little person. She slipped it free and made it waddle playfully toward the dragon pastry.

"Then one day," Ruby continued, "a small boy ran into him. He was terrified at first, but when Naram spoke to calm him, the fear faded into curiosity. The boy wanted to know everything about this invisible creature."

She smiled softly. "They became friends. Lifelong friends. Years later, when the boy was old and about to cross into the Borderlands, he told Naram there was only one thing he wished for—that he could see his friend at least once before he died."

"Naram went to the Faerie Queen and told her he would give anything to make that wish come true. She said she could craft a ring that would let the boy see him… but the cost would be part of his tail."

Ruby slid the Dragonscale ring toward the charm and the pastry.

"The dragon agreed. The Queen gave him one of three rings, and Naram gifted it to the boy. In his final moments, the boy finally saw his friend."

She looked up at Lizzy.

"And that," Ruby said gently, "is why dragons have such short tails."

"Is that true?" Lizzy asked as Ruby passed the ring back to her. She looked at her ring with new appreciation.

"That's what I was told," Ruby smiled. "Sorry, I'm not a very good storyteller. I get too excited to get to the end."

"No, I loved it," Lizzy replied.

"Cool, cool," Ruby said and took a long drink of her coffee. "So, your great-grandmother knew of our world?"

"Apparently, but she never told me it was real. She told me stories about it all the time, but I always thought they were just that, stories. In the past couple of days, though, I've discovered the truth.

She noticed Ruby was distracted by the barista at the counter's frantic waving. He looked frazzled as he tried to take orders from a long line and make their drinks.

"Uh oh, looks like Arely is late for her shift…do you mind… I'm just going to help him out for a minute."

"Yeah, no problem."

"Don't eat all the pastries without me!" Ruby called over her shoulder as she slid behind the register and began chatting with the customers.

Lizzy perused the other customers while she enjoyed her coffee, and warm sunlight shifted onto her table. Near the windows in the first room, a man with large feathery wings, folded against a vintage jean jacket, sat alone. He was radiant; the gold tone of his umber skin contrasting with the white feathers. Luckily, he was too absorbed in a small book of poetry to notice Lizzy's lingering stare.

Lizzy turned around in her seat and felt guilt tickling the corners of her mind. She fiddled with the blue stone around her neck. She shouldn't be sitting here enjoying herself when she could be trying to figure out how to bring *Him* back. The profound sadness she had been free of for several hours loomed over her. She didn't want to be overwhelmed by it, so she did her best to ignore it by choosing which treat to try next. After a sip of coffee, she was reaching for her half of the dragon bread when she sensed someone standing behind her. She prayed it wasn't Xeilan.

"You made it!" a deep voice said.

Lizzy looked up to find Leondyas standing beside her table. He wore a crisp white button-down and black slacks, as though he'd stepped straight out of a business meeting.

Lizzy choked slightly as she stared up at him. He lingered there, uncertain, waiting for a reply or an invitation to sit.

Remembering his companion, Lizzy twisted in her seat and scanned the café. The tall woman he'd called Xel sat at a table across the room. When their eyes met, Xel fixed Lizzy with an unmistakable glare.

"I am sorry once again for the other day," Leonydas said. "You have my word—she will keep her distance."

"Okay," Lizzy replied.

"Did you have any trouble finding the place? The card worked for you?"

"Yes—no. There was no trouble," Lizzy corrected herself. "I actually came by yesterday."

Leonydas's expression softened. "You were able to find your way back, then. That is good to hear." He paused. "I had meant to come yesterday as well. To thank you. Saving my life is not a small thing."

"It really was no problem," Lizzy said, taking another sip of her coffee. She leaned back, glancing toward the counter to see if Ruby was close to finishing up, but she seemed busier than ever.

"Still," Leonydas said, "I find myself indebted to you. If there is anything I might do to repay that debt, you need only ask."

Lizzy smiled. "Honestly, introducing me to this place was more than enough. It is amazing."

"Is it not?" Leonydas said. His hands shifted at his sides, as though searching for something to occupy them. His gaze flicked, more than once, to the empty chair across from her. At last, he reached for it. "Would you mind if I joined you? You are surely not intending to eat all of these by yourself."

Lizzy bit the side of her mouth while she considered telling him no. It was obvious he liked her, but she wasn't interested in that. He was attractive, though, and had a genuine smile. She would never use someone's interest in her to get something, but she did save his life. Since Ruby was busy, she hoped he would be willing to answer her questions about this world and the necklace.

Lizzy blushed when she realized she had been staring at him without saying anything. She glanced at Xel again, still glaring, then nodded to Leonydas.

"Thank you," he said. He sat, and the chair groaned softly beneath his weight. "You were not meeting someone else, were you?"

"No," Lizzy said. "Ruby and I were hanging out, but she had to go help out." She gestured to the pastries. "Would you like one?"

"Oh no, thank you." Leonydas patted his stomach with a self-conscious smile. "I have let myself go a bit of late. I am attempting to correct that."

He did have a bit of a belly, but it suited him.

Lizzy nodded and glanced down at her coffee. It was nearly empty. Just as she started to stand for another, Ruby appeared at the table with two mugs—coffee for Lizzy, tea for Leonydas.

"Here you go," Ruby said, setting them down. "Hey, Leonydas!"

"Ruby," Leonydas said, dipping his head politely. "How are you this day?"

"Busy, busy," Ruby replied, resting a hand on Lizzy's shoulder. "I see you two have already met?"

"Yesterday," Leonydas said. "Lizzy saved my life. In return, I offered her an Invitation."

"Oh!" Ruby laughed. "Well, that explains everything. I love it."

Lizzy shot her a questioning look. "Are you still stuck working?"

"Yeah, I'm sorry, honey. But it shouldn't be much longer." Ruby squeezed her shoulder. "Besides, you are in very good hands. Right, Leonydas? Maeve asked me to keep an eye on her."

"Of course, Guardian," Leonydas replied, solemn.

Ruby winked at Lizzy and glided back to the counter.

Leonydas watched her go. "Maeve and Ruby. You have formed strong connections to our world in a very short time."

"It is an evolving story."

"I would imagine so," he said. "I have crossed paths with the Princess only a handful of times. Each encounter was…

memorable."

Lizzy blinked. "Princess?"

"Maeve," Leonydas said. "Lady of the Fairie Heart. High Princess Maeve Dornwisp."

Lizzy stared. Tita had never included that detail.

"And Ruby?"

"No. She is not royalty," he said. "She is Torwynne—a guardian-warrior."

"Warrior?" Lizzy exclaimed, watching Ruby dance around a coworker to snag an empty cup. "What does she guard?"

"The gateway—" Leonydas paused, then sighed lightly. "Forgive me. These are common matters to us. I forget how unfamiliar they must sound. I have rarely spoken at length with a Shimmerkind."

Lizzy narrowed her eyes. "Is that like Dullren?"

"No. Not at all," he said gently. "A Shimmerkind carries a spark of magic. One newly awakened to our world."

Lizzy huffed. "Why are there so many names for people like me and none for the rest of you?"

"We are called Thraewen."

"Yeah, I heard that one already," Lizzy said. "Naturally, you all get the cool name."

Leonydas smiled. "What would you prefer to call us?"

"Is there a word for know-it-all?" she asked, lips twisting.

"Frechud," he replied, amused.

"Frechud," Lizzy repeated thoughtfully. "That works. So, care to use all that Frechud knowledge to help me learn more?"

Leonydas laughed heartily, and Lizzy found herself laughing with him. From behind the counter, Ruby grinned as she watched them.

"Of course," Leonydas replied. "You already possess a connection to ilThren. It is visible to me."

"What can you see?"

"The ilThren around you. Some of us are more attuned to it and can sense its presence in others."

"And that's you?" Lizzy said, raising an eyebrow. "Very attuned?"

"Not in any exceptional way," Leonydas said, hesitating slightly. "There is, however, something about you that draws attention."

Lizzy let her brow drop into a doubtful frown.

"Not in appearance," he added quickly. "That is not what I mean."

She gave him a look.

"Though you are beautiful," Leonydas continued, his voice steady now, "there is something deeper. The ilThren moves wildly around you, as if it waits for you to accept it."

Lizzy had heard Ruby's explanation, but wanted to hear his as well. "I have to acknowledge it?"

"Yes. IlThren is not a tool. It is a relationship—one of giving and taking, of cooperation. Together, it creates something greater."

"Oh," Lizzy said, at a loss for words.

As he spoke, a faint shimmer stirred in the dark green of Leonydas's eyes. It was not a trick of the light, but something alive—kindled from within. She wondered if it was ilThren stirring within him. Lizzy realized she had been silent for far too long. Her thoughts scrambled for an escape.

"Faeries!"

Leonydas blinked. "Faeries?" He glanced over his shoulder, as if expecting one to be hovering nearby.

"Yes, faeries," Lizzy rushed on. "Why are some of them completely unhinged, and others just…mean?"

She grabbed a pastry and stuffed it into her mouth, as if that might stop the question from sounding ridiculous.

Leonydas tilted his head, considering. "Are you referring to Flitterlings?"

Lizzy shrugged, cheeks full.

"Until they reach roughly one hundred years," he explained, "faeries are called Flitterlings. Humans often label them 'crazy.' I would describe them as mischievous or simply playful. I have not known a truly cruel faerie."

He paused. "If you are thinking of Maeve, she can be… abrasive. She was not always so. Times have grown difficult for the Fae. I do not fault them for their stress."

"Why do you say that?" Lizzy asked, swallowing the last of the pastry and washing it down with coffee.

Leonydas's expression darkened. "There is a sickness spreading through our world."

"The Hollowing?"

"Then you have heard of it?"

"Only that it affects the lower class of the magic world."

"The lower class," Leonydas repeated, a faint edge entering his voice. "Yes, that is one way to name it. But it also affects the Fae who visit this realm. If they contract it outside the Sylmarch, they cannot return home."

He looked down at his tea. "In truth, I believe it harms them more than any others."

"Because it prevents them from going home?" Lizzy asked.

"No," Leonydas said quietly. "Far worse than that."

He folded his hands together. "Fae are more ilThren than

physical form. For a Thraewen, the disease is terrible; it severs the connection to ilThren. I have heard it described as losing all senses at once."

His gaze darkened. "Some are driven to madness. Others sink into a despair so deep they do not recover. For beings more entwined with the il, it is a death sentence. A Fae who contracts it simply withers—drained until nothing remains."

"That's horrible," Lizzy said, the weight of it crushing her.

"Ruby mentioned something about Betela's necklace," she added. "That—it's important to those who are sick?"

Leonydas stiffened. "Betela's Blossom?"

"Yes," Lizzy said, glancing toward the wall where the replica hung. "That's the necklace, right?"

Leonydas laughed softly. "No. Such an artifact would not be left hanging in a coffee shop. That piece is only a replica."

"Are you sure?" Lizzy pressed. "Stranger things have happened. Million-dollar paintings have turned up in thrift stores."

"I am certain," he replied. "I loaned that piece to the café myself. It has been in my family's possession for centuries."

"That's a long time," Lizzy said. "Where is your family from?"

"From the Realm," Leonydas answered. "Though I am the last."

"Oh," Lizzy said gently. Then, after a beat, she nodded toward Xel. "Is that why you have a bodyguard? Miss…Xena?"

"Xel," Leonydas corrected with a quiet chuckle. "Yes."

Lizzy eyed his arms skeptically. Even beneath the loose white shirt, his build was hard to miss. "You don't really look like you need one."

"Even if I told her to stay behind," Leonydas said, glancing in Xel's direction with faint amusement, "she would follow all the same."

"Well," Lizzy said, "she's not bad-looking. I am sure you don't mind the company."

"It is not like that," he replied evenly. "She *is* more than a guard to me, but not in a romantic sense. She is family."

"Uh-huh," Lizzy said, unconvinced. "So…where is the real Betela's Blossom? In the Realm?"

"I do not believe so," Leonydas said, noticing Lizzy's persistence regarding the necklace. "Though it remains possible. It has been lost for a very long time."

"How long?"

"At least a thousand years."

"Oh."

Doubt crept in, unsettling Lizzy's earlier certainty. Had Tita only ever possessed a replica?

"Then where could it be?"

Leonydas hesitated. "There were rumors that it crossed briefly into the Realm. When I attempted to track it down, it was gone again. But that was, oh…a hundred years ago."

Lizzy's eyes lit up, too focused on the necklace to catch his fantastic age. Leonydas studied her with a curious suspicion, and Lizzy realized she was showing too much interest in the necklace. Fresita and Cendryn were right. She wasn't the only one looking for it. Leonydas seemed friendly, but she could tell he was holding something back.

"Where is this Realm?" Lizzy said, quickly changing her line of questioning.

"A land far from your own, though closer to where we are here in the Inn."

"You lost me," Lizzy said, as she glanced out the window. "Are we not still in Houston?"

"We are. From a certain point of view."

Lizzy frowned. "How does that work?"

"Very difficult to explain in terms you could comprehend."

Lizzy made a face. "Because I'm 'Dull', Frechud?"

"No," Leonydas said with a laugh. "Because I don't even understand it, and I'm from the Realm."

"How would I get to the Realm?"

"Using the Gateway," Leonydas said, glancing towards the café's counter. The only thing that looked like a gateway was a door in the wall at the end of the counter. Past that, around the corner, an open doorway appeared to lead to an employee area.

"Which one?" Lizzy asked. Ruby, as if she could hear their conversation from the other side of the room, made a game-show-worthy flourish to the door behind the counter. Around the frame, rune-like symbols glowed softly in response and then faded as Ruby smiled and moved away.

"Is that what you were referring to when you said Ruby was a guardian of the Gateway?"

"Exactly," Leonydas nodded. "It forms a connection between this world and the Realm."

"Like a magic portal?"

"Yes," Leonydas said, and then paused. "From a certain point of view."

"Why is everything here described like that?"

"Magic, as you name it, resists description. Yet when it is experienced, understanding follows."

"Show me."

"What do you mean?"

"Do some magic," Lizzy said, leaning back and motioning towards the table in front of them. "Do some ilThren."

Leonydas looked rattled. Lizzy thought perhaps she had offended him with a wrong use of the term, but he quickly smiled and waved Ruby over to the table. There were no customers now, so she playfully tossed her towel to her co-worker and wove her way over, moving the rhythm of a song only she could hear.

"Hey, guys," she said cheerfully.

"Join us," Leonydas said and slid a chair from a nearby table to theirs. She plopped down and excitedly grabbed a pastry half. "Liz and I were just talking about ilThren."

"So many questions, right?" Ruby said, feigning an annoyed look, and then bumped Lizzy's shoulder.

"As would any Shimmerkind," Leonydas replied and smiled warmly at the ladies. "Ruby, could you show Liz something. Maybe Essenwend?"

Ruby nodded with the excitement of a kid being offered candy. She looked around the table and then peered into Leonydas' cup.

"Done with that?"

He responded by finishing the last bit of tea and sliding the ceramic mug towards the barista. She grinned at Lizzy and then splayed her fingers over the mug. Lizzy stared, but nothing happened.

She flashed a questioning look at Ruby, but found her eyes were shut. Between slightly parted lips, Ruby lightly bit her tongue, then opened her eyes. Lizzy gasped. The whites of her eyes were brilliant, turning her honey-colored irises milky before erasing them altogether.

A prickling sensation like a hundred tiny static shocks swept

Lizzy's skin. It was as if the air itself had been electrified. Ruby closed her eyes again but moved her silver ringed fingers as if pulling at the strings of a harp. The cup began to glow.

Small pieces, particles even, of the cup floated away from the rim of the mug and swirled in concert with the fingers that were conducting them. Lizzy's eyes grew wider and wider as the field of the now glowing particles expanded and the mug dissolved into non-existence.

It was unexplainable, breathtaking, and world-altering. This was magic, and it was happening on the table in front of them. Something inside Lizzy shifted, settled into place, as if, for her entire life, she had unknowingly been out of place.

Lizzy was too focused on the magic happening in front of her to notice that Leonydas' gaze was fixed on her. He stared at her with awe. The particles' light danced in her eyes, her face softening as she wondered at its beauty, as did he at hers.

Ruby twisted her lips in a goofy smile as if she could see both of their faces with her eyes closed. She moved her hand, as if gliding along the curves of a wave, guiding the particles into something new. On the table, the swarm of twinkling atoms began to alight back onto the table. It was too bright to make out what shape they were taking, but it wasn't another mug. After a moment, the glow brightened one last time before fading as Ruby opened her eyes.

She leaned back and revealed a glossy porcelain rose where the mug once existed. If not for the glaze, Lizzy would have thought the satiny red flower was real. Though she had seen mass-produced shelf-sitting flowers like it before, it was apparent this rose was a handcrafted marvel. But Ruby hadn't even touched it.

"I don't believe it," Lizzy muttered, reaching for it, but paused for permission.

"Go ahead, it's yours to keep," Ruby said, and peered into the coffee mug she had left earlier. "I'm going to get a refill."

As Ruby left with her mug, Lizzy pulled the amazing flower towards her and ran her fingers over the surface. It was cool to the touch and as smooth as glass. She turned it over and giggled when she discovered Ruby's signature etched into the bottom.

"Beautiful," Leonydas muttered. Lizzy glanced up and caught his entranced stare before he changed it. "*It* is beautiful. Ruby is indeed talented."

"Yes, she is," Lizzy said, cradling the flower in her palm. "It's amazing that this is even possible. That magic…ilThren exists. What other things can it do?"

"Many things. Almost anything you can think of."

"Like healing the sick?" Lizzy said.

"Almost everything," Leonydas said. "IlThren has never possessed the ability to heal. It may ease pain and soften certain symptoms, but by itself, it cannot restore."

"But the necklace can?"

"The flowers on the necklace are part of a sword. The sword, in tandem with the right person, can heal."

Lizzy was quiet for a moment as she considered her next question. Leonydas, lost in thought for a moment, played with a large ornate ring on his finger. The silver band was adorned with a fox-like creature standing proudly on a peak.

Lizzy cleared her throat. "Could it heal anything? For instance, what if someone dies?"

"Are you asking if it can restore a life lost?" Leonydas whispered. He squinted his eyes and furrowed his brow as if trying to determine if she was joking or not.

"Yes."

"No," he responded emphatically. "No, absolutely not. It was never intended for that and would take the life of the one who uses it in that manner." Leonydas' face had changed into a severe glare as if what Lizzy had asked was anathema.

"Oh," Lizzy said. *So, it was possible, just not accepted.* His response to the topic seemed to be the most honest she had encountered. "I was just curious."

"No, it's ok," Leonydas began, letting his face ease. "I—

Before he could finish, a hand wrapped around Lizzy's wrist and jerked it upward. As happened the day before, Xeilan stood at their table, but this time he didn't hide his disdain. His anger. His brow was contorted, and he bared his teeth.

Suddenly, Leonydas was on his feet and grabbed Xeilan's wrist in return. Though he winced, Xeilan did not let go. He yanked down Lizzy's sleeve and twisted her arm towards Leonydas. Lizzy's face bent with pain.

He released Xeilan, and his mouth fell open. He stammered as his eyes flashed across it, then to Lizzy's face. She was too frightened to wait for what he might say and quickly thrust her knee sharply into Xeilan's groin. He released his grip on her as his hand thudded onto the table for balance.

The world rushed at her. Ruby was headed her way, Leonydas and Xeilan both reached for her, and out of the corner of her eye, she saw that Xel was almost on top of her.

Lizzy pulled at the leather pouch in her hoodie pocket, tearing it open as she did. Fortunately, the pouch caught inside her pocket, but the powder that fell into her hand she chunked towards the ground.

A deafening crack split the air.

A shockwave thrust Lizzy, shattering through the window and out onto the street. She landed and rolled to a stop at the feet of a bewildered pedestrian, then scrambled to her feet. Reality spun, and her ears whined.

She squinted at the café, now missing one of its large window panes, and saw that everyone, everything around where she had been, was overturned.

"Stop her!" shouted a pair of men, wearing security guard uniforms that matched the colors of Xeilan's hotel. She sprinted down the street, pinballing off of bystanders as she went. She ran past the Celestine, dodging out of the grasp of a doorman trying to block her path, and turned down the next street. Ahead, it curved around a park, and behind her, the approaching footfalls of her pursuers grew louder. She had no idea where to go to escape.

While she was deciding where to run, a cold hand, with rings tattooed on the fingers, clamped over her mouth and dragged her into an alley. Lizzy struggled, but she was only held tighter against someone else's body. They stepped backwards into a shadow and disappeared from view.

Lizzy tried to pull away again, but she only tightened her grip.

"Wait," Cendryn hissed in Lizzy's ear.

The men skidded to a stop at the alleyway and looked inside. The two that had been outside the café paused only for a moment before continuing down the street. The doorman cautiously peered into the dark alleyway, waiting for his eyesight to adjust. He took a step in and scanned the area, looking straight into Lizzy's eyes but apparently not seeing her. After a moment, he shook his head and ran after the others.

Lizzy used her bottom this time to push against her savior captor until Cendryn shoved her away. Lizzy spun around and glared. Still unable to see her face, Lizzy could feel her smug grin with a shrug of her shoulders.

"I just saved your ass," Cendryn said in a haughty tone.

"Thanks," Lizzy mumbled, backing away.

"I won't do it again," Cendryn warned her with a wag of her index finger.

"I'll be fine."

Cendryn shrugged and headed towards the back of the alley. Quick footfalls echoing from the street sent Lizzy jogging after the woman.

"Wait, is there another way out of here?"

"You'll be fine," Cendryn said over her shoulder.

Urgent voices joined the footfalls, prompting Lizzy to grab the woman's arm. She felt an armlet just underneath the woman's clothing before Cendryn jerked out of her touch. She spun around and glared at Lizzy from within her darkness.

"Please help me," Lizzy said as apologetically as she could sound. The woman cocked her head and stared. "I need your help."

The woman grabbed Lizzy's hand tightly, reached into her cloak, and then threw something onto the ground. At her feet, an ink-black portal four feet across gaped open, letting a cold shaft of air shoot upwards.

As the footsteps ran up to the alleyway entrance, Cendryn jumped into the hole, pulling Lizzy behind her. Lizzy's head wacked against the opposite edge of the escape route, knocking her unconscious before she could see Leonydas, Xel, and Ruby round the corner.

CHAPTER 8

Raucous laughter jarred Lizzy back to consciousness and pain. She winced as her fingers discovered a large welt on her forehead. Lizzy rolled onto her side and found the walls of a small tent. The thin leather tarp glowed amber with light from outside, and though she was warm, a cold knife of air leaked in where the tent met the grass. She eased herself upright, wincing again at a throb of pain and hugged her knees as she took a moment to remember why she was there.

She sighed. For a moment, she was living a dream that had plucked her from a nightmare. Now she was stuck somewhere in between. She could see the horror in Leonydas' face as he laid eyes on her tattoo. She was sure Ruby would feel the same. She thought she had made new friends, but she was alone again. Now she would give anything to have *Him* lying here beside her like when they were kids.

She didn't hold back the memory of a sticky summer night when they sneaked out of Tita's old house. Barely ten years old, and they couldn't stop giggling as they ran through the uncut, grassy-smelling yard. Behind a storage shed in that large backyard, they lay cradled in the rooty arms of an ancient tree. With sticks, Pecan husks, and little mounds of dirt, they created their own stories of magic, horses, and Vic's addition: wrestlers. Lizzy didn't mind because, in return, she had freedom to direct the story as she wanted.

Lizzy's reminiscence naturally triggered a laugh that crumbled into a sob. The blue stone was a choking reminder against her throat. She grabbed a handful of flattened grass and pulled until the roots ripped free. She thought she was free, but it was back. Even if he hadn't told her, she knew it was her own fault. Everything.

A sudden thump against the tent startled her out of her thoughts. Lizzy paused and waited to see if she had imagined it. Another thump landed dangerously close to her head. She rubbed her face dry and clambered out of the tent.

Overhead, a field of brighter-than-normal stars splattered across the night sky. Even an arm of the Milky Way was visible. Sharp pines framed the starry tapestry stretching down to the ground to create the small clearing where her tent and a few dozen others sat. The clearing formed a semi-circle that on one side butted up against a group of neglected but clearly occupied mid-rise commercial buildings. Someone had taken a street block and dropped it into the middle of the forest, far from the city. It didn't seem to surprise anyone visiting the businesses.

Someone intentionally clearing their throat pulled Lizzy's attention to the tree line behind her. Cendryn, who was tossing and catching a pine cone in one hand, was backlit by an enormous bonfire deeper in the woods. She let the cone fall and lifted her palms as if to say, "Took you long enough," as she sauntered over.

"Must be nice to be able to sleep so well, Liz," Cendryn chided.

"Where am I?" Lizzy asked, ignoring the comment.

"The Nightcamp," Cendryn replied, heading towards the buildings. Lizzy looked back at the roaring bonfire. She could feel the warmth from here, and the air was thick with the crisp, smoky smell of wood and resin burning. "Are we splitting up here or...?" Cendryn said, already entering a walkway between the buildings.

Lizzy shook her head and followed. They passed between walls covered with layers of hastily sprayed street tags, but also works of art that must have taken hours, possibly days, to create. Cendryn weaved her way between the press of vendors and patrons, but Lizzy fell behind, her attention lured at every turn.

Stalls and stores overflowed with daggers, colorful potions, and strange but appetizing foods. Even stranger were the burner phones, wristwatches, and knockoff toys thrown in the mix. Even if the wares hadn't been distracting, the people alone were distraction enough.

A knot of goblins, barely four feet tall, one of them in a pair of jeans and a wife-beater, shoved past her. One flicked a gnarled tongue at her in a leering gesture before vanishing into the crowd. Lizzy barely noticed. She had already been distracted by a deer walking upright, in a yellow dress. The deer snorted at her in return.

Flustered, Lizzy turned and promptly tripped over someone's tail. She fell against a large, half-man, half-dragon being. She stammered an apology. He rolled purple eyes at her and went back to haggling with a cell phone vendor.

As she turned to catch up with Cendryn, a tickle against her belly startled her; the pocket of her hoodie was squirming. She cautiously peeked in and found a pair of Flitterlings gathering up some of the dust Fresita had given her.

"Hey!" Lizzy yelled and grabbed at them. They easily invaded her fingers and darted into the open air. She frowned at their cackling and tried to shoo them away. She was in no mood to be pestered by them. Two of them paused to coo at the unicorn on her hoodie and then darted off, but the third folded her arms on her chest and hovered up to eye level. It was the same pixie she had a run-in with the day before, and if possible, she was more grubbier than before.

"You," Lizzy said, recognizing her. She flashed her an angry look. "I'm not in the mood."

The Flitterling narrowed her eyes, ready to retort, but her companions returned to yank her to their next victim. She fluttered after them, then glanced over her shoulder. Lizzy rubbed her neck, and her sleeve slipped to reveal a glimpse of the tattoo beneath. The sight made the Flitterling's face brighten with sudden curiosity. She changed course and followed Lizzy from afar.

Almost losing sight of Cendryn, Lizzy hurried to catch up as they entered a tight cross alley and then exited into an area that was a mixture of forest and buildings. Stretching ahead, the buildings appeared less and less between groups of trees.

"Where are we going?" Lizzy asked, peering into windows as they walked. Few had displays, and none had signs. This wasn't a place for window shopping; customers already knew where to go. A popular establishment had shelves and counters lined with glass canisters filled with a variety of sands and small wooden chips. Some were labelled with familiar places like Rome or Vietnam. Others, "Aiur's Throne," were more remarkable. Lizzy frowned at one marked "Betel's Keep."

"Someplace where we can talk. We're almost there. Oh, and don't believe everything you see here," Cenrdyn warned over her shoulder as they passed a street vendor with a table of new-in-box smartphones.

"Fake phones," Lizzy said, adding a humorless laugh. "Yeah, we have that in the real world, too."

"That's not what I meant. The phones are real. This world is real, too," Cendryn said, with an annoyed tilt of her head.

"Sorry, I didn't mean it like that."

Cendryn pointed out a vendor beyond the phones. An older man with a tarp full of flowers spread on the sidewalk haggled with someone over a wilting bouquet.

"The people that come here can't afford the beauty of the Inn or the convenience of your world. This isn't some back-street, shady market; this is life."

A small family of dwarves, ruddy, mother and father both bearded, passed in front of them heading for a table of clothes around the corner. The children excitedly picked through outfits that looked as if they had had several previous owners.

"Doesn't ilThren help? I saw someone reshape a coffee mug earlier. Is that not possible with everything? I thought it was everywhere?"

"Everything has its costs and rules," Cendryn said. "Even ilThren…especially ilThren. Here, there are fewer rules, and the cost is low." Cendryn gestured towards the dwarf family. "That's why they're here."

They continued walking until they came to a rundown bar

at the edge of the Nightcamp. Beyond, there were only trees and darkness. Lizzy had seen many bars like this around Houston, but never in a forest. A flickering neon beer sign hung crookedly in the window, and a Hornthal leaned next to the entrance. Lighting a cigarette, he nodded to Cendryn as they entered, but avoided Lizzy's eyes.

Inside was typical: pool tables, a jukebox, and a bar. Most of the occupants were women waiting around for someone with more money than the ones racing towards the bottom of a bottle. They eagerly looked up as they entered, but anxiously turned away when they recognized Cendryn.

Sitting at a booth near the door were Cendryn's dark companions, whom Fresita and Lizzy had seen on the rooftop. They sat facing each other, hands folded on the table like posed and forgotten mannequins. Strange tattoos peeked out from the sleeves of their ponchos.

Black hooded ponchos hung over jeans and t-shirts, but unlike Cendryn, the lower half of their faces was visible. Their pale, stretched skin made Lizzy wonder if they were alive or a horrific display of someone's idea of art. A twitch in one of their mouths answered her question.

Cendryn led them to a booth in the back corner. As they slid in, Lizzy facing the rest of the bar, a woman and a male faun hurried over to them with eager smiles. Both were evocatively dressed, with what little they had on. With an agitated wave, Cendryn sent them away to find solace in each other's caress.

"Ok, so…," Lizzy said, trying to keep her focus on Cendryn.

"I need your help," Cendryn said in a reluctant tone. "And in exchange, I will help you heal your friend without losing your power."

"What do you need me to do?"

"When I was younger, I was attacked by a powerful creature," Cendryn explained. "My face disfigured, but even worse, it robbed me of my connection to the il."

Lizzy stared at her for a long moment, frowning.

"What kind of creature?" Lizzy finally said.

"A demonic animal that leeches ilThren from its prey. I was trying to help a friend."

"But I've seen you use ilThren."

Cendryn shook her head and continued.

"I couldn't live without it. No one born with ilThren can. So I devised a way to connect to it technologically. It is crude, not as reliable, and very painful." Cendryn shoved her sleeves up and laid her arms on the table. The ring tattoos Lizzy had seen before extended along the back of her hands and up her forearms, framing jewel-shaped nodes. Like a computer chip, thin geometric lines, gilded with a thin layer of gold, rose slightly from red-irritated skin.

From the window beside them, half-hidden by the blinds and a narrow gap at the top, the fairy who had followed Lizzy watched. Her eyes widened, then her brows knit with concern as she studied Cendryn's tattoos.

Lizzy stared too long. Cendryn raised her hand, and with a twist of her wrist, the lines pulsed, and the jewels flared. A black beer bottle hovered from the bar to their table. Stylishly, it slid into Cendryn's opposite hand. She took a long swig, and surprisingly, Lizzy caught a glimpse of her lower lip. It was full but pale.

"Ok," Lizzy said. "How exactly are you going to keep me from losing my power? How does that work?"

"With these," Cendryn replied, showing Lizzy her arms again. "I will give you the same setup I have and connect it to me." Lizzy flashed her a horrified look. "This will give me the ability to channel away the negative effects while you heal your friend. This isn't just a tattoo, it's a path to redemption."

"I don't know," Lizzy said, staring at the tattoos while she massaged her arms.

"I'm not going to beg you; I can find another way to heal myself. But I'm surprised. You wouldn't do that for *him*?" Cendryn asked in an accusing tone.

"Yes, of course, anything," Lizzy said, "But how do you know for sure it will work?"

"I have run some tests on others and have been successful at dividing parts of the ilThren," Cendryn explained. "I haven't failed yet."

"Has anything like this ever been done before? Are there others that have that?" Lizzy pointed to Cendryn's arms.

"No. I struggled for years to come up with this. It's not something that the rest of the Thraewyn would approve of… especially not the Aurenthal." Lizzy opened her mouth to ask another question but Cendryn cut her off. "And before you ask, no, it is not considered legal. But sometimes breaking the rules is important."

Lizzy stared at the table top and frowned hard.

"It'll be ok, Lizzy."

"I just need some time to think about it."

Lizzy could feel Cendryn's frustration tighten from within her hood; however, she only took a deep breath and nodded.

"That's understandable. However, I'm afraid your time is short. They know now you are marked. Word will spread fast."

"I know. It's just…"

"A lot? Yes, I know," Cendryn said. "But I trust you to make the right decision. We are both hurt and suffering. We deserve to be whole again."

Lizzy nodded. Cendryn took another drink of her beer and then led Lizzy back into the commercial buildings. They took a different path and came to a stop in front of a tattoo parlor, but a long line of people wrapping around the corner of the building across the street caught Lizzy's attention.

Guards in outfits similar to Xeilan's men but armed with swords stood under a large wooden carved crest that hung above the door. Lizzy huffed in disbelief. It was the same symbol that Leonydas had on his ring: a proud fox on a peak.

"What is that place?" Lizzy asked.

Cendryn was already headed in the door, but turned to see what Lizzy was asking about. She shook her head and shrugged.

"It is a so-called 'clinic' for the Hollowing, but there are only two ways to actually get treated. First, you wait all day for a lottery ticket. If your number is called, you're given a prescription. Six weeks of doses, at the cost of a month's wages…per dose. And the best part? It can only be filled here, at this clinic. It's a sad joke. The treatment doesn't even work for everyone."

"Are you serious?" Lizzy said, her brow wrinkled. "How is that allowed?"

"Because Xeilan and the Aurenthal run it. They get to say that they are helping."

"And if I start healing people…"

"They lose control," Cendryn said, nodding. "And, more importantly, they lose money."

"They can't be making that much money if they are limiting

access to the treatment."

"That's where the second method of getting treatment comes in. For 100 times the price, you can skip the line by using the other entrance AND get luxury treatment while you are administered each dose."

"Where is the other entrance?" Lizzy asked.

"Through the Celestina Hotel."

Lizzy rolled her eyes. "Also Xeilan's."

"Correct," Cendryn said, motioning for Lizzy to follow her into the tattoo parlor. Lizzy cast a last look at the line of people—tired, frustrated, and sick, but unwilling to give up. Her stomach fluttered with a feeling she had been trying to forget over the last few weeks. She turned away and went inside.

They walked into a room that looked like a cross between a Victorian steampunk artist studio and a gentleman's barber shop. Richly stained, vintage wood lined the walls and floors. Framed tattoo designs suffocated the walls with mythical creatures, pin-up girls, and the like. Pencils, charcoal, and stacks of yellow paper littered the counters with unused ideas. Beside tufted leather upholstered benches and stools sat mechanical monstrosities—arms fitted with needles and inkwells. Lizzy shuddered.

A red-haired woman in a pair of worn cuffed overalls sat atop one of the reclined chairs, absorbed in painting her toenails the same shade as her hair. Lizzy liked the color but became more interested in the pair of twisting horns curving back from her forehead and disappearing into her frizzy hair. The woman jumped when Cendryn spoke.

"Where's Matthew?" Cendryn said, peering towards an entrance into the back of the parlor.

"Shit, dude," the woman complained. "You almost made me mess up."

"Where's Matthew?" Cendryn repeated tersely.

"He quit," the woman said, returning to her toes, biting her lip for better precision.

"What? When?" Cendryn said. "Did he leave something for me?" The woman huffed and closed the bottle of nail polish. She hopped off the chair and went over to one of the tattoo stations. She grabbed a roll of paper that had been tied with a short piece of twine and handed it to Cendryn, who snatched it from her.

"He quit this morning, he said some Dullren place offered him a chair there. Better pay, I guess. Whatever. Gairloch's taken his place. Wanna talk to him?"

Cendryn nodded and sighed. Lizzy wondered if that was a common name as she opened a scroll with a line drawing of a muscular unicorn flexing. The image winked at her and flexed even more. Lizzy chuckled and dug through the other designs.

"Gair, you got someone here to see you!" the woman shouted, then hopped back onto the chair to resume her task.

Cendryn muttered to herself as she opened and flipped through the roll of papers. Gairloch, the same dwarf Lizzy had met at the party, stepped into the room.

"Hello," he greeted them with a business-like smile that twisted with confusion as he recognized Lizzy. "Well, Miss Elizabeth! You found your way into our world after all."

"Gary! It is you," Lizzy exclaimed and smiled. "And *you* didn't think I'd remember."

"I've never seen a beginner even remember their own name after taking on three honey meads."

"You two know each other?" Cendryn asked, suspicion

coating her tone. She closed the roll of papers and held it tightly.

"We talked briefly at a party a few nights ago," Lizzy explained.

"That we did," Gairloch said.

Cendryn remained quiet and then walked to the window to look out. While she had her back turned, Gairloch pointed to himself and then placed his finger to his lips. Lizzy understood and nodded. If she had the same curse, she probably wouldn't want people to know either.

"Are you good at what you do?" Cendryn asked, still peering out of the window.

"I'm not half bad," Gairloch said with a proud smirk.

Cendryn turned back around and looked in the horned girl's direction.

"Yes, he's good," she said, without looking up. "I wouldn't have hired him otherwise."

"How good?"

"More than half of these drawings are his. He worked here years ago."

"I needed a break," Gairloch said with a shrug. "Now I'm back."

"Fine," Cendryn said, pulling up her sleeves. "Can you do this?"

"Huh, Matty wasn't exaggerating," Gairloch said, moving closer to inspect Cendryn's tattoos. "He said you might be back for more work."

"I guess the extra fee I paid him to keep quiet was bullshit," Cendryn growled.

"He only told me because, as I said, he thought you'd be back. He even left the gold ink with me." Gairloch pointed to the machine at the end, where one of the glass bottles was filled with gold ink.

"So, you can do it?" Cendryn said, inspecting the bottle. Lizzy followed and peered at it with a dubious raised eyebrow. She poked at the machine, causing the needled arm to wobble with a squeak.

"I can. In fact, I can do it faster and with less pain than he did."

"I like that part," Lizzy commented. *"I like that color,"* Lizzy mouthed to the girl, pointing at her nail polish, when she got her attention. The girl smiled in return and continued painting.

"I don't need it done faster," Cendryn said sternly. "I need it done right."

"My work has always been better than his."

"Fine," Cendryn said. "But I expect this to be kept between us. You don't leave until the work is done."

"I don't have plans to leave anytime soon. Like Matty, I need the money."

"Matty will discover that honoring his word was more valuable than money," Cendryn said, looming over Gairloch. She tightened her hands into fists, drawing heat into the gold on the backs of her hands. They burned like orange embers. "Don't make me teach you the same lesson."

"I understand," Gairloch said, squinting as he leaned away. "I have heard of you. I know what you can do. Don't worry, I'll get the job done."

"You'll be doing her this time," Cendryn said, motioning to Lizzy. "But with some alterations."

"Ah, eh…," Gairloch said, turning to Lizzy. "Sure about this?"

"Not yet, no," Lizzy responded, avoiding looking at Cendryn.

"I need some time."

"Yes, we are going to wait for her to be ready, but it should be soon," Cendryn said, notably controlling her tone.

"Well then, I'll be around most days, and when I'm not, Isley here can get in touch with me."

"Fine," Cendryn said and pointed towards the door. "Let's go."

"It was good seeing you again, Gary," Lizzy said as she followed Cendryn out. "Bye, Isley."

"See ya," Isley said and then looked at Gairloch. "Gary? Heh."

As Lizzy and Cendryn exited the tattoo parlor, Lizzy thought she caught sight of a fairy darting away from the windows. Before she could be sure, it vanished around the corner. Cendryn led her past the clinic, where Lizzy found herself frowning once more at the wooden symbol carved above the door.

"Was that Xeilan's symbol hanging over the entrance to the clinic back there?"

"No," Cendryn replied. "He just uses it to garner trust. It is a symbol for the family he used to serve."

"Used to? He doesn't anymore?" Lizzy asked hopefully.

"I don't know," Cendryn said, annoyed. "But I wouldn't be surprised if they didn't still back him. He had to get his money from somewhere; he was only a general before."

Lizzy's heart sank at the thought of Leonydas being involved with this. She wondered if Ruby and Fresita knew. They continued past it into a vacant lot where the line jumped across the street and emptied into it. Writhing bodies littered the ground. It was a triage area, but no medical professionals were working it.

The skin under Lizzy's tattoo felt warm. She wondered if it was glowing again.

"Elizabeth."

Lizzy looked around, but realized it was the same call she had heard in the alley, and from the sky when she met her future self. Was it now in her head, or was the necklace actually calling for her? Could it be close by?

Lizzy tripped over her own feet, snapping herself out of her thoughts.

As they circled the perimeter, Lizzy made a mental list of the symptoms: dry skin, hair loss, and possible fever. Most of them lay on their sides, tightly curled up and shivering. Some had family members caring for them who obviously suffered with their own, less harsh symptoms. The smell of cold stone permeated the area.

"Why does it smell like that?" Lizzy asked.

"One of the side effects."

"Will they die?" Lizzy said, afraid of the answer.

"The ones more closely tethered to il'Thren will," Cendryn replied in a cold tone. "The rest will be useless after the disease has stripped them of it. They'll be lost to memories of the relationship they used to have with it."

"I still can't believe anyone has done anything about this. I hate it."

"Elizabeth, you could have discovered this long ago," Cendryn snapped. "Haven't you felt the call to heal your entire life? You should have known to search for the necklace. You should have found the sword—"

Cendryn's head snapped back in pain, and her knees doubled as she staggered. Lizzy caught her and tried to keep her on her feet, but Cendryn shoved her away. After a moment of fighting against an unseen weight, she finally fell to her knees with a growl.

"How can I help?" Lizzy asked. She was worried about her. She knew Cendryn might be dangerous, but she had to trust her. She did trust her, though she didn't understand why.

"I'm fine. I just need something to drink," Cenryn declared as she got to her feet. "Wait for me here, I need to pick up something, and he won't want to talk to me with you around. I won't be long." She wobbled slightly as she walked away. Lizzy watched as she met up with the men from the bar.

The three headed back to the other buildings, so Lizzy began walking around the perimeter of the block again. The patient nearest her, curled on her side, was a Humanoid, dragon-like female, similar to the one Lizzy had seen earlier. Her scaly skin was dry and flaky, and her breath was rapid and short. Unlike the others whose eyes remained squeezed shut in pain, she stared longingly towards the nearby treeline.

Lizzy followed her gaze and discovered a small dragon girl in a purple dress barely ten feet from her. She had her face pressed against a tree as she stared back at the woman. She glanced over at Lizzy and mustered up a sweet smile.

"That's my mom," the little girl said in a shaky voice.

"Are you here by yourself?" Lizzy asked as she went over to her. The girl nodded, using one hand to rub her nose; her other arm was in a makeshift sling.

"It's just my mom and me now. Daddy was taken by the Hollowing yesterday." There were tears in the girl's eyes, but she held them back.

"I'm so sorry, sweetheart," Lizzy said and put a hand on her head.

"Thank you," she said. Lizzy caressed her head, surprised it was cool, and the scales were almost satin-like.

The race's name suddenly dawned on her. Tita once told her about the descendants of the first dragons that held dominion over the skies. The ancient beasts were most likely extinct by now, but the half-human, half-dragon Drakesint are numerous. Lizzy wondered if they were descendants of the dragon from Ruby's story.

The little girl, possibly seven years old, had legs bent into a permanent predatory crouch. Her upper body was more human-like, except for glossy scales that shifted from aqua blue to gray as they spread from her chest and face outward. Short but sharp extrusions framed her flat-nosed face, and when she turned, reptilian eyes twinkled with tiny blue flakes in a sea of liquid silver.

"Momma told me to be brave until my Aunt gets here tomorrow or the next day," the girl explained as Lizzy crouched beside her.

"Where are you staying?" Lizzy asked, looking around. "Do you have food?"

"Mmm-hmm," the girl nodded, and pointed behind them. Spread out on the ground next to a tree was a thick homemade blanket, a pillow, and a plastic lunchbox. On the cover of the pink box was one of the cartoons Lizzy remembered watching when she was little.

"I love your lunchbox!"

"Thanks," the girl said without looking back. "Are you hungry? I can share some of my sandwich with you."

"No, but thank you for offering. That is very sweet of you," she said, squatting beside the girl. "I'm Lizzy."

"I'm Grecka," the girl said, offering her hand. Lizzy shook it and smiled at her.

"How long has your mother been sick?"

"A couple of days."

"How long was your dad sick?" Lizzy asked, afraid of the answer.

"A couple of days."

Lizzy's heart sank.

"Wait here for me, ok?"

"Mmm-hmm," the girl replied with a nod. Lizzy went over to the woman and knelt beside her without blocking her view of Grecka. She had no idea what her physiology was like, but could see a stark difference between the two.

"Who...?" the woman said, moving only her eyes to look at Lizzy.

"I'm a...," Lizzy said, stopping herself before she could say nurse. She couldn't believe how easy she had almost said it. "I'm a friend. My name is Liz. Is there anything I can do to help? Anything you need?"

"I am Rheema. Thank you, but there is nothing to be done," the woman replied with a slight shake of her head.

"Is there anything that will ease your suffering?"

"Only the il'Thren could do that, but it has abandoned me... left me empty. The only thing I feel now is my daughter."

"Her aunt is coming for her?"

"Yes, but I'm afraid I won't last long enough for her to arrive. I will try to hold on as long as I can. But if I can't, she'll be left alone."

Lizzy's face wrinkled with worry. "There's nowhere else for her to go? Friends? Shelter?"

"Here? No. We only came for supplies we couldn't get back home. We didn't realize how bad…we've lost everything." The woman choked; her throat had gotten too dry to cry. Tears ran down Lizzy's face as she glanced back at Grecka.

"Can I take her somewhere, or if nothing else, stay with her?"

Rheema lifted her head and did her best to focus on Lizzy. She let her head collapse back to the ground and nodded slowly.

"Clinic," Rheema said weakly.

"Are you sure? I don't think it's a safe place for her to be."

"No…clinic in the Inn. Her arm."

"You want me to take her to a clinic in the Inn and have her arm looked at?"

Rheema nodded.

"Ok, give me a second. I'll bring her closer to say goodbye."

"No, don't risk. Said goodbye"

"I understand," Lizzy said, and then met her eyes. "Rheema, I promise I'll take care of her. I won't let her out of my sight until her aunt arrives."

"She's a good girl," Rheema whispered. "Tell her…love her." The corners of Rheema's lips turned up with the slightest hint of a smile and then relaxed. Her eyes closed, and her body settled. She had passed.

Lizzy's chest tightened, and she gasped. She couldn't breathe, and then she was breathing too rapidly. She sat up on her knees, but they were trembling too much for her to stand. She was so far from home; the distance trapped her. She closed her eyes and tried to push the thoughts aside, but she was so hot. She pushed up the sleeves of her hoodie and tried to focus. Grecka had just lost her mother, but Lizzy was too wrapped up in herself to console her. Minutes that were mere seconds passed until Lizzy was able to get to her feet and draw in a deep breath of cold air. She forced a smile and turned to go to Grecka.

The little girl had been playing with pine needles, but looked up as Lizzy kneeled beside her.

"Momma's resting?" Grecka said, studying her mom.

"Yes, sweetheart," Lizzy said, maintaining her smile. "While she rests, we are going to go on a trip."

"A trip?"

"Uh-huh," Lizzy nodded, trying to look as friendly as possible. "Your momma asked me take you to get your arm looked at."

Grecka's eyes quivered for a moment but then grew wide, and her face relaxed.

"Lady Betela!" Grecka said. "That's why she trusts you."

Lizzy choked and gave Grecka a wide-eyed stare.

"You have her symbol," Grecka explained, pointing at Lizzy's tattoo. She had forgotten she rolled her sleeves up and quickly yanked them back down.

"I...," Lizzy began to deny it, but then worried Grecka wouldn't go with her otherwise. "Yes, well, your momma wanted me to take you to get your arm looked at while we wait for your aunt to get her."

"That's silly," Grecka said with a cute smile. "Why don't you just fix my arm?"

"Uh...," Lizzy stuttered. She didn't know how to explain to her that she had no idea how her powers worked or if she could even heal her arm. And then the next logical leap came from Grecka.

"And then you could heal momma!"

"Grecka," Lizzy said, deciding on partial truth. "I don't know if I can yet. I'm new to this, and I don't know how it works. Besides, I have to find a necklace—

"Betela's Blossom?"

"Yes, exactly. Without it —

Grecka nodded, as if she understood everything. "You don't have all of your power yet."

Lizzy let a half smile ease her stressed face. Grecka probably knew more about it than she did.

"Yep, that's true. I'm sorry."

"It's ok, but I bet you could still fix my arm, and then I could help you find Betela's Blossom."

"I wish I could, but I honestly haven't got a clue how to do it. I know it works, because I cut myself…on accident, and it healed very quickly. But it still took a while."

"The storyteller told us that the Lady only had to think about healing someone, and they would be healed. You could try that."

Lizzy wasn't sure what to say and could only give Grecka an exasperated sigh.

"Here," Grecka said, and placed her broken arm under Lizzy's hand. "You can practice on me."

Lizzy nodded. It couldn't hurt to try; she was sure she couldn't make her arm any worse. Lizzy gently removed Grecka's brace and supported her arm with one hand while she gently placed the other against her scales. Lizzy froze when Grecka shivered in response.

"Your hands are cold," Grecka said

"Sorry," Lizzy said and rubbed her hand on her leg a few times. She touched Grecka again and waited. Nothing happened. Lizzy looked it over; it was swollen but showed no other signs as far as she could tell in the dark. "Are you sure it's broken?"

Grecka nodded. "There was a very loud crack when I fell, and then I couldn't stop crying. It hurt more than anything I've ever felt. It still hurts a lot, but I'm being brave for Momma."

"Ok, let me try again," Lizzy said. She gently pressed against a few places on her arm until Grecka flinched and tears filled her eyes. "I'm sorry, sweetheart, I'm just trying to figure out where to heal it."

"It's ok," Grecka said, with a sniffle.

"Can you wiggle your fingers for me?"

Grecka barely moved her fingers but flinched as she did.

"Ok, that's ok. Now, let me try again."

"Don't forget to close your eyes," Grecka reminded her.

"Got it," Lizzy said, closing her eyes. She truly had no idea what to do next. She thought about how she treated patients. Normally, she would get X-rays, cast the arm, and prescribe painkillers. This wasn't science, though; this was healing. Magical healing. Lizzy tried something different. She thought about the pieces of the bone coming together and—

CRACK

"Oh god!" Lizzy yelped as Grecka screamed and fell onto her back. She wailed, rocking back and forth as she cradled her arm. Lizzy reached for, but Grecka curled up around her arm.

"No, no, please don't touch me!" Grecka cried out.

"I'm so sorry, Grecka, please let me look at it," Lizzy said, trying to calm her down. The crunch of pine cones behind her made her look back. A pair of older men had rushed over to see what had happened.

"What are you doing to that little girl?" one of them demanded and yanked Lizzy away. The other knelt beside the girl and examined her.

"I was trying to help her," Lizzy stammered. "I don't know what happened."

"I think she broke her arm," the one kneeling beside Grecka said. "That's what that crack was."

"We heard it all the way over there," the one standing over Lizzy exclaimed.

"It was an accident," Lizzy said.

"I think we'd better take her to the clinic," one said, motioning to the clinic nearby.

"No!" Lizzy shouted and reached for Grecka. "Her mother wants me to take care of her."

"Where's her mother?"

"She's over there, but—"

"That woman's dead," the one man said.

"Momma's dead?" Grecka wailed and sobbed even louder as the man picked her up.

"No, you can't take her," Lizzy said, reaching for her. The other man grabbed her from behind and yanked her back.

"Get away from her," the man said. "I'm not going to let you hurt her—"

The man's words crumpled into a choke as a flat hand landed against his throat. One of Cendryn's men followed up with an elbow to the back of his head as he doubled over. He fell unconscious to the ground as the other man sat Grecka on her feet, still wailing, and lunged for the attacker. Another of Cendryn's men caught him by the arm and ran him headfirst into a tree.

Past the men, Cendryn strode toward the skirmish, and behind her, a larger group of angry men and women was coming.

"Get out of here," Cendryn said. She sounded angry. "We'll

deal with them, and I'll come find you when it's safe."

Lizzy immediately scooped up Grecka and ran into the woods.

Lizzy did not stop running until the commotion dwindled behind them. She clutched Grecka as she slowed and fought to catch her breath. Grecka's cries had sunk into sobs and then quiet as sleep claimed her. Relief had settled over Lizzy; she couldn't stand the thought of her being in pain. Pain she had caused.

She scanned the woods, but it was an endless wall of trees and inky darkness. Even the cool light from the night sky was swallowed up by it. She trudged forward but stopped again and looked at Grecka. If she got lost, it wouldn't just affect her. She looked back; the faint golden light from the bonfire was enticing, but most likely not safe for her anymore.

She was about to continue into the woods when a squiggly light orbited a nearby tree. A squeaky voice called out to her.

"Psst, Dullren!"

Lizzy carefully approached the tree. The light came to a stop, hovering between Lizzy and the tree. It was the Flitterling that had been pestering her.

"Oh, shit," Lizzy said, her shoulders slumping.

The Flitterling gave the corner of her mouth an annoyed twist and placed her hands on her hips. Lizzy shrugged. The Flitterling nodded and held up her hands in a surrender gesture, and then held up a single slender finger. She appeared to be thinking for a moment and then nodded to herself. Straightening her posture, she gave Lizzy a tiny curtsey and then pointed to herself.

"Cerisetta," she announced with a perky squeak.

Lizzy's expression relaxed. She glanced around quickly and

then bowed her head as much as she could while still holding Grecka.

"Liz," she whispered.

"Ah, Liz La Dame Betela," Cerisetta said, beaming and shaking her hips in a gleeful little dance. She paused and thought again before speaking. "Come, oui? Follow, follow. Aide..help?"

"Help?" Lizzy asked, and then nodded. "Yes, we need help."

Cerisetta blinked at her briefly as she processed Lizzy's response and then shook her head.

"Mmm...help Fées," Cerisetta said, pointing at her wings.

"You need help?" Lizzy asked, frowning.

"Yes...yes. Regarde, regarde..." Cerisetta said, fluttering with excitement as she circled to the back of the tree. Lizzy scanned the woods once more. She half-remembered stories in human books about fairies stealing children, but never heard Tita speak of such things. She hugged Grecka close and followed the Flitterling around the tree.

Light flared, forcing Lizzy to squint until it softened. A platform appeared, formed from a thick slice of tree trunk, its far corners supported by twisty vines. On it were rows of fairies, Flitterlings perhaps, Lizzy wasn't sure of the difference yet, tucked under little blankets woven of moss. Most were still, but some rocked back and forth.

They were all very pale, and a few were barely skin and bones. The sight of it made Lizzy profoundly sad. Tears rolled down her cheeks without her realizing.

The trunk beside the platform was hollow, and towards the back, what looked like an image of a spring field dotted with wildflowers shimmered. Lizzy was quickly surprised to find that it wasn't an image at all. A fairy, healthy and energetic, flew from within the image out over the platform.

She landed and began offering the sick fairies nectar from her upside-down flower bud. The air was filled with the scent of grassy, sweet flowers drifting from the meadow within, only to be quickly tainted by the same cold, stony smell she encountered earlier. These fairies were infected, and as Leondyas warned her, they were most likely dying.

"Aide," Ceristetta said, sadly.

"Help *them*," Lizzy said as the Flitterling's request dawned on her.

"Yes—yes, please," Cerisetta nodded. Tears trickled down her face now as well.

"I can't," Lizzy murmured. She wanted to, but the memory of Grecka's arm cracking made her stomach twist again. She continued louder. "I don't know how to do it yet without hurting someone."

Cerisetta looked distraught, staring at the sky, she searched for words again. Finally, she hovered closer to Lizzy and touched her hand where she had bitten her the day before.

"So sorry. Very sorry," Cerisetta cried, and placed a gentle kiss on Lizzy's skin.

"Oh," Lizzy said and cried. "No, it's not that. I promise it's not. It's me. I hurt people."

Cerisetta stared at her with a blank, confused look.

"You don't understand," Lizzy said. She pointed at Grecka's arm. "I did this. I hurt her when I was trying to fix her."

Cerisetta frowned and hopped over to Grecka. She put her ear to her arm and frowned again.

"Je ne comprends pas. Arm… mieux now, yes?"

Lizzy breathed out through her mouth and shook her head.

"I don't understand," Lizzy said.

"Please, please, Dame Betela, I bind myself to you—si tu aides us," Cerisetta pleaded, tugging at Lizzy's finger.

Lizzy sighed and leaned closer to the Flitterlings. They were so small, too easy to hurt if she made a mistake. But they were suffering. So badly.

Another fairy slipped out of the shimmering portal, but stopped short at the sight of Lizzy bent over the platform. She zipped back and forth, chattering in a shrill, panicked voice. Heads lifted. Wings stirred. For the first time, the other fairies and Flitterlings noticed Lizzy, and agitation rippled through them.

Cerisetta darted over to the others, chittering back to them. She pointed to Lizzy and at her arm. The unrest only worsened. The recently arrived fairy flew forward and flung a pink powder at Lizzy. It flashed, and she stumbled back as her eyes watered and burned.

Lizzy turned away, protecting Grecka, and blinked hard to restore her vision. Behind her, fairy voices rose in an argument until finally a pop snapped in the air. Everything was quiet.

Her vision clearing, she peered over her shoulder. The platform and its patients were gone, as was Cerisetta. Lizzy's shoulders slumped. She had done it again; she had caused more harm than good.

He was right. This is all her fault.

She frowned and ran for a few minutes before reaching exhaustion. There seemed to be a storm coming; the trees swayed, and needles fell. Lizzy hurried to a nearby fallen tree, its twisted roots scraping out a crater deep in the forest floor.

She slid down into it and pressed her body against the dirt

wall. She gulped air, filling her lungs with the smell of old rain and ancient roots, as she strained to listen for pursuers. The woods replied with creaks and groans of the pines' arms as the wind grew harsh. She was glad that Cendryn had not shown up—yet.

It was cold, but it didn't penetrate the overexertion of Lizzy's body. She was overheated but didn't dare move Grecka to slip off her hoodie. She pressed her head back against the side of the crater and stared at the sky. She didn't have a clue how she was going to get home.

A gust of wind sent a scatter of pine cones thudding onto the forest floor, before diving into the hollow to whip Lizzy's hair across her face. As if carried by the wind, a tune popped into Lizzy's head: *Rhapsody in Blue.* Maeve's favorite song. Tita claimed that if you whistled it into a gust of wind, the Flapper Fairy would track you down. Lizzy prayed that, like everything else, this was not just a story.

Tita played the old record endlessly. The original 1924 pressing was scratchy and warbly, but she loved it. Lizzy wet her lips and waited for the next rise of wind. The branches swayed again, she covered Grecka's ear, and then whistled the opening bars to the tune. The wind swirled into the hole, caught the tune, and danced away with it.

Lizzy relaxed, keeping a firm grip on the wounded little girl. She felt an overwhelming warmth again and sat up far enough to draw a breath of cooler air. Lizzy gasped and froze. A pair of glowing eyes framed by black fur peeked over the edge of the crater. Heavy paws stepped onto the edge of the crater, sending crumbling chunks of dirt around Lizzy's feet. The monster that had attacked her found her again.

Lizzy didn't understand why it had chosen now or any

other time to come for her. She was frustrated and tired of the returning threat looming over her. She bared her teeth at it and stepped forward. The creature responded in kind, narrowing its eyes and dropping into a crouch. It was going to attack.

Before it could leap, from nowhere a small white fury of claws and teeth wrapped itself around the beast's neck. Fresita had arrived. The monster rolled and thrashed as it tried to free itself. Lizzy scrambled out of the crater, heart pounding, and watched as Fresita tore at its face. It shrieked and growled until, with a violent twist, it slung Fresita off. It was back on its feet immediately.

Fresita landed, ready for a second attack, but the monster galloped away. Lizzy, covering Grecka's ears again, hurried to the cat's side.

"Arrre you ok?" she asked.

"Yes, you?" Fresita said, following the monster in the distance with her eyes. It had long since gone past Lizzy's ability to see it.

"Yeah, we are," Lizzy said. Fresita's head jerked around, noticing Grecka for the first time.

"A Drakesint Lizzy? Please tell me her motherrr knows. They are relentless hunters and unforgiving when it comes to family."

"Yes, she—

"Shhh!" Fresita hissed and tilted her head, listening. Behind them, shouts that even Lizzy could hear, sounded out as they were spotted. "I was too focused on that creature. They're on top of us! Run!"

Fresita waited until Lizzy ran before taking off herself.

"What did you do?" Fresita said.

"They think I hurt her," Lizzy replied between breaths. "I did, but it was an accident."

"Oh, Lizzy!" Fresita exclaimed, looking back.

Fresita galloped ahead, leaving Lizzy running desperately to keep up. The commotion behind them faded into echoes until Lizzy could only hear her gasps for air. She hesitated when she realized she couldn't see Fresita anymore. She turned one way and then the other. Panic tightened her chest, and then fear as a large bush nearby rustled.

"Come on!" Fresita whispered, poking her nose out from between some branches. Lizzy crouched to peer into a tangle of leaves and stiff branches. Lizzy squatted, tucked Grecka under her chin, and pushed her way inside, dodging small finger-like branches reaching for her face.

It grew darker, and just as she felt like she couldn't move forward anymore, the branches thinned out. The leaves crunching beneath her hands gave way to warped floorboards. She struck something hard; it clattered across the wood, rattling like a metallic baby's toy before spinning to a stop.

A spray paint can.

They were inside an abandoned building.

Still on her hands and knees, Lizzy found herself in a room, its windows and doors missing, littered with spray paint cans. They had obviously been used to paint, tag, and layer color on top of color until the walls were a jumble of designs. Lizzy's nose itched from the moldy air as she got to her feet.

"One more passageway...," Fresita said, standing in the doorway. Her white fur glowed with moonlight pouring in through a jagged hole in the ceiling.

"Sure," Lizzy relented. She was beyond exhausted.

Fresita led them, carefully choosing where to place her pristine paws amongst cigarette butts and beer cans, down a hallway to another room. The designs and smell followed them as they creaked across the old floors.

Lizzy was quiet. Though she was curious about the place, she was tired of asking questions that only garnered cryptic or empty answers. They finally stopped in front of a closet whose door was still attached.

"Riftnach!" Fresita exclaimed, and a series of symbols glowed to life. They mirrored what had appeared around the doorframe inside the café earlier in the day. Between the frame and the door itself, light spilled into the room until everything else darkened.

"Open it," Fresita said and stepped back. Lizzy did as she was told, and another place appeared before them. Café Calacoayan.

CHAPTER 9

Lizzy and Fresita walked through the doorway and into the comfort of the coffee shop. A male barista, whom Lizzy hadn't seen before, nodded at them as he wiped down the counter. The café appeared to be closed for the evening, but a roaring amber fireplace hugged the room with its warmth. The decor and furniture were different somehow, as if someone had switched out pieces like a rotating exhibit. The framed necklace, however, was where it hung before, and the window she had blown out earlier looked as if nothing ever happened.

Lizzy stood in the middle of the room and just breathed. She wished she didn't know about magic, and more than anything, she wished she didn't have the hope that *He* could be saved. It wasn't even hope, it was a chance—an idea. For all she knew, it could already be too late.

Quick thudding down stairs gave Lizzy enough time to blink back to reality and turn. Ruby rushed out of the back room and enveloped Lizzy in an emotional hug.

"Lizzy!" Ruby said, clinging to her as if she were a long-lost relative. "Honey, I'm so glad you're back." When she finally pulled back, she rubbed Grecka's back. "Who's this little one?"

"Her mom asked me to take care of her," Lizzy explained, focusing herself to focus on Ruby. "She, uh…" Lizzy paused and then mouthed the word 'passed' in case Grecka was half awake.

"Oh, sweet thing," Ruby said, touching her heart. "She must be exhausted. You too. Are you ok?"

Lizzy nodded and rolled her neck.

"We have a bed upstairs with its own fireplace. It's really cozy. I sleep there sometimes. Why don't you let me lay her down while we talk?" Lizzy frowned, but she was sure it would be more comfortable for Grecka.

"Just be careful with her arm," Lizzy said, carefully rolling Grecka into Ruby's arms. "It's broken." Ruby nodded and rested her head on Grecka's, gently rocking her as she took her upstairs.

"Sean, can you make Lizzy a Lindwarm?" Ruby whispered as she passed by on her way upstairs.

Lizzy sank into a velour-reupholstered antique chair near the fireplace, staring straight through the frenzied dance of the flames. She was exhausted, and her arms numb.

Fresita wandered over, planning to scold Lizzy, but thought better of it and settled into a watchful silence. Roasting coffee from some other part of the café mingled with the deep, incense-like aroma of woodsmoke that hung in the room. The atmosphere lulled her to the edge of drowsiness. But as the fire crackled before her, she realized the heat stirring her back to life did not belong to the hearth—it was radiating from her arm.

"Elizabeth."

The voice called to Lizzy again, but it did not come from her arm. She turned towards the necklace. It did not originate from it either. The voice was somewhere far away, and yet she could almost pick out a direction. Like a dream, it slipped away, and she was left frustrated.

Lizzy lifted an annoyed eyebrow at her sleeve, irritation flickering through her. It hadn't worked. Grecka's arm was proof. She glanced at her hand again, there was no trace of the scar, as if cutting herself was only in her imagination. The truth came to her along with *His* words. It wasn't the tattoo's fault Grecka was hurt—it was Lizzy's

"It's all your fault…"

She blinked away frustrated tears as Sean came over with a golden brown steaming drink in a glass mug.

"That won't keep me awake, will it?" Lizzy said, shaking her head. "I really just want to rest," Lizzy said.

"It's not strong like coffee," Sean explained. "Just something to perk you up so y'all can all talk."

"Who's we?" Lizzy asked. The answer came as a quick, melodic knock against the Gateway door. Sean crossed the room and set his palm against the knob, murmuring under his breath. He stepped back as the symbols flared in quick succession, and seams of light slipped between the door and the frame. The door swung open, pushing light into the room. Lizzy squinted, and then Leonydas stepped through. He scanned the café and sighed as he caught sight of her.

"Are you ok?" Leonydas asked, the concern in his voice unmistakable. He looked Lizzy over, checking for injuries, lingering on her arm, where the tattoo lay hidden but now known. She pulled back and frowned. He gave her chilly response a worried smile, and backed off.

Xel had jogged through the door, directly behind him, glaring. Both were still in their business attire, though disheveled now. Close behind her, someone Lizzy did not expect to see emerged: Mykayla.

"Good, everyone's back," Ruby said, returning from upstairs. "Have a seat, guys."

Lizzy stared hard at Mykayla, who tried to appear distracted by a bronze statue of a Dwarf riding an Elk. Lizzy held her stare until Mykayla finally raised her eyebrows and pursed her lips in an annoyed face. She met Lizzy's eyes, but only responded with a shrug and looked away.

Ruby waved Sean over as she settled in cross-legged on the orange chair. The others pulled chairs around to form a circle around a roughly hewn wood coffee table. Fresita hopped onto it. Sean brought over drinks for everyone, seemingly knowing exactly what each person needed. Black tea for Leonydas, whiskey for Xel, coffee for Ruby, and a craft beer for Mykayla.

Lizzy looked around the room at their faces. They all stared back, full of questions, but thankfully no anger or judgment. Except maybe Xel, but Lizzy wasn't surprised.

"What's new, guys?" Lizzy finally said, eliciting a chuckle from Mykayla and a smile from Ruby.

Before anyone could speak, the café door opened, and Xeilan marched through. His face set like a teacher pleased to assign weekend homework. Lizzy bolted to her feet, her eyes darting around for an escape. Ruby, though, placed a reassuring hand on Lizzy's arm and leaned close.

"You're safe, honey," she whispered. The tightness in Lizzy's body eased, but she remained standing, ready to run.

Leonydas stood and moved to block Xeilan from entering

the circle of chairs.

"Xeilan, this is a private meeting," Leonydas rumbled. Xeilan's eyes flinched, almost imperceptibly, but his mouth stretched into a thin smile.

"I brought an invitation," he replied, nodding over his shoulder.

Entering the café behind him was the winged man Lizzy had seen reading poetry earlier. Gone was the vintage jacket; in its place, elegantly crafted leather armor, etched with knotwork, hugged his body. His eyes were milky and unmoving, his gaze fixed on the room as a whole, only slightly twisting his torso to take everything in. As he turned, a glimmer caught on the razor edge of his Grimmklin, a tonfa-like baton on his hip.

"Master Sentinel, what business have you here?" Leonydas said, his tone edging toward a growl.

"*I,*" Xeilan began, "brought—"

The Sentinel placed a heavy hand on Xeilan's shoulder and answered for himself.

"We have been made aware that the sigil of the Lady Betela has manifested." His voice was even, yet it reverberated with a dangerous supernatural harmony that set Lizzy's nerves on edge. Ruby put herself in front of Lizzy, posture stiffening, and shot a glance at Sean, who looked back with a raised eyebrow.

"That has not been made clear yet," Leonydas replied, shifting his focus to Xeilan. "We were about to discuss the issue —privately."

"This matter is not yours to keep, Lord Leonydas," Xeilan said. "The people of the Realm have a right to it. Especially the Aurenthal."

Leonydas remained focused on Xeilan as he addressed the

Sentinel. "Is that your opinion on the matter as well, Sentinel?"

"I apologize, I was led to believe that we were invited to this gathering as well," the Sentinel said, narrowing his eyes at Xeilan's. "However, this revelation is important to the Realm. I would like to see the sigil."

Leonydas remained in front of the intruders but turned his head enough to see Lizzy shake her head in response.

"The bearer is new to our world," Leonydas said. "And wary of those she has not met or has been threatened by."

"A Dullren, Sentinel," Xeilan said, his cheeks flushing red. "This is reason enough. The Aetherwilde belongs with the Aurenthal. She does not know how to wield it. Guidance and protection are required."

The Sentinel's form blurred, stretching as it reached across the circle of chairs before snapping back in focus in front of Ruby and Lizzy. Lizzy stumbled, collapsing back into her chair. The others spun to face them but kept their distance, except for Fresita, who leaped into Lizzy's lap.

"She is under my protection," Fresita hissed. "Do not dare touch herrr."

The Sentinel ignored the cat and stared into Lizzy's eyes.

"What is your name?" The Sentinel said, his tone forceful. Lizzy looked at the others; no one spoke up to stop his interrogation. They waited for her.

"Liz," she replied. Now that the Sentinel was closer, her fear sank into unease. His presence pricked at her anxiety like a drop of water in hot oil.

"Liz, I am Jorba, a Sentinel. Have you heard of the Sentinels?"

"No, but I remember seeing you here yesterday."

"Yes," Jorba smiled. "I do enjoy coming here on my days off.

Now, Liz, the Sentinels are guardians of the Realm and areas like the Inn Between."

"A guardian, like Ruby?"

"No, Guardian Ruby defends the Gateway. I keep an eye on everything else."

"So, what, you're like the magic…the il'Thren police?"

"In a manner of speaking."

Her anxiety edged towards anger as she rolled her eyes at his response.

"But really," Lizzy said, coating her words with defiance, "you work for Xeilan and his group?"

"It is true," Jorba said, his jaw twitching, "that the Aurenthal advises the Sentinels; however, we come to our own conclusions. We merely seek to protect the Realms and its people—even its newest members. The manifestation of the Lady would be of interest to all Thraewen; however, it is not imperative for it to be made known. Especially if it is only the sigil."

"What does that mean?"

"It means that you are under no mandate to show me the symbol, but it would be helpful to be aware of its existence. If only to inform others that the Lady Betela is at hand."

"No," Lizzy said simply, staring past Jorba to Xeilan.

"I understand," Jorba replied with a professional smile. He turned and glided to the door. "I am sorry to have interrupted your meeting."

"Sentinel Jorba," Xeilan said, walking quickly to keep up. "I insist that you escort her back to the Celestine. Do not leave her here with *these* people."

"I apologize, Master Xeilan, but I must report my findings. Besides, the path of the Lady is not ours to guide."

Jorba continued until he reached the street. He peered through the door Xeilan was still holding open, locking eyes with Lizzy. She answered him with a critical lift of her eyebrow.

Jorba unfurled his wings; they glowed like a snowdrift under winter moonlight. With a single beat, he rose and vanished out of sight.

Xeilan turned to glare at Lizzy and then Leonydas.

"I will return," Xeilan said, his voice trembling past his control.

"You disappoint me, General," Leonydas said.

"Like you once disappointed me...," Xeilan said, slamming the café door.

The group watched him walk past the windows back towards the Celestine before they settled back into their chairs. Fresita hopped from Lizzy's lap to the coffee table and paced.

"Lizzy, could you show *us* your tattoo?" Ruby asked. A serious but concerned expression replaced the joy of her relaxed smile. "Please?"

Lizzy sighed, looking from face to face, finally meeting eyes with Fresita, who gave her a reassuring nod. Tita had once told her that of all the fairies, Maeve was the one she trusted with her life. A fairy tale, then, Lizzy hoped that sentiment held up in this new reality she found herself in. She slid forward in her chair, rolled up her sleeve, and held out her arm.

An air of quiet awe swept the room. Even Xel's grimace flickered with reverence.

"May I?" Leonydas asked, reaching toward her arm. His eyes locked onto Lizzy's, and the desire to trust him surged, sudden and overwhelming, though she couldn't have said why. His family symbol should have been enough to spark serious doubt. Yet, he and Xeilan clearly stood at odds.

She relented and, with a nod, stiffly held out her arm. His fingers barely touched her skin as they inspected the raised lines of the design. His touch was warm, reassuring—*right*. She clenched her jaw to remain annoyed. As he sat back in his chair, he looked relieved. "It's true."

"What's true?" Lizzy said, getting to her feet. "And before anyone says anything. I swear, the first person who answers me with a question is getting punched."

Mykayla snickered.

"It's crazy but true," Ruby said. "That tattoo is world-changing." She paused, letting the words sink in. Around the room, heads nodded in agreement. "It's the mark of Betela's Blossom, and it means that you will be the next Lady Betela." One by one, they bowed their heads towards Lizzy. Even Sean, who had been sweeping nearby, gave a deep bend at the waist.

"I apologize, Liz," Leonydas said as he raised his head. "If I had known sooner, I would have never left your side."

"I already know a little about this," Lizzy said, holding up her arm. "And that," Lizzy continued, pointing at the replica of the necklace. "But I need to know everything: the whole story. Not bits, pieces, and hints that I'm somehow supposed to puzzle together." Lizzy finished and stared firmly at Fresita.

"You must understand," Fresita said, her tail snapping. "I was forrrbidden. Had I been free to speak, you would have known long before now. This is why I am a cat."

"Yes, I know," Lizzy said. "You're tired of being a cat. And I'm tired of being Lady Betela, and I haven't even done anything yet. I've just been running around like a chicken with its head chopped off while everyone watches. I thought I was supposed to be healing people."

"You did! You healed me!" Grecka interjected from the stairs, drawing everyone's attention.

"You healed her?" Leonydas asked. As Grecka walked over to Lizzy, rubbing her eyes, she held up the arm that, no more than an hour ago, had been broken. She twisted it one way and then the other as she wiggled her fingers.

"No, I mean…," Lizzy said, examining Grecka's arm. She pushed against it softly at first, watching Grecka's response, and then harder. "I don't know. Her arm was broken; now it's not."

"Because you *are* the Lady Betela," Leonydas said.

"But I hurt her," Lizzy said, her brow bent with concern. "Grecka, I'm so sorry it hurt so much. I've never used these powers before. I must have done something wrong."

"What happened?" Ruby asked. Lizzy frowned and shook her head. Just thinking about it made her sick.

"It went CRACK!" Grecka said, emphasizing the sound and making Lizzy jump. "And then I cried a lot. But I fell asleep. Then just now, when I woke up, it was all better."

"I don't know what happened," Lizzy explained. "I just thought about healing her, about making the bones come back together, like I learned in school. Progressive callus formation and remodeling."

"The power of Lady Betela is not in science, Elizabeth," Xel chided her. "It is based on caring and love."

"I guess I skipped that chapter in the Lady Betela manual?" Lizzy replied, glaring at Xel.

"You did a remarkable thing, Lizzy," Fresita said, her tail giving a slow, thoughtful flick. "Those who bore Betela's name before you were trained for months before they could wield such power. But you must be careful. What you have now is limited."

"And if I use it up?" Lizzy asked, prodding again at Grecka's arm, who responded with a giggle.

"It will make the necklace far harder for you to find," Fresita said. Ruby motioned to Sean to bring the framed necklace over.

"That is typically part of the training period, finding the necklace and the sword," Leonydas explained.

"And what happens when I find the sword?"

"Full power!" Grecka exclaimed, and the room brightened with laughter.

"What can you tell us about the Lady Betela, sweetheart?" Ruby said, her light smile and demeanor returning. Sean handed Ruby the frame; she took it out and passed it to Lizzy to examine.

"It's her," Grecka said,pointing at Lizzy. "She's the Lady Betela."

"Mmm-hmm, but do you know about the first one?"

"Of course, Guardian," Grecka said and then beamed at Xel. "Miss Xel, the storyteller, told me *alllll* about it."

"She did?" Leonydas said, surprised, and turned to look at his bodyguard. Lizzy held back a satisfied smile at the sight of the usually stern woman turn ever so slightly pink with an embarrassed blush.

"I did," Xel explained. "I visit the clinics every so often to assist however I can."

"Every week!" Grecka added exuberantly.

"Yes, well, they needed a new storyteller for the children. I don't know any, so I just gave them history lessons."

"Last week, she told us the story of Lady Betela. Can you tell it again, Miss Xel?"

Lizzy watched Xel, whose usually frigid white skin glowed

in the light of the fireplace. Xel flashed Leonydas a questioning look. He replied with a brief nod.

"Ild Anda Tormer...," Xel began, her gaze fixed on the fireplace as if the story itself was being forged within. "Once, in a realm of wonder, during the times of the Birth Kings, a great sickness swept the land. A mighty nation was laid low, and countless souls were carried to the Borderlands prematurely. We were—"

"Stubborn," Leonydas murmured.

"—a proud people," Xel insisted. "And in those days, in the province of Gryn, there lived a common woman named Betel. The sickness took her father and mother, kith and kin, until only her young brother remained. She could not endure the thought of losing him as well."

"One night, she cried out to the creator for healing, offering her own life in trade for her brother's. But no answer came. The suffering and sadness of the people were many and loud; she feared her voice was lost among them. So, on the following night, Betel climbed the highest mountain in the land. There she called upon the Creator once more, not only for her brother, but for all the people. She swore to bear their sickness upon herself, to carry it for a thousand years if need be, if only the people may be preserved."

Lizzy glanced around at the others. Though she was sure they had heard the story before, they seemed captivated. Whether it was the story itself, Xel's voice, or the magic of the firelight dancing in the empty café, Lizzy didn't know. It was lovely, though.

"Then," Xel continued, "the brightest star of the night fell from the heavens and struck the earth in a valley near the mountain's peak. Betel followed its light and found a still pond, upon which floated blossoms of deep purple hue. Star Blossoms," Xel paused, nodding to Lizzy's tattoo. Lizzy held her arm out for everyone to see again as Xel continued, her voice softening.

"Its grip was bound in living vines. Its silver guard was carved in the likeness of those same star-born flowers. It was no weapon of war, but a blade made for guarding life. Betel waded into the water and took it up."

"As she journeyed home, she healed the people she passed, village by village, wound by wound. Yet when at last she reached her own, she found her brother had already crossed into the Borderlands. He had hidden his illness from her, fearing she would stay behind."

Xel paused. "Betel mourned him, but she did not lay down the blade. She healed the rest of the land, and when the sickness was gone, the people named her Queen. She ruled long and well, forever to be remembered."

The group leaned back, only then realizing how close they had drawn, as Lizzy turned the pendant over and over in her fingers. The weight of the story, and the responsibility it carried, tightened her shoulders. She was connected to all this, and it sent a chill through her. This was about more than curing a handful of people. It was a legacy that now rested in her hands.

"Betela's Blossoms," Xel said, staring at Lizzy. "The pendant is a piece of that sword."

"Why did she remove it?" Lizzy asked.

"Betel did not," Xel explained, her voice shifting back to its stoic iciness. "It was a later Queen who removed them so the sword could be hidden. Together they emit so much il that they would be too easy to track down."

"If the sword was so important, if it could help people, then why was it hidden?"

"The power of the sword," Leonydas said, "was turned into a weapon years after Betel's reign. It became a temptation to abuse. Unfortunately, even to her. She gave her life to heal someone close to her who had died."

Lizzy's mind raced.

"When she died," Leondyas continued, "the sword was passed to her brother, but he was not like her. He was war-minded and discovered the sword could be willed to aid his armies. Blessed by the power of the Bright Sword, his men were stronger, battled longer, and recovered faster. He was eventually defeated, but the sword no longer worked for just anyone. The sword itself deemed who was worthy to wield it. Decades passed before another Lady Betela came into the world, and it has been hundreds of years since the sword last appeared."

As they listened, Xel's eyes darted every once in a while to the wall beside the fireplace.

"There are those who believe," Fresita said, her tail giving a slow, uneasy flick, "that the next Lady Betela will be the one to use it as it was meant to be. That she will set both Realms upon a path of healing and bring them together again." Everyone turned their attention to Lizzy. She laughed.

"And y'all think that's me? Now that *is* a fairy tale. I can even get a broken arm right."

"Liz," Fresita said, walking to the edge of the coffee table to face her. Grecka, who had been leaning on Lizzy's chair, bit her lip. Her fingers mimicked a petting motion. "I have watched you since you were small," Fresita said, ears angling forward. "You are a healer. With or without the sworrrd or the pendant, that has always been true."

"I just studied hard in school."

"It's more than that," Fresita said. "You know it."

"Not any more. That part of my life is over," Lizzy said and fell back into the chair. However, all eyes remained on her. "Even if I thought I had it in me to really do some good, I have no clue where to begin. How would I find the real necklace?"

"How did you come by the mark?" Xel asked in a stern tone, her eyes still drifting to the wall occasionally.

"It just *magically* appeared," Lizzy said, closing her eyes as the image of Tita lying still on the hospital bed intruded. "I was with Tita when she passed. Afterwards, something happened."

Silence pressed in as she stared into the fire. She tried to focus on the moment, but the memory of the gurney sliding into the ER forced its way back. Her throat closed. She had done nothing. Again, her fault.

A sharp tap on Lizzy's arm caused her to jerk aside. Mykayla had knelt beside her and began signing.

"There was nothing more that you could have done that they didn't. Remember, I was there. Fresita too."

Lizzy nodded and cleared her throat to continue.

"It happened just after she passed," Lizzy said, grimacing against the memory. "Her ring…I took off her ring." Lizzy held up the hand that had the Dragonstone ring on it. "Right after that, my tattoo appeared, and her scar disappeared."

"Her scar?" Leonydas asked, leaning forward. "Was she a bearer of the mark?" He flashed a look at Fresita. The white cat swished her tail and shook her head.

"I cannot help," Fresita said.

"Bad cat," Mykayla signed.

"I can understand you," Fresita growled. Mykayla made a face in response.

"Aww," Grecka cooed, and finally mustered the courage to pet Fresita. "Poor kitty." Fresita purred and rubbed against her palm.

"She had a scar in the same place as my tattoo on her arm," Lizzy continued. "It was the same shape and size."

"Wait," Ruby said. "Are you saying that there was no hint or trace of the tattoo at any point in your life? Even just like an accidental glimpse?"

Lizzy shook her head.

"And you did not live with your great-grandmother?" Xel asked. Lizzy shook her head again. Leonydas looked quizzically at his bodyguard and then at Ruby.

"Huh, so…it's a Dragonstone Ring, right?" Ruby said as she sat on the arm of Lizzy's chair. "Sure, it could have been hiding Lizzy's mark, but she would have at least had to be near her all the time. None of the rings are powerful enough to hide it for that long and across those distances."

"It would have had to have been a potent spell," Leonydas added. "A Fae-based spell."

The room focused its attention on Fresita, who could only be bothered to yawn and curl up under Grecka's caresses.

"Also, when did she get it?" Ruby asked. She turned her attention back to Lizzy and rubbed her shoulder. "Honey, can you think of anytime in your life when something might have happened. Something to do with ilThren? With magic?"

Lizzy stared at Fresita for a long time, hoping to prod her into sharing anything that could help.

"The only thing I can think of is the dog attack," Lizzy finally said. "When I was little, a dog chased my sister and me. It bit me there."

"It bit you were the tattoo rests now?" Xel said, scooting forward in her chair.

"Yes, actually, there used to be two scars exactly where the flowers are now."

Leonydas and Xel stared at each other with almost an excited energy.

"I still see the dog monster sometimes," Lizzy added. "Fresita saved me from it in the woods tonight."

"Bloom and blight," Fresita said, pacing again. "I did not know. I should have."

"That was no beast," Xel explained. "It was a Veilkin. Guardians of the Bright Sword when no Lady Betela presides."

"Then why did it attack me?" Lizzy said, with a doubtful glare.

"It may have seemed so, but in truth, it was marking you."

"*That's* when she got the tattoo," Ruby said.

"Yes," Leonydas said. "Lizzy's great-grandmother used the Dragonscale ring, bolstered by fairy power, to conceal the sigil. The Faerie Queene must have helped her. No one else could have crafted a spell with such potency."

"Why did it mark me back then?" Lizzy said, running her hands over the tattoo. "And why has it been appearing to me in the past few days?"

Leonydas stared at the mark before responding.

"What were you doing before you encountered the Veilkin?"

"I don't remember," Lizzy responded quickly. She had tried to remember that morning too many times before to attempt it now. Even Tita had counselled her to let it go. "It's a blank."

"If her great-grandmother was marked and refused it," Xel pondered, "Would that have created her scar?"

"Yes," Leonydas said, deep in thought. He refocused on Lizzy. "Your great-grandmother may have had Betela's Blossom."

"I think she did," Lizzy said. "There was a drawing of it in the sketchbook, along with the sword. In the drawing, the hand that was holding it wore a Dragonscale ring. There's not a lot of them, right?" Lizzy glanced at Ruby.

"That is correct," Ruby said. "In my lifetime, I have only seen two. Even that is rare."

"Agreed," Leonydas said. "Where is the sketchbook now?"

"Stolen," Lizzy replied. "Someone broke into my apartment and took it."

"I tracked the thief for some time," Fresita said, her tail flicking sharply. "He did not wish to be found."

"It did not help that he was invisible," Lizzy added.

"Not invisible enough," Xel said.

Everyone turned. Xel now stood near the wall, her hand clenched around something unseen.

"Urghk," a voice gasped as her grip tightened.

"Reveal yourself," Xel hissed, pulling her capture closer to her face.

A dark distortion rippled in the air. Then a hoodie appeared, followed by arms, legs, and finally the rest of a young man. He clawed at Xel's hand, struggling for breath, and forced up onto his toes.

"Xel," Ruby said firmly, rising to her feet. "Let him breathe."

"He is a spy," Xel snarled.

"Then we should learn what he knows," Ruby replied, stepping closer to the boy. Her tone softened into a dangerous threat. "Do not worry. He will cooperate."

She brushed a charm on her bracelet. A sword gathered itself into being across her back, forming in a shimmer of light. It was massive, so large it hung sideways to keep from scraping the floor.

Xel released her grip. The boy collapsed to his knees, coughing and wheezing. Ruby offered him a hand; when he took it, she hauled him upright with ease. His gaze fixed on the blade behind her.

"Is that Twilight's Lament?" he rasped.

"Abenlieth," Ruby corrected, a hint of pride lifting one corner of her mouth. "Yes." She straightened. "I am Guardian Ruby. And you are?"

"Evren, I'm—"

"A thief," Lizzy cut in.

"I am sorry," Evren rushed out. "Truly. I had no idea who you were until I saw the mark that night. If I had known, I would never have taken it. You are Lady Betela."

"And yet you still ran off with Tita's sketchbook," Lizzy said.

"I panicked," Evren said weakly. "Your cat is terrifying."

Fresita responded with an exaggerated hiss, making Evren jump.

Suddenly, Leonydas was behind him. Lizzy had not seen him move.

"Wow," Grecka breathed.

Leonydas loomed over the boy. "Why are you following Lizzy?"

"Master Xeilan sent me," Evren said.

Leonydas's jaw tightened at the name.

"When I stole the book, I was working for him," Evren continued.

"And for whom do you work now?" Leonydas asked.

"No one," Evren said more quietly. He looked up, meeting Lizzy's eyes. "I wanted to return it to you."

Lizzy stepped forward. Behind her, Mykayla and Fresita closed in, wary.

"Please tell me you have the sketchbook," Lizzy said.

"I am sorry," Evren replied, reaching beneath his hoodie.

Leonydas moved. In the blink of an eye, his hand closed around Evren's wrist, stopping him cold.

"Slowly," Leonydas warned him. Lizzy caught a glimpse of Leonydas' eyes. At first, she thought they were like the Drakesint, liquid and sparkly, but they were different. The contrasting hues within his pupil clashed intensely—a hurricane of raw power swirled within. It was only a brief distraction, because the boy carefully produced Tita's sketchbook.

"Thank you!" Lizzy exclaimed and grabbed the book from him. She hugged it and backed away as Ruby and Leonydas cornered Evren.

"Why did you bring it back?" Ruby asked.

"Because I was sorry that I stole it. Like I said I didn't know who I was stealing from. I didn't realize who she was until I saw the mark."

"You saw the mark before you left her apartment," Fresita said, a low growl threading her words. "Why did you not leave it?"

"I was scared," Evren responded.

"As you should have been," Fresita said, sitting upright, tail curling with satisfaction.

"Not just of you. I was more afraid of what Xeilan would do if I returned without it."

Fresita's eyes narrowed. "You should have fearrred me more," she said. "I was restrained."

"Not me...my brother. I promised my mom I'd look after him when she was gone...but he...I told him not to go out. I told him...anyway...he got the Hollowing. Xeilan has him in his clinic. We made a deal, if I did some favors for him he would make sure my brother got better."

"Clinic?" Leonydas asked. Lizzy stared at him hard.

"The one just outside of the Night Camp."

"Xeilan operates a clinic?" Leonydas asked again, confused.

"It's not a clinic," Mykayla signed and motioned to Lizzy to translate for her. "It's just another source of income for that fucking rich pig." Lizzy translated, only briefly hesitating at the end.

"Let me guess, he's charging exorbitant prices to *help* people?" Leonydas said. Lizzy glanced at his ring before looking back at Mykayla.

"Yeah," Mykayla continued, noting Lizzy's focus. "And Lizzy thinks you're working with him."

"I'm not translating that," Lizzy said out loud.

"What did she say?" Leonydas asked.

"She said that Lizzy thinks you are working with Xeilan," Fresita said and approached Leonydas. She stood on her hind legs and looked him over. "Why Lizzy?"

"That symbol," Lizzy said, pointing to Leonydas's ring. "It was hanging over the entrance to the clinic."

Leonydas went very still. For a heartbeat, Lizzy thought he might shout but instead, he rose from his chair and turned toward the door.

"Leonydas, wait," Xel said, moving quickly after him.

"Where are you—where is he going?" Ruby asked.

Leonydas stopped at the threshold, his voice low and tightly controlled. "How dare he use my family's crest to prey upon others. This ends now."

"You should not do this," Xel said.

Leonydas turned, anger flashing in his eyes. "You knew."

Xel held his gaze. "I had suspicions. I told you I had been to the clinic."

"You did," Leonydas said. "But you did not tell me why."

"I was investigating," Xel replied. "I wanted answers before bringing this to you."

"You should have told me," Leonydas said quietly.

Xel's expression softened. "I knew you would react like this."

"Lord Leonydas," Ruby interrupted. "I understand your anger, but right now there are more important matters." Leonydas spun around to reply, but met Lizzy's eyes. She looked tired, frustrated, and done with everything. He swallowed his anger and returned to the group.

"I apologize," Leonydas said, meeting everyone's eyes and ending with Lizzy. "I let him get the better of me. I will take care of that matter at a later time."

Lizzy nodded and sank into her chair again.

"Evren, you said Xeilan could help your brother?" Ruby said as everyone settled in again. "He has a cure?"

"For some," Evren replied. "Unrae affects my kind slower than others, but they'll still be Hollowed in the end. His clinic, though, has ways to slow it even more and reduce some of the pain."

"How many others are in this hospital?"

"Not many, maybe a dozen."

Ruby and Leonydas exchanged glances.

"That," Leonydas said, "is why he is so interested in Liz. He is making a profit by easing the suffering of the few Aurenthal that contract it."

"Not just the Aurenthal," Lizzy said. "Thraewen as well. When I was at the Night Camp, I saw at least a hundred people waiting in line for a chance to be treated. He's charging them more than they earn in months."

"Disgusting," Fresita growled, trotting over and leaping up to look out the front windows. She peered at the Celestine Hotel down the street.

"But it doesn't matter now," Evren said, looking at Lizzy. "She will fix everything, right?"

"What a minute," Leonydas said, ignoring Evren's question. "Liz, what were you doing at the Night Camp? How did you even know about it?"

Lizzy frowned as she began flipping through the pages of the sketchbook.

"I don't know. I just sort of fell into it, trying to get away from Xeilan." Lizzy flashed him an angry look. "Why?"

"I apologize. That is none of my business," Leonydas said, his confusion slipping to embarrassment. "I was surprised to hear you had been there."

Lizzy kept her focus on the sketchbook and hoped he wouldn't push any further. She wasn't ready to tell anyone about Cendryn. They wouldn't understand. Lizzy felt Fresita's eyes study her; she was sure Fresita was wondering the same as Leonydas.

"Evrrren, Xeilan doesn't know?" Fresita asked, turning the attention in the room away from Lizzy. "The book is gone?"

"No, he's been too busy trying to get support for harassing

Liz," Evren said, with a smirk. "Besides, I'm really good at stealing things."

"May I look at it?" Leondyas asked, kneeling beside Lizzy's chair.

"Sure," Lizzy replied, avoiding his eyes. "I was just looking for the drawing of the necklace."

"It's ok to say 'no', honey," Ruby assured her. "I know we seem powerful or in control, but we are just like you. And we want to help you, so that you can help others."

"It's ok," Lizzy said, finally flipping to the page with the sword. "Here it is."

"IlBetela," Leonydas said, in an awed tone as he took the book. His eyes lit up again. "It has been too long since I last saw a Bright Sword." Xel came over and admired the drawing with him. For the first time, Lizzy saw something other than a stern expression. Her face relaxed into wonder with a hint of excitement tugging at the corner of her lips. It faded as she reached across and flipped forward and back a few pages.

"Nothing more?" Xel asked.

"I don't think so," Lizzy responded. "There are some pages missing, though."

Leonydas nodded as he came across the torn remnants of a page.

"Tita didn't tell you anything before she passed?" Mykayla said, waving first to get Lizzy's attention.

"No, nothing about any of this...," Lizzy said, as she thought again about her last moments with Tita. Tears filled her eyes as she remembered her last words. Then, as it suddenly dawned on her, she grabbed the book from Leonydas.

"The end of the story," Lizzy said, excitedly. She flipped to the final page and stared at it. It was blank. She turned to the inside back cover, but there was nothing. "Dang it."

"What is it, Lizzy?" Ruby asked.

"Tita's final words were something about the end of the story. Originally, I thought she meant that she was at the end of her story, or that there would be no more stories from her. But now I'm thinking she meant something different. She said it out loud…she was deaf, but she said this—out loud. It was important. There's nothing here, though, at the end of her stories."

"Can I see?" Ruby asked. Lizzy set the book on the table. Ruby came over and, together with Leonydas, stared long and hard at the pages. Leonydas flipped to the front of the book and then back again.

"Can I try something?" Ruby asked Leonydas. He nodded, and Ruby tapped one of the charms on her bracelet, closing her eyes. When she opened them again, they had turned a soft, cottony white—the same as when she had crafted the rose for Lizzy. She held her palm above the book's inner cover and stared straight ahead, unblinking.

At last, she leaned back and blinked until her honey colored pupils reappeared. Leonydas immediately bent closer to the book. "There it is," he said excitedly. "Xel?"

"I see it," Xel responded with a nod. "Fortunate tonight is an Aethruen Moon."

"I can see it too!" Grecka gasped. She leaned forward, twirling her feet in excitement.

"I don't see anything," Lizzy said, frowning at the blank page. She squinted, then opened her eyes wide, but saw no change.

"You have to be pretty tight with il'Thren to see it," Ruby explained. "But Xel's right. It's an Aethruen Moon night, and we will all be able to see it." Ruby picked up the book and, with a grin, winked at Lizzy. "Come on."

The group, Evren included, with Xel close at his back, climbed a flight of stairs, followed a narrow hall, and entered a meeting room lit by two large skylights. Above them, the stars of the evening sky glittered brightly through the glass, untouched by the city's light pollution.

Ruby stepped into the center of the room and lifted her hands. She murmured a few words under her breath, and the ceiling stirred. Like the mug that had become a rose, the wood and glass above them dissolved into countless shimmering particles. Within seconds, they swirled and reshaped, expanding outward into a single vast opening, its edges framed by wood carved into blooming floral designs.

"You honor us," Leonydas said with a nod to Ruby. She bowed her head in return.

"We couldn't have timed it more perfectly," Ruby said, pointing to the full moon that was beginning to rotate into view.

"Open the book," Xel said, more excited than demanding.

"Please," Leonydas added with a displeased glance to Xel.

Ruby opened the book to the back. Everyone gathered around and stared intently at the page.

"There's still nothing," Lizzy complained.

"It'll take a moment, honey," Ruby reassured her. "The moon will need to be in full view."

Lizzy glanced around the room, the familiar twist of guilt squeezing her insides. They were all watching her—waiting, hoping. That weight was not new. She carried it nearly every day as a nurse, felt it in the way patients looked at her as if she alone could make things right. Once, it had been a responsibility she welcomed. Now it weighed on her painfully. Worse still were her possible plans with Cendryn. If she agreed, she could be risking everything: herself and all of them.

"Your great-grandmother was an exceptional artist," Leonydas said, releasing her from her spiraling thoughts.

"Thanks," Lizzy said. "She was an amazing woman and apparently lived an extraordinary life. I knew she traveled a lot when she was younger, but I didn't realize just how much."

"Yes, it definitely looks as though she experienced a great deal of our world."

"Look!" Mykayla said out loud.

Lizzy and Leonydas bent over the page as a cold column of moonlight poured through the open ceiling. The light haloed the notebook—a holy tome of hope. Along the inside back cover, tiny points of light gathered and drifted, dancing across the paper until they drew together. One by one, letters began to form.

Each word flared softly as it formed, then dimmed, leaving behind Tita's familiar, cheerful cursive. When the writing was finally complete, Lizzy stared at the page, puzzled.

"It's gibberish," Lizzy said, still trying to decipher the page. "It's her handwriting, but I've never seen a language like that before."

The writing was a mix of letters, many foreign, and a host of dots accenting each line. One by one, each of her companions looked it over and shook their head. Even Grecka peeked at it and declared it was "scribble-scrabble."

"Certainly *you* have seen this before," Leonydas said to Fresita. She trotted over and leaped onto Lizzy's shoulder to peer at the page. She chuckled after she scanned it.

"Show off," Fresita said under her breath.

"Who?" Lizzy asked.

"Your great-grandmother," Fresita said, hopping down to the book. "A human writing *this*, is spectacle. Not secrrretive."

"But what does it say?"

"I can not say," Fresita said.

"Can't or won't," Lizzy said, with a glare.

"It is not a failurrre. Prudence. Hornthal takes years of schooling."

"Ah," Leonydas said, pulling out a thin notebook from his back pocket and flipping through it.

"What is Hornthal?" Lizzy asked.

Mykayla answered by holding her fingers to her head like horns and letting out an exaggerated bray.

"Not goats," Ruby said dryly. "They may resemble half-human, half-goat, but the Hornthal are a proud people—and fierce warriors."

"I know where we can go to get this translated," Leonydas said as he compared the sky to a series of circles and lines on the pages in his notebook.

"You? Friends with a Horrrnthal?" Fresita scoffed.

"No, but I know someone who is," Leonydas replied.

"Did not think so," Fresita said, twitching her whiskers satisfactorily. "Were cannon fodder for your people and Hornthal have a long memory."

"I am aware of that," Leonydas said and motioned to Xel. They huddled together to look at his notebook and then Xel's phone. As they talked, Fresita produced a blue Art Deco glass perfume bottle from her backpack and angled its opening toward the moonlight.

"What's that for?" Lizzy asked.

"To reveal the message later," Fresita explained, replacing the cap and handing it to Lizzy. "Just a dash, yes?"

Lizzy nodded as she looked over the pretty bottle. She was sure Tita had a few similar to it in her bathroom.

"Where are you planning on taking her?" Ruby asked, concern distorting her usually calm face.

"The Dragon's Breath."

His reply eased Ruby's face but brought a frown to Mykayla's.

"I can't go with you," Mykayla signed to Lizzy.

"Why, what's wrong?"

"I just can't, I'm sorry," she said and hung her head.

"It's fine, but when I get back, we are going to talk…how am I the only person that didn't know Tita knew about all this?"

Mykayla shrugged guiltily.

"Be careful," Mykayla warned Lizzy. "The place you are going is safe, but there are a lot of people there. Stay close to them."

Lizzy shot her a doubtful look.

"You can trust them," Mykayla signed, meeting Lizzy's eyes.

"How do you know?"

"I trust her," Mykayla said. "I…know her."

Lizzy raised her eyebrows.

Mykayla grinned.

"Liz," Leonydas said, interrupting the women's silent conversation. "I would like to take you to meet a man I know. He is friends with the Hornthal and may even know some of the language himself."

"Ok," Lizzy replied. "But what about Xeilan's men?"

"The Dragon's Breath is protected by rules," Xel said in a dismissive tone.

"It is safe there," Leonydas explained. "Weapons are forbidden. Fighting is permitted only by sanction, and any trouble is ended swiftly. We will travel briefly outside its protection, but Xel and I will keep you safe. I believe this journey is necessary."

"Hmmm, an idea that may help," Fresita said, stretching her front paws as if she had just woken from a long nap. "The boy must agrrree."

"What is your plan?" Leonydas asked. Xel motioned sharply for Evren to join them, and he quickly complied.

"The boy's chameleon-like ability. I can create an echo of the Aetherwilde in Lizzy's tattoo," Fresita said, her whiskers twitching as she stared at Evren. "Not perrrfect. Adequate."

"You will have to stay on the move," Leonydas said, giving him a stern stare. "Or they will catch you."

Guilt flickered across Evren's face.

"I can't. I have to get to my brother. Once Xeilan discovers what I've done, he'll hurt him."

Xel opened her mouth, but Leonydas shot her a warning glance.

"Liz," Leonydas said. "Your friend—can she handle herself?"

Mykayla lifted an annoyed eyebrow as she stepped closer, straightening her posture. She folded her arms across her chest and flexed. Lizzy realized she had never really noticed it before. Mykayla was strong. The muscles were lean and sinewy, subtle when relaxed, easy to miss beneath her skin until she chose to show them.

"She can," Xel interjected, giving Leonydas a quick glance before leaving the room.

Leonydas raised his eyebrows.

"Ok, ask her if she thinks she can get into the clinic and get his brother out."

"I'm right here," Mykayla said outloud. Lizzy stifled a laugh; she wasn't sure she had seen a person more annoyed.

"She can read lips," Lizzy said.

"I apologize," Leonydas said. "Can you—

"I can," Mykayla signed, with a nod.

"Evren?" Leonydas said, giving him a questioning look.

"Ok, ok…," Evren said, as he dug in his pocket and produced a toy car. It was metal but dented and missing decals. "Give him this. He'll know I sent you."

Mykayla nodded, looking the toy over before sticking it in her pocket.

"Liz?" Leonydas said, looking to Lizzy.

"All right," Lizzy said. "If it will give me answers, then let's go." She nodded to Leonydas.

Their eyes met, and the instant stretched into a moment. Warmth stirred in her chest and pushed up towards her cheeks. It would have been easy to linger there, but she did not let herself. It wasn't right.

Lizzy dragged her thoughts elsewhere, back to guilt, to loss. To Tita. To *Him*. The familiar ache closed around her like armor. Lizzy broke eye contact, frowning as she turned back to the book. She scanned the strange writing one last time, then closed it with more force than necessary.

"I'm so sorry I can't go with y'all," Ruby said, frowning. "But right now my duty is here. I'll keep an eye on Grecka."

"I understand, Torwynne," Leonydas said, honoring her with her title. "What do you suggest for the quickest route to the Pirochettes?"

"The Snicket," Ruby said, nodding. "Near the end of

Nythera's Walk."

"That doesn't sound safe at all," Lizzy complained.

"Got it. Thank you," Leonydas said, motioning to the others. "We should go."

Ruby held Lizzy back and watched until the others were out of sight. She grabbed an embroidered, brushed leather backpack and gave it to Lizzy to carry the sketchbook. Removing a charm from her bracelet, she pressed it into Lizzy's hand.

"If you need to get back in a hurry: hold this tightly, think of this face…" Ruby pointed at her face and tilted her head with a cheesy grin. "And knock on the first door you can find."

"Got it," Lizzy replied with a tired smile. Ruby smiled and planted a warm kiss on Lizzy's cheek. Her chest tightened. She envied Ruby's joy and affection; they were a sharp reminder of the distance between who she used to be and who she was now. As if reading Lizzy's thoughts, Ruby wrapped her arms around her neck and held her close. "You'll be fine."

Lizzy nodded and then looked to Leonydas, who had come back for her.

"I'm ready when you are."

CHAPTER 10

The group emerged from the back of Café Calacoayan into the dim, pink light of early morning. Lizzy shivered as her breath drifted away in a pale cloud. It was getting colder. She could not tell whether another cold front had moved in or whether the weather here, in the Inn, simply followed its own rules.

Before they had stepped outside, Fresita had fashioned a fuzzy echo of Lizzy's mark onto Evren's arm. He had turned invisible and slipped out through the front door. Mykayla followed the rest of them out the back, flashing Lizzy a thumbs-up before scrambling onto the roof and disappearing from sight.

Lizzy craned her neck up to watch her go and stumbled over a stack of empty burlap coffee sacks with a loud grumble.

"Shh!" Xel spat. She stood at a bend in the alley with her head tilted, listening ahead.

"Is someone nearby?" Leonydas asked.

"No," Xel replied. "But if there were, she would have given

us away."

"Do not forget who she is," Fresita warned, her words edged with a hiss. "Orrr who *I* am."

"She is new to this, Xel," Leonydas said calmly. "Show restraint."

Xel answered with a short, disgruntled exhale before bending down to meet Lizzy's gaze.

"Listen carefully, little one. Stay with Leonydas. Do not wander off. Do as we say."

"Whatever you say, Xena," Lizzy said, narrowing her eyes into a threatening glare.

"Let's go," Xel said, glancing at Leonydas before disappearing around the corner.

"Sorry," Leonydas said, leaning his head closer to Lizzy. "In times like these, it is best to listen to her. She is the best there is—even if her attitude is not."

"Uh-huh," Lizzy said, and squatted down beside Fresita. "Will my healing powers cure bad attitudes?"

Leonydas frowned down at her.

"Though the Lady Betela's powers are unrivaled," Leonydas said. "Healing deep emotional trauma is one of the few things she is not recorded as healing. Xel has endured much."

"Oh...," Lizzy said. Leonydas gave her a half smile and then rounded the corner. "Shit."

"Come," Fresita said as she followed Leonydas. "They arrre emotional."

"They who?"

"Soon. Come."

After a few turns, the alley ended at a cobblestone street

similar to the one in front of the café. There were fewer businesses on this one, though there were many doors. Lizzy wondered if people lived in the Inn as well.

Xel crouched beside a dwarf-sized doorway on the opposite side of the street and motioned for the others to follow. Lizzy tried to look in but was met with a rotten waft of air.

"Ugh, what is this place?"

"It was a passageway used by the Halflings," Xel explained. "They had a fishing operation down the street. It's been out of use for a few decades."

"Is it safe?" Lizzy asked.

"It's not the dark. It's the Grrrinnels," Fresita said, with a sly grin. Xel chuckled and then ducked inside.

"What the hell is a Grinnel?"

"Tasty," Fresita purred as she trotted inside.

"There are none here," Leonydas said evenly. "They are only teasing." He bent to enter, then looked back at her. "Stay close, all the same."

Lizzy twisted her mouth in a mocking echo of his words as soon as his back was turned. She rolled her neck and, with a sigh, leaned down a little to follow.

Something dropped down beside her.

Lizzy looked up, startled. One of the dark, long-limbed men who had been with Cendryn loomed over her.

"It's time," he said, his voice low and gravelly.

Lizzy couldn't speak; she only shook her head.

Leonydas emerged from the entrance. "Who are you?" he demanded, stepping in front of Lizzy.

The man retreated a single, measured stride and reached to his side.

"*Svaenwyr*," he said.

Sand spilled from his empty hand, falling only inches before lifting again. The grains whirled, tightening and hardening as they took shape, until a long sword rested in his grip.

"I am taking the woman," the man growled.

Leonydas answered by charging him.

The man lifted his sword, but Leonydas crashed into him before he could react. They hit the ground hard, rolling in a tangle of limbs.

"Leonydas?" Xel's voice snapped from the entrance. Her head appeared, seeing the struggle, she grabbed Lizzy and shoved her into the passage before stepping out herself.

The man rolled with Leonydas for a heartbeat, then sprang backward, breaking free. Xel reached behind her neck. As her fingers closed, a staff appeared in her grasp, silver-capped at both ends. She drew it free and spun it once, smoothly.

Two more of Cendryn's men dropped from the roof above. As they landed, swords coalesced into their hands in a similar magical fashion as the first.

"Do not mistake this for an advantage," Leonydas warned, moving to Xel's side.

"Hey! What's going on over there?" a voice called from farther down the street. A patrolling guard from the Celestine had happened on them.

One of Cendryn's men spun, a dagger flashing from his sleeve. He hurled it.

The blade crossed the distance in a blink and buried itself in the guard's throat. He collapsed backward, clawing at the hilt as shouts erupted nearby.

"We will lose our advantage if they find us," Xel said sharply.

"Let Xeilan's men deal with it," Fresita growled, appearing at the entrance. "Come. Come!"

Leonydas nodded and dove into the passage, narrowly avoiding Lizzy. Xel followed close behind. As she crossed the threshold, Fresita raked her paw across the dirt floor.

"Drinwyr."

The earth lifted, hardened, and sealed the passage in a rising wall of stone.

"Keep moving," Xel commanded, already rushing ahead into the darkness.

Fresita bounded after her, leaving Lizzy alone with Leonydas. Lizzy reached for the flashlight on her phone, but Leonydas caught her arm gently.

"I will guide you," he said.

Lizzy was surprised to find she did not pull away.

"All right."

"Xel and I see well in low light," Leonydas continued. "Besides, it is better not to disturb certain creatures that make their homes in the dark."

Without quite realizing it, Lizzy nodded and slipped her hand into his.

The tunnel, if it could be called that, sloped downward for a few steps before leveling out. Loose gravel crunched beneath their feet. Lizzy had to jog to keep up with Leonydas' pace.

"Who do you think those men were?" Lizzy asked. She knew. She hoped he didn't.

"I cannot say," Leonydas replied. "Yet it seems clear that Xeilan is not alone in wishing to bar your path to the necklace."

"I guess so," Lizzy said, glad he couldn't see her face.

After several minutes, a faint glow appeared ahead, and

as they drew closer, Lizzy could make out a sheet of plywood covering an exit. Light leaked in around its edges, revealing crumbled beer cans and trash on the floor.

"Dullrrren," Fresita said, tilting her head to hear better.

"I hear him," Xel whispered. "Asleep." Lizzy tried her best to listen for whatever it was that alerted the others, but couldn't hear anything over their breathing. Xel put her hands against the exit and listened a moment more before finally throwing her shoulder against it.

A sheet of plywood slammed open, sending a homeless man tumbling down a cement embankment. Xel shot out after him. He came to a stop at the bottom, where a sidewalk ran in front of the incline. He grumbled angrily until Xel loomed over him. He scrambled to his feet and took off running.

Fresita snickered, but Leonydas gave Xel a displeased look.

"I probably saved him," Xel excused herself. "Nastier things than us could come out of the Snicket."

"There is a right way to do things," Leonydas chided her, as he helped Lizzy get her footing on the steep incline.

"That was not a concern before," Xel said, giving an indifferent shrug as she turned to inspect the bayou that ran alongside the sidewalk.

"Now, where are we?" Lizzy asked. She squinted, but the street running overhead blocked out the morning light. "I can't see a thing."

"Not much to see," Fresita said, plucking a leaf from the mosstragel on her back. The little satchel only appeared as she reached for it. She whispered to the leaf, and it bloomed with a soft amber glow. The light revealed that they stood atop the lower structure of an overpass leading into downtown. A four-foot section of wall bridged the incline to street level, and set into it was the narrow, rectangular doorway they had just emerged from. Even in daylight, it would have been easy to miss.

Fresita handed the leaf to Lizzy, but she instantly let it go, thinking it was hot. It fell to the ground, evaporating as it landed. Fresita shook her head and trotted down the sidewalk.

"We are near the northern edge of downtown," Leonydas said, offering Lizzy his hand to steady her. "From here, a boat will carry us to the gateway that leads to the Dragon's Breath."

"Thanks, I got it," Lizzy said, with a shake of her head, and headed down to the sidewalk. "Do some gateways go places others can't?"

"Do all doors?" Xel snapped. Lizzy glared back, wondering if she could shove her in the water before she had time to react. Probably not.

"That's right," Leondyas said, ignoring Xel. "The café gateway can go to and from a lot of places, but some are restricted. Others are private."

"Got it," Lizzy said, and glanced back to Xel. She was talking with a rugged-looking, portly man.

At the waters edge, where previously there was nothing, a long boat had appeared and rocked lazily against a bronze post it was tied to. The man helped Xel step on board and encouraged the others to follow.

"Hurry, we should go," Fresita insisted as she rejoined them. "Ill intentions are nearby."

The captain welcomed Lizzy and Leonydas as they boarded before heading back to steer. The vessel drifted away from the dock, and then, with a casual push of the captain's hand against the empty air, the boat surged forward, gliding down the center of the bayou.

"You saw those men following us?" Lizzy asked.

"I saw no one," Fresita said, her pupils wide as she scanned the banks of the bayou. "I felt them. Their intention is a sickening aroma."

Lizzy nodded, but wondered about Cendryn and her men. She knew they probably weren't the best of people, but until now, she hadn't considered them to be evil.

They soon passed the man whose sleep they just disturbed. He dragged a large piece of cardboard behind him as he lumbered down the sidewalk, grumbling. Lizzy expected him to react to the boat as it passed him, but he stared through them. Leonydas saw her expression.

"We're invisible to him," Leonydas said.

"How does that work…invisibility?" Lizzy asked.

"It does not take much to hide from the Dullren," Leonydas explained. "Usually, they do not want to see us or magic."

"I did," Lizzy said. "At least, when I was little, I did. I was always looking for something from the fairy tale realm."

"Ah, a child's eyes will find the ilThren in everything. Even when not necessarily 'magic.' But time and maturity rob the memory of those things, even when a Dullren has done their best to hold on to them."

Lizzy nodded and grabbed hold of the wooden railing of the boat as it swept smoothly around a log in the bayou. Fresita paced back and forth, inspecting the buildings as they passed overhead at street level. Xel stood at the front of the boat, the breeze making her blonde hair dance behind her.

"Do all cities have Thraewen areas?" Lizzy asked.

"No, not like this. Only some of the bigger ones," he

explained. "However, there are Thraewen everywhere, and most will have their hidden spaces."

Lizzy nodded as she tried to imagine the fairy tale world of her childhood intermingled with modern society. It excited her; she wished she could explore it all. But she had to make things right.

The boat carried them deep into the bayou, far deeper than Lizzy had ever imagined it went. Leonydas assured her it was not magic; people just didn't travel that far anymore. Eventually, they emerged at the far edge of Memorial Park and disembarked on muddy, undeveloped banks. They pushed through dense brush until they reached a narrow, rugged bike trail where they came upon a Vietnamese man with salt-and-pepper hair seated on a bench.

The man, wearing a worn woolen jacket over a matching vest, was reading a well-read paperback book and wasn't startled by their sudden appearance. He merely smiled as he looked up at them.

"Good afternoon," Leonydas said, handing the man a pair of silver coins. The man accepted them automatically, then paused. He turned the coins over in his fingers, studying them more closely.

"Oh, I haven't seen any of these in at least a hundred years," the man said, turning the coins over.

"There are not many of us around to spend them," Leonydas said.

The man nodded, eyes still on the silver. After a moment, he reached into his trouser pocket, withdrew a handful of gold coins, and tucked them into his vest.

"I'm gonna hang on to these for my own collection," the man said, playing with the coins in his hand.

"Enjoy," Leonydas said, stepping back as the man rose.

"Oh, most definitely." The man smiled and ran his hand along the back of the bench. He leaned close and spoke a single word.

"*Molam.*"

The bench groaned and scraped as the cement platform it was anchored to swung upward. Dirt and clumps of grass tumbled away, revealing a passage hidden beneath.

Lizzy blinked and shrugged. It fit neatly with everything else she had encountered so far. What intrigued her more were the coins Leonydas had given the man.

"Thank you, I—

Leonydas stopped abruptly as the man's face became grave. He followed his stare and found the men who had attacked them back in the Inn racing towards them down the trail.

"Hurry!" Leonydas said, gesturing for her to follow Xel and Fresita down the newly revealed stone steps. Lizzy and Leonydas ran down them as the closing cement platform rained dirt, pattering against the steps and their shoulders.

"Can they get in?" Lizzy asked, breathlessly.

"Not until after we have left the passageway," Leonydas said, hurrying her forward. "The payment only covers the ones paid for."

"But they have an idea where we are going now," Xel called back from further ahead.

They hurried through the passageway, brushing past finger-like roots reaching in from the walls and ceiling. At the far end, Lizzy passed through a door; like a trap door, the world fell out from under her. The sensation hit like the first plunge of a roller coaster. Her legs buckled before she understood what was happening, and she pitched forward. Leonydas caught her around the waist, steadying her before she hit the floor.

"What was that?" Lizzy gasped, struggling not to throw up.

"I am sorry, I should have warned you," Leonydas said. "Are you ok?"

"Yeah," Lizzy said, stepping away from his touch to lean on the wall. "I just feel like I fell off a building."

"She should know," Fresita said with a sharp laugh.

"Shush," Lizzy said. The feeling passed, and she straightened her posture. "I'm ok now."

"Good," Leonydas said. "Usually, travelling by Gateway is no different than walking from one room to the next. However, when you travel great distances, you will feel the displacement more. You will grow accustomed to it with practice."

Lizzy nodded as they continued through a stone hallway. Flickering with torchlight, it reminded her of a medieval castle. They came to a stop at an oak door, large enough for a car to pass through. Xel looked to Leonydas for approval and then lifted a basketball-sized iron ring hanging from the front of the door. Though she hid it well, Lizzy could tell it was extremely heavy.

A moment passed before the door swung slowly inward, and they stepped into a new chamber. Lizzy braced herself for another drop, but nothing came. The stone-walled room hummed with muted laughter and conversation drifting from somewhere past a velvet curtain. The rich scent of roasted food hung thick in the air, and Lizzy's stomach answered with an unhelpful growl. She couldn't even begin to remember the last time she had a full meal.

The chamber itself was small and largely bare, save for an oversized wooden farmhouse chair tucked into one corner. Lizzy eyed it, certain that whoever sat there must have been enormous.

"Weapons," a baritone voice boomed.

Startled, Lizzy jerked back into Leonydas. Behind them, the door swung shut under the weight of an immensely bulky man. He was at least twice the size of any weightlifter she had ever seen—tall enough that even Xel had to look up at him. His arms and legs were thick as tree trunks, supporting a torso that was broad and unexpectedly soft.

He might have been terrifying, if not for the stretched, threadbare Halestorm concert T-shirt and the jeans he wore. She shifted subtly, keeping Leonydas and Xel between herself and the mountain of a man as he slowly raised one massive hand, palm outstretched.

Xel, without hesitation, stepped towards him and produced the staff Lizzy had seen her use earlier. She was closer to it now and admired deep but flowing etchings in the silver caps. Xel placed it in the steady behemoth's hand in front of her and stepped back. Without moving his head, the man looked at Leonydas.

"These are the only weapons I have," he joked, holding up his hands. The man was not amused and shook his large head slowly to show it. His eyes narrowed at Lizzy, who was still sheltered behind Leonydas.

"I…I don't have any weapons," she responded in a small voice to his steady stare. She opened the backpack Ruby had given her and showed it to him. The large man took a long look at it and then finally nodded.

The man lumbered toward a thick orange curtain, from behind which the ambient noise seeped through. He raised one massive arm and took hold of the fabric.

"Do not start…what you cannot…finish," he boomed, his

voice flat and emotionless.

He drew the curtain aside. Warm, golden light spilled into the room, and the muted murmur of voices and laughter swelled into full volume. Xel stepped back, gesturing for Lizzy and Leonydas to go first.

"Come on. This is it," Leonydas said quietly, giving Lizzy's hand a gentle tug as he stepped through.

Lizzy followed, keeping one wary eye on the large man as they passed. But the moment they crossed the threshold, her attention was swept away by the sudden cacophony of conversation, music, and movement.

CHAPTER 11

The group moved down a short stone corridor that opened into a vast, arched hall—wide enough for multiple rows of long tables and crowded with jovial figures. Lizzy guessed it must have been half the length of a football field and nearly as wide. The scent of roasted, buttery meats and vegetables wrapped around her, making her even hungrier. They were pressed for time, but she hoped they were going to grab a bite before leaving.

The warmth that permeated the space was so thorough that she briefly wondered if the food was being cooked in the same room. She stood on her tiptoes to look around and found that the hall's main source of light came from the far end of the room. Even at a distance, the heat flushed Lizzy's cheeks. The scale of the hearth was impressive enough, but it was the mantel that held her gaze. A dragon's snarling snout and massive claws, carved from the same gray stone as the hall, cradled the flames. Smoke billowed from hollow nostrils, and in the shifting light, the creature seemed almost alive.

The Dragon's Breath

December 1921
The Dragon's Breath! A magnificent experience that all should behold. It's a gathering place to end all gatherings. So many people. So much food!

My favorite thing was this fire place. Big enough for a large man to stand inside.

The craft work!

It seems alive. I would not be surprised if it was....

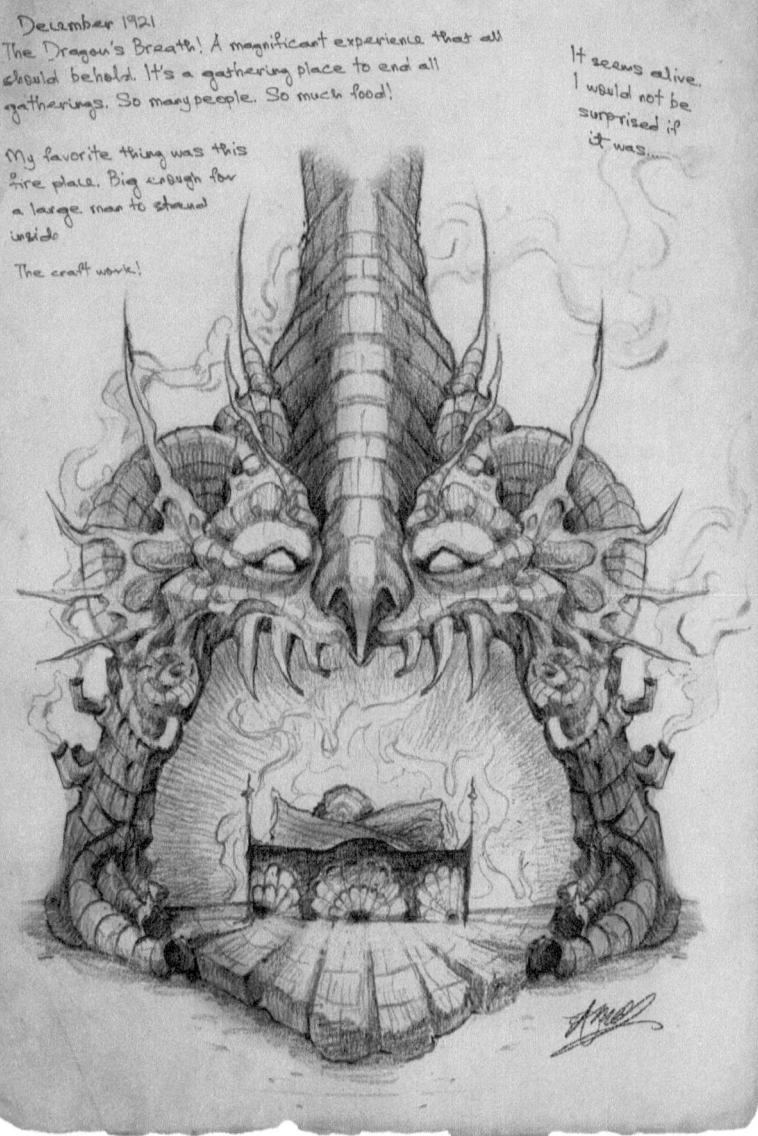

Lizzy stopped short. She had seen it before.

A drawing of it had lurked in Tita's sketchbook. It was one of the pages Lizzy had always skipped as a child because it frightened her. It had been an older sketch, dated years before Tita ever began telling her stories. And now it stood here, real and roaring.

Leonydas and Xel continued on, forcing Lizzy to break her stare and hurry after them. They passed one of six enormous pillars supporting a vaulted stone ceiling. Set high within each were oval inlays of amber, glowing with a soft, flaxen light that chased away the shadows the hearth did not reach.

The room had no windows; Lizzy looked for them but only found massive roots. They curled around the pillars, bursting through the ceiling at the hall's center. The largest were as wide as tree trunks, sprawling across the stone overhead in every direction. Lizzy stared, trying and failing to imagine the size of the tree they belonged to. Wherever they were, it was definitely not under Houston anymore.

They wove past long tables crowded with people deep in conversation, laughter rising and falling around them. Between the tables, more patrons wandered freely. Near one spread of food, Lizzy caught sight of an enormous arrangement, better yet, a charcuterie board of meats, cheeses, and fruits laid out for anyone to take. The whole place felt like the most jubilant holiday gathering she had ever seen.

She instinctively smiled, checking out everyone's outfits. Just as at the café and the Night Camp, some people wore garments suited to a time long forgotten, but just as many wore modern clothes. The mix made her think of a Renaissance fair, but if possible louder, warmer, and alive in a way those never were.

As they moved deeper into the crowd, Lizzy noticed Xel nodding a greeting every once in a while. One caught Lizzy's attention, someone who looked like they might be from Grecka's people, but the moment she tried to focus, he vanished into the press of bodies.

"Watch it, you tall-ass giraffe!"

Lizzy blinked, startled. First, at being called tall for the first time in her life, and then at the source. A grey-skinned goblin barely four feet high, with sagging ears and sharp eyes, shook a fist at her as it stormed past. It kicked her foot for emphasis.

"Sorry," Lizzy said instinctively.

Her second run-in with goblins. Apparently, she wouldn't be making friends with them anytime soon. The goblin shot her a glare.

"Whatever," Lizzy muttered, frowning.

She turned and sighed. Leonydas and Xel had left her behind. For a moment, she considered staying put, surely they'd notice she was missing and come back—but a familiar face caught her eye.

Gairloch had just passed her. He turned, recognition lighting his face. "Liz!"

"Gary, we keep meeting like this…" Lizzy said, offering a half-smile.

"You get around almost more than I do," Gairloch said with a hearty chuckle. "What brings you here? Wait—she's not here, is she?"

"Oh. No. I'm with Leonydas and Xel."

"Leonydas?" His brows shot up. "*The* Leonydas?"

"I guess?" Lizzy shrugged. "Big guy. Beard. Eyes that…" She hesitated, catching herself before revealing too much. "…that are different."

"Yeah," Gairloch said slowly. "That's probably the one. I've never met him myself. I steer clear of the Aurenthal, too stuffy and controlling for my tastes." He gave her a sideways look. "I'm surprised you're with him."

"Aurenthal?" Lizzy frowned. "I don't think my…the Leonydas I'm with is part of them. Maybe we're talking about different people."

Gairloch laughed. "Could be. Though there aren't many Leonydas running around."

"Huh," Lizzy said, thoughtful. "So what are you doing here?"

"Trying to drum up new clients," he said with a shrug. "Isley doesn't advertise much, and I'm commission-based, so…"

"Well, if I don't end up getting the Cendryn special," Lizzy said, "I'll definitely come by for a normal tattoo. I've always wanted one."

"Absolutely," Gairloch said, pointing at the unicorn on her hoodie. "That little fella there would suit you."

Lizzy glanced down. "Yeah… that might actually be kind of cool."

"Well, I'd better run," Gairloch said. "Gotta make a living."

"I'm sure I'll see you around again," Lizzy replied.

He waved over his shoulder as he left. Lizzy laughed softly—and jumped.

Xel was suddenly beside her, leaning down close to her ear.

"Be careful who you speak to," Xel whispered sharply. "Not everyone is as kind as I am."

"I know," Lizzy murmured, rolling her eyes. "I get it."

She followed Xel back toward Leonydas.

"Everything ok?" Leonydas asked.

"Yeah, just overwhelmed," she said.

"It is amazing, is it not?"

Lizzy almost gave him a cynical reply, but stopped herself. A few months ago, this would have been the most exciting and joyful event of her life. Now it was being tempered through pain, grief, and anxiety. She hated it. And so, stubbornly, she made herself try to enjoy it anyway.

"It's unbelievable, Leonydas," she said quietly.

He smiled at her use of his name, a warmth she did not notice.

"Even after everything," she said, shaking her head, "I cannot believe it exists."

"I will see if they have any private tables for you," Xel said to Leonydas. She pushed past them and headed toward the long bar. Behind it, on a raised platform, dwarven men and women worked with practiced ease, filling heavy mugs with a golden drink too thick to be beer.

Relieved to be free of Xel's glare, Lizzy watched her go. Only then did she notice a silver-and-pearl star blossom brooch pinned at the back of Xel's hair. Against all that thorn and steel, it looked like a single rose.

Leonydas gestured for Lizzy to follow, and together they moved closer to the massive hearth.

"It's amazing," Lizzy said when she finally got a clear view. Up close, the dragon-faced hearth was even more imposing. Leonydas could have stood inside its open maw with room to spare. Yet the heat was not overwhelming; somehow, the temperature was perfect, no matter where one stood in the hall.

"Has this place been here a long time?" Lizzy asked. She vaguely recalled the date on Tita's sketch, somewhere around the turn of the century. "Like...a hundred years, at least?"

"A hundred?" Leonydas laughed, loud and rich. "More. Far more. That is why they call this place The Dragon's Flame. It was lit by dragon breath a millennium ago and has never gone out. It burns wood from trees as old as the earth itself. Each log they add lasts a decade."

"A millennium?" Lizzy scoffed, raising her voice to be heard over the din.

Leonydas leaned down at the same moment she rose onto her toes. They stopped short, faces suddenly only inches apart. The roar of the hall seemed to fall away.

His smile faltered as he took in the way the firelight caught in her eyes. Lizzy opened her mouth to repeat her question—but the words never came. The closeness set her stomach fluttering, and despite the crush of smells around them, all she could sense was the faint trace of rosewood from his coat.

Almost without thinking, he reached for her hand.

Then a broad shoulder slammed into them, breaking the moment as abruptly as it had formed.

"Move it," a meaty, mostly goat-shaped man grunted, shouldering sharply past them. It was a Hornthal. "Get a room."

"Careful, my friend," Leonydas replied, his voice low but edged with warning.

The shift in his tone drew attention. Nearby conversations abruptly stopped as the Hornthal turned to face him. Lizzy's eyes widened despite herself. The creature's lower half was unmistakably goat, while his upper body was vaguely human. Thick curling horns, small flattened ears, a blunt nose, and rectangular pupils contrasted widely with the camouflage utility pants and vest he wore.

"I am not the one who needs to be careful," the Hornthal growled. He leaned in close, sniffed Leonydas, then grinned, his cadence lifting into something that almost bleated. "Banished one."

Leonydas straightened. Lizzy could have sworn he grew taller, his presence hardening. Around them, faces brightened; cheers and jeers rose, eager for a show to accompany their dinner.

"Master Hornthal," Leonydas said instead, his tone deliberately softer as his shoulders eased. "We are not here to cause trouble. Let us both go on our way."

The Hornthal held his gaze, then his eyes slid to Lizzy.

"And what is this runt doing here?" he sneered. "You dragged a Dullren into our world?" His gaze roamed over her with open disdain. "At least she is a pretty one. I could use a new farm girl—delicate hands, good for milking."

With a sharp smack, Lizzy slapped his calloused, long-haired, three-fingered hand as he reached for her.

"I don't think so, asshole," Lizzy snapped.

The Hornthal laughed at first, but jeers prodded him into restoring his pride. He reached for her again, but before it could touch her, Leonydas struck it aside. The blow sent the Hornthal's drink sloshing to the floor. Snarling, he lunged, then yelped as his wrist was wrenched violently sideways.

Xel emerged from the crowd, her grip precise and merciless. Using his arm as leverage, she shoved him backward into a cluster of startled onlookers.

With a roar, the Hornthal charged her.

A gleaming silver axe slammed down between them, biting into the stone floor.

"Ya know how I feel about fightin' instead o' fun?" a gravelly voice roared. Holding onto the handle of the axe was a fiery-red-haired, jean-jacket-wearing dwarf. He looked from the Hornthal to Xel.

"This idiot made me spill my drink!" the Hornthal shouted, jabbing a finger in Leonydas' direction.

"Well then, he can buy you another," the dwarf said, looking at Leonydas.

"Happily," Leonydas replied without hesitation.

"And that Witch tried to break my arm," the Hornthal continued, as he cradled his wrist over-enthusiastically.

"If that were true, it would indeed be broken," Xel countered, her eyes fixed on the Hornthal.

"I have been disgraced! Personally attacked! I demand retribution. I demand Harthgelt!"

The last word doused the flame of conversation throughout the entire establishment and brought all eyes to them.

"Well, ma'am, do ya agree to face off with this one in Ilion's Belt? The consequences are shame if you do not."

"Let's go, Xel," Leonydas leaned over and said to Xel.

"I will gladly enter the belt with *it*," Xel answered the dwarf while still staring into her opponent's eyes.

"Very well—

"On one condition," Xel interjected. The entire place erupted in hushed shock and excitement.

"Go on," the dwarf said as he yanked his axe from the splintered floor with ease.

"Can he read Hornthal?"

All attention turned to the Hornthal, who blinked in surprise and then indignation.

"Of course I do, what does that have to do with anything?"

"Then if I win, you will translate something for me."

The Hornthal scoffed. "And if I win?"

"*I* will be your new 'milk maid,'" Xel said, scowling.

"Deal!"

"Fine then," the Dwarf said, after a mighty laugh. "In thirty minutes ya can sort out yer differences, until then," the dwarf paused as he slung the battle-worn axe onto his shoulder. "Have fun!" He nodded at Leonydas but gave the Hornthal a stern look before leaving.

"You need not have done this, Xel," Leonydas said, his disappointment evident. "The historian would have known where to find a suitable translator."

"He will not be any trouble," Xel replied, breaking her gaze from the Honrthal. She offered Leonydas a confident smile. "This will be quicker than sending the historian on a search. Come, the table has a clear view of the Belt."

The Hornthal snorted as they passed him. Lizzy held his gaze a moment too long, then quickly looked away when he growled low in his throat.

They followed Xel into a connecting room where a pair of dwarves were shooing patrons back from a slightly raised circular space at its center. Beyond it, up a few steps, were wooden booths set into the stone walls. This area was lit more by the glowing lights around the ceiling than by the fireplace, though the heat could still be felt.

Xel led them to a booth already occupied by an older man who bore a striking resemblance to Leonardo da Vinci, right down to the flowing robes Lizzy recognized from old paintings. Down the front of the robes were symbols similar to what framed the gateway doorway at the café.

"Felicis," Leonydas said, breaking into a wide smile.

"Leonydas!" Felicis replied, sliding out of the booth and pulling him into an enthusiastic embrace. His grin only widened as he turned to Xel and drew her into an even warmer hug.

"Tirithwen," he said with evident respect. Lizzy guessed it was a title. "How you have grown since last we met…not only in stature, but in beauty. Truly breathtaking."

Xel's composed smile cracked into a laugh that Lizzy thought was surprisingly close to a giggle.

"I have not seen her since she was half that height," Felicis added as everyone settled into the booth.

"Liz," Leonydas said, gesturing toward her, "this is Felicis. The greatest historian the Realms have ever known."

"Ha!" Felicis laughed, lifting his glass in salute. "I was not terrible once, that is true, but that was many sunsets ago. These days, I am more storyteller than scholar."

"Well, it is a pleasure to meet you," Lizzy said, offering a small wave.

"The pleasure is mine," Felicis replied with a courteous nod. As he moved, Lizzy noticed his hair, soft and straight, like pale strands of cotton. He smiled thoughtfully at Leonydas. "My word. You do surround yourself with remarkable women. How long have you two been together?"

"Oh—no," Leonydas said quickly, clearly flustered. "We are only—"

"Friends," Lizzy finished for him, suddenly very interested in the table.

"Are you sure?" Felicis asked with a knowing chuckle. His expression grew thoughtful as his gaze moved from Lizzy to Leonydas and back again. "Sometimes il'Thren tangles two lives together, whether they intend it or not."

They laughed, a touch too nervously, as Felicis winked at them.

"What'll you tall folk be havin' tonite?" a bellowing feminine voice said, causing Lizzy to jump. She wished she could get used to unexpected things happening; she was sure her heart rate was all over the place lately.

A female Dwarf with a thick blond beard stood beside their table, patting the pockets of her bright blue apron in search of a pen before remembering the one tucked behind her ear.

"You used to serve something called Larffy's Platter," Leonydas said.

"That we do," the woman replied, eyeing Lizzy. "But it is a whole lot o' food—and the lot of you look a bit skinny. Especially this one."

"I remember it as some of the finest food I have ever eaten," Leonydas said calmly. "And it is her first visit here."

"Well then," the waitress said brightly, "she absolutely should have the best o' the best." She jotted a few notes down on her palm.

She turned to leave, then stopped short as a young Dwarf waiter passed by carrying a tray stacked with hefty steins. Without missing a beat, she plucked one free and set it firmly in front of Xel.

"I will bring more Honey Fig mead shortly, but this one is for you," she said with a grin. "The fight will be starting soon, and you will need the energy. Do not let me down—my money is on you, love."

"You're not really going to fight that goat creature?" Lizzy asked once the waitress had gone.

"Honrthal," Xel replied flatly, lifting the mug. "Yes."

"Xel," Leonydas said, his gaze steady, "this is not something you must do. Felicis is here now. The message may be translated without bloodshed."

"Oh!" Felicis said, eyes lighting up. "A translation? What do we have?"

Leonydas inclined his head toward Lizzy. She pulled out the sketchbook, opened it to the back, and set the perfume bottle beside it. Only then did she realize she had not seen Fresita in some time. She glanced around, even ducking beneath the table.

"She is nearby," Leonydas said gently. "You need not worry."

Lizzy nodded and shook a dash of moonlight from the bottle across the page.

Nothing visible emerged, but moments later, the writing in the sketchbook flared to life. Lizzy slid it toward Felicis, who squinted thoughtfully.

"Honrthal," Felicis said, shaking his head. "And an older form, at that. The only word I recognize is Blossom. I am afraid it is among the least-documented tongues. Their scholars guard what little exists."

"Then do not concern yourself," Xel said, clapping Felicis lightly on the arm. "I will win the fight and bring back a translation."

Lizzy could not help noticing how different Xel seemed around him. Xel must have felt her gaze, because her expression hardened.

"I must prepare," Xel said, turning to Leonydas. "With your permission?"

"Yes," Leonydas replied, fully aware that refusal would mean nothing. "Go, with care."

Xel smiled, mischief sparking in her eyes. "If I were careful, little of interest would ever occur." She winked, then glanced at Felicis. "Watch over him."

"I will," Felicis said solemnly. "Nothing will happen to him unless it happens to me first."

"My thanks," Xel said, bowing slightly. She flashed Leonydas a grin and headed toward the ring.

"How can you let her do this?" Lizzy said, making her displeasure obvious. "She could be hurt!"

Leonydas smiled faintly. "I would not deny her joy. And if she were unable to protect herself, she would not have gone."

Lizzy huffed and turned her attention back to the ring, where Xel, still dressed in business attire, looked entirely out of place.

Xel stood in the center, rolling her shoulders and loosening her arms before cracking her neck. Around her, the crowd thickened. From the main hall, more people poured in, forming a tight circle around the ring as coins and bills began to change hands.

"Maybe he won't show up," Lizzy mused.

"Ha!" Felicis laughed. "Not likely. The Hornthal are as stubborn as rock is solid. In the Great Wars, they served as the first line of defense. Not a single one ever turned away in fear. I've heard that watching them sweep across the battlefield was like watching the ocean rage against the coastline. It did not matter how many died or if they were successful; they kept at it until the battle was over."

"Do we even have time for this?" Lizzy said, looking for any excuse to prevent the fight. "What if those hooded men show up, or Xeilan's guard?"

Leonydas remained focused on Xel but leaned his head

towards Lizzy to respond. "They would not be permitted to carry weapons, if they were granted entry at all," Leonydas said. "The doorman judges trouble well."

"As for time," he added, "it does not behave here as it does elsewhere. Hours may pass for us, while only moments slip by outside."

Before Lizzy could ask more, the sound of a horn bellowed. The buzz of the crowd flattened.

"Prepare for battle!" A voice shouted from somewhere in the room.

The Hornthal shoved through the crowd and stepped into the ring with an overconfident pride. Glaring at Xel, he took off his vest and tossed it into the crowd behind him. His hooves clacked on the floor with every step he took.

Xel ignored him as she slipped out of her a pair of shiny black flats and carefully placed them just outside of the ring.

"I will return for these," Xel said, glaring at a group of onlookers near them. They gave her shoes plenty of space.

"Ergh," the Hornthal said, making a face at her feet. "Soft-footed creatures are nasty. You should keep them covered."

"Only if you cover those ugly smooth horns," Xel replied without hesitation. The Hornthal roared, threatening to charge her.

"The horns, and their rugged texture, are the pride of every Hornthal," Felicis said, leaning over the table to give Lizzy some context. "That insult was worse than calling his mother a whore."

Lizzy nodded, keeping her focus on the ring.

The same dwarf who had stopped the confrontation earlier emerged from the onlookers and stood at the edge of the ring between the two opponents.

"Fine peoples of the Realms!" he rumbled. On his shoulder, he carried the great silver axe with one hand and cupped his other hand around his mouth. His voice quieted the room and the hall beyond it. "The rules are simple. No magic. No enchanted weapons. No quitting. The fight ends when one o' the fighters is either unconscious or dead."

Lizzy spun around in her seat and gave Leonydas a dissatisfied, questioning look. He patted her arm and mouthed, 'It will be ok.' She jerked her arm out of his reach and turned her back on him.

"Do the fighters acknowledge these rules?" the Dwarf asked, making eye contact with each of the fighters. Xel nodded. The Hornthal grunted. "Very well then. When the rat reaches the center, the fight may begin. Be well and good luck!"

No sooner had he stopped speaking than the crowd roared—cheering and jeering the fighters. Lizzy watched, fascinated beyond belief but also concerned. The Hornthal was like a sharp hunk of rock compared to the Xel's honed prowess.

"Xel!... Xel!... Xel!" an excited voice chanted over the roar of the crowd.

It did not take Lizzy long to spot the source. At the edge of the ring, a colorful young woman waved both arms wildly, doing everything possible to catch Xel's attention. Her arms were covered with tattoos. She wore her hair in blue-and-pink space buns, paired with a vintage ringer tee and high-waisted plaid pants—all carefully coordinated.

Xel glanced her way, a faint smile tugging at her mouth.

Lizzy watched as the animated woman tugged an earring free from her upper ear, then wiggled her fingers in the air. Lizzy grinned as a burst of small fireworks shot from the woman's hands. She made 'jazz hands' in an arch in front of her and a shower of pastel-colored fireworks, matching the woman's outfit, exploded to form the letters X - E - L.

The crowd marvelled at the impromptu show as Xel shook her head in amusement and mouthed 'thank you.'

The crowd's attention shifted at once as a chubby rat waddled into the ring. The scruffy, ear-notched rodent scurried along the perimeter. Each time it drifted closer to the center, the cheers swelled, startling it back again. Its eyes darted wildly, searching for an escape from the madness.

Xel never looked at the rat. Her gaze stayed locked on the Hornthal. He snarled under his breath, fists clenching as his eyes flicked between her and the animal.

The mounting noise and tension made Lizzy's stomach churn. She glanced at their table. Felicis was practically bouncing in his seat, craning for a better view. Leonydas leaned forward, concern etched into his face, but when he caught Lizzy watching, he forced a smile. She frowned at him and turned back to the ring just in time to see the rat hesitate, then step into the center.

The crowd erupted.

The rat bolted, vanishing into a frantic sea of stamping feet.

The two fighters circled each other, neither one breaking their gaze. Xel's face displayed no emotion, and her movements were smooth, calculated, and calm. The Hornthal, on the other hand, took each step with a threatening suddenness. After a few circles around each other, he began to periodically fake lunge at her.

"Elf witch," he heckled her. "Or is it Elf bitch?" The crowd oohed at his attempt at an insult.

Dominic Dragomyr

Being: Hornthal
(Faunus Magnibellus)
Height: 1.5 meters
Age: 43 years
Location: Brooklyn, NY
Occupation: Dock Worker

December 1921
On a hidden dock in Brooklyn we had 'dealings' with a being known as a Hornthal. They are somewhat similar to the Satyr of Greek mythology. Half man. Half goat. Though, in appearance they seem closer to goat. But their attitudes are all man. Chauvinistic. Loud. Prone to violence. Handsy.

I have been told that the Hornthal were once great warriors. They were employed by kingdoms to act as a first line of attack. I can imagine that having a horde of them running at me would be quite terrifying!

"You know, I had a goat once," Xel quipped. "It tasted like shit." The Hornthal roared and finally dove for her.

She sidestepped easily, sending him careening into the crowd. They shoved him straight back into the ring. Using their momentum, he charged again. Xel dodged, but this time she left her leg in his path.

He tripped and slammed face-first into the floor.

Laughter roared as his hooves clacked and skidded against the wooden boards. Before he could recover, Xel seized one of his horns and swung him in a tight arc. When he crashed into the crowd again, several people went down with him.

Lizzy watched in awe. Xel moved with effortless speed and precision, every dodge perfectly timed, every motion clean and elegant. Lizzy would blink, and Xel would be in an entirely different part of the ring. As the realization settled in, just how skilled she was, Lizzy felt her tension ease. She even joined the crowd laughing at each of the Hornthal's failed attempts. She glanced at Leonydas. He was watching with a pleased expression.

"See," he mouthed.

Lizzy frowned, but she was relieved he was right. Then his expression changed.

Lizzy turned back just in time to see the Hornthal tip the contents, an orange glowing liquid, of a small, pear-shaped vial to his mouth. Boos and chairs swept the crowd. He hurled the empty vial to the floor, where it shattered and then dissolved into a curl of vapor, leaving nothing behind.

He laughed, the sound edging close to maniacal as Xel circled him warily. The potion worked fast. His face contorted as every muscle in his body swelled, tripling in size like overinflated balloons. Thick veins bulged beneath his skin, pulsing darkly as his frame broadened.

He did not grow much taller, but he did grow heavier. Bulk replaced agility. When he stamped a hoof, the floor groaned beneath the impact, the sharp clack replaced by the ominous creak of strained wood.

"You wanna eat goat? I've got something to feed you!" he said, an eye twitching as he moved towards Xel. She remained confident but countered his steps to keep space between them.

"That's not fair," Lizzy shouted urgently to Leonydas. "You've got to stop the fight."

"Patience," he said calmly but with a creased brow of concern. "She has faced much worse than this fool."

Again, the Hornthal lunged, and somehow, even though he was bulkier, he was faster. Xel slipped by, but he managed to grab a fistful of her hair. She grunted as he yanked backward and tossed her across the ring. She gracefully twisted herself so that she landed on her feet.

She slid to a stop. She rushed forward and slammed her open palm into his gut. He grunted and answered with a fist to her jaw. Xel's head snapped to the side, and she went down hard.

Instantly, she pushed herself up on hands and knees, blinking, dazed.

Lizzy's stomach dropped. A blow like that could have shattered bone, at the very least left her concussed. Dark blood spilled from Xel's nose, dripping onto the floor in thick drops.

The Hornthal laughed and danced around her, fists raised in triumph as the crowd roared its approval.

Xel got to her feet and tried to loosen her muscles, but felt restricted. She pulled off her jacket and her loose blouse underneath. Underneath, she wore a pale blue sports bra. Lizzy noticed Xel's lean, sinewy muscles first. Then she gasped.

A jagged scar carved its way from the top of Xel's shoulder down across her torso, disappearing beneath the top of her pants. It was old, long healed, but its severity made Lizzy's skin crawl. Whatever had done that had not merely wounded her—it had tried to tear her apart.

"Go, Xel! You got this, girl," the colorful woman shouted from the sidelines. "Kick his ass!"

Lizzy watched Xels for signs of head trauma but found that she moved as smoothly and as calculating as she had at the start of the fight. The Hornthal grinned as he tried to fake her out again. Not once did she fall for it. Finally, he rushed at her, but instead of diving or hitting her, he threw his goat legs forward with a powerful kick.

As if she knew exactly what he was going to do, Xel moved out of the way. She reached out and yanked at his horn playfully as he went by.

"Oh, you want my horns, do you?" he threatened, charging again. She tumbled around him, this time yanking his stubby brush-like tail.

He snarled and lunged again. This time, his fingers caught her arm, wrenching her off balance and slamming her back to the floor. He followed immediately, driving a fist down onto the scarred shoulder.

Xel grunted and grimaced from the pain.

But she reacted instantly—bringing her feet up and kicking him square in the chest. The blow knocked him off his feet. He crashed down on his side and rolled away, out of her reach.

He rolled onto his side, eyes wild, searching for her. She was behind him.

Snarling, he swept his hooves around in a brutal arc. They caught Xel's legs and sent her crashing onto her back. Her head struck the floor, and her vision exploded into black stars.

The Hornthal was on her instantly. He hauled her upright by the back of the neck. Dizzy and disoriented, she struggled to focus as he hooked an arm beneath her chin and squeezed.

Xel clawed at his forearm, fighting for air as pressure crushed against her throat.

"Do something!" Lizzy insisted as she reached back and dug her fingers into Leonydas' arm.

"Xel!" Leonydas yelled as he shot up from his seat. "Find your way!"

Xel's head cleared as she heard his voice. She planted her feet firmly on the ground. Using her height as her weapon, she thrust her torso forward. The Hornthal flipped heels over head onto the floor with a smack.

She brought her knee down on his neck, pinning him in place. Raising her fist high above her head, with all her force, she slammed it down hard on one of his horns. There was a loud 'crack' and a scream of pain as the horn broke and clattered across the floor.

Xel stepped away, massaging her hand as the Hornthal cradled his head.

"Do you yield?" she hissed at him. He blinked at her, the pain in his head sharp, and leaned forward as if ready to make another attack. However, the great silver axe slung down between the two opponents.

"Ya have forfeited yer half o' the fight Hornthal!" The dwarf shouted, stepping back into the ring. "I warned ya, magic is forbidden."

"Lies!" the Hornthal spat. "Did anyone see me take a potion?"

"Potion! Potion!" the crowd chanted at the angry creature.

"The crowd has spoken," the Dwarf said, eyeing the Hornthal. "What say ya Elf warrior? Live o' die?" The Hornthal looked around wildly for some way to escape, but the crowd was thick in all directions.

"I do not need or want his life. I've already taken from him what I wanted," she replied with a smile as she held up the horn that she had broken off. The crowd cheered.

"Yer opponent is an honorable warrior," the Dwarf said, slinging the axe onto his shoulder.

"I give you time to recover from your wounded head and pride," Xel said. "But do not go far. You have a promise to fulfill."

The Hornthal cradled his head but nodded. He gave Xel one last dirty look before pushing his way through the crowd towards the main hall. Xel turned beaming and raised the horn again.

"Xel! Xel! Xel!" The crowd chanted, pushing in closer to congratulate her.

"She looks so happy," Lizzy said to herself, watching from her seat. She was truly impressed by Xel's endurance and courage. Lizzy turned to the table as she lost sight of the victor and saw Leonydas proudly chatting with Felicis.

"I attest," Felicis eloquated, as he raised his glass in the direction of the ring. "That this was one of the most magnificent fights the Dragon's Flame has ever witnessed since its foundations were laid,"

"It was something, all right," Lizzy said as she looked back at the crowd to locate Xel. "Is she going to be alright? Is there a doctor here who could check her out?"

"Yes, she will be fine," Leonydas said, scooting closer to

Lizzy so she could hear him over the noise as it got closer. "She heals quite fast. Besides, I would have to carry her to go to an apothecary. She would never go of her own accord."

Xel appeared at the table in a blur and slid into the seat beside Felicis. One side of her face was swollen and red, her hair plastered to her face with sweat, but she grinned ear to ear as she slammed the goat-man's horn onto the table like a trophy.

"Congratulations to the victor," Felicis praised her with a clap of his hands.

"Thank you," Xel replied, proudly. Seeing the mugs, she grabbed one and guzzled.

"Well done, Xel," Leonydas said as he reached over and grabbed her arm briefly. "I'm proud of you."

"Thank you, Leonydas," Xel said, pleased with his praise.

"How do you feel?" Lizzy shouted over the noise of the crowd. "How is your head?"

"I feel amazing, little one."

"You should see a doctor; you could have a concussion."

"Ha!" Xel said as she took another drink. "I'll be ok."

"Xel! Oh my god!" An excited voice exclaimed. The woman who had created the fireworks bounded up to the table.

"Saoirse!" Xel replied as the woman threw her arms around her neck in a hug. Lizzy cringed at the pain Xel must be in.

"Leonydas!" Saoirse said in a chipper tone and excitedly waved as she noticed him. She stopped suddenly as she noticed the horn and grabbed it. "Holy shit, Xel, is this it? This is so badass…you're so badass."

"Is…," Xel started, but paused to look around at her table companions. She frowned before deciding to finish her question. "Is Diego here too?"

"Yep, he's around here somewhere with the girls. We had a meeting with someone, but when I heard you were gonna fight, well, I wasn't going to miss that." Saoirse took a whiff of the horn and wrinkled her nose. "Do you think it will get too smelly?"

This woman fascinated Lizzy. She was heavily tattooed with both cutesy cartoon animals and beautifully intricate designs. But more than anything, Saoirse exuded an infinite childlike energy that saturated the area around her.

"The girls?" Leonydas asked.

"Oh yeah, we're on this whole mission-quest thing with these two super cool girls," Saoirse said as she handed the horn to Xel. "One grew up in our world, the other has just been introduced to it. I think she has a lot of promise, though." Saoirse's eyes jumped from one person to the next as she talked and then paused on Lizzy before she suddenly turned and leaned to face Felicis. "Oh, hi! Shit, I'm sorry I didn't notice you," she said as she grabbed his hand and squeezed it lovingly.

"Hello, Saoirse," Felicis said. "It's no problem at all, we're all excited about Xel's victory."

"Huzzah!" Saoirse exclaimed loudly as she threw up her hands.

"Huzzah!" The crowd near the table responded.

"Saoirse…Saoirse," Leonydas said, waving to get her attention. "I'd like you to meet our friend Liz."

"Hey, girlie!" Saoirse winked at Lizzy as she leaned across the table to grab her hand and squeeze it. "Oh! I looove your freckles. Sooo freakin' cute!"

"Oh," Lizzy said, flattered. "Thanks!"

"O… M… G!" Saoirse shouted, eyes wide as she pointed at Lizzy, who leaned back, suddenly unsure of what was happening.

"That hoodie is so amazingly awesome. Let me see!"

Before Lizzy could respond, Saoirse sprawled across the table and grabbed the front of her hoodie, tugging it straight to admire the design of the cuddly unicorn. "He is so fat and cute. I love him!"

"Uh—thanks," Lizzy said. "I found it at a vintage store in the Heights."

"Ooo. Ooo. Ooo!" Saoirse squealed as she slid off the table and bounced into the seat beside Lizzy. "This little guy would look uh-mazing with the rest of my art. Can I make a copy?"

Lizzy glanced down at the pink unicorn, then back at Saoirse's eager face, and shrugged. "Sure. I guess."

"Hell yeah!"

"How are you going to—oh." Lizzy's question died as Saoirse began whispering softly, waggling her multicolored fingernails over the stitched image.

Saoirse's eyes glowed faintly. At the same time, Lizzy felt that familiar, crisp tingle prick across her skin—the same sensation she had felt earlier with Ruby. She watched as a translucent, sticker-like version of the unicorn peeled free from the fabric. It drifted upward like a leaf on a gentle current.

Saoirse followed it with delight, scanning her arms for the perfect spot as the glowing copy hovered patiently nearby.

"Here... no—here... wait... wait—here!" Saoirse exclaimed as she finally found the perfect spot on the back of her hand.

The glowing sticker drifted down and settled where she indicated, flattening slowly. One corner remained curled, as if peeking up at her for approval.

"Yup. Go for it," Saoirse said, her eyes wide with excitement.

The corner smoothed down. There was a brief flash of light,

a soft sizzle, and the image fused into her skin. Lizzy blinked, realizing the tattoo looked less like ink and more like actual yarn stitched beneath the surface.

"Can I touch it?" Lizzy asked, hopeful.

"Here," Saoirse said, thrusting her hand toward her.

Up close, Lizzy caught the sweet scent of cotton candy. She touched the tattoo lightly at first, then let her fingers trail over Saoirse's warm skin.

"It looks so real, but there's nothing there!" Lizzy said, astounded.

"Cool, right?" Saoirse responded happily, popping back into her seat beside Xel. "Hey Xel, do you want to hang out for a while? I'm not sure when I'll get a chance to visit with you again. It's been so long!"

"I should stay close to Leonydas," Xel said. "We are actually here on our own mission."

"What?" Saoirse said with an exaggerated pout. "You can't be serious. There's no way anything will happen to him here. You know mister 'big axe man' wouldn't allow it."

"She's right, Xel," Leonydas said, shooing her off. "Get out of here, go celebrate your victory. You deserve it. We have a little time."

"Ok," she said hesitantly, and after glancing around the room, was more sure of her response. "Ok, let's go then!"

Lizzy watched the two women leave reluctantly. She had never seen the smiling side of Xel before, and Saoirse seemed like she would be a fun friend to have. Maybe someday.

"Are you ready for this?" A deep female voice bellowed. Lizzy turned just in time to see a large tray of food being lowered onto the table in front of them. Her eyes widened as she looked across an amazing spread of food that took up most of the table. There was a roasted chicken with crispy golden skin that was larger than a Turkey, visibly seasoned and buttered vegetables that were twice the size of any veggies she had ever seen, and steaming fresh loaves of bread.

The two men quickly grabbed plates and started picking out pieces of the steaming food as Lizzy peered into one of the mugs that had been brought with the food. She stuck her finger into the mug to get a taste of the golden, sweet-smelling Honey Fig Mead. It was smooth and hearty like a lager, but was sweet and rich instead of bitter.

"Here you go, Liz," Leonydas said as he slid a plate of food in front of her. She almost laughed at the amount of food in front of her. She didn't usually eat that much in a week. "Now dig in!" Lizzy wasn't hungry as she took her first bite of a potato, but the flavor was so delicious that she found she couldn't hold back from eating and then eating some more.

CHAPTER 12

After eating for what felt like hours, Lizzy could not stomach another bite. Not that she didn't try. She had never tasted food this delicious before, and it was the biggest meal she had in weeks.

The men picked at food from the platter as they chit-chatted about current events, some she knew about, and others were obviously from their world. She thought it was interesting how they switched between talking about the different worlds as if it were nothing to them. She hoped to learn more by listening, but ended up confused by places and names that seemed alien to her.

"Doing ok?" Leonydas asked her as he pushed his plate back. Felicis did the same and patted his round belly.

"Oh yeah," she responded, peering into her now-empty stein of Honey Fig Mead. "Everything was so good, I'm just too full to eat anymore."

"Do you mind," Felicis said, wiping his mouth with a napkin, "if I inquire about the writing you wanted help translating? Xel mentioned something about a mission?"

"Ah....yes," Leonydas replied hesitantly. "It is a sensitive matter." Lizzy was glad he wasn't going to share everything about what they were doing with him. He seemed trustworthy, but she couldn't handle someone else treating her like she was someone special.

"Understood," Felicis said, clearly unbothered by the secrecy. "Well, if there is anything I can do to help, I am always at your disposal, Lord Leonydas."

"Ok," Lizzy said, holding her hands up to stop the conversation. "Lord? Can you please explain why people refer to you like that?"

Felicis chuckled and glanced at Leonydas, who was fidgeting with his utensils. He took a moment and then nodded to Felicis. "You can tell her, but start from the beginning."

Felicis raised an eyebrow. "The beginning?"

"Yes—of everything."

"Ok," Felicis said, clearly excited. He brushed off some crumbs from a spot in the middle of the table with his hand. "I'll be discreet, Leonydas."

Lizzy watched as Felicis leaned toward the edge of their alcove. He pressed his fingers to the wall, tracing a loose, squiggled line, and murmured a few words under his breath. As she had seen earlier with Ruby, the stone responded, part of the wall breaking apart into tiny, glowing motes that stretched outward across the opening.

The air prickled with energy, and Lizzy felt it spark against her skin again.

Unlike Ruby, Felicis did not pause to watch the magic finish its work. He leaned back almost immediately and continued speaking as if nothing unusual were happening. The particles obeyed whatever command he had given, weaving themselves together until they hardened into a latticed privacy screen, its repeating patterns sealing off the alcove.

"Once in a Realm of wonder..." Felicis began—then paused until Lizzy finally tore her attention from the magic of the wall.

"Once in a Realm of wonder, so long ago that the world itself was young, things were very different."

As he spoke, he drew a small pouch from his robes and loosened its tie. Inside was something like sand. He whispered to it, then tossed it toward the center of the table as casually as one might throw dice.

The grains never touched the surface. They rose instead, swirling and gathering until they fused into a slowly turning globe.

"You may remember from your earliest science lessons," Felicis continued, "that there was once only a single continent."

The globe rotated, the familiar ancient landmass forming, one Lizzy recognized from old textbooks.

"So, too, were its people once united. Humans, Hornthal, Dwarves, Orcs, and many others, including Elves. They all lived together. Not always in harmony but for sure cooperatively."

As each race was named, pale, glowing figures shaped themselves from the sand around the globe: three-dimensional, monochrome statues standing in quiet harmony.

"And ilThren was everywhere," Felicis said softly. "It was shared freely. Used to care for one another and for the world itself. For thousands of years, the Earth flourished."

The globe shifted, drawing closer. Ancient cities bloomed into view, bustling streets, laughter, thriving lands.

Leonydas watched Lizzy as she absorbed it all, her attention utterly captured by the living history unfolding before her. He found himself less interested in the images than in the way wonder softened her grief, if only for a moment.

"But then," Felicis went on, "some humans were born without a true connection to ilThren. They could see it. Feel its effects. But they could not wield it."

The images darkened.

"Many accepted this difference and lived alongside ilThren users, benefiting from our shared strength. But others, both gifted and not, grew resentful. And some among the ilThren-born began to exploit those without power. These humans came to be called the Dullren."

Figures formed again, people turned away, driven from their homes.

"They were confined to certain places. Made to serve. It was forgotten that there had ever been a time when they stood beside us as equals."

The scenes shifted to suffering: bowed heads, cruelty, despair. Lizzy's stomach twisted. Even here, in a world of magic, the same darkness had taken hold.

"When some of us recognized the injustice, laws were proposed to protect them. But too many had grown comfortable with the Dullren's subjugation. Debate became argument. Argument—violence."

Scrolls of law appeared, then crumbled beneath marching feet. Armies swept across the land. Lizzy watched Dullren flee, stumble, and fall; trampled beneath the tide.

"The wars spread," Felicis said quietly. "They threatened to tear the world itself apart."

The globe reformed once more into the single great continent. It trembled. Cracks split its surface. With thunderous force, it shattered. Continents drifting apart as glowing motes of il'Thren were drawn upward from the land, lifting away like sparks from a dying fire.

"At last, a decision was made. The Thraewen would be removed from the world they were destroying."

The sparks faded.

"We were separated into a Realm apart, yet still connected. The Dullren were given the Earth, in recompense for what they had endured. We, the Thraewen, were charged with tending the il'Thren that still flows through your world… but forbidden from ever revealing ourselves, or il'Thren, to Dullren again."

Lizzy took a deep breath and leaned back as the globe gradually came to look like the Earth she knew.

"How do Thraewen care for the planet?" Lizzy asked thoughtfully.

"il'Thren is like the blood of existence," Felicis said. As she listened, Lizzy remembered Ruby's explanation. She liked it better. "It flows everywhere and keeps everything alive."

Felicis waved his hand again, and the sand jumped to life and created a glowing orb. It throbbed like a beating heart, and then veins of glowing 'magic' stretched out in every direction.

"In the beginning, everything was ordered, like a completed puzzle. But, as time went on and the Great Wars occurred, everything fell into disarray."

Some of the veins in the image wilted and shriveled, while others veered sharply. The beats of magic became irregular and labored like someone struggling to breathe.

"The flow of il'Thren became chaotic and needed assistance

to balance it—keep it in line. That is what the Thraewen, well, most, do. We tend to the flow of ilThren and the things it affects."

Lizzy leaned back, her eyes roaming over the table as she tried to absorb everything she had just seen. A young man ran up to the table and stuck his arm through the lattice. He held out a folded piece of paper. Leonydas took it, and the young man sprinted off.

"It is from Fresita," Leonydas said, reading the note. "She says the 'Checking on boy. Meet at café.'"

Lizzy nodded. She glanced at the note; it was addressed to 'Lord Leonydas.'

"Wait," she said. "So what does all of this have to do with 'Lord' Leonydas?"

"Ah—my apologies," Felicis said with a chuckle, waving his hand over the image still hovering above the table. "I have wandered a bit."

The particles shivered, then leapt upward. They gathered and reshaped themselves into the base of a mountain. About a quarter of the way up, the stone transformed, rising into a magnificent castle carved directly from the rock. The detail was so intricate it seemed impossible that it had been sculpted from stone at all. Towers soared skyward, some stretching high enough to brush the undersides of clouds.

At first, Lizzy thought it might be the castle nestled between the cloven mountain she had seen before, but as she studied it more closely, she realized this was something else entirely.

"Of all the peoples who lived during the Former Times," Felicis continued, "the Elves were the most powerful, both in physical strength and in their mastery of ilThren. Their bond with it was innate, surpassed only by the Fae. Elven children, at birth, could do what others would labor years to achieve."

A multitude of hardy beings emerged from the glowing sand, arrayed in elegant garments and adorned with finely worked jewelry—most prominently along long, pointed ears that swept back toward their skulls. Their faces were rugged, carved by hardship and age, yet carried an alien, arresting beauty.

They bore little resemblance to the delicate elves of storybooks. If anything, they looked more like warriors of old—Viking in bearing, forged rather than crafted.

"They were noble and great leaders of the world," Felicis said. "Their ruler at the time of the Great War was Inhyrsa Starshower, the Mountain Queen. Daughter of the First Kings, she was loved and revered... as much as she was feared."

The sand that formed the mountain and the Elves flowed together, rising into an elevated throne. Before it stood a single figure regal and unyielding. A mighty goddess gracing the face of the earth. Her straight, silken hair fell to her thighs. A simple crown rested upon her brow. She wore elegant armor, unadorned yet unmistakably royal, and in her hand she held a great sword that glowed from within, its pulse slow and powerful.

"During the onset of the Great Wars," Felicis continued, "she led the Elves in neutrality for as long as she could. But within her court, opinion was sharply divided over the fate of the Dullren. Voices rose. Pressure mounted."

The image seemed to darken.

"In the end, the Mountain Queen chose to lead her people against those who sought to defend human freedom."

Felicis fell silent. His gaze shifted to Leonydas, who was transfixed, staring at the Queen's likeness, his eyes glassy with a longstanding grief.

Inhyrsa Starshower
The Elven "Mountain Queen"

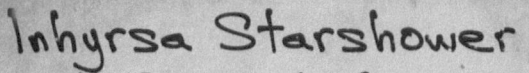

Being: Elf
(Alvus Sylvarum)
Height: 1.9 meters
Age: 400 years

March 1922
In all my travels, so far, I have only come across a few Elves. They keep to themselves and trust almost no one. I have come to understand that their kind was exiled long ago, due to something this woman did many thousands of years ago. There are few that are willing to talk about them or that time.

I came across a painting of Lady Starshower in an abandonded Elven abode. She appears sad, but very formidable. It is rumored her son has been sighted in the states! He must be thousands of years old.

"It was only with the help of her son…" Felicis said softly.

"Betrayal," Leonydas interjected. "The betrayal of her son."

"It was *because* of her son that she was able to be defeated, and the Elvish armies forced to surrender." The image of the Queen faded. "Due to their actions, though, the Elves were severely punished. Their ability to manipulate ilThren was stripped from them, and any weapons imbued with il were cursed and made untouchable by them. The ruling Council of the Realm exiled the entire race into the Formless Void to remain imprisoned until the end of time."

"What does that mean?" Lizzy asked, her stomach tightening. "Were they all killed?"

"They might as well have been," Leonydas muttered as he fidgeted with his mug.

"The Formless Void is an empty land, shrouded in constant darkness and bone-chilling temperatures. Over the ages, some of the most evil creatures have been sent there as punishment. The banishment of the Elves, most believe, was unwarranted."

"Oh," Lizzy said, frowning as she thought over everything she just heard. "Wait, so then you aren't an Elf?"

Leonydas looked at Lizzy and forced a smile.

"Not all Elves were punished," Leonydas explained. "A small group were rewarded for their aid in stopping the Mountain Queen and her forces. They were forewarned about the coming punishment and allowed to escape. It was supposed to be a secret and peaceful exodus, but many held grudges against the Elves for their part in the Wars. *I* was allowed to lead my people as they escaped and have since spent many years afterward fighting for them and helping them create new lives."

"*You* did? I thought this took place thousands of years ago."

"It did," Leonydas said with a grimace. "But we were sent forward in time. It was hoped that letting time pass would help old wounds heal. That was not the case."

"Ok…," Lizzy said, letting a short huff of air out. "So, you *are*…an Elf Lord?"

"He is *the* Elf Lord," Felicis clarified with pride. Lizzy looked at Leonydas for clarification, but he only stared down at his cup. After a moment, he looked into Lizzy's eyes solemnly.

"I am Prince Leonydas Starshower," he said quietly. "Lord of the Elves. Firstborn son of the Mountain Queen."

As he spoke, Felicis lifted his hand—this time with a deliberate flourish. The sand stirred and surged back to life. It reshaped itself into the image of a young man clad in armor similar in style to the Queen's, though less ornate. He stood tall, a sword gripped in his left hand, a bow in the other.

The resemblance to Leonydas was unmistakable.

"That's you," Lizzy said slowly. "When you were younger?"

"Yes," Leonydas replied. "Many long years ago." He did not look at the image.

Lizzy frowned, unconvinced, and pointed. "What about your ears?"

Leonydas's mouth curved into a wry smile. "They are still there."

Felicis chuckled softly.

"Though we are restricted from using ilThren," Leonydas continued, "Xel secured special dispensation for a handful of protective measures. We both wear enchanted jewels that disguise us. They were far more useful when we first arrived, before anyone knew who we were."

"Yes," Felicis added. "Over time, Leonydas has aided so many that he has become… recognizable."

"It still serves its purpose," Leonydas said, casting Felicis a pointed look. "Those who do not know Xel and me are less tempted to linger on our features and less inclined to cause trouble."

Lizzy glanced at her Dragonscale ring. She wondered why it so rarely worked to reveal magic.

"So, you don't look like this?" Lizzy said, turning her attention to his ears.

"I look similar; it doesn't change my features completely, but it does hide my ears."

"Yes, they would be a dead giveaway," Felicis explained. "The elves that remain in this realm always stay together in their protected areas. It is extremely rare to run into one. And never in the Realm itself."

"Oh," was all that Lizzy could manage to respond. The table was again quiet for a while as Lizzy took in everything that had been said. She leaned back in her seat and thought for a moment. Everything that she had read or seen about fairy tales and fantasy creatures was always so lovely. Everything she had just been told, though, was very dark and unjust.

"Why is your world like that?" Lizzy asked, jumping from her thoughts to the conversation.

"Like what?" Felicis asked, unaware of her thoughts.

"So, dark," she explained. "Your world sounds so unfair and dangerous."

"Not everything can be cute, Unicorns," Felicis responded, nodding at her hoodie. She frowned at him and sat up to hide the cute design.

"Liz, I understand what you mean," Leonydas said, coming

out of a dark fog of memories. "But your world is much the same. Your world is extremely dangerous, and there have been so many times when we were sure you were going to destroy yourselves. Wars, plagues, and hatred have at times infected the face of the Earth. It's everywhere, not just in our world. History books tend to only capture the big events, and those are usually bad or destructive things. But our world, as well as yours, is so full of beauty and wonders, and happiness, and love. You just have to be willing to risk looking for it and enjoy the moments you have with them while you can. That is what makes them beautiful, the rarity of it all."

Lizzy nodded and unconsciously smiled at Leonydas.

A body slammed against the table. Lizzy nearly jumped out of her skin this time.

"Look who I found trying to duck out," Xel growled, pressing the Hornthal's head onto the table. He moaned in response. She pulled his head up and held him in place by his neck. The potion had worn off; he was back to his normal size.

"Xel, he's hurt," Lizzy said, hopping up to examine his broken horn. "Let him go." Lizzy didn't ask.

Xel's eyes narrowed, but the hint of a smile flickered at one corner of her mouth. She released the Hornthal but stayed close to him.

"Let me see," Lizzy said, tiptoeing to look at his wound. Blood and pus trickled down the side of his head. The Hornthal jerked back but flinched when he bumped into Xel.

"Leave me alone," the Hornthal grumbled. "I've been embarrassed enough by all of you. Give me this text you want me to read for you so I can leave."

"Maybe I can help you with the pain," Lizzy insisted with a

glare. "It needs to at least be cleaned."

"Who do you think you are, a nurse?" the Hornthal said in a dismissive tone. As he talked, he leaned close to Lizzy's face and then paused. He sniffed around her and then pulled back. Surprised. He blinked a few times and then looked away. "Give me the text. I shouldn't be here."

Leonydas looked at him, fearing he might have realized who Lizzy was.

"What do you mean?" Lizzy demanded.

"I can smell the Aetherwilde plain as day," the Hornthdal whispered, leaning close to her again. Xel grabbed his arm to prevent him from getting any closer. "I am not worthy of the likes of you. Besides, I can tell how little is left. To use it on me would be a waste."

"Liz, show him the text so he can leave," Leonydas said, glancing at Felicis, who was watching the conversation transpire with great interest.

"I can help him, I mean, he's already in pain, I'm sure there's not much more I could hurt," Lizzy said, reaching for the Hornthal's wound. He jerked back, running into Xel again. This time, she let him move further away, but kept a grip on him.

"No, thank you, but no," Hornthal said, shaking his head and wincing. "Show me the text."

Lizzy frowned, then set the sketchbook on the table and opened it. A flash of panic swept across her; the page was blank.

Leonydas reminded her of the bottle of moonlight. She took it out and poured it onto the page. Glittery light tumbled out and once again revealed Tita's writing.

The Hornthal studied it for a moment and snorted.

"It reads: Maeve holds the answer to what you seek."

Lizzy's mouth dropped open, and then she closed it, and her eyes narrowed.

Xel released the Hornthal, and the group exchanged quick goodbyes with Felicis. He understood well enough what was unfolding and promised his silence.

They hurried toward the exit, only to find many others doing the same. Though the Dragon's Breath never truly closed, it moved in tides—waves of patrons leaving as food ended and entertainment reset.

"She's had it all along?" Lizzy said, confusion flashing briefly before fury took its place. Leonydas instinctively stepped back. "This isn't a game."

"I think it may just be the wording," Leonydas offered, glancing to Xel for support.

"Maeve did say Elizabeth needed to discover things for herself," Xel replied evenly. "Whether she believes that is a necessary part of the journey or just to remove her own curse, I do not know."

Leonydas frowned at her.

"I don't care about the journey. I need to find the necklace. Now," Lizzy snapped. She stood on her toes in a futile attempt to see over the crowd. "There isn't another way out of this place? I need to leave!"

A few people from the departing mass turned to stare, smirking. Leonydas placed a steadying hand on her shoulder.

"Liz. We'll get out," he said gently.

"There isn't some kind of magic that can take us to Fresita quicker than this?" she pressed.

"Patience, little one," Xel said, stepping in front of her. "Rushing into things can lead to a bad outcome. I have learned—

Lizzy didn't wait. She closed the distance until she was toe to toe with the towering bodyguard.

"Screw patience!" she shouted, fists clenched, neck craned back to meet Xel's eyes. "It's easy for you to be smug when you don't have someone sick…dying. My—"

Lizzy paused, catching herself.

"It doesn't matter to you. You aren't hollowed out by this disease," Lizzy continued, changing course. "And you don't have the responsibility of helping all these people on your shoulders. They are counting on me, and I'm stuck in a line. And besides," she added bitterly, "you can't even use magic anymore, so what does it even fucking matter?"

Xel stared at her, eyes slightly widened, jaw locked tight.

"Now," Lizzy said, voice shaking but unyielding, "if you aren't going to help me, then get out of my way."

Xel stepped aside, and Lizzy immediately began pushing through the crowd.

"Please excuse us," she called loudly. "It's an emergency. We need to get out."

Reluctantly, patrons shifted and parted until a familiar splash of color appeared directly in their path. Saoirse was deep in a one-way conversation with an older man who was trying to finish his drink before they reached the exit.

"Saoirse!" Lizzy said.

"Heya girl," Saoirse said, hugging her as if they hadn't seen each other in ages. "Fancy meeting you here. Where are you headed?"

"I'm trying to get out of here so I can find my cat."

"Oh no! Your cat is missing? That's so sad. My Diego is missing…and the girls. Well, not really missing, I just wandered off." She paused and then grinned. "I guess that means I'm missing."

"Saoirse, we are looking for Maeve," Leonydas clarified. "She is disguised as a cat currently. Would you be able to help track her?"

"Looky, looky, long-lost pets are my specialty," Saoirse said, beaming. "Come on."

She waved them toward an empty table and hopped up onto it, legs swinging. She rummaged through her pockets, producing an assortment of trinkets, frowning, shoving them back, and trying again. Finally, she rolled her eyes and laughed.

"Oh!"

She lifted a ruby-red crystal from beneath her collar, the stone suspended on a necklace of thin, desiccated vines. Closing her eyes, she extended one hand.

"Alright," she said. "Give me something that belongs to your cat."

"Like what?" Lizzy said.

"Mmm, like a favorite toy, or outfit," Saoirse said, opening one eye and giggling. "Like a little pirate outfit…have you seen those? It fits over their head and front legs, and when they walk around, it looks like a little pirate person waddling around. Oh my gosh, they are so cute!"

"Sursh," Xel said. "She is not actually Elizabeth's pet. I do not think we have anything of hers."

"…Elizabeth's pet…," Saoirse said, in a mock deep voice, and then laughed. "You are so funny when you're on the job." Saoirse's smile faded when she caught Lizzy frowning at her. "Ok, then anything else? A photo? Uhmm, twig? Fae always have a favorite twig."

Lizzy looked at the others for help and then recoiled as Xel reached for her.

"Do not move," Xel said, plucking a white hair from the neckline of Lizzy's hoodie. She presented it to Saoirse.

"Nice!" Saoirse said, shooting finger guns at her with a wink. She examined the hair for a moment, closed her eyes, and then tossed it into the air to float freely. Saoirse lightly placed two fingers on the crystal, eliciting a fuzzy glow in response. The tiny hair hung in the air for a moment, frozen in time, and then twirled around as if caught up in a lazy breeze. It danced here and there until finally shooting off towards the front entrance.

"So where are you off to next?" Saoirse said, her eyes following the hair behind her eyelids.

"We hope that is what you are about to tell us," Leonydas responded, amused.

"Oh yeah," Saoirse said, punctuating with a cackle. Her head turned this way and that, seemingly following the path of the white hair as it searched for its owner.

"Are you sure that was one of Fresita's?" Lizzy said, looking up at Xel.

Xel shrugged in response.

"Right? That would be hilarious if it took me to some old white-haired old lady taking a shower," Saoirse said, and closed her eyes tighter as if focusing on something. "But I don't think it is....woah!" She jerked backwards and then fell off the table.

"She's in trouble!" Saoirse exclaimed, immediately popping up to her feet and wide-eyed. "There's like a thousand guys she's fighting."

"A thousand?" Lizzy said.

"Well, you know, ALOT."

"Where?" Leonydas asked.

"Mmm, the Inn, Bracken Row, not far from Calacoayan."

"Is there a fast way to get there?" Lizzy asked.

"Maybe, someone here has a scheduled trip back to the café," Leondyas said, as he turned to look through the crowd.

"I can get you guys there faster," Saorise whispered into Lizzy's ear. "But you have to promise to keep it a secret." Lizzy nodded quickly.

"Follow me," Saoirse said, and ran towards the back of the hall.

"Come on," Lizzy called over her shoulder as she followed. The dwarf with the silver axe emerged from the kitchen as they rushed by.

"Where are the lot of you off to in such a hurry?" he asked.

"Sorry, our friends are in danger," Leonydas said. The dwarf's smile faded, and he dashed back to the kitchen.

The group hurried into a seating alcove facing away from the crowd. Saoirse shoved the table out and motioned for the others to stand back.

"Gosh, Diego's gonna kill me," Saoirse mumbled, pulling a flat circular rock, about palm-sized, and tossed it onto the floor. "I can get you there, but I can't go with. You'll be ok on your own?"

"Yes, Sursh, thank you," Xel said.

"Thanks," Lizzy said, nodding as she touched Saoirse's arm.

"Anytime," Saoirse replied, dropping to her knees before the stone. She leaned close and murmured to it, her voice low and coaxing. "Ohtzali."

Using both index fingers, she spun the rock in place. Saoirse sprang back as it began to rotate faster, the motion blurring until the stone began to form a cloud of dust. Still spinning, it shrank and shrank until only the dust remained, billowing upward between them.

She tapped the crystal at her throat. The cloud split cleanly down the center.

Lizzy realized then that it wasn't the dust dividing, but reality itself. The air crackled as the space before them tore open, revealing a fractured image of a rainy street in the Inn Between. Wind rushed past them, drawn violently into the break.

"Go, hurry," Saoirse shouted, "Good luck!"

Xel stepped through first. She immediately spun around and darted out of sight.

"Lord Leonydas," the dwarf said, coming around the corner of the alcove. In his hands, he carried Xel's staff. "She'll be needing this."

"Thank you," Leonydas said, taking the staff. "Liz, stay right behind me."

Lizzy nodded. Leonydas stepped through, turned, and tossed the staff to wherever Xel was.

"Be careful, new friend," Saoirse said with a reassuring smile. "See you soon!"

Lizzy nodded and followed Leonydas through. Her stomach lurched and then plummeted worse than she experienced before. She stumbled forward and fell with a splash onto the rain-slick street.

"Walk it off," Saoirse yelled through the portal. Lizzy looked back in time to see the split in reality rejoin and form a new scene.

Slow, heavy drops of rain fell onto the street of the Inn Between. In the middle of it, Xeilan and Leonydas stood deep in conversation. Beyond them, a line of Xeilan's guards waited, their attention fixed on Lizzy. Evren was being held by one of them, his hands tied behind his back. As she pushed herself upright, Xel crossed the street toward her.

"Wait here," Xel commanded.

"What's going on?" Lizzy asked.

"Leonydas is trying to talk his way out of this," Xel replied, nodding toward Evren, who knelt on the sidewalk. "Xeilan caught them inside his suite. I do not know why he was there and not leading them further away."

"Mykayla and Fresita?" Lizzy said.

"It sounds like Mykayla and the boy's brother escaped safely. Fresita is there," Xel said, pointing to a small cage on the sidewalk.

Fresita lay on her side, trapped in an enclosure of dried plant vines. Rain streamed into her eyes, and from where Lizzy stood, it was impossible to tell if she was breathing.

"What did he do to her?" Lizzy cried. "We have to help her! She knows where it is, Xel!"

Xel grabbed her arm and held her back.

"Just wait," she snapped. "It's not safe."

"Xel," Leonydas called, gesturing for her to join him.

Xeilan shifted his weight and smiled faintly at Lizzy—self-satisfied, smug.

"Stay here until this is settled," Xel said, softer now. "Please."

Lizzy nodded, though her gaze never left Fresita. The rain began to fall harder. Xel joined Leonydas, and after a few moments of quiet conversation, the three of them laughed. Lizzy's chest tightened.

Something was wrong.

From farther down the street, a group of finely dressed individuals carrying umbrellas approached Xeilan and Leonydas. They greeted one another cordially. Lizzy knew these must be members of the Aurenthal, and now she was sure—Leonydas was one of them. Gairloch was right.

She took a step forward, anger flaring, ready to confront them, when her phone buzzed violently in her pocket. She pulled it free, blinking rain from her eyes. Dozens of notifications flooded the screen after being out of range for so long, but one message froze her in place. Galloway.

"Hey Lizzy. I've tried calling a few times. I know you don't want to talk. I just wanted to let you know that Vic's family has decided to let him go. It's tomorrow at noon. I'm so sorry. You know it's for the best…for everyone."

Her heart dropped into her stomach. Painful goosebumps rippled over her skin. Still staring at the screen, she reached out and grabbed a lamppost to steady herself, afraid her legs would give out. Her time was running out. He would truly be gone in only a matter of hours.

She looked up again. Soldiers, distinct from Xeilan's guards, marched in behind a hooded woman who led them with quiet authority. Lizzy squinted through the rain as the woman approached Leonydas. Then she threw back her hood and embraced him. It was hard to be certain in the downpour, but Lizzy was almost sure it was the woman who wore the other Dragonscale ring.

Lizzy pressed her forehead against the lamppost, trying to clear her thoughts. She reread Galloway's message. She had the power to change things, to fix *her* mistakes, but everyone else seemed determined to decide how she should use it. Maybe it *would* be better if she used it to heal only him. The world was unbearable without him in it. If it killed her, then at least he would live, and the pain would finally stop. And if it only stripped her of her power, then everyone would leave her alone.

Her hand struck the pole with a dull thud.

She ran for Fresita.

The vines forming the cage looked dry and brittle, fragile enough to break. Lizzy dropped to her knees beside it and began pulling at the vines.

"Lizzy, no! Get back!" Leonydas shouted as he spun and sprinted toward her.

Behind him, Xeilan's guards drew their swords, steel flashing in the rain, though they held their positions. Lizzy shoved a hand into her hoodie pocket. The small pouch of dust was still there, though nearly empty after all the jostling and fairy thieves. She prayed it would be enough.

She hurled it toward the street, farther from herself this time, but she had no way of knowing that water would amplify the powder's explosive force. The pouch split open midair, spraying dust into the pounding rain. Instantly, the air erupted in a chain of sharp pops, like firecrackers snapping all at once. As more powder spilled free, the explosions built on top of each other—brighter, louder—until flashes of the chaotic white light blinded the street.

Shielding her eyes, Lizzy grabbed the cage and tried to rise. The pouch struck the ground near Leonydas and the others, flinging its remaining contents across the street. With a concussive boom, the air itself seemed to detonate in light.

Lizzy was thrown forward, skidding across the wet stone before rolling to a stop, the cage landing nearby. For a heartbeat, she lay still, rain splashing cold against her cheeks, pinning her to consciousness.

Then she pushed herself up and reached for the cage. Inside,

Fresita stirred. The vines, once brittle and lifeless, twitched. Long, sharp thorns broke through the dry skin of the vines and stretched inward, creeping toward Fresita's body.

"What have you done!"

The voice boomed from above, riding on slow, powerful wingbeats. Lizzy looked up. Two Sentinels hovered in the rain-soaked air, their wings beating steadily as they brandished their deadly Grimmklins. Rain streamed along the razor-curved edges, catching the light in cold flashes.

"The Dullren has attacked our Queen!" Xeilan shouted, shaking his head to clear his senses. "She's taken the Fairy Queen's daughter hostage in that cage!"

Lizzy opened her mouth to contradict him, but one of the Sentinels, a dark-haired male, descended first. He landed beside the woman wearing the Dragonscale ring, the Queen, and helped her to her feet.

The other Sentinel, a female, drifted closer to Lizzy. She leveled her weapon at her, the edge humming faintly.

"Release the Fae at once," the Sentinel commanded.

Like the most intense headache Lizzy ever had, the Sentinel's voice rang through her skull, sharp and punishing. It made her queasy and doubled the fog she still had from the blast.

"No!" Lizzy cried, hands still tearing at the cage. "I can't let them have her!"

The Sentinel drew her Grimmklin back and lunged.

Xel surged up from the ground and threw herself between them, staff snapping up just in time to deflect the blow. The silver cap of her staff connected with the edge of the Sentinel's weapon, throwing sparks through the rain-slick air.

The Sentinel halted mid-motion. Then a slow, pleased grin

spread across her face.

"Xel Illwvyen," she drawled. "The *mighty* Frostwind." She let out a soft, mocking laugh.

"Sentinel Yar'la," Xel replied, drawing in a steadying breath and blinking hard to clear her vision from the blast. Her grip tightened on her staff as she glanced toward Leonydas, who still lay unconscious in the street.

"What business do you and the Elf Lord have here?" Yar'la demanded.

"The Dullren is under our protection," Xel said evenly. "She bears the sigil of Lady Betela."

Amused, Yar'la watched as Lizzy tried to stand, only to wobble and sink back to the street, dazed. When Lizzy stopped pulling at the cage, the thorns receded, curling back into stillness.

"What insignificant protection this Dullren has managed to secure," Yar'la mused.

She lowered herself until she hovered just above the street—still a head taller than Xel.

"Do not make this about you and me," Xel warned. "There are far greater matters at stake."

"You are correct," Yar'la replied coolly. "She is holding the Fairy Queen's daughter captive and has just attacked the Queen of the Realm."

Xel glanced toward the other Sentinel as he drifted closer. Behind him, the Queen was already being escorted away by her soldiers. The members of the Aurenthal scurried away as well. Xeilan stepped forward to join the Sentinels, all of them looking down at Xel as though judgment had already been passed.

"The Queen has requested that the Dullren be taken into custody," the male Sentinel said, "until we determine what has occurred and if she indeed is marked."

"Yes," Xeilan added smoothly, righteousness coating every word. "That seems best for everyone. I'll take Lord Leonydas to the Celestine to be treated so he may attend the Aurenthal's meeting. He's a… valuable voice there."

"I'm not going anywhere!" Lizzy shouted. She staggered to her feet, fury keeping her upright. "All of you can go straight to hell," she spat. "Especially you and you." Her glare flickered from Leonydas to Xel. "You betrayed me."

"Elizabeth," Xel said sharply, meeting her gaze. "You do not understand what has happened."

"Lizzy!"

Ruby rounded the corner at a run, rain tracing her face and tugging a few loose strands of hair free, though her bun held fast.

"Let's not make this any harder than it needs to be," Yar'la said, drifting toward Lizzy.

Xel stepped in front of her once more, pointing her staff as a warning.

"I was hoping you would try me," Yar'la murmured.

She touched the jewel set into the pommel of her Grimmklin. Xel gasped and collapsed to her knees with a strangled grunt.

"The scar we gave you the last time we met was more than just a reminder. It was a restraint to make future encounters go smoother."

Xel ignored the pain and pushed herself back up as Ruby dropped beside Lizzy, hands gentle but urgent as she looked her over.

"Are you hurt?"

"Yes…no," Lizzy said shakily, eyes burning. "They're with the Aurenthal. They trapped Fresita in that cage, and I can't get her out."

Ruby's gaze flicked to the cage, then to Xel, who was struggling to rise.

"That can't be right," Ruby said softly. "I know Leonydas is part of the Aurenthal, but—"

"What?" Lizzy snapped. "You knew too? You're with them?"

"No," Ruby said quickly, pain flooding her expression. "That's not true."

She didn't get the chance to say anything more.

Xel screamed. Hovering over her with a pleased stare, Yar'la twisted the jewel, increasing the pain. Xel ripped her blouse to one side and looked down. The dormant scar stretched open, tissue and flesh straining against the pressure, and pulsed red. It was as if she were being torn asunder.

Ruby sprang to her feet and rushed to Xel's side. Xel clutched her for a heartbeat before forcing herself upright, her body trembling violently. Her sweat beaded across her skin, streaked pink where blood had begun to seep through.

"Stop!" Ruby screamed, tears burning at the corners of her eyes. "Please—please, you're hurting her!"

"I've only begun to hurt her," Yar'la growled, a smirk of naked pleasure twisting her mouth.

"Yar'la, that is enough," the male Sentinel said calmly, casting her a displeased look. "Guardian Ruby, while we acknowledge your concern, you hold no authority here. Your domain is the Gateway."

"And our domain," Yar'la added smoothly, "is protecting the Inn from those who would disrupt the balance of ilThren."

She turned the jewel back slowly, deliberately. The crushing pain eased just enough for Xel to drag in a breath.

Ruby stepped closer, fists clenched. "Xel has defended Thraewen across the Earth for centuries. She does not deserve this punishment…this torture."

"It's alright, Ruby," Xel rasped through clenched teeth. "Let her enjoy herself. When she's finished, I'm going to rip off her fethskarn wings."

Xel took a step forward. Yar'la twisted the jewel again. Agony ripped through Xel's body in convulsing waves, forcing a cry from her throat. Ruby's eyes narrowed. A low growl gathered in her chest.

She slipped one ring from her finger and raised it where the Sentinels could see. It was made of bone, its center band set with pale crystal. Stark white, it glowed softly in the moonlight. Yar'la dismissed it with a glance. The male Sentinel did not. His eyes widened.

"Skarweng," Ruby said.

She spoke the word softly, no louder than her normal voice, but it rolled outward like distant thunder, reverberating off the surrounding buildings. The sky answered in kind. Lightning was cast down, striking the ring, with a blinding flash. The air hummed with fuzzy static.

When the light vanished, Ruby stood holding a massive sword. This was not Abenlieth, the blade Evren had once marveled at in the café, though it could now be seen resting across her back.

The sword Ruby now wielded bore a hilt and grip carved from aged bone. At the pommel, wings were etched in stark relief—bone feathers flared outward, frozen at the instant flight was forever severed. Rising from the hilt was a single blade of pale blue crystal rock, translucent and cold. Within it, faint fractures shimmered like trapped lightning.

The blade was nearly as wide as Ruby's shoulders and stood a full foot taller than she did. Yet she held it with ease, as though her will alone outweighed gravity's claim. She shifted into a ready stance and fixed Yar'la with a calm, unwavering stare.

Without needing to be asked again, Yar'la touched the gem on her weapon and released Xel from the torture. The pressure vanished at once; Xel collapsed onto her hands and knees.

Lizzy stared at Ruby, her attention breaking only briefly when she noticed Leonydas struggling to his feet behind the Sentinels.

"You wield..." the male Sentinel began, but was unable to finish. It was a name the Sentinels themselves did not speak. It was a name they feared might hear them and remember their wings.

"Skarweng," Ruby said evenly. "The Wing Splitter."

Yar'la sneered. "How dare you display that weapon before us."

"Yar'la—enough," the male Sentinel snapped. "Leave us."

Yar'la shot him a look of startled fury. He answered by narrowing his eyes, never once looking away from Skarweng. With a sharp huff, she cast Xel one last look of disgust, then launched herself skyward, vanishing into the night.

Leonydas hurried to Xel and wrapped his arms around her, carefully examining the wound left by the Sentinel's magic. She stirred, trying to push him away, but was exhausted.

"Sentinel Ruby," the male Sentinel said, measured but wary, "may I ask where you obtained that weapon?"

"It was a gift from the former King, following the incursion last year," Ruby replied evenly. "He said it would be safest in my care. It is not something I ever wished, or imagined, I would have to wield." Her grip tightened slightly. "But what happened here tonight was unjust. Sentinel or not, you do not have the right to torture someone. Especially someone like Xel."

"I regret my companion's...zealous response to a perceived threat," the Sentinel said stiffly. "You must understand, we have not yet determined what truly occurred."

"What has occurred," Leonydas said, his voice cutting cleanly through the rain, "is that Xeilan manipulated the situation to cast doubt between Lizzy and us." He took a step forward. "She is Lady Betela. She does not deserve this treatment. And while Xel and I have had our disagreements with the Sentinels over the centuries, we have long since made peace with you."

"Lord Leonydas," Xeilan began, "I take offense at—"

His words were smothered under Leonyda's booming voice.

"Enough." He paused and stared sternly at Xeilan.

"As heir apparent to my mother's armies, the Mountain Queen's armies, I formally strip you of any authority you claim through my family," he said coldly. "Master Sentinel, I request that the former General Xeilan be detained."

Xeilan's clenched fist trembled. His face twisted with rage.

"Lord Leonydas," the Sentinel replied, equally cold, "you have not yet ascended your mother's throne. More importantly, you are an Elf. You hold no authority to make such a demand. The Queen's order to take the woman must be obeyed."

Ruby adjusted Skarweng in her hands, just enough for light to glint along its crystal edge. It was only a reminder of her presence, not a threat. The Sentinel's jaw tightened.

"I demand," Xeilan snapped, striding to where Evren lay unconscious on the street, "that this boy be taken into custody. He was caught breaking into my hotel."

"He was trying to ensure his brother's safety," Ruby countered. "He is being held by Xeilan inside the Celestine."

"He is being *treated*," Xeilan said sharply, "very graciously, I might add, by my physicians for the Hollowing."

"I am curious," Ruby said, narrowing her eyes at Xeilan. "How it is that your physicians have been so successful in treating a disease so many Menders have failed to cure. It almost lends truth to the rumors that the Hollowing was created and spread by you, Xeilan."

Xeilan scoffed but offered no reply. The Sentinel's gaze moved slowly from face to face before settling on Ruby, then Skarweng.

"I will escort the boy and Xeilan back to the Watchhold for questioning," he said at last.

Xeilan surged forward in protest, but the Sentinel's sharp frown stopped him cold.

"And Liz?" Leonydas asked.

The Sentinel glanced toward the spot where Lizzy had been kneeling beside Fresita. "She has already fled. She remains free until we are able to locate her. Later."

Leonydas turned slowly, scanning the street. Lizzy was gone, but he heard her scream nearby.

While the others argued, Lizzy had seized the cage holding Fresita and escaped around the corner. The vines were brittle at a glance, but every time she pried at them, the thorns twitched, ready to drive themselves into Fresita's body. Lizzy had no idea if she would have enough of the Aetherwilde left to save Fresita from so many potential wounds.

The call of the necklace was faint now, barely a whisper. If she healed Fresita, the path to the necklace could be lost forever, unless she truly knew where it was. Lizzy felt her phone vibrate against her leg, the reminder jarring her thoughts back to Galloway's message. Tomorrow afternoon was rushing towards her.

Desperation took over. She shoved her arms between the vines and forced the cage apart with everything she had. The thorns reacted instantly. Faster than the cage could break, they shot outward, driving deep into Lizzy's arms. The jagged tips burst through on the other side, slicing into Fresita's body as they emerged.

Lizzy screamed.

Fresita groaned as the pain dragged her back into consciousness.

"Liz! What did you do?" Fresita gasped, trying to push herself upright before slipping back onto her side.

Lizzy tore the thorns from her arms. Blood streamed down, spattering the street. Shaking, she stared at the wounds, then at Fresita.

"What do I do?" she sobbed. "How do I heal myself?"

"Blessed Mother!" Fresita said urgently. "Focus. Calm. Contrrrol."

"It hurts," Lizzy whimpered. "It hurts so much."

Leonydas came running around the corner, Xel close behind him, barely managing to stay upright.

"Liz, here, let me help," Leonydas said, dropping to his knees beside her.

He reached for her. Lizzy collapsed backward and scrambled away, landing hard on the stone.

"Don't!" she cried. "Stay away from me!"

"She is losing too much blood," Xel said grimly. "Too fast."

"Lizzy," Fresita said, forcing herself upright as she reached into her Mosstragel. She pulled free a handful of tiny flower petals and reached for Lizzy's arms. "This will slow the bleeding."

Lizzy nodded weakly. The world was already starting to tilt. Fresita pressed the petals gently against the wounds, then hesitated.

"I'm sorry," she whispered. She pressed them in hard.

Pain burned through Lizzy's arms. Her eyes flew open as it threatened to overwhelm her—then it faded, tapering into something warmer. The tattoo flushed with comforting heat, loosening the tension in her body. That warmth rolled down her arm and into Fresita's paws, knitting through the wounds that matted her fur with blood. Then it rebounded.

Fresita's pain surged into Lizzy all at once. She groaned, and the world slipped away. The last thing she saw before darkness was the Veilkin, that dark familiar monster, watching from a rooftop.

CHAPTER 13

The dream from the morning she lost *Him* repeated in broken pieces. The rush of victory after saving the victim. The look on his face. His head. Sidewalk.

"It's all your fault…"

After too many repetitions, the memory blurred and finally faded, loosening its grip. She was able to rest. When Lizzy became dimly aware of her surroundings again, she felt eyes on her. She couldn't remember what had happened, so she kept still, pretending to sleep. Peeking through her lashes, she took in a small, bluish-white room.

Vines of fall-colored leaves traced the corners, edges, and doorway like the living molding of the café. Nearby, a stethoscope and a ceramic tray bearing dried copal sat atop an antique wooden cabinet. The warm, earthy scent of the copal drifted up, a familiar blanket around her. Tita had used it often.

Something sticky clung to her fingers. She rubbed them together and remembered the blood.

"Fresita?" Lizzy said, pushing herself upright and instantly regretting it. Again, she was waking up with a throbbing head. Lizzy let out a frustrated groan.

"It's alright, cupcake. She is safe," an ancient voice said nearby.

For a fleeting moment, the familiarity brought hope until Lizzy remembered where she'd heard it before. She turned her head.

Flo, the old woman from the alley, sat beside her. She looked friendlier now. Calmer. Less wild-eyed than before. The bathrobe was gone, replaced by a white linen mumu and a shawl of golden moss. She twirled a strand of her cottony hair around one finger.

"You," Lizzy said, sitting up again—carefully this time.

"Yes, it's me," Flo replied pleasantly. "You likely have a great many questions. Much has occurred since we last spoke." She chuckled. "Shall we begin with a cup of coffee?"

"Please," Lizzy said honestly. "I would actually love that." She scooted over to rest her back against the wall.

As if summoned by the words, a boy appeared in the doorway. He moved with careful, nervous steps, carrying a tray with two overfilled mugs. He approached Flo, but she waved him toward Lizzy instead.

"Guests first."

Lizzy offered him a small, reassuring smile, but he didn't notice. His eyes were locked on the trembling surface of the coffee. When he finally stopped in front of her, she reached eagerly for a mug, then hesitated.

The cup was carved from a solid piece of pine, its exterior still rough with bark. Sap glistened along the rim. The boy's eyes silently begged her to save him. Lizzy took the mug anyway, searching for a safe place to sip. She made a face at the sticky edge, doubting she'd find one.

The woman took her cup and drank, leaving the boy waiting for a command.

"Something wrong?" Flo asked mildly.

Lizzy poked at the edge of the coffee. "I don't usually take sap with my coffee."

"Ah." Flo nodded and turned to the boy. "Be a dear and fetch a mug from this world for our guest."

The boy shot Lizzy a defeated look before hurrying from the room.

"No! Wait," Lizzy said quickly. "It's ok, this will be just fine." She brought the cup to her lips and took a quick sip. She faked a smile afterward, even though the coffee tasted like wood and bitterness. It almost hid the fact that the coffee was probably from an instant brewer, too.

The woman shooed the boy away and then looked at Lizzy expectantly.

"Is this...are we in the Inn?" Lizzy asked as she looked for a place to abandon her cup.

"Yes," the woman answered patiently. "Just down the street from Calacoayan."

"And you are...are you the...?" Lizzy wanted to say 'Faerie Queene,' but it was still odd to her to say fantastic things out loud, even to people who were used to hearing them.

"Ah!" the woman exclaimed. "I'm sorry, cupcake, my mistake. I've known about you for so many years...I forgot you don't know me. So many do. I am indeed Floressa." Like Fresita declaring she was Maeve, the woman said her name as if Lizzy should instantly know everything about her just from those few words.

"Floressa...The Faerie Queen?"

Being: Faerie
(Aetheria Vivax)
Name: Floressa
Age: Older than
the dirt (her own words!)
Height: 1.8 meters
Location: Everywhere

November 1921

If I had already been
flumoxed by the reality
of faeries, then the Faerie
Queene herself became
incomprehensible.

I'd like to say that she
is the embodiment of joy,
but in reality, she is an
amalgamation of all
emotions. A torrid tempest
of passions.

Her laugh enthralls
and infects. Her anger
wreaks havoc upon the
senses.

Only once have I
witnessed it, and only
because I was the
cause. I will not
discuss that here.

— Ansel

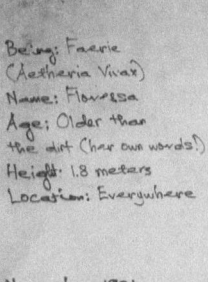

While the fae are small cute beings, (perhaps
only 12 cm tall) Lady Floressa is human size (1.8
meters. Taller than me of course.) and there is
nothing cute about her. Her beauty is powerful.
A force — not a feature.

Grace of the Fae Realm, Life Giver and Protector
Lady Floressa -- The Faerie Queene

"Yes," Flo replied with a warm giggle. "That is what some name me. Others, my children, call me Mother, but please, I am just Flo."

"Ok, and this is your clinic?" Lizzy said.

"The clinic belongs to anyone who needs it, but yes, I set it up."

"An ilThren clinic?" Lizzy said, leaning over to try to see into the next room.

Flo tilted her head to consider Lizzy. After a moment, she sat down beside her.

"Not in the way that you are thinking," Flo finally replied.

"Don't you mean 'from a certain point of view,'?" Lizzy said, making a face.

Flo tilted her head as she considered the phrase for a moment and then smiled. "Why, yes, that is a good way of putting it."

Lizzy rolled her eyes.

"I understand our world can be frustrating," Flo said, patting Lizzy's leg. "But at least you were a little prepared for it by Tita's stories. Not everybody has that. For most, discovering that our world exists is just too much to accept. I remember a young lady who did everything she could to avoid getting to know our world. She traveled halfway across the world trying to escape it."

"Did it work?"

Flo laughed heartily. She hopped to her feet and grabbed Tita's sketchbook from Lizzy's backpack on the floor.

"If it had…," Flo replied as she sat back down beside Lizzy and opened the book to the page with the drawing of the younger-looking fairy queen. "Then she would never have drawn this or anything else in this book."

"Tita? Jules."

"Oh yes," Flo smiled, staring at the portrait fondly.

"How did she discover your world?"

"Our world discovered her," Flo said, flipping through the pages. "And as I told you, she wanted nothing to do with it. At first."

"I find that hard to believe," Lizzy said. "All she ever talked about were fairy tales and the magic hidden in the world."

Flo huffed softly as she closed the book. "It took some effort. But once she accepted it, she became an unstoppable force in the Realms."

"What do you mean?"

"Jules…" Flo began, then stopped. She pressed her lips together, choosing her words with care. "We did not always get along. But she and Maeve were very close."

She paused again, then nodded to herself. "In the end, I believe things turned out as they needed to—but that is a story for another time."

"Maeve—Fresita," Lizzy said quickly. "Is she all right?"

"Oh yes," Flo replied. "She is recovering just fine."

"And the others?" Lizzy asked, her jaw tightening as the moment Leonydas and Xel talked with Xeilan flashed through her mind. "They are still here?"

"They are," Flo said. Her expression sobered as she studied Lizzy. "And they were very concerned about you. Leonydas especially."

"That's…nice," Lizzy said slowly. "But I don't know if I should trust them. He is tied to the Aurenthal."

"By their choosing, not his," Flo said firmly. "Xeilan used Leonydas's family name to force his way into their ranks."

Lizzy rubbed the back of her neck, staring at the wall. "He

seems like a good man, Flo. But everything in this world feels… layered. Like nothing is exactly what it appears to be."

Flo nodded. "Leonydas may one day become a great king. Until then, he is simply a good man—reliable, resolute, and deeply compassionate. Not only toward his own, but toward anyone in need."

"Okay," Lizzy said, nodding—though the uncertainty clouded her thoughts.

Remembering the wounds, Fresita's and her own, she looked down at her arms. Simple bandages covered her arms. They felt sore as she twisted them.

"When I healed myself," Lizzy said, still staring at her arms. "There was a moment when it felt like Fresita's pain transferred to me?"

"Yes, that is how it should work. I'm sure it is uncomfortable, but the Aetherwilde weaves two beings together so that the body's natural healing process can be assisted. You did a beautiful job healing her. You are coming into your destiny nicely."

"My destiny? Does that mean I have no choice in becoming this great person everyone is expecting?"

"I'm sorry, poor choice of words. I forget not everyone can see what I do. At this point, the choice is yours. You can still go down a different path. We all can."

"I don't understand."

"It's ok. You don't have to. But suffice it to say, the choice is and must be yours. You almost have all the information before you."

"Do you mean the necklace?" Lizzy said, flashing Flo a hopeful look. "Do you know where it is?"

"No, dear, the necklace is still within you," Flo said, tapping

Lizzy gently on her forehead. "It will become clear when you decide you are ready."

"Within me? But Tita left a message that Fresita has it."

"Is that *really* what she said?"

"Yes…I don't know," Lizzy said, frowning. "Everything in this world is so secretive—maybe the message was a code."

"Not to worry, dear, you will figure it out when the time is right."

"But people are suffering," Lizzy said. "They need help now."

"There is always someone who needs help. Always. Even if you had all the power now, you could not save everyone. You can help so many but never everybody, and sometimes not even those, or the one that you want to help, can be healed."

Lizzy sighed.

Flo tilted her head as if listening to something in the distance. She winked and hopped off the bed. Xel appeared in the doorway and nodded a greeting to the women.

"Xel, come in," Flo said. "I have some matters to attend to, maybe you could keep Lizzy company?"

"I only wanted to look in on her," Xel said, avoiding Lizzy's eyes. "However, if she would like me to, I will of course stay."

Lizzy nodded. Flo chuckled and squeezed Xel's arm as she left the room, leaving the two women staring at each other.

"So…," Xel said.

"Uh, yeah…I'm doing ok," Lizzy said, and motioned for her to sit. Xel hesitated and then awkwardly sat beside Lizzy. "I guess I'm going to have to get used to the healing thing."

"Healing is tough. Even with 'magic.'"

"It is," Lizzy said.

"Especially when the wound is deeper than the flesh."

"Yes."

A silence of understanding carried the conversation for a moment.

"Eliz—Liz, I would like to clear up any misunderstanding you have about what happened out there."

"It's ok, Xel," Lizzy nodded. "I was confused, overwhelmed, and I get it; Xeilan manipulated the moment."

"Yes," Xel said, then paused. "Leonydas is, through no choice of his own, a member of the Aurenthal. But he has nothing to do with them." Her gaze didn't waver. "He is not that kind of man, or I would not serve him as faithfully as I do. I decided long ago that I would give my life to protect his."

"Ok," Lizzy said. "I believe you."

Xel tried a smile, but it was awkward. She let it fade and stared at the ceiling instead.

"I know we aren't… friends," Lizzy said, choosing her words carefully.

Xel lifted a dubious eyebrow and glanced at her.

"Okay," Lizzy amended quickly. "So maybe we at least tolerate each other. But is it alright if I ask—well… Leonydas mentioned you went through something. And I…" She hesitated. "Is that how you got your scar?"

"This?" Xel said, tugging her shirt aside to reveal the edge of the wound. "No. This was nothing compared to what came before. I would endure this a hundred times over if it meant avoiding—"

She stopped.

Lizzy nodded and didn't push. She wasn't about to reopen a wound just to help herself.

"What is it you want to know, Liz?" Xel asked, casting her a sideways glance.

"How did you get through it?" Lizzy said softly. "The pain from your past?"

Xel's jaw tightened. For a moment, Lizzy thought she'd gone too far, but then Xel's expression eased. She shifted closer, leaning back against the wall beside Lizzy.

"I was fifteen when I dedicated my life to protecting Leonydas," Xel said, staring ahead as the memory unfolded. "I was just an Elf girl with *in-Anil*, 'starry eyes,' and dreams of becoming the future King's Captain of the Guard. I already followed the Prince everywhere, even when he didn't know it."

A small smile touched her lips; she clearly found a specific memory.

"I trained with the guard. And when I wasn't training, I trained more. I skipped time with my family. I never made friends. Everything was in service of that oath." Her voice steadied. "I swore my life to defend his, first in private, then publicly when the time came."

Her smile faded.

"Then the Realm fell apart. War came. When we fled from the armies chasing us, I did not leave his side."

Xel inhaled deeply and held the breath.

"I did not leave his side even when those armies overtook us and murdered my parents—right in front of me."

"I'm so sorry, Xel," Lizzy whispered.

"I could have stopped it," Xel said, turning to her. Guilt twisted her features. "Even then, I was fast. Strong. If I had gone back, if I had left Leonydas, I could have saved them."

Her gaze dropped to her hands, clenched in her lap.

"I could have killed every one of those soldiers before they ever saw me." Her voice wavered. "But I saw my parents' eyes. My father's: stern, furious, telling me not to come back for them." She swallowed hard.

"And my mother…" Xel's breath caught. "She mouthed, 'Everything will be okay in the end, little one.'"

A single tear slid down Xel's cheek. She looked at Lizzy and offered the faintest smile.

"And it was," Xel said quietly. "It has been."

She exhaled slowly.

"We've endured terrible things since then, but it was all for the good of our people and others. My parents traded their lives so *that* future could exist. If I had gone back, Leonydas might have died. Maybe all of us."

She paused.

"For years, I believed I had to forgive myself for choosing to let them die." Her voice softened. "But that wasn't the truth. What I had to accept… was that it was their choice to make."

Xel looked at her and saw how close Lizzy was to breaking. The sadness of Xel's story pressed in on Lizzy, an ache so deep it blurred the line between grief for Xel and for herself. Lizzy couldn't imagine a future where the choices she was being forced to make would end with everything being okay.

Her jaw trembled. Her cheeks quivered as she fought to hold it together, trying desperately to emulate Xel's composure.

"Oh, little one," Xel murmured. Xel wrapped her strong arms around her. Lizzy collapsed into them and sobbed.

Xel had stayed with Lizzy until she drifted back to sleep. Later in the morning, Lizzy woke and stretched. Her arms felt better. She felt better—lighter somehow.

She got up and stepped into a larger room that looked as

though it had once been a bakery. Long wooden tables ran in rows down the center, with counters lining the surrounding walls. Several of the tables held patients suffering from various ailments, though none appeared to have the Hollowing.

A sudden jab to her thigh made her jump. Mykayla sat on the floor beside the doorway, half asleep. She shot Lizzy a crooked, sleepy sneer.

"Hey," Lizzy signed. "Where is everyone?"

"Around," Mykayla said, pushing herself to her feet with a yawn. "How are you feeling?"

"Not bad," Lizzy replied, scanning the room again. "Evren's brother is safe?"

"Yep, they never even knew I was there. He should have trusted me," Mykayla said, glancing at Lizzy's bandaged arm. "None of this would have happened."

"Is he still with the Sentinels?"

"Last I heard," Mykayla said. "Xeilan too. They are taking a serious look at his clinic, though I wouldn't get my hopes up about anything serious happening to him. He has too much sway over too many people."

Lizzy nodded. "Has anyone talked to Fresita about the necklace?"

"Leonydas asked. She didn't tell him anything," Mykayla said. "Honestly, I don't think she knows. She's had that confused look on her furry little face all evening."

Across the room, she spotted Leonydas seated on a bench. Xel slept beside him, her head resting on his shoulder. He noticed Lizzy and lifted a careful hand in greeting.

She smiled back and meandered through the room. As she passed the tables, patients and their companions watched her.

Some faces held recognition. Others, hope. The weight of it made her frown.

She stopped before a door rimmed with warm golden light.

"That's where the Fae with the Hollowing are being treated," Mykayla said quietly. "We can't go in. It's partially tethered to the Fae realm."

Lizzy wondered if Cerisetta was inside. The next doorway stood open, revealing a small playroom bright with flowers and childish drawings. Two toy chests lay open on the floor, and three children played among them. One was Grecka.

Grecka grinned and waved. Lizzy waved back and continued on.

The next door opened into what had once been the bakery's warehouse. Empty flour sacks were stacked in the corners. In the center lay dozens of patients—all afflicted with the Hollowing.

Men and women of many species tended them, including a few Fae. Lizzy tensed at the lack of protective gear, then relaxed as the air around a patient glittered when a nurse reached out with a spoon of medicine. The shimmer clung briefly to her hand before evaporating.

"She made it sound like no one was helping," Lizzy said softly. "I thought… I thought they were abandoned."

"Barely helped," Mykayla replied, frowning as she tried to read Lizzy's lips. "Small clinics like this do what they can, but it's not enough. Xeilan could make his treatment free. He won't." Her jaw tightened. "People like these don't have much time."

Panic and guilt twisted together in Lizzy's stomach. She turned away.

The thought that she could help these people if she could just find the necklace clashed painfully with the fragile, desperate hope of saving *Him*. Trying to justify choosing him over them only deepened the ache. These people were still here. *He* was already gone.

Lizzy clenched her hands into fists until pain bit into her palms. She squeezed her eyes shut, blood rushing in her ears.

"I can't do this—"

"That is why you must find the necklace," Fresita said softly as she stepped beside her. "But it is not with me."

Lizzy opened her eyes to Mykayla staring at her with a worried look and Fresita calmly grooming herself at her feet.

"Tita's clue said that you did," Lizzy said, and sat down on the floor with her back against the wall.

"I know," Fresita said, tapping the back of her head with her tail. "I have spent the day seeking the meaning of her worrrds."

"How are you feeling?" Lizzy said, looking the white cat over. There were no obvious signs of injuries.

"Better…thank you," Fresita said, and hesitated briefly before rubbing up against Lizzy's leg. "Still, you must perrrserve the Aetherwilde that remains within."

"So, why would Tita say you have the necklace if you don't?"

"I think it's the words that we need to pay attention to: The answer lies within Maeve," Mykayla said, emphasizing the sign for within.

"Right," Lizzy said, turning her attention back to Fresita. "I figured that if you didn't have the necklace, then that meant that you would know where it is."

Fresita shook her head thoughtfully.

"When did you last speak to her?" Mykayla asked.

"A year ago," Fresita said. "Time…slips by so fast for humans. For me, only a day or two, and then I sensed it. I returned, but she was already gone. Too soon. I wished forrr one last adventure."

"I'm sure the two of you will have many more adventures in the Time To Come," Flo said, rejoining them. There was a white halo around her and an afterimage of her younger form that softened the lines of her elder face in this realm. Lizzy gave her a puzzled look.

"Sorry, cupcake," Flo said. "I just had to pop over to the Feywald for a bit. The ilWunne usually fades quickly enough, but..." She paused and shivered her body. The glow and afterimage tumbled to the ground like a shawl falling from her shoulders, fading. "There we go."

"Motherrr," Fresita said, in an obedient greeting.

"I see you're back to your normal prickly self," Flo said, with a wry smile. She reached down and patted Fresita's head a little harder than one should pat a cat. Fresita yanked away from Flo's touch and glared at her briefly before trotting off.

"Flo!" Grecka exclaimed, running forward and throwing her arms around her.

"Grecka," Flo laughed, returning the hug.

Lizzy smiled at the sight. "Are you having fun with the other children?"

"Yep! And I found this doll. She's so cute—look!" Grecka held it up and shook it, making the doll bounce in a clumsy little dance.

It was shaped like a fairy, its crinkled wings made of cellophane that caught the light.

"She is cute," Lizzy said softly. "When I was little, I had a fairy doll too."

"Really?" Grecka's eyes lit up. "I named mine Whispy. What was yours named?"

Lizzy's breath caught—her eyes widened. She knew where the necklace was.

"Excuse me," Lizzy said suddenly, turning to Flo. "I need some fresh air."

She caught Mykayla's arm and gently steered her toward the door. Flo merely shrugged as they glanced back, then smiled knowingly as they turned away.

"What is going on?" Mykayla asked as they stepped outside.

"Myk," Lizzy signed excitedly, barely containing herself, "I figured it out. Grecka's fairy doll. I had one too."

"Okay…" Mykayla said slowly, studying her like she might have finally snapped.

"I named her Maeve."

Mykayla froze.

"Maeve," she signed. "That's it, isn't it?" Then, more carefully, "Are we… not telling the others?"

"I don't want anyone else to know yet," Lizzy signed. "I'm not sure what I am going to do."

"What do you mean?" Mykayla asked. "You are still getting the necklace, right?"

"I am," Lizzy said. "I just don't know what I am going to do about Vic."

"Oh." Mykayla hesitated. "I kind of thought you had decided not to try to heal him."

"I never said that," Lizzy snapped, keeping her voice low. Her eyes flared.

"I just got that impression."

Lizzy clenched her jaw and turned away.

"Wait," Mykayla said, catching her arm. "It's okay. Whatever you decide, I'm with you."

Lizzy exhaled. "Okay… thank you. Can you get me to Tita's place?"

Mykayla's mouth curved into a sly smile. She took Lizzy's hand and led her down the street.

CHAPTER 14

They hurried down a side street and slipped through Café Calacoayan's back door. The surly barista, Yarely, was scrubbing the espresso machine when they burst inside. She scowled at them.

"Cleaning the machine," she said sourly. "Half an hour. Longer, maybe. If you're desperate, there's batch brew." She jerked her chin toward a coffee dispenser on the counter.

Lizzy and Mykayla were already heading down the back hallway—the same one Lizzy had first entered days ago.

Moments later, they were back in the Dullren world, sneaking down an alley half a block from the café's hidden entrance. At the darkest end, Mykayla grinned and signed an elaborate symbol Lizzy didn't recognize. With a dramatic flourish, she pulled something back.

A red motorcycle shimmered into existence. Two helmets rested on the seat—one black, one matching red.

"You kept it?" Lizzy asked.

"Nope. This is where Xel hides it."

"It is Xel's," Lizzy said. She remembered them roaring off on it after she'd saved Leonydas's life.

Mykayla ran a hand lovingly along the bike's sleek body, like smoothing silk over a hip. "Yes. And it's a masterpiece. Especially now that I've tuned it up."

"I don't think this is a good idea," Lizzy said. "Besides pissing her off, won't she be able to track us? She's got to have this thing lo-jacked."

"Nah," Mykayla said. "It's too fast. By the time they figure it out, we'll be long gone." She shot Lizzy a look. "And do you really care about pissing her off?"

Mykayla grabbed a helmet and handed the other to her. Lizzy shrugged. A day ago, she might have relished the idea. Now... she understood Xel a little too well. She checked her phone. 5:00 a.m.

"Okay," Lizzy said. "Let's go."

Mykayla was already swinging a leg over the bike. Lizzy hesitated, searching for a foothold, then awkwardly clambered on behind her. She pulled on the helmet; it smelled like Leonydas.

"Hang on," Mykayla signed, twisting around with an enormous grin.

Before Lizzy could respond, the engine roared to life. Lizzy yelped and wrapped her arms tightly around Mykayla's waist, pressing herself close.

The tires squealed, and the bike launched forward, leaving Lizzy's stomach somewhere behind them. She squeezed her eyes shut and held on for dear life as they whipped around corners and zipped down straightaways. Mykayla's excited breathing and the occasional laugh crackled through the helmet's intercom.

"Fun?" Mykayla asked.

Lizzy answered by shaking her head frantically against Mykayla's back.

Far too soon for Mykayla and an eternity later for Lizzy, the bike slowed to a stop in front of Tita's house. Mykayla bumped her helmet lightly against Lizzy's a few times with no response. She glanced back. Lizzy was still curled against her, unmoving. Mykayla rapped her knuckles on the top of Lizzy's helmet.

Lizzy finally leaned back shakily and pulled the helmet off, gulping in air.

"That was not fun," Lizzy said, still shaken.

She hopped off the bike and immediately wobbled. Mykayla's loud laughter echoed off the old house.

"Sorry," Mykayla said with a wink, giving Lizzy's shoulder a light punch. "Your first time was a little rough. It's been a while since I rode something like that—I couldn't help myself."

Lizzy rolled her eyes and grabbed the fence until her legs steadied.

The porch light flickered on, and the front door opened to reveal Martin. He yawned as he squinted at them, clearly unimpressed by the early-morning chaos.

"You're waking up half the city," he muttered. "Con tanto ruido."

"Sorry," Lizzy said quickly as she and Mykayla walked up the sidewalk. "But I need to get into Tita's room upstairs. There's something I'm looking for."

"You're welcome to go up," Martin said, rubbing his face, "but if you're looking for those old boxes, they might be gone."

"What?" Lizzy's heart jumped. "Gone where?"

"Your mom came by late last night with your sister. Took a load of them."

"Why?" Lizzy blurted. "She said she was leaving that for me."

"Quién sabe?" Martin shrugged. "Maybe because your sister was there to help. She wasn't happy about it, though. Complained the whole time."

"Damn it," Lizzy muttered, already pulling out her phone. She hated to call her mother anytime; five in the morning was going to be even worse. "Of all the times—"

"*Elizabeth.*"

The voice, which had barely been audible the last time, now reached out to her from the house. Loudly.

"It has to be here," Lizzy said, excitedly, and dashed into the house.

When Lizzy was little, she'd spent hours exploring this house. Doors that seemed to appear out of nowhere, hallways that shifted, and rooms that didn't exist the day before, excited her little heart. One door led to endless books. Another to a hallway she swore had never been there. She vaguely remembered an adventure with another child and her Maeve doll—discovering a room with forest wallpaper and paintings of fantastical creatures. For the life of her, she could never remember who the other child had been. She'd always told herself it was imagination.

Now she was slightly out of breath by the time they reached Tita's door. Her mother had left it cracked open, but Lizzy still pushed it wider with care. Tita's presence seemed to spill out into the hallway. As Lizzy stepped inside, her favorite floral perfume wrapped around her, warm and familiar. It had been months since she'd last been here.

Toward the end, Lizzy would often find her peering from behind furniture and digging through old chests. Tita was nearly as short as Lizzy, which never helped as she turned their visits into a one-sided game of hide-and-seek. Now the room was mostly bare. A few shelves of knick-knacks remained. Books still lined the walls.

"It's so empty," Mykayla said, with a frown. "There used to be so many cool things up here."

"Oh, you should have visited her ten years ago," Lizzy said. "She lived in the WHOLE house, and had 1000 times more things." Mykayla laughed out loud at the thought.

For a moment, the happiness of being there faded. There was almost nothing left, certainly no doll. Then Lizzy peeked behind the door—three boxes sat stacked neatly against the wall. Her breath caught. She lunged for the top one and dragged it onto the floor. Mykayla grabbed the second, and together they tore into them.

Mykayla's box held old papers and a handful of loose drawings. Lizzy had her set those aside to add to the sketchbook later. Lizzy's box was filled with figurines wrapped in yellowed tissue paper. She unwrapped one to find something like a saint's statue, only this figure had pointed ears and carried a sword and shield.

They exchanged a look and turned to the final box. Mykayla hauled the heavy thing between them. Lizzy paused, then slowly lifted the lid, silently begging the universe to be kind.

Nothing but books.

Lizzy growled in frustration and leaned back against the wall. She was going to have to call her mom and she'd need an excuse for why she suddenly needed those boxes back. Mykayla flopped onto the floor beside her, stretching out and staring at the ceiling. After a moment, her head tilted.

"The doll we're looking for," she signed slowly. "It's a fairy doll, right? With wings? And glitter?"

"Yes," Lizzy said. "Why?"

Mykayla pointed upward.

From where Lizzy stood, the small shelf above them looked ordinary, books lined up neatly, and a dying plant drooping at one end. But from Mykayla's angle, the shelf didn't quite meet the wall. There was a narrow gap behind the books. And in that darkness, something glittered—without any light to catch.

They both scrambled to their feet. Lizzy jumped, stretching uselessly. Mykayla, with her height and long reach, slipped her hand behind the books and pulled something free.

Lizzy's vision blurred with tears. It was Maeve.

The twelve-inch doll was made of cloth, with Spanish moss hair dyed black and a sequined 1920s flapper dress. A pair of floppy fairy wings sparkled from her back. She was dusty, but after a quick shake and brush, she looked almost exactly as Lizzy remembered. Lizzy hugged the doll to her chest, then hesitated.

She had avoided thinking about what might be hidden inside, but Mykayla's questioning look made her nod. Lizzy squeezed the doll.

Nothing.

She pressed harder, holding her breath. There was definitely something inside. She turned the doll over and over, searching for a seam, but there was none.

"How do I get it out?" Lizzy murmured.

Mykayla reached into her pocket and produced an old yellow pocketknife. She flipped it open and handed it over.

"Careful," she warned. "It's sharp."

Lizzy nodded, studying the doll, then gently pressed the

blade against Maeve's cloth side with no result. She pushed harder, but the cloth would not break. Frowning, Lizzy ran her thumb along the blade to check it.

"Ow!" she yelped.

The knife sliced cleanly through her skin, and a bright drop of blood welled up.

"Stupid," Mykayla said immediately. "I told you it was sharp."

"I know, I know," Lizzy said, squeezing her thumb. It was a deep cut. "But it didn't cut through the doll."

"Because it's probably protected—"

Lizzy's tattoo flared to life, and then a faint glow answered from the doll's chest. Lizzy shivered as the cut across her thumb sealed shut—seconds instead of hours. The light faded, and the two of them smiled at each other.

"I think we found it," Mykayla said.

She had barely finished signing when hurried footsteps pounded toward the room. Both of them jumped. Mykayla shoved Lizzy behind the door, her body tensing as she planted herself in front of her.

The footsteps reached the doorway.

Mykayla threw her shoulder into the door. It slammed into whoever was on the other side but was immediately driven back with even greater force. For the first time, Lizzy registered that Mykayla might have magic of her own. She was stronger than she looked. Faster, too.

Mykayla caught the door before it could fly open and braced herself against it. She managed to force it halfway closed before the pressure surged back. Her boots slid on the wooden floor, only an inch, as she held her ground. Clutching the doll to her chest, Lizzy raised the pocketknife, her heart hammering.

A sudden streak of white light darted around the door and into the center of the room. Lizzy spun, blade raised, and froze. Fresita stood there, laughing.

"Fresita!" Lizzy gasped, relief flooding her.

Mykayla shook her head in disbelief, but didn't ease her grip.

"Is that Liz?" Leonydas's voice called from the hallway.

"It's okay, Mykayla," Lizzy said.

Mykayla only grinned wider and pushed harder.

"Not a time forrr showing off," Fresita said dryly.

Mykayla abruptly leapt back from the door. Xel stumbled into the room. There was a brief, awkward flail, then Xel recovered with effortless grace. She straightened and folded her arms across her chest.

Mykayla mirrored the stance, answering the bodyguard's frown with a smug grin.

"Liz," Leonydas said, stepping in and ignoring the rest. "Are you alright?"

"Yeah," Lizzy said quickly. "Sorry for disappearing. I wasn't sure if this was going to turn into a wild goose chase." She hugged the doll closer. "I didn't want to wake you."

"Next time," Leonydas said quietly, genuine worry in his voice, "please do."

"I know," Lizzy replied. "But I found it." She lifted the doll. "It's within—Maeve."

"Of course," Fresita said, trotting over to sniff the doll. Dust puffed up, making her sneeze, but she nodded. "Yes. It is there."

"How do I get it out?" Lizzy asked.

"Set her down," Fresita said.

Lizzy placed the doll between Fresita's paws and sat cross-legged in front of her.

"*I* am much cuterrr," Fresita insisted.

"Maeve, please," Leonydas muttered, already moving to the window to scan the street.

Fresita flicked a furry eyebrow, then sat back on her haunches and lifted her paws. The pink pads glowed softly as she traced slow patterns in the air. The doll shuddered.

Its cloth front rippled, turning fluid, swaying with the faint breeze that Fresita's movements stirred. From within, a thin gold chain drifted into view. Lizzy's heart pounded against her chest. The necklace floated before her.

She forced herself not to grab it. The chain continued to rise until a pendant emerged: twin Star Blossoms cradled in delicate leaves. Like the one Lizzy had examined in the café, only smaller, finer. Every etched line shimmered, as if alive. She could have stared at it forever.

Then warmth bloomed in her arm. The lines of her tattoo ignited, glimmering in a rhythm that matched the pendant's pulse. Her hand clenched as the warmth sharpened into searing pain.

"It hurts!" Lizzy cried, clutching her arm.

"Sorry," Fresita said, quickly shifting her attention. The necklace's glow reflected in her eyes, making her seem even more otherworldly. She lowered her paws. The doll settled back into solid cloth, though the necklace remained suspended in the air.

The burning receded, easing into that familiar healing warmth.

"I believe my ilWunne irritated it," Fresita said thoughtfully. "Aetherwilde preferrrs to work alone."

"Okay..." Lizzy murmured, barely listening.

The necklace drifted closer, hovering near her face. She

started to ask what she was supposed to do, but she realized she already knew. She felt the pull—the invitation. If she put it on, she was choosing a path: helping others, healing the world. Letting *Him* go.

Everyone watched in silence, breath held. Xel was the first to break the spell. She blinked, scanning the room and then to the window to search the street below.

At first, everything seemed still. Suddenly, the shadows shifted, leaning toward something moving down the street.

"Time to go!" Xel shouted, drawing her staff from her back. "Something is coming."

Lizzy snatched the necklace from the air and closed her fist around it.

"Keep Liz between us," Leonydas said to Fresita and Mykayla. "We need to get back to the café, now."

"We borrowed your bike," Lizzy blurted to Xel, guilt flashing across her face.

"I know," Xel said without slowing, already leading them down the stairs. "You did not think I would miss that?"

Mykayla chuckled as she followed close behind. They spilled onto the lawn, Martin and his sister close behind.

"¿Qué pasa?" Martin demanded.

"Do you have a car we can borrow?" Fresita asked.

Martin barked out a laugh. "Not if you plan to drive it the way they drove that motorcycle up here. They almost took out the mailbox!"

Xel shot Mykayla a brief, sharp look, then she turned to Martin and loomed.

"Give me the keys to your car," Xel said evenly, her stare cold. "This is more important than personal property."

A low growl rumbled deep in Martin's chest. Then his body expanded. Coarse hair burst from his skin as his frame swelled, bones shifting, muscles bulging. In seconds, a massive bear towered over Xel, breath steaming from its snout. Lizzy flinched as the bear snorted, hot air rolling over her. Martin's sister crossed her arms and regarded them all with a sharp, unimpressed look.

"Please," Leonydas said calmly, stepping forward. "We need to get Liz safely back to the Inn. Can you help us?"

"We do not have time for this," Fresita hissed. "Liz, show her your arm."

Lizzy hesitated, then pulled up her sleeve. Her tattoo was still glowing faintly. The bear immediately took a step back, posture easing. His sister leaned closer instead, squinting at Lizzy's arm. She let out an irritated grunt and shrugged.

"Claro. We can help," she said. "But we haven't driven that thing in years. The starter's bad or something, right?"

The bear responded with an agreeing-sounding snort.

"Give me a few minutes," Mykayla said. "I can have it running."

"No," Fresita snapped, already trotting toward the street. "We'll fight."

"Xel," Leonydas said sharply, pointing toward the motorcycle. "Get Liz back to the Inn."

"Absolutely not," Xel replied.

"This is not a request," Leonydas said, his voice hardening. His posture straightened, and though Xel stood his equal in height, he somehow looked down at her. "You will do as I say."

"I do not leave you."

"I will be fine," Leonydas said without hesitation. He glanced toward the bear. "I am sure Martin would not mind assisting us in the fight."

Martin glanced at his sister. She shrugged, then nodded once.

"Right now," Leonydas continued, turning back to Xel, "Liz is more important than I will ever be. She carries not only the legacy of our people but the hope of all people. Do you understand?"

Xel's jaw tightened.

"Yes," she said curtly.

"Get her back to the café. We will hold them here and regroup with you in thirty minutes." Leonydas held her gaze. "Everything will be okay in the end."

Xel's jaw tightened as the words landed, but she understood.

"Herrre they come!" Fresita shouted.

A thick fog rolled down the street, crawling toward them. At its edges, dark boots marched in unison until the figures emerged. Guards, but maybe not Xeilan's. The same uniforms as before, but something was off. They were larger. Broader. Even without il'Thren, the evil they carried with them was discernible.

"Go!" Leonydas commanded, pointing toward the city.

"Come, little one," Xel said, gripping Lizzy's arm and guiding her toward the motorcycle—and for the first time, the words carried warmth instead of disdain.

As Xel mounted the bike, Lizzy caught Mykayla's eye. Mykayla was already loosening her shoulders and rolling her arms.

"Hang on tight," she signed with a wink. "See you soon."

Lizzy nodded, shoved the necklace deep into her pocket, and jammed the helmet on. She climbed on behind Xel, hesitating to grab her.

"Hold on to me," Xel said firmly, reaching back to take

Lizzy's hands.

Lizzy wrapped her arms around her as tightly as she could. Xel glanced once more at Leonydas and nodded. Behind them, Martin lumbered forward in his bear form and let out a thunderous roar. Xel leaned forward, and they shot off.

Mykayla was undoubtedly an excellent driver, but her handling of the bike had been rough and aggressive. Xel, by contrast, was smooth, slipping through traffic as though the cars were standing still. Buildings blurred past, and for the first time, Lizzy felt steady enough to ride with her eyes open.

She glanced down at the shape of the necklace pressing into her thigh and thought of the others. They were risking their lives for her. Or was it for the necklace? No, it was the hope of what she could become. The future she and…Vic had once dreamed about in idle, impossible conversations. The future he had given his life for—whether he had known it or not. The decision became clearer, simpler, though still just out of reach, waiting for her to grasp it.

"They're going to be okay, right?" Lizzy asked.

Xel didn't look back, only nodded as she brought the bike to a stop at a red light. They had blown through several intersections already, but a police cruiser cut across the street ahead.

Lizzy twisted in her seat, scanning for pursuit. The street behind them was empty; then something moved overhead. At first, she thought it was a low-flying plane until she noticed the glint as city lights slid beneath it. The object angled toward them.

"Xel?" Lizzy said, flipping her visor up.

The shape dipped. It wasn't a plane or a drone. It was a bird, black and massive, gull-like, and nearly the size of a military drone. Its talons were extended, locked on them.

"A Tar-Gull," Xel said, glancing back. She swore under her breath, and gunned the engine. Lizzy scrambled, throwing her arms tight around Xel as the bike lunged forward. They blasted up the block and dropped low into a sharp turn. Lizzy pressed her helmet to Xel's back and twisted to look behind them.

The bird swept wide around the corner, scraping against the buildings and leaving a thick black smear along the brick. Its wings thundered as it surged back into the air closer than before.

The creature was coated in a rippling layer of oily tar that streamed in the wind. Droplets flung loose, splattering across cars and pavement. Everywhere the substance touched, it hissed and steamed.

Lizzy shuddered and clung tighter. They banked into another turn, but this time, the Tar Gull didn't follow. Lizzy scanned the sky wildly.

Nothing.

Then Xel wrenched the bike sideways. The bird plunged straight down in front of them. Lizzy jerked back as talons tore past her shoulder. They missed but the tar rained down across both of them.

It ate through fabric instantly, searing the skin beneath. Xel flinched but didn't slow. Lizzy screamed. She'd once splashed hot oil on her hand while cooking—this was infinitely worse. Nausea surged as the pain burned and spread. She fought the instinct to pass out.

Then warmth bloomed along her arm. Her tattoo flared. Through her jeans, the necklace glowed, and like cool water poured over fire, the pain receded.

The Tar Gull saw it. It screeched and rolled sharply, flipping in the air before diving again. Xel glanced back and saw the attack coming.

She flattened her body over the bike, dragging Lizzy down with her, and twisted the throttle as far as it would go. The bike leapt forward. Lizzy pressed her face into Xel's back and never saw the semi-truck trailer sliding across the intersection ahead of them.

"Keep your leg tucked behind mine!" Xel shouted.

Lizzy obeyed just as the bike skidded sideways, grinding them against the asphalt. The motorcycle and Xel took the brunt of the impact, sparks screaming as they slid beneath the trailer.

Lizzy's already wounded shoulder, protected only by her burned hoodie and shirt, scraped along the pavement until Xel slammed her arm down, shielding her.

For a breathless moment, they tilted upward as they cleared the far side of the trailer. Behind them, the bird slammed into the truck, but Lizzy's view was wrenched away. The street ended abruptly. The motorcycle struck a fire hydrant and spun violently. Momentum ripped them from the bike and hurled them into a nearby vacant lot.

Lizzy hit the ground, rolled, and the world went black.

Lizzy started as she was shaken awake. Xel was kneeling beside her. Feeling claustrophobic, she desperately pushed off her helmet and gasped.

"We have to keep moving," Xel insisted, pulling Lizzy reluctantly to her feet.

Lizzy cowered closer to Xel; nearby, the Tar Gull was lying on the ground, flailing and gurgling. It had been impaled by a support from the trailer's frame. They took a few hurried steps away, but Xel stumbled and fell to her knees. Her hand shook as it clutched Lizzy's arm.

"What's wrong?" Lizzy said, evaluating Xel's injuries. Her jeans and leather jacket were shredded on the side they skidded on and smeared with blood. She had a bruise on her chin, which must have happened when they were flung off, but Lizzy was more concerned with her shoulder. The tar had splattered on the site of Xel's scar.

"Oh no, Xel," Lizzy said. The scar looked almost as bad as it had earlier when she faced Yar'la. It still sizzled from the tar, and the edges around it were raw and moist.

Lizzy quickly pulled the necklace from her pocket and reached for the injury. Xel grabbed Lizzy's wrist and shoved her away.

"No!" Xel said and tried to get back on her feet. She stumbled before finally forcing herself to stand upright.

"Xel, don't be stupid. I can help you," Lizzy chided her.

"There is no time for that," Xel said, scanning the skies. "There will certainly be another attack, and we still have blocks to go." Xel leaned against the wall of a nearby building and caught her breath. Next to her, a boarded-up doorway gave Lizzy an idea. She pulled out the charm that Ruby had given her earlier and held it up.

"I can get us there quicker," Lizzy said, and gestured at the door. Xel's eyes lit up, and she did something Lizzy rarely saw her do. She smiled. Xel turned and used her uninjured arm to rip the boards, screws, and all off the door.

Lizzy closed her eyes and pictured Ruby's joyous smile. She rapped her knuckles on the door and stood back. Only a few seconds passed before the edges of the door glowed. Blinding light poured out as Xel opened the door, before fading to reveal

Ruby on the other side in the café. Ruby's welcoming smile dropped when she realized Xel was injured.

"Blessed Milda!" Ruby exclaimed, stepping outside with them. "What happened?" She helped Xel into the café. Lizzy paused before she followed them through.

"Liz...," a whisper floated through the air behind her. Lizzy spun around, but there was no one. The door slammed. Lizzy turned back; Cendryn was there pressing her hand firmly against the closed door.

"So, you've found it," Cendryn said, her voice slipping into excitement. "The necklace?"

"I—

Cendryn didn't wait for her to finish; she grabbed Lizzy's arm and pulled her along with her.

"It's time for both of us to heal," Cendryn said, as Lizzy shuffled to stay on her feet.

"Wait, where are we going?" Lizzy said. Cendryn took a long look at her before answering.

"Someplace safe." Cendryn turned Lizzy and pointed to the sky. A pair of dark shapes, still far away, pounded the air furiously. "There are more of those birds coming."

"Shit," Lizzy breathed, nodding. "Who is sending them? Xeilan?"

"Possibly," Cendryn said, releasing her to jog ahead to a convenience store. She stormed inside and down an aisle. Lizzy hurried after her, avoiding the owner's suspicious stare.

"Hey! You can't go back there," the owner barked as Cendryn strode through the stockroom's plastic strip curtains. Lizzy froze for half a second when the owner reached beneath the counter.

"He's got a gun!" Lizzy hissed, shoving through the curtains.

She spotted the exit further back, but Cendryn was focused on the bathroom door. "What are we doing? Cendryn!"

Cendryn ignored her, pressing her palm flat against the door. The gold on her hand turned fiery red as the gap around the door glowed in turn.

"Open it!" Cendryn said sharply.

The plastic curtains slapped together as they parted behind them. Lizzy grabbed at the handle as if it would shield them from harm. It was hot, but she turned it anyway, shoving the door open. A blast of cool air rushed past Lizzy, and where the toilet should have been, a line of trees stretched ahead.

Behind her, Cendryn turned, yanking something from her cloak. She thrust her arm forward just as the owner pointed his gun at them. A tongue of fire leapt from her palm, widening as it crossed the room. He was barely able to cover his face before the flames rolled across him, catching his sleeves on fire and sending him screaming as he stumbled backwards.

Cendryn grabbed her and ran through, closing the door behind them.

CHAPTER 15

It didn't take long for Lizzy to realize they were back at the Night Camp. Her stomach tightened as she scanned for anyone who might be looking for her and Grecka. Cendryn, however, was immediately on the move, trudging towards the entrance of the tattoo parlor. Lizzy hurried to catch up.

"Wait," Lizzy said, but she was too late and followed Cendryn inside.

"Gairloch," Cendryn called out, before she spotted him working on a client.

"He's busy," Isley said, glancing up from the book where she was perched on a stool behind the counter. She was clearly annoyed.

Cendryn stormed over to Gairloch and loomed over his client

"You're done," Cendryn commanded. "Come back later."

The man looked offended, but as Cendryn stared down

at him, his eyes trembled in fear. He cowered back from her, bumping against Gairloch's belly.

"You'd best come back later. I'll give you a discount."

The client nodded, keeping his eyes fixed on Cendryn, and bumped into Lizzy on the way out.

"Be sure to give us a like online!" Isley called after him, rolling her eyes at Lizzy.

"So," Gairloch said, glancing up as he reset the tattoo device. "I guess we're doing this?"

"Yes—"

"No!" Lizzy said, stepping forward to cut Cendryn off. "I haven't decided yet. I need more time."

Cendryn whipped around and moved closer to Lizzy.

"You've already found the necklace; there isn't time to be scared."

"I *am* scared, because this doesn't just affect me.

"Exactly. It affects me as well."

"It's bigger than just the two of us. Just here, in the Night Camp, there are dozens of sick." Lizzy shook her head. "If something goes wrong, they'll be left with nothing. No, I have to do this right if I'm going to heal the world."

Cendryn exhaled slowly through her nose, her voice dropped an octave as she spoke.

"You can't just do that."

A chill crept down her back for reasons she couldn't understand.

She stepped back.

"I'm not going to make another mistake that will lead to someone getting hurt," Lizzy said. "Not when I may be *so* close to changing things."

Cendryn turned toward Gairloch, who had paused mid-prep. He held up his hands and began screwing in the bottle of gold ink into the machine.

"You're nervous," Cendryn said, her voice returning to its deeper tone. Her words slipped out, stained with urgency. "It's understandable, but you don't have to be. Since we last spoke, I have tested my design on someone else, and it worked beautifully."

Lizzy shot a look at Gairloch.

"She did. Just a few hours ago," Gairloch said, meeting Lizzy's eyes. "I wouldn't have believed it if I hadn't seen it with my own eyes. This lady was able to siphon off a portion of the il while maintaining the rest. Remarkable!"

"Ok," Lizzy said slowly. Something was very wrong. "But isn't the ilThren in the necklace different? Aetherwilde?"

"Different but the same," Cendryn said, moving closer to Lizzy. The air in the room tightened. Lizzy was sure the building anxiety wasn't hers.

"No," Lizzy said with a sigh of finality. "Not like this. I believe you can control ilThren, but the necklace is different. I can feel it. I don't know enough about it, and I don't think you do either. Let me bring the others here, they can—

Cendryn growled under her breath and seized Lizzy by the wrist.

"Come with me," Cendryn said, her voice forced through her teeth. "I'm going to show you something that will change your mind."

Lizzy jerked free of her grip, sick of her wrist being used as a leash. When Cendryn looked back, Lizzy offered a defiant look.

"Lead the way," Lizzy said, waving towards the door.

Cendryn let out an amused huff and continued outside.

"Gary," Lizzy said, pausing at the door, "you are still cursed, right? To always tell the truth?"

Isley let a doubtful laugh, but continued focused on her book.

Gairloch didn't respond but stared at her with a guilty look.

Lizzy flashed him an angry look, nodding as she spun and left.

Lizzy caught up and walked beside Cendryn as she maneuvered through the buildings of the Night Camp. Like the other business, the one they finally entered had no signage, but it was very clear what they sold. Hanging from the walls by wooden dowels and piled on top of tables were hundreds, maybe thousands, of pairs of underwear.

Not lingerie or silk boxers; only tighty whities and granny panties. Lizzy gawked. By the thick odor of bleach burning her nose, they had been cleaned and were stain-free, but the waistbands and leg holes were stretched or loose. Some had holes.

"What the…," Lizzy muttered as they walked past a table of fairy or gnome-sized undergarments. "Why are we here?"

Cendryn ignored her as well as the guy behind the register as she strode past him.

"You think this is weird?" the man chuckled. "There are actually people who shop here." He shook his head and reached under the counter. A sharp click followed by a whining groan echoed from the back. Cendryn continued through sloppy piles of garments labelled 'Cleaned but Stained: Buy One Get One."

Lizzy couldn't help but cover her nose as she tiptoed behind Cendryn towards a now open trap door. As they entered, Lizzy brushed against one of the piles, setting off a mini avalanche of permanently stained underwear.

"Ack!" Lizzy complained, shaking a yellowed bra from her shoulder, almost slipping down the ramp. The room they entered was stocked with crates of alcohol, mostly vintage wine bottles caked with dust. It smelled like formaldehyde, though. It made her nauseated.

"Is this...?" Lizzy's voice trailed off as Cendryn stepped straight through a brick wall. It shimmered like liquid after she had passed through. Lizzy passed her hand through. Finding nothing solid, she closed her eyes and followed.

She winced as her toes struck uneven stone. When she opened her eyes, she was standing on the uneven floor of a cavern. From the stony ground to a ceiling shaved smooth of stalactites, dozens of doors covered the space. Some stood alone—others were stacked, leaning, even piled atop one another in impossible arrangements.

At the cavern's center, a shimmering pool glowed with a soft, holy light, illuminating even the darkest corners. Its surface quivered, as though something stirred just beneath. The air was thick with humidity, and Lizzy tugged absently at her hoodie.

She moved to stand beside Cendryn, intending to peer into the pool, half-expecting to see fish, but her curiosity was cut short as two women coalesced.

Both wore layered robes of sheer fabric. One was fully corporeal; the other drifted, her body semi-transparent, as though carried by an unseen current. An ethereal strand tethered the spirit to a nearby door left slightly ajar.

The solid woman greeted Cendryn, then turned her attention to Lizzy—slowly, deliberately appraising her from head to toe.

"I am Cirsta," she said at last. "Mother of All Doors."

"I am Versula," said the spirit, her voice echoing faintly.

"Priestess of Passages."

Cirsta gestured toward the glowing pool. "And that is our sister—Amula, Prophetess of Arrival."

"Uh… hi," Lizzy said, shrugging. "I'm just Liz."

"Lady Betela-in-waiting," a reverberating voice rose from the pool itself.

Cirsta's gaze shifted back to Cendryn. "So. You have not yet come to fulfill your promise."

"Not yet," Cendryn replied evenly. "She is not ready. But she soon will be."

"She will see the truth," Versula said, pointing toward the pool.

"What truth?" Lizzy asked, leaning closer.

"As Amula carries you," Cirsta said, "the truth of the consequences of your passage will be revealed."

Lizzy glanced at Cendryn.

"She means," Cendryn explained, "that when you pass through the pool, you will witness a prophecy of what will follow as a result of the journey."

"Okay," Lizzy said, straightening, trying to summon her inner Xel. "I'm ready."

She was not.

"Until you fulfill your promise and free us," Cirsta warned, "this will be your final passage, Cendryn."

"I understand," Cendryn said, her eyes fixed on the water.

"Then present a piece of your destination," Cirsta said, taking position at one side of the pool. Versula hovered opposite her. Together, they raised their arms. A breeze spiraled upward from the pool. Robes tangible and spectral alike lifted and fluttered.

Cendryn produced a small glass vial filled with fine grayish-brown sand and tipped it over the water. For a moment, the grains hovered, suspended in the current, before falling into the pool. The surface rippled then stilled with an image: a shoreline, tides rolling in and out, alive with motion.

Cendryn looked at Lizzy.

"Hurry," she snapped, her voice drenched in an annoyed, impatient tone, and stepped into the pool. She slipped beneath the surface and vanished.

Lizzy stood frozen, the hair on the back of her neck prickling. Her mother had used that same tone a thousand times. She had always hated it.

Now it terrified her.

Lizzy stepped forward and stood at the edge of the pool. She glanced at Cirsta.

"I don't suppose you can send a message to someone for me?"

Cirsta stared at her for a moment before answering. "You do not have to pass through. You are welcome to return the way you came."

"No," Lizzy sighed. "I think I actually do have to follow. It's my path."

Cirsta nodded.

Lizzy took a deep breath and held it. Then she stepped forward—and fell.

She expected water as she passed through the pool's surface. Instead, there was only nothingness and wind. It tore past her as she dropped, stomach lurching with that familiar, dreamlike sensation of falling from a great height.

She leaned forward and looked down. A pinprick of light raced up toward her. It swelled into a brilliant globe, and Lizzy plunged straight into it.

She squinted against the brightness. The falling had thankfully stopped. Now she hovered, standing, somehow, and before her stood her sister.

"Ashley," Lizzy breathed. She was glad to see her. She expected to face their mother.

Ashley laughed brightly, her golden skin and blonde hair glowing as though lit from within by the sun itself. She opened her arms, inviting an embrace. Lizzy reached for her, and the light burned.

Ashley's body blackened instantly, charred as if scorched by the very sun that illuminated her. Flesh crumbled beneath Lizzy's fingers, breaking apart into ash. The remains slipped through her hands, tumbling onto the ground, and were swept away by the wind.

Lizzy screamed.

The vision shattered. She pitched forward and slammed onto sand. The beach from the pool stretched around her, real and solid beneath her palms. Lizzy gasped, chest heaving, trying to breathe through the terror and the images still seared behind her eyes.

"It's a bitch, huh?" Cendryn said, standing over her, holding out her hand. Lizzy glanced at her and then back to the ground. She needed another moment.

"I don't understand what I saw," Lizzy said.

"Eh, you probably won't until it happens," Cendryn said. "Try not to think about it, it'll drive you crazy."

"What did you see?"

"You wouldn't understand," Cendryn said, tapping her shoulder with her extended hand. "Come on."

She looked around. She knew this place. The beach stretched wide and flat, the gray-brown sand damp and compacted beneath her hands. The Gulf rolled in with steady waves, capped with white foam that hissed as it collapsed and slid back into itself. The air smelled of salt and iron and something faintly decaying, seaweed rotting in unseen piles somewhere nearby.

Lizzy finally stood on her own. "Galveston?"

"Yes, come on," Cendryn said. "We're almost there."

Cendryn turned and trudged across the sand toward a line of dunes set back from the tide.

The moment fluttered in Lizzy's stomach with déjà vu. She watched Cendryn walk away, unease tightening her chest. The weight of who she concluded Cendryn was pressed down on her shoulders and squeezed at her temples. She didn't want to think about it. She wished she didn't know. But the truth had been closing in on her for some time now.

No one else disliked her enough to do this.

Lizzy followed. "Where are we going?"

"I am going to show you why you were born to accept this power," Cendryn said, without slowing, "and why you must claim it, to heal what was broken long ago."

Lizzy nodded, though her throat had gone tight.

They walked until they reached a towering dune, its slopes stitched with long, dry grasses whipping violently in the wind. Cendryn stopped and reached beneath her hood, drawing out a necklace.

The morning sun caught a green gem at its center, just for a moment, before a passing storm cloud dulled its glow.

Lizzy shivered. Her chest constricted. She recognized the necklace. It was her mother's.

"Kyr'eth Val," Cendryn said.

The gem darkened from within, stained by an inky shadow.

Tendrils writhed inside it until the stone turned completely black. The ground beneath them trembled with a low, ancient roar, and then the dune itself began to rise. Slowly, as though an enormous hand beneath the earth was lifting it. Sand and broken shells trickled down as a great hollow gaped open, revealing a cavernous mouth plunging into darkness.

Lizzy should have been shocked, but the déjà vu deepened.

When the opening reached nearly ten feet high, the movement stopped. Cendryn stepped into the darkness.

"Come," she said.

"Tell me who you are," Lizzy demanded.

Cendryn paused and turned back. She stood swallowed by shadow, while Lizzy remained in the thinning daylight. Slowly, Cendryn reached up and pulled back her hood.

It was too dark to see her face, but Lizzy already knew. She stepped into the darkness.

"I already knew it was you, moth—"

The word died in her throat. She froze. She had been so certain. Who else carried that much disappointment? That much cold certainty? Who else spoke to her like that?

But it was not her mother.

It was her sister.

It was Ashley.

"Hello, sister," Ashley said, staring at Lizzy with a calm void.

Lizzy couldn't speak. There were no words large enough for how impossible the moment felt. She stood there, waiting for more. For a further explanation or another reveal. This couldn't be the final reality—it just couldn't be her sister.

"I could try to explain," Ashley said lightly, already turning away, "but it'll be easier if you just remember." She gestured for Lizzy to follow. "Hurry up."

That tone again. It made Lizzy wonder just how much of their mother infected both of them, undiagnosed.

Lizzy followed, floating, though her steps were real. The world had taken on the soft distortion of a dream. No, a nightmare pretending to be one. As they moved deeper, she took in the cavern. The sandy floor sloped gently downward. Smooth, curved walls of pale sandstone arched overhead, brickwork fitted so precisely it reminded her of photographs she'd seen of ancient tombs.

Ashley reached into her cloak, murmured to something unseen, and a flame sprang to life. It floated ahead of them, casting just enough light for tongues of fire to lick back the darkness.

Up ahead, broken shapes lay on either side of the passage. Statues—or what remained of them. They would have towered over Lizzy, had they not been shattered into massive chunks. Only their pedestals remained intact.

Ashley stopped. She nudged a fallen piece with her foot and looked back at Lizzy.

"Not ringing any bells yet?"

Lizzy frowned, stepping closer. She tilted her head, studying the fragment from another angle. A long snout, angry eyes, and curling horns erupting from the sides of its head. Her breath caught. If it had been black, she would have recognized it instantly. The thing that had hunted her for years.

The memory slammed into her. The statue was whole, towering, and she was so small, pressed back against someone. A hand had found hers and guided it forward, helping her touch the stone paw. Tiny fingers. A child's hand.

"There's nothing to be scared of."

Ashley's voice snapped Lizzy back. She realized she'd backed into her sister without noticing. Lizzy's hand was clenched around Ashley's arm. She dropped it quickly and stepped away.

"Remember? That's what I told you," Ashley continued, quieter now. "I was wrong." Her mouth tightened. "That's on me."

"I don't understand," Lizzy said, her voice finally finding its way out. "We were here?"

"Yes."

"When?"

Ashley tilted her head. "What is the only time in your life you have never been able to remember?"

"The dog attack," Lizzy murmured.

She turned back to the statue fragments, and for the first time in years, she pushed against the wall inside her mind that had kept those memories out. This time, there was no resistance. The images came, blurred, incomplete, but real.

She and Ashley, small again, stood on the beach before they reached the statues. Lizzy fretted over a fish trapped in a tide pool while Ashley waited impatiently behind her. She tugged Lizzy's hand, eager to show her something.

"Even then," Ashley said softly, pulling Lizzy forward in the present, "you cared too much. About everyone. About everything." She turned and walked on.

Lizzy hurried to stay within the glow of the floating flame, the memories catching up with the present. Little Ashley had pulled Lizzy along until they came to a dune. The same dune. As had happened earlier, Ashley…Ashley made the dune rise up.

"You used magic," Lizzy said suddenly, stepping into Ashley's path.

The firelight threw sharp shadows across Ashley's face.

"When we were young," Lizzy pressed, "you used ilThren. You knew about it."

"I did," Ashley said. Her jaw tightened. "I was a natural."

She stepped around Lizzy and continued down the slope.

"Was."

The passage steepened as they descended deeper into the dark.

Lizzy sank deeper into her memories.

As she had just recalled, they had found the statues, and Ashley had told her not to be afraid. They had gone farther around the next bend where a vast, well-like structure waited, its interior ringed with staggered platforms descending like a spiraling stair. But, there had been more light.

"It's darker than I remember," Lizzy said, as they approached the corner. Ashley stopped. "The walls had shimmered."

"You're right," Ashley said, the memory finding her as well. She lifted her hand, and the floating sphere dimmed to a dull red, flickering weakly. An unsettling, absolute darkness pressed in around them. There was no shimmer, no glow ahead. There was supposed to be a blueish glow.

"Give me your arm!" Ashley snapped. She lunged forward. The red light cast Ashley's face in harsh shadow, twisting it into something unfamiliar—something frightening. For the first time, Lizzy felt real fear of her sister. She stumbled back until her head struck the stone wall. Ashley grabbed her arm and shoved up her sleeve, exposing the tattoo.

"It's not glowing," Ashley growled. "It should be glowing.

Where's the necklace?"

"In my pocket," Lizzy said, putting her hand over it.

"Take it out, I need to see it," Ashley said.

Lizzy hesitated.

"I'm not going to take it from you," Ashley said, through her teeth. "I'm not even allowed to touch it."

Lizzy waited until Ashley took a reluctant step back and pulled the necklace out. The delicate designs caught the red light and glittered faintly.

"Allowed by who?" Lizzy asked.

Ashley ignored her, gawking at the necklace.

"It should be responding," Ashley said, glancing to the corner. "We are so close…unless—no!"

Ashley broke into a run, disappearing around the corner, the sphere bobbing alongside her, leaving Lizzy in the darkness. She pulled out her phone and, using the flashlight, followed. The well opened before her just as she remembered: enormous, at least the length of a bus across, with broad platforms staggered down into the depths.

In her memory, Ashley had surprised her again by touching the sand and speaking a word to it. It hardened into a large disc that they stepped onto. Her sister's hand guiding them unsteadily down into the well.

Now, Ashley stood at the edge, fists clenched, shaking as she stared into the black. Something was very wrong.

"What is it?" Lizzy said as she came alongside her.

Ashley didn't answer. Again, she touched the sand at their feet, forming a disc. She yanked Lizzy onto it and guided them over the edge. They smoothly floated downward, ten, thirty, and finally eighty feet, where they neared the floor. Before they even came to a stop, Ashley leaped down and dashed ahead through a doorway.

"No!" Ashley screamed.

Lizzy stepped off the platform and walked towards the doorway, her memories guiding her.

Before, they had entered a dim cavern full of softly glowing crystals and waterfalls that reflected their light. Coral-colored sea shells embedded in the moist rocky walls formed a natural wallpaper of mosaics. Up a few natural steps, a rocky pedestal rose from the ground between two streams of water tumbling down the rocks. Floating above the pedestal in its own light was the sword.

ilBetela.

That was before. Lizzy knew the truth of the present before she even crossed the threshold. She entered the cavern anyway. It was dry. Dead. The waterfalls were gone. The crystals were cloudy and dull. The shells had lost their luster. At the pedestal, Ashley was bent over, hands braced against the stone, growling low and furious.

"It's not here anymore," Lizzy said quietly.

"No shit."

"Did we take it?" Lizzy said, frowning as she tried to recall. Her memory was fuzzy again, but trying to resolve. Ashley raced, in bounds, down from the pedestal, grabbed Lizzy by the front of her hoodie, and shoved her to the ground.

"Remember!" Ashley screamed. "You stupid bitch!" Her face trembled with fury as she leaned over Lizzy. Lizzy cried out and threw up an arm, bracing it against Ashley's chest to keep her

back.

She saw her own hand and remembered a hand reaching for the sword. The weapon was beautiful, more beautiful than anything she had ever seen or dreamed of before. As a child, the magic her sister had displayed was amazing, but she was so close to Tita's stories that it wasn't unreal. It was just something that she expected to encounter someday. The sword, however, was beyond that. It was not of this earth and teemed with an energy that called to her—reached for her.

The hand that reached for it in her memory, however, was not her own. It was Ashley's. She had tried to grab it, wield it. But it rejected her. It had hurled her sister backward and slammed into the cavern floor. The impact ripped the breath from her lungs. The sword hovered, untouched.

ilBetela spoke.

"It is not for you to wield," the heavenly voice had echoed through the cavern, each word layered with harmonies that resonated in air and bone. "But the one who will wield it is present."

Ashley had flipped over, staring at Lizzy, shock flashing across her face before curdling into rage. She had lunged for the sword again and met the same invisible force, slammed back as though struck by judgment itself. She collapsed onto the stone and sobbed as the sword drifted lower, turning toward Lizzy.

"Elizabeth Luna, the power of the Lady Betela will pass to you," the sword had sung. The light in the chamber pulsed, humming in time with its voice. "You only need to accept it."

"No," Lizzy had said immediately. She was terrified by what it was doing to Ashley. "I do not want it."

She knelt beside her sister, wiping blood from the heels of Ashley's hands where she had fallen.

"As should be," the sword answered. "You have not yet completed your journey."

"Lizzy, take it," Ashley had begged her, the words spilling out in a frantic tone. "Take it and give it to me. I know about magic. I can use it to give you magic, too."

Lizzy shook her head. She wanted to go home. She wanted Tita.

Ashley shoved her aside and charged the sword once more, shouting words Lizzy could neither understand nor later remember. Fire burst from Ashley's palm but vanished before it could reach the blade.

This time, the force did not throw her back. It drove her to her knees.

"Why do you insist on claiming what is not yours, Ashley Luna?" the sword asked, its voice suddenly cold.

Ashley looked up, tears streaking her face, fury twisting her features.

"Because I found it," she said hoarsely. "I knew where to look. It should be mine. It has to be."

Her voice broke.

"Mom will be so proud."

The sword did not respond. Instead, a great sadness filled the cavern. Lizzy remembered the weight of it. At the time, she had thought it belonged to Ashley, but now she understood. It had come from the sword itself. It did not want to do what it was about to do.

The stone beneath Ashley's knees stirred. Rock crept upward, crawling over her legs, locking her in place. Ashley struggled, sobbing. Lizzy rushed forward and grabbed at her, trying desperately to pull her free, but a blast of force struck her squarely in the chest.

Lizzy was thrown backward, skidding across the cavern floor.

"Ashley Luna," the sword sang, its voice resonant and final. "You have attempted to claim what was never meant for you." Light gathered around Ashley. "As punishment, all connection to ilThren is severed."

The beam engulfed her. Ashley thrashed, head thrown back in a silent scream. Her body convulsed as the light intensified, then abruptly vanished. She stared at the sword, eyes wide and empty, blinking as though she no longer understood the world around her.

"Any attempt to speak of these events to Elizabeth Luna," the sword continued, firmer now, "will result in pain."

Then its attention shifted.

"You have come too early, Elizabeth Luna. Until you have completed your journey, the events of this morning will be hidden from you."

She raised her arms too late. Warm light washed over her, turning her arms limp. Drowsiness settled in, and the day was erased. She would awaken, face down, on the beach with the Veilkin charging towards her. It would attack her—scarring her for life, and she would never understand why.

Until now. Ashley no longer loomed above her. She sat cross-legged on the stone floor, just as they had when they were children. She was crying quietly.

"Ashley," Lizzy said and reached for her. For an instant, Ashley reached back wanting to embrace her sister, love softened her face, but she caught a glimpse of the tattoo. Her face shattered with anger—fury. She pulled back and drove her fist into Lizzy's jaw.

Lizzy fell to her side, pain shooting across her face.

"Now you remember," Ashley growled, getting to her feet. "Now you see why you have to heal me. You owe it to me!"

"I'm so sorry, Ash," Lizzy said, her voice breaking. "I didn't know. I couldn't...the sword took my memory."

"But you had the chance," Ashley snapped. "You could have accepted the sword back then. I would have never had my power stripped from me. Do you even understand what that felt like? It was worse than an injury. Worse than losing a limb. It was as if my very soul was peeled apart from my body." Her voice dropped, raw and hollow. "You don't get over that, you can't forget it. That's why I studied so hard in school and spent so many hours researching. I had to get it back." Ashley ran her fingers over her tattoos. "It's not the same, though, and it hurts so much. Every time I use it, the pain claws into my bones, but it's worth it. Just for a taste."

"I'm so sorry," Lizzy said. It was all she could say.

The darkness pressed in, thick and suffocating. The red glow cast Ashley's rage into sharp relief, and Lizzy felt the cavern fill with sorrow, but this time, it was her own.

"Words do nothing," Ashley said coldly. "It doesn't change anything. It doesn't help." She stepped closer. "I hoped that losing Vic, then Tita, would finally give you some idea of what I felt."

"Ashley... no," Lizzy whispered, horror piercing her. "You couldn't have."

"Vic?" Ashley said quickly. "No." But the disappointment on her face betrayed her. "Even though you stole him from me."

"No, that's not true, I didn't take him from you," Lizzy said, and flinched as Ashley raised her fist again. She let it drop and continued.

"He was always in love with you," Ashley spat. "Even before we knew what love was. Then, when I finally had him, I gave him everything. My love. My body. I would have given my soul to keep him, but like the sword…" Her voice broke into a scream. "…he belonged to you!"

They both cried in the dark. Ashley wiped her face roughly and continued, faster now, as if afraid to stop.

"It was just luck that he was killed and even moreso that you were there with him." Ashley paused, and her anger turned to an evil, self-satisfied smile. "It only took the slightest nudge of a whisper, echoing in your ears to drown you in despair. And I probably didn't even have to, you believed your own lie and sank so low so quickly—but I wanted to. I enjoyed it."

"Whisper?" Lizzy croaked.

Ashley lunged.

Lizzy tried to pull away, but Ashley was faster. She seized Lizzy by the throat and ripped the corded necklace with the small blue stone from her neck. Holding it close to Lizzy's ear, she let it speak.

In Vic's voice. "*It's all your fault…*"

"No!" Lizzy whimpered, knocking the necklace from Ashley's hand and wrenching free. She sobbed. "Why? How?"

"I needed you to suffer. It would never be as much as I have, but at least it would be close. Besides that, I needed it to drive you to Betela's Blossom—"

She stopped abruptly, bracing for pain, but none came. Ashley's eyes widened. Then she smiled, slow and triumphant.

"The sooner you sank low enough, I knew the sword would call to you. History is full of Lady Betelas who answered it at the lowest moment of their lives."

Lizzy stared at her sister, still crying. It was too much. It was as bad as losing Vic all over again.

"And Tita," Ashley added lightly. "She was easy. Didn't take much to get her heart racing."

"No!" Lizzy screamed. "Please, don't tell me you did that."

"I did," Ashley said, simply. Peacefully. Lizzy's stomach turned—she had to force herself not to throw up. "Do you know I went to her after that morning on the beach? I was just a kid—lost and hurting. I begged her to help me get my connection back, but she wouldn't. So did mom. You know, Mom, she was so pissed. She demanded to be taken to wherever it was that we had gone, but Tita refused. I couldn't take her or even tell her exactly what happened. Ever since then, she lost interest in me and was so pissed at you all the time. Because…like Vic said. This was all your fault."

Lizzy stared at the ground blankly. "Mom knew. She knows."

It hurt so much, and she didn't want it to. She wished she could go back in time and change it all. Make herself say yes to the sword. But she was just a kid then. She was scared. Lizzy knew it wasn't her fault. It wasn't even the sword's fault. She could feel the necklace against her leg, whispering to her.

"Ash," Lizzy said hoarsely. "I am so sorry. You're right—those words don't fix anything. I wish I could change it for you. More than anything." She lifted her gaze. "But the sword was never meant for you."

"Are you insane?" Ashley snapped. "It was my right to take it. I knew magic. I was powerful. Mom told me so."

"Ashley," Lizzy said quietly, anger hardening her voice, "Mom is a bitch." Ashley slapped her, as her mom had done to both of them on many occasions. Lizzy's head snapped to the side—but she turned back, jaw clenched, eyes blazing.

"Sorry," Ashley said with a huff, more irritated than remorseful. "I don't know why I did that." She rolled her shoulder. "You're right. She is a bitch. But she's also been right all along." Ashley straightened, lifting her chin. "I'm the powerful one. I'm the attractive one. I'm the one who should have had the sword—not punished for it."

She held out a hand. Lizzy stared at it. She wanted to lunge at her—to pound her face with everything she had. Ashley had murdered Tita.

The thought shattered something inside her. The building rage was there, but it crashed into everything else she had just learned and broke apart. Her mind recoiled, slipping into shock before the rage could take hold. The world became distant.

She let her sister pull her to her feet. They were both silent for a long while—staring into the darkness around them.

"Ash…," Lizzy finally started, but paused. She knew what she needed to say, and it frightened her.

"I know it was a lot," Ashley said quickly, mistaking her hesitation. "But it will be worth it. For both of us." Her eyes gleamed. "I'll get my power back—and you can have Vic. Together, we'll find a way to bring him back."

Lizzy stared at Ashley.

"You lied," Lizzy said flatly. "You don't know how to save Vic without losing my power." Her insides, though, crumpled.

Ashley shook her head.

"But Gairloch," Lizzy said, confusion bleeding into her voice.

"He said that you did it."

Ashley couldn't help but let a smile break across her lips. "I'm sorry, but that part was too easy. All he had to do was tell you he couldn't lie, and you believed him."

Lizzy's face crumpled. It felt like everyone in her life had been lying to her forever.

"Lizzy, I did this for both of us," Ashley said, putting an arm around Lizzy. "Between the two of us, we will make it work. Together."

"No, Ashley," "No," Lizzy said, firm. She pushed Ashley away. This was not the sword's will—it was her own. "I will not help you. I'm sorry, but what you've done is…" Lizzy's voice cracked, and she sobbed. "Unforgivable."

Lizzy paused for a heartbeat. She waited—hoping, foolishly, that Ashley would say something. Beg. Flinch. Show even the smallest sign of regret. She prayed for it, but there was nothing.

Ashley stared blankly at first, and then her cheek twitched, followed by her eye. Anger was building. Without waiting for Ashley to say or do anything else, Lizzy turned and walked to the exit.

At the edge of the well, she stopped and stared up. The platforms rose into darkness, staggered and uneven. She gauged the distances between them, wondering if she could make the climb. She flinched when, behind her, Ashley growled and then screamed.

Over and over.

An explosion thundered through the cavern. Fire bloomed into the well, furious and violent, then vanished, only to flare again with Ashley's rage. Heat washed over Lizzy in waves, but she ignored it. She grabbed the first ledge and hauled herself up.

The jump to the next platform looked further than what she would have been comfortable with, but she had to get back to the others. Besides, she was sure that Ashley would leave her here once she had taken her anger out on the cavern. She wanted to at least get out of the well before she did.

Lizzy backed up and ran. At the edge, she pushed off and sailed through the air. She dropped too soon. Her breath left her in a sharp grunt as her stomach slammed into the edge of the next platform. Pain flared, but she clung on, fingers finding shallow grooves in the stone. She kicked, swung her hips, and managed to hook a leg over. With a final heave, she dragged herself onto the platform.

She sat there, out of breath, and looked up into the darkness.

This was going to take forever.

CHAPTER 16

Lizzy lay on the cold stone of the platform listening for Ashley. The fire and brimstone had ceased. Lizzy rolled over and looked toward the cavern. Ashley was there, the globe casting light across her face. It wasn't angry, like Lizzy expected. It was fixed with resolve.

Lizzy rolled back over and half-wished that Ashley *would* leave her there.

She did not.

Ashley floated up to the platform Lizzy was at and stared at her. Lizzy gave in, pushed herself up, and stepped onto the platform. In silence, they floated up and then walked out of the cave and onto the beach.

The storm clouds now stretched as far as the eye could see up and down the beach. Wind tore through the dune grass and whipped the sisters' hair around their faces.

Just beyond the cave entrance, two orderly rows of men, nearly sixteen in all, waited. They wore the same outfits Lizzy remembered from when Ashley had still called herself Cendryn. Nearby, a pair of Tar Gulls perched along the dunes, shifting and flexing their wings as they watched. They were all with Ashley.

"You've got your own little army?" Lizzy scoffed.

"They are called Nyrdin, and yes, they are *mine*."

The way that she stressed the last word sent goosebumps down the back of Lizzy's neck.

"Ok. Now what?" Lizzy said as they joined the men.

"Now we begin the search for the sword," Ashley said, as casually as if announcing an errand. "The necklace alone is not enough to undo what was done to me."

Lizzy pulled the necklace from her pocket. "I don't even know where to start."

"Put that away," Ashley snapped, spinning toward her. "You must not use it." Her eyes flicked downward. "Just like your healing before, its power is limited. Use it too much without the sword, and it will be gone. Without that power, I will never reclaim IlBetela."

"Fine," Lizzy said, stuffing the necklace back into her pocket. "So?"

Ashley seized Lizzy's arm and twisted it sharply, forcing her sleeve up and exposing the tattoo.

"Now that you carry the necklace," Ashley said tightly, "the mark will respond. At night, under starlight, it will glow. You will feel the sword pulling you toward it."

Lizzy glanced up at the ominous clouds. "Doesn't look like that's happening here."

"We will be travelling to a better place to start from soon," Ashley said, "Until then, we will search the old woman's place here on the beach. Maybe she left clues or even hid it there."

"Tita's beach house?" Lizzy said, startled. "Didn't she move everything to her house in Houston?"

Ashley didn't answer. She signaled for her men to stay back and started down the beach. After a moment, Lizzy followed. If Fresita or the others were tracking her, they would have found her by now. That meant she would have to escape on her own or contact them herself.

The powder was gone, but the charm Ruby had given her was still in her pocket. Lizzy curled her fingers around it, holding it tight.

After a few minutes' walk, they crossed a line of dunes to a lone beach house perched on tall supports, lifted to survive high tides and storm surges. Lizzy hadn't been there in nearly twenty years, but it looked exactly the same.

The small yellow house wasn't as old as her home in Houston, but it had weathered plenty. Like Tita's other place, it needed a little TLC, but the paint was still bright and cheerful. Lizzy couldn't help but smile.

Ashley led her up the stairs to the screened porch and around to the front door. The windows and screen were boarded over. Ashley placed her palm against the plywood and whispered a few words. The gold tattoos flared hot orange. She yanked her hand back as the wood exploded outward. Lizzy dodged just in time, missing a spray of splintered boards and bent, rusty nails by inches.

"Be careful," Ashley hissed, casting her an annoyed glance. Lizzy bit back a retort. A part of her almost wished she'd been hurt so Ashley would be forced to let her heal, draining the Aetherwilde.

Ashley repeated the process through a second layer of boards.

The screen door tore free, leaving only the solid oak front door behind. A large iron knocker comprised of a pair of mischievous fairies swinging from a tree branch hung on the front.

Lizzy stepped forward, hoping to touch the doorknob, but Ashley made sure she was the one to open it. She waved Lizzy in and then followed her. Lizzy stopped short.

There was so much here. Most of which were things Lizzy remembered in Tita's home before. Nothing was set out as decoration or for use; it seemed she was using it more as a storage unit than anything else. Boxes were stacked on top of each other, furniture too.

There was a little bit of everything here. Brass candlesticks, statues, and lamps. Glass orbs, apothecary bottles, and figurines. Wood bowls, trinket boxes, and utensils. And books—stack upon stacks of books. It would take Lizzy months, maybe longer, to truly go through it all. It gave her something to look forward to, easing the weight of everything else.

Ashley took a few steps in and sighed. She poked around at a few things and then turned to Lizzy with an impatient look on her face. She nodded to Lizzy's arm. Lizzy lifted it, and they both stared at the tattoo.

"Do you feel anything?" Ashley asked. "Sense anything?"

Lizzy shook her head.

Ashley nodded towards the necklace in Lizzy's pocket. Lizzy took it out, but it showed no signs of change either.

Ashley scowled and swept her gaze around the room again. "It would take too long," she snapped, "to dig through all this on the chance there's a clue."

She turned and gestured toward the door. Lizzy hesitated. Could she close it, call Ruby, and reopen it before Ashley stopped her? Or should she wait?

As they moved to leave, a stack of papers toppled deeper in the house. They both turned. Ashley frowned and wove through the clutter toward the fallen pile. She knelt and began flipping through the pages.

Lizzy's heart hammered.

This was it. She put the necklace in her hoodie pocket and readied Ruby's charm.

She carefully grabbed the door and tiptoed outside. She had almost pulled the door completely shut behind her when Ashley popped back up from her digging.

"Huh, look, this was my favorite coloring book—

Lizzy shut the door and pulled on the handle with all her weight. She heard boxes and furniture being shoved aside as Ashley raced towards her. She thought of Ruby, knocked quickly, and braced herself.

Ashley made it to the door and began pulling. She was far stronger than Lizzy, and the door popped open an inch. Lizzy braced her knee against the frame and strained until it closed again. She grunted as she fought to keep it closed.

"Come on…," Lizzy said, through her teeth.

Light flickered around the frame, but Ashley gave the door another powerful tug, and it came open a few inches again. Lizzy pushed hard against the frame with her knee, and the knocker made a sharp clank as the door snapped closed.

Light poured from around the frame, and Ashley's resistance vanished.

She carefully let go and turned the knob. The door swung open, revealing the interior of Café Calacoayan.

"Lizzy!" Ruby and Fresita cried. But reality bent. The café

fractured, splintering like glass. Fresita dove through. With a thunderous crack, the image shattered, and wooden shards blasted outward as Ashley kicked through the door.

Lizzy was thrown backward, through the porch, and down into the sand. Pain tore through her as she rolled, clutching her arm and side. Ashley landed beside her in a heartbeat, driving her fist down inches from Lizzy's head.

"Do not try that again!" Ashley snarled. "Leave your friends out of this."

"Too late!" Fresita hissed.

She launched herself at Ashley's face, claws slashing. She ripped open Ashley's cheek and chin before Ashley tore her loose and hurled her aside. Fresita hit the sand hard, rolled, and sprang back to her feet—already yanking Suckerwirl from her pack. She ignited it with a word and flung a glowing pink sphere of energy.

Ashley barely managed to block it but screamed as it scorched her palm.

"Lizzy!" Fresita shouted, already furiously charging again. "Grab the knocker! Get inside!"

Dazed, Lizzy spotted the iron knocker half-buried in the sand. The carved fairies no longer looked playful; their faces were twisted in pouts. She snatched it up and pushed herself to her feet, and nearly collapsed.

Pain hammered through her side, preventing her from taking a full breath. Then her tattoo flared—the pain eased. She could breathe.

Lizzy ran, but a Veilkin, once a monster, now a caretaker, caught her eye. It sat on a nearby dune waiting, watching. Fresita hissing somewhere behind her forced Lizzy to pick up her speed and focus. She circled to the back door.

Her heart stopped as one of Ashley's men turned the opposite corner. He drew his sword, slowing to a stride as he came between Lizzy and the stairs. Lizzy tightened her grip on the knocker. She ducked through a narrow gap in the wooden trellis between the house supports.

Splinters scraped her arms as she desperately forced her way through. Her hoodie snagged on a piece of wood. She was stuck. The man seized her arm and yanked, trying to drag her back out. The wood bit into her spine, knocking the breath from her lungs as she struggled, trapped between escape and capture.

"Let go!" Lizzy shouted, clawing for his face. Her hand snagged his hood instead and yanked it aside.

Now revealed, his face was like the ones she'd seen in the Night Camp: gaunt, pallid, stretched thin over bone. But now she saw his ears, long, pointed, and swept back. An elf.

He slammed the heel of his fist into the trellis. Wood cracked and split, and they fell apart in a spray of splinters. Lizzy turned and ran out from under the house just as he rounded the corner again.

"Come on, man!" she yelled, her eyes darting wildly for an escape.

Fresita streaked past her in a flash of white fury, claws raking the man's face in a vicious flurry before she leapt away again. The man staggered and looked down. Suckerwirl clung to his chest.

His scream tore through the air as it detonated, but Lizzy and Fresita were already racing up the steps.

"Inside—hurry!" Fresita shouted.

They tore along the porch toward the front of the house. Below them, Ashley struggled as beach grass writhed unnaturally, coiling around her legs and reaching for her arms. From the dunes, the rest of her men were closing in.

Inside, Fresita shoved a broken door fragment towards Lizzy. "Put the knocker on it."

Lizzy pressed it into place, and Fresita lifted the handle with her tail and let it fall. The knocker trembled as the door fragment rattled until the iron fairies moved.

They lifted themselves by the ring, hovering where the knocker had once been. In a blur of motion, boards knitted together, and nails slid into place. The door rebuilt itself in seconds.

Lizzy stared, then her gaze dropped past it. Through the last narrowing gap, she saw the necklace lying in the grass below. The final piece slammed into place, and through the door they could hear the fairies clanking back into stillness.

Silence fell on the other side of the door.

Fresita had been frantically nudging through items in a short bookcase sitting by the door.

"The bell jar, quickly," Fresita said as she pulled out a miniature ceramic duplicate of the beach house. Lizzy grabbed the glass-domed display from a box behind her, placed it on the floor, and Fresita placed the little house underneath the glass.

A hum rattled the house, and then everything dropped to silence. The wind that had been intensifying outside was gone; only the sound of their breathing remained.

"We are safe," Fresita sighed, sitting back on her haunches and licking her paw. "Forrr now."

"I lost the necklace," Lizzy said. "I just saw it in the grass. It must have fallen out when the door exploded."

"No," Fresita said, and then hung her head. Lizzy sat on some boxes but jumped when a roar shook the house. Ashley wasn't going to wait for them to come back out. Fresita hopped up to a windowsill and peeked out. Flames shot out from Ashley's hand and fell against the invisible shield protecting the house.

"Still have Ruby's charm?" Fresita said, looking at Lizzy hopefully.

Lizzy nodded and went through the process of creating the doorway. She pushed open the door to reveal Leonydas and the others at the café, looking on hopefully.

"Come," Leonydas said, holding out his hand.

"She lost the necklace," Fresita complained, prowling through the house. "We cannot leave. There are men here trying to get to us."

Leonydas nodded and walked out of view as Mykayla crossed over.

"You ok?" Mykayla asked.

"I'm not hurt," Lizzy said, though her face gave away her turmoil. Mykayla gave her a quick hug and rubbed her arm.

"Well, I'm here now, so...," Mykayla bragged, flashing a cheesy grin. Lizzy chuckled and mimicked the shoulder punch her friend usually gave her.

They were still laughing together when Leonydas entered the room. Since the last time she had seen him, Leonydas had changed into clean clothes, similar to what he'd worn before, though slightly less fitted.

Xel followed close behind. She wore billowing pants gathered low at the waist, ideal for quick movement, and a loose, well-worn black-and-red leather jacket. She stood as straight as ever, composed and unyielding, but the deep crease etched into her face betrayed how much pain she was in.

Ruby came in last and closed the door behind her. Like Xel,

she had opted for loose clothing: corduroy overalls, sneakers, and a light jacket. Abenlieth rested across her back.

"You didn't bring that ginormous sword, too?" Lizzy asked.

"Oh no, honey," Ruby said with a smile as she peeked out the window. "That wouldn't do much good unless we were up against Sentinels."

Ruby leaned away from the window as a roar from outside pulled everyone's attention to the windows. Orange light flickered across Ruby's face, and the air in the room grew warmer.

Ruby looked back at everyone. "Someone's trying to burn their way through."

Leonydas stepped forward. "What are we facing?"

Everyone gathered closer. Lizzy looked around the room, at the quiet readiness in their stances, the way they all seemed prepared to fight for a power they believed could save the world. She hoped that someday she might live up to that kind of resolve. Right now, she just wanted to survive the day.

Flames slammed against the shield again. Beads of sweat formed on Lizzy's forehead. They couldn't stay in there forever.

Lizzy glanced at Fresita, who was staring back at her. Again, she realized everyone was waiting for her. She jumped as another rumble shook the house and then gave them a quick account: Ashley, the confrontation, the beach house, the men. She ended with the revelation of the elf who had attacked her.

"That would explain the guards we fought outside Tita's house," Leonydas said, glancing at Xel. "They fought as we do, but with the aid of il'Thren."

Xel nodded, silent.

"Is that even possible?" Ruby asked. "With the curse and all?"

"It sounds like Ashley's tattoos circumvent it," Leonydas

replied.

"I saw the tattoos on them, too," Lizzy added.

Leonydas frowned. "It should still cause them pain, though." He was silent for a moment as he puzzled over the other elves. Finally, he straightened and met the other's eyes. "We can figure that out later. Right now we need to get that necklace and get Liz out of her safely. Xel and I will keep Ashley's men busy. Ruby, can you and Maeve take on Ashley?"

Ruby looked at Fresita for confirmation and then nodded.

"Mykayla," Leonydas continued. "Stay by Liz's side no matter what."

"Lizzy, take this," Ruby said, handing her a different charm. "But you must guard this with your life. It is a key to the Gateway door. It works like the other, but you don't have to think of me. Just use it to open any door, and it'll get you to Calacoayan."

"I will," Lizzy said, examining the silver charm of a tiny door before tucking it into her pants pocket.

"Do not wait for us," Leonydas said, "Get the necklace and get out of here. We will meet you there later."

Lizzy nodded. Outside, Ashley's voice shouted for her.

"Are you sure?" Lizzy asked, her eyebrows drawing together. "Ashley is very powerful. Couldn't we contact the Sentinels? I know you don't get along with them, but this is something that affects the Thraewen. Right?"

"We will be fine," Leonydas said, flashing her a confident smile. "I'm sure the Sentinels will be steering clear of us for now. Skarweng did the job."

"It'll be fine, Lizzy," Ruby said. "We got this."

"I'm sorry, guys, that I was going behind your back with Ashley. I didn't know who to trust, and with her, there just seemed to be a natural trust. I didn't realize she was using that against me. She offered…" Lizzy's voice broke off.

"It's not your fault," Ruby said. "This was all your sisters' doing. She took advantage of you."

Lizzy nodded but still felt sick to her stomach with guilt. She was worried.

Lizzy noticed Xel hide a flinch and pulled her aside as the others made plans of attack.

"Are you ok?" Lizzy asked, leaning to one side to get a better look at Xel's scar. Blood and sweat already stained her new top. The Tar Gull's black poison was relentless.

"Of course, little one," Xel said, stoically pulling her jacket over to hide it.

Lizzy shook her head. "I know you're not. Xel, it's ok if you sit this out. I don't want you to get hurt."

"Elizabeth…Lizzy," Xel said, her face softening slightly. "Thank you, but this is my job—my responsibility. Besides, I've been through worse before, Leonydas and I both have. Everything will be ok in the end."

Lizzy smiled and squeezed her hand.

"Alright, everyone ready?" Leonydas said.

Xel looked out the window and spotted the necklace.

"She has not seen the necklace yet," she said, turning to Leonydas. "We must push her back enough for Lizzy to get it. Perhaps diplomacy this time?"

Leonydas smiled. "Agreed. Also, Ruby, let's not tip our hand quite yet."

"Got it," Ruby said and stood to one side of the door.

"Liz?" Leonydas said, motioning to the door.

Lizzy opened the door carefully and peeked out. Ashley was

in the midst of launching another wave of fire at the house when she spotted her sister and stopped. Her men formed a semi-circle behind her, their swords drawn and readied.

Lizzy opened the door the rest of the way, allowing Leonydas and Xel to step out first. She followed with Fresita and Mykayla down the stairs. The thundering of the sea and sharp whips of the wind returned as they passed outside the bell jar shield. Dark clouds still held back the sun.

Leonydas approached Ashley, keeping his eyes locked on hers. He tried to push her back by continuing until he was within arm's reach, but she fearlessly held her ground.

"Lord Leonydas," Ashley said with a grin. "I've heard so much about you—from your family."

She gestured to her Nyrdin. Almost in unison, they lowered their hoods. All were elves, and all had the same sickly, hollowed look. Leonydas and Xel took them in, momentarily taken aback despite Lizzy's warning.

Leonydas signaled Xel to stay where she was, then stepped forward and slowly circled the group, studying each face. He stopped in front of one elf in particular, taller and younger than the rest.

"Xerandys?" Leonydas said quietly. The Nyrdin stared through him. Leonydas shook his head, disbelief tightening his features, and moved on. The moment he passed, Xerandys's eyes sharpened. They broke their empty stare and tracked Leonydas's back, narrowing with cold intent.

Leondyas approached Ashley from behind, forcing her to turn to face him.

Lizzy eyed the necklace.

"What have you done to them?" Leonydas demanded.

"I have returned to them what was taken," Ashley replied. She lifted her arm, baring the gold tattoos etched into her skin. One by one, the others followed, revealing the same marks. "Because of me, they can taste the sweetness of connection to the il again. And in gratitude, they follow me—serve me."

"You're controlling them," Leonydas said coldly. "They are Nyrdin now."

"The Nyrdin," Ashley scoffed. "A name given to elves who dared disobey their rulers. Who refused to kneel." Her smile sharpened. "But in doing so, they freed themselves from punishment, from restraint. From your rules."

She gestured dismissively at Leonydas.

"You would condemn them to a hollow life, cut off from the il. A life of meaninglessness."

"I would have them serve their people," Leonydas replied evenly, "by helping others, not just themselves. Or you."

"But they are," Ashley countered. "By reclaiming the Sword, all elves can be healed. Is that not the power of the Lady Betela? To heal? To restore?"

"I do not believe that is your true goal."

"I told him what you've done," Lizzy said.

Ashley smiled faintly. "What I've done is help his kinsmen. Did you tell him what *you* planned to do?"

Lizzy frowned. "What do you mean?"

"Bring it," Ashley said sharply, motioning to the Nyrdin behind her.

They moved at once, cresting the dunes and signaling to someone out of sight. Moments later, two more Nyrdin appeared, hauling a door and its frame up from the sand.

"While we wait," Ashley said lightly, "why don't you pick up the necklace, Liz?"

Lizzy eyed her warily.

"What?" Ashley shrugged. "You didn't think I wouldn't notice it lying right in front of me. Go on. Besides, it's not like I can do anything with it without you."

Lizzy met Xel's gaze. Xel stood squarely between her and Ashley, then gave a small nod.

Lizzy stepped forward with Mykayla at her side and retrieved the necklace. She closed her fist around it, then backed away several steps, glancing toward the beach house.

Ashley smiled. "Before you go, you might want to see this."

The Nyrdin set the door upright, wedging it into the sand. It was cinder-gray, as if torn from the front of a house and hastily altered to stand alone. The men stepped back as Ashley approached and placed her palm on the knob.

"This," Ashley said, "is what she was planning to do with all that power."

She bowed her head. Her tattoos flared, gold bleaching into white, as she whispered,

"*Grathûn.*"

The knob turned, and the door swung open. Lizzy's gasp came out as a choke.

Beyond the threshold lay Vic, still in the hospital, tethered to machines and life support. A familiar lock of hair fell across his forehead, the one he was always fussing with, the one Lizzy had brushed aside for him more times than she could count.

"There's still time," Ashley said, retreating a step.

Lizzy moved forward. Mykayla caught her arm, trying to pull her attention back. Fresita darted ahead, blocking her path.

"Liz, don't fall for this," Fresita pleaded.

Lizzy barely heard her. She continued forward, eyes locked on Vic. Tears spilled freely now, her shoulders trembling as she fought to breathe.

"This is him?" Leonydas asked quietly. "Her friend?"

"Yes," Ashley said smoothly. "Her best friend. The one she loves." She tilted her head. "And she's the reason he's like this."

"That's not true," Fresita snapped. "It was not her fault."

Ashley's gaze never left Lizzy. "That's not what he said. Remember?"

Lizzy stopped and turned slowly. "*You* made me believe that."

Ashley shook her head. "No. I only amplified what *you* already knew. He did say it."

The words echoed in Lizzy's mind, over and over. Not like before—inflicted by Ashley's cursed whispering stone. However, they were still sharp, still real. His words. She took another step.

"Stop her," Mykayla said urgently, looking to Leonydas.

Leonydas did not move. "This is her choice. Her path."

Lizzy reached the doorway. All she had to do was step through to be close to him again. Just once more. She drew in a shaking breath.

"Everything will be okay in the end," Lizzy said softly, glancing at Xel from the corner of her eye. Xel stiffened, tension rippling through her stance.

Lizzy stepped into the threshold. One foot inside. One still in the sand.

"I'm sorry, Vic," she whispered.

Her hand closed around the doorknob and she jumped back, slamming the door shut instead. The gateway charm burned against her palm as she pressed it flat to the wood and twisted the knob.

Light flared.

Ashley had expected the deception. As the doorway began to glow, she flung a handful of sand toward it. The grains ignited midair, swelling into a rolling ball of fire that roared forward.

Mykayla didn't think; she reacted, slamming Lizzy into the sand as heat and light detonated where the door had been. The gateway's glow vanished. With a loud crack, the door exploded. Sharp splinters grazed Lizzy's cheek, and she tasted blood.

Fresita ducked beneath the fire and twisted back, panic flashing through her eyes as she checked on Lizzy. Instead, Ashley's foot sent Fresita tumbling, a sharp cry torn from her chest. Ashley raised her hand again and stopped. Ruby was suddenly there, silent as a held breath.

Steel flashed, Abenlieth yearned to taste her blood. Ashley barely managed to react, wrenching the sand upward into a jagged wall just in time. The impact rang out, deep and jarring, echoing across the dunes.

Lizzy held her breath. For a heartbeat, everything froze. She gasped, and the fight exploded outward— shouting, movement, and magic filling the air. Ashley fell back toward her followers, no longer smiling. Ruby advanced without hesitation.

Leonydas moved through the chaos like a force of nature. Xerandys watched him from the edge of the fighting, momentarily arrested. Leonydas had no weapon at first, only speed, timing, and an unrelenting calm. Blades missed him by inches. He struck with open hands, elbows, and momentum, turning his opponents against themselves until one fell and another's sword clattered free. Leonydas caught it without breaking stride and kept moving.

Ashley reached the shelter of the remaining Nyrdin and met Xerandys's gaze. The message was clear. Xerandys inclined his head and turned away from Leonydas and went for Xel.

Xel was already bleeding. She dropped her first attacker with brutal efficiency, wrenching his shoulder out of place and crushing his ankle beneath her heel. The second didn't last much longer. But each movement pulled agony from the old wound, still irritated by Yar'la's torture and the Tar Gull's attack. It showed now etched into the tightness of her jaw, the hitch in her breath. Her body pleaded with her to stop. She refused.

Lizzy was still on the ground. Something heavy slid off her chest, and she sucked in air, disoriented, only realizing it had been Mykayla when she rolled clear. Lizzy pushed herself up and froze.

A Nyrdin loomed over her, his sword already attacking its prey. Lizzy twisted away on instinct. The blade buried itself in the sand where her head had been a heartbeat before.

Mykayla was there instantly. Her speed was near that of Xel's. Without hesitation, she used her fist, knee, then a bone-shaking blow that dropped the Nyrdin at her feet. She flashed Lizzy a quick, breathless grin and reached down and screamed. Steel tore across her back. Mykayla arched in pain and collapsed forward.

Fresita saw it, but she had her own enemy to finish first. Whispering to her claws, she fed them ilWunne. They flared white-hot. She carved through the Nyrdin in front of her in a blur of motion; legs, bodies, and throats were slit before they even realized they were dying.

She turned and hurled a thorn she had kept from the cage. It struck the Nyrdin going after Lizzy mid-step. Vines exploded from it, coiling tight, driving thorns deep as he thrashed and screamed himself silent.

As Ruby approached Ashley again, she whispered to the

arm of her jacket. It flowed into a silver gauntlet around her arm as she advanced, Abenlieth ready. The Nyrdin guarding Ashley surged forward, trying to keep Ruby back. They were faster, but Ruby was relentless. Abenlieth hunted again. Blood sprayed. One fell. Another staggered.

Then Ashley dropped to her knees and drove her hands into the beach. The sand rose in a shrieking spiral, blinding, battering, lifting Ruby off her feet and hurling her away like something weightless.

Xel turned ready to take on another easy target, but Xerandys was already on her. His confident stare gave him away. He was not controlled. He was angry. They collided in a storm of motion too fast to track: strike, counter, pivot, roll. Xel read him effortlessly, her experience guiding her where his youth overreached. She knocked his sword away and broke contact, breathing hard.

Xerandys straightened, smiling. He reached beneath his poncho and drew another blade. This one gleamed and had runes that crawled along half its silver length, catching the light even in the chaos.

Xel's blood ran cold.

"A Bright Sword," she said.

Xerandys glanced down at it, almost bored.

"Is that what it is?" he replied. "I just thought it looked cool."

"Even with whatever you have become," Xel said, her voice tight, "the curse against all elves and the Bright Sword together should destroy you."

Xerandys smiled, almost indulgent.

"Then I suppose that proves how strong I really am."

He swung, and for a heartbeat, Xel hesitated, caught by the blade's terrible beauty and history. It was a sacred legend come to life, issuing its judgment against her. At the last second, she leaned away, but the sword nicked her chin.

Pain flared, sharp and bright, clearing Xel's head. She surged forward in a blur of motion, staff and fists striking again and again, driving Xerandys off balance before he could fully recover. He swung wildly. She slipped inside the arc and slammed the base of her staff down on his knuckles.

The sword flew free, striking the sand and skidding to a stop at Lizzy's feet.

Lizzy looked up just as Leonydas went down, his blade knocked away, his body crashing hard into the beach. Without thinking, she snatched up the Bright Sword. It was heavier than she expected.

"Leonydas!" she cried. "Sword!"

She hurled it the best she could. Leonydas caught it without looking and rose in the same motion, but the moment his hand closed around the hilt, he screamed.

Smoke curled from his palm. The curse flared violently, burning up his arm, yet he held on long enough to parry a strike and cut his attacker down. Then the sword fell from his grasp, hissing in the sand. Leonydas collapsed to one knee, clutching his scorched arm, staring at the weapon. It had been a hundred years since he last saw a Bright Sword, his mother's, but this was not that one.

Around them, the battle faltered. Lizzy dragged Mykayla upright, hands slick with blood, while Fresita positioned herself between them and the others, petals and magic working desperately against the damage. Ruby staggered back into the fray, sand still clinging to her clothes, jaw set with fury. Xel regrouped beside Leonydas, breathing hard. They were still outnumbered, but just barely.

Ashley stepped forward, unhurried and pleased.

"Why continue this?" she called. "I want Lizzy to find the sword just as you do. Let us work together. She heals my men and me, and then she is free to do whatever she wishes."

"Ashley, enough!" Lizzy shouted, her voice breaking as she pressed flowers against Mykayla's wound. "Why didn't you just talk to me? You know I would have helped you. We were sisters."

For a moment, Ashley only stared.

"...But I will not heal you now," Lizzy continued, shaking. "Not after what you've done. Not to Vic. Not to them. Not to Tita."

Ashley's anger twisted, then softened into a smile that made Lizzy's stomach drop.

"You do not need to help me willingly," Ashley said. "I will take you. I will make you find the sword. And I will decide who you heal."

"I will never help you."

Ashley turned away from her and pointed to the sand. One of the Nyrdin stepped forward and dropped to his knees. Ashley slipped a dagger from her sleeve and placed it in his hand.

"Cut your throat," she said calmly. "Give me your life."

The Nyrdin hesitated. His hand trembled. His eyes flickered with fear, doubt, and something elven struggled to surface.

Ashley leaned closer and raised her glowing arm.

"Obey."

The hesitation vanished, and the blade slid across his neck. Blood spilled onto the sand as he remained kneeling, body shaking, eyes already empty. Then he fell forward and lay still.

The beach went silent.

"What control do you have over my kinsman that you can force them to take their own lives?" Leonydas demanded, his voice raw with fury. Ashley's only answer was to raise her eyebrows.

Leonydas turned to the remaining Nyrdin and extended his hand toward them. "Proud elves of the Realm—fight her. Fight the chains she has wrapped around you. Stand with me."

"I control them all," Ashley said, pride ringing in her voice. "And there are many more like them. They were eager to trade freedom for the taste of ilThren again." Her gaze slid sideways. "All except Xerandys. He was happy to help hurt you."

Leonydas turned, disbelief flickering across his face as his eyes found Xerandys.

Ashley gave a sharp look. The Nyrdin lifted their swords.

"I won't let you have it," Lizzy said, her voice steady despite the terror clawing at her chest. "I'll use it all."

She pressed a hand over the necklace in her pocket, then planted her palm against Mykayla's wound. Mykayla cried out. Lizzy shut her eyes and focused not on the pain, but on her: the girl who laughed too loudly, fought too fiercely, and stood beside her no matter what. The tattoo flared. Heat surged through Lizzy's body and poured into Mykayla, stitching flesh together as agony echoed back into Lizzy's own nerves. She bent forward, gasping, refusing to pull away.

Ashley answered with fire. Sand tore from her grasp and bloomed into flame midair. Ruby met it head-on, hurling her own sand upward, her eyes flashing white as it hardened into a blazing shield. The two forces collided— Ashley's fury driving the inferno harder, pushing Ruby back step by step.

Then Ashley dropped to one knee and plunged a free hand into the earth. Sand surged beneath the shield and burst upward into Ruby's face. It struck her at such a speed that each grain drew blood. She screamed, clawing at her eyes as she fell.

Fresita leapt for Ashley, but flames coiled at Ashley's gesture, wrapping around the Fae Queen's daughter in a ring of heat. Fresita hit the ground, rolling and hissing, fighting to keep her fur from igniting.

And then the Nyrdin charged. Leonydas and Xel moved without hesitation. Xerandys went straight for Xel. He didn't bother with a sword. He took her blows, staff cracking against bone, strikes landing clean, absorbing them with a grim, almost reverent focus. When Xel overextended, he slipped inside her guard and slammed his fist into the back of her head. Her staff flew from her grip.

An arm locked around her throat and lifted her clear off the sand. Her feet kicked uselessly as another Nyrdin rushed in, fists hammering her ribs until breath fled her lungs.

Leonydas roared and tore into the attacker, dropping him in a fury of blows, but pain exploded through him as another blade cut deep into his arm, then his leg. He staggered, forced back into the fight.

Xel saw Leonydas' blood. She quieted her mind and the pain. She stopped struggling. Then she struck, driving her skull up into Xerandys's chin again and again until his grip broke. She dropped to her knees, vision swimming, lungs screaming. But her hand found the star-blossom brooch at the back of her head.

She turned. One clean, vicious swipe. The brooch, a weapon in disguise with a razor-sharp edge, bit deep. It split flesh, tearing away Xerandys's scream along with his face. He fell back howling, clutching what was left of his nose.

Xel stayed kneeling, breath ragged, blood dripping down her

jaw.

The battle raged on around her.

Xel surged to her feet, already turning toward Leonydas, but then she saw Lizzy.

Lizzy was still kneeling over Mykayla, so consumed by healing that she didn't notice Ashley closing in. Mykayla sagged into unconsciousness, and Lizzy felt the pull to follow her into the dark. She tore her hand away. The wound was closed now—raw, livid, but sealed.

The beach came back into focus. Bodies littered the sand. The Nyrdin lay broken or still. Her friends, every one of them, were bleeding, staggering, barely standing. A shadow fell over her. Lizzy looked up.

Ashley stood above her, dagger raised, her face alight with cold purpose.

"I may have to wait longer," Ashley said calmly, "but I will find a way to tap the Aetherwilde for myself. You have caused me pain for far too long." Her lips curved. "It will be worth it to kill you now. Now that you've lost everything. Now that it is all your fault."

Lizzy couldn't move—she couldn't speak. She watched the dagger fall.

Xel was there.

She slammed into Ashley, catching her wrist mid-strike. Bone snapped. Ashley screamed as Xel hurled her aside, but Ashley only smiled through the pain. With a flick of her fingers, she summoned her second blade. The dagger tore through the air and buried itself in Xel's scar.

Xel gasped and staggered, clutching at it, but the blade fought her, driving deeper, sawing through flesh slick with blood.

She couldn't grip it. It wouldn't stop.

"Xel!" Lizzy screamed, scrambling forward.

It was too late. The dagger found her heart, and Xel collapsed into Lizzy's arms.

Lizzy caught her, screaming, sobbing, pressing her face into Xel's chest as blood soaked through her hands. Xel coughed, dark red spilling from her lips, her weight going slack, terrifyingly heavy.

"No—no—no—" Lizzy choked.

She fumbled, frantic, trying to decide: heal, pull the blade, stop the bleeding, something. Anything. But there was too much blood, too much damage. Even in the most well-equipped ER, she would have struggled to save her.

Lizzy pressed her hands over the wound and squeezed her eyes shut. Xel struck her wrist aside.

"Don't," Xel rasped.

"You're dying," Lizzy sobbed. "Please—please let me heal you."

Xel shook her head, eyes locked on Lizzy's, fierce even now.

"Can't… let her win," she whispered. "You must… become Lady Betela."

Blood bubbled at her mouth. Her breathing stuttered, and Lizzy broke.

"Xel—"

"It's alright, little one," Xel breathed. "Everything… will be okay."

Her body convulsed once. Lizzy cradled Xel's face, wiping blood from her lips, sweat from her brow. She pressed her forehead to Xel's and cupped her temples, pouring everything she had left into one desperate wish. *Ease her passing.*

Agony ripped through Lizzy's chest. For a heartbeat, it felt as though the dagger had pierced her heart too, pain vast and consuming, dragging her under with Xel. She tried to let go. She couldn't.

Darkness swallowed her. Pulling her deep down—or was it up?

Into light.

CHAPTER 17

As Lizzy began to surface, she tried to gather the pieces of the day before. Surely she had been sleeping. The memories slipped through her grasp like water, as if reality were the dream fading away. She couldn't remember falling asleep, but wherever she was, it felt as safe and gentle as her own bed.

Still, something was wrong. The thought made her hesitate, afraid to open her eyes.

"Elizabeth," a commanding voice said nearby.

She tried to sit up, to look, but her body refused. Or perhaps she no longer had one. The sensation was strange, like distance without direction. Was it her body that was far away... or her mind?

"Lizzy," the voice said again.

This time it was warm. Affectionate. But the tenderness didn't quite fit the voice that carried it. She drew a slow breath. Honeysuckle filled her lungs.

Lizzy smiled despite herself. A breeze whispered nearby,

teasing leaves she could not see. Blades of grass brushed her arm, soft and playful, and a quiet laugh escaped her before she could stop it. It was peaceful. Like what heaven must feel like.

Heaven.

Death.

The beach. The battle slammed back into her all at once.

"No!" Lizzy screamed as she jolted upright. "Xel!"

She spun wildly, heart pounding, until her gaze landed on her. Xel stood before her: alive, whole, radiant.

"Give me your hand," Xel said.

Her voice flowed like honey over stone. She looked nothing like the woman Lizzy had cradled in blood-soaked sand. The tension, the armor, the pain, all gone. Xel wore a soft, flowing gown that seemed woven from light itself, nearly translucent, drifting around her as if moved by a current only it felt. Underneath, her body was like pure marble lovingly set free by some great artisan. She stared down, her face joyful and free.

She was a goddess.

Lizzy's mouth fell open as Xel smiled and gently pulled her to her feet.

"I thought—" Lizzy stammered. "I thought you were dying."

"I was," Xel replied calmly. "I am."

The words struck like ice.

"In a few seconds," Xel continued gently, "my body will die in your arms on that beach."

"No," Lizzy said, panic rising fast and sharp. "No, tell me what to do. Tell me how to save you."

"It's too late, little one." Xel cupped Lizzy's cheek, her touch warm and solid. "That moment has already passed."

Lizzy broke. She threw her arms around Xel, clutching her

as if she could anchor her here by force alone.

"I'm sorry," Lizzy sobbed. "I'm so, so sorry. This is my fault."

Xel wrapped her long arms around her, holding her as Lizzy shook with grief.

"It is not your fault," Xel said softly, stroking her hair, resting her chin atop Lizzy's head. "It was my choice."

Lizzy cried for a long time, but Xel didn't let go once.

Eventually, the sobs eased into shuddering breaths, and Lizzy's gaze drifted past Xel's shoulder. She froze. A city stretched across the horizon.

At first, she thought her vision was blurred. She blinked but realized the city itself glowed softly, edges shimmering as though seen through light mist. It was vast beyond comprehension, spread across a long grassy plateau that rose gently toward it.

Waterfalls poured from either side of the land or perhaps flowed upward, defying sense. Stone buildings rose like towers, smooth and gleaming, as if carved from porcelain and polished by time itself.

Lights moved everywhere. Tiny, living sparks drifted through the air like summer fireflies, weaving between buildings, gathering and scattering in patterns that felt purposeful… alive.

"What is this place?" she whispered.

Xel gently took Lizzy by the shoulders and turned her until they stood side by side.

"We are in the Borderlands," Xel said, gesturing to the grass beneath their feet. Then her arm swept upward, graceful and unhurried, toward the luminous city on the horizon. "And that," she added softly, "is Evnwyn—the Infinite."

Lizzy looked up at her, confusion knotting in her chest. Xel smiled, patient and kind.

"We stand between life and death," she said. She hesitated, as if weighing her words. "And that… is the life to come."

The meaning struck all at once.

"No," Lizzy said, panic flaring hot and sudden. "No—no, Xel. I won't let you. You can't go there."

Xel did not pull away.

"We all have a destined time to become citizens of the city," she said gently, lifting her free hand to brush Lizzy's cheek. "And this is mine."

Her thumb lingered, warm and steady.

"It is irrevocable," Xel continued, her voice calm, almost peaceful, "but it is not unwelcome."

Lizzy shook her head, tears spilling freely now. The city behind them glowed on, indifferent and eternal.

"Xel," Lizzy said as she began crying again. "I don't understand why this is happening."

"It's ok," Xel said with a smile. "One day you will."

Xel paused and looked off to the city. She let go of Lizzy and stepped towards it.

"Xel?" Lizzy said, clinging to her arm—afraid she was already leaving.

"I'm sorry. The city and its…my people, our people, are calling to me. I don't have much time to linger." Xel looked a moment longer towards the city, finding it hard to pull her gaze away. Finally, she turned back to Lizzy. They began to walk slowly through the field parallel to the city. The tall grass tickled her fingertips as they walked. "I understand things more clearly now."

A scary thought struck Lizzy. "Wait, if I'm here? Am I dying too?"

"No, little one," Xel said with a light, airy laugh. "You still have much time left in the physical Realms—many things yet to do with it. Your visit here is only temporary."

Lizzy's shoulders sagged with relief and sorrow all at once.

"When you tried to ease my pain," Xel continued, "we formed a connection. I pulled you with me as I crossed."

"How do I get back?" Lizzy asked, suddenly afraid of the answer.

"I will break the connection and send you home."

"Wait—" Lizzy said quickly. "Not yet. Please. Let me stay a little longer… with you."

Xel nodded, her smile soft and full. Seeing her like this, unburdened and joyful, felt almost unreal. This is how she was always meant to be.

"I don't know what to do next," Lizzy admitted. She stared across the wide plain, as if the swaying grass might offer answers. "If we survive… how do I find the sword? What do I do with it? How do I heal the world?"

Xel laughed gently. "Your questions are racing far ahead of the present." She rested a hand on Lizzy's shoulder. "Take one step at a time. Live through the process. Enjoy the journey and learn from it."

She turned, meeting Lizzy's eyes fully.

"Do you understand? Take what you are going through and use it. Turn sadness into conviction. Pain into power." Her voice softened. "But temper it all through your heart. That is your strength, Lizzy. You have an enormous heart. Do not let it burden you, let it guide you."

Lizzy nodded, swallowing hard. "I understand."

Together, they looked toward the glowing city. It radiated a peace so deep it ached. Lizzy felt the pull again—the wish to remain.

"You cannot stay," Xel said gently, as if hearing the thought itself. "I know it is tempting. But you still have much to do."

"I have to heal the world," Lizzy said quietly.

"Yes." Xel squeezed her hand. "And I have one favor to ask."

"Anything," Lizzy said without hesitation, turning fully toward her and taking her hand again.

"Watch over Leonydas for me," Xel said, brushing a loose strand of hair from Lizzy's face. "I fear he will seek revenge for my death. Do not let him surrender to anger; it will pull him away from what he is meant to become."

Her gaze lingered, full of trust.

"Promise me."

"Of course," Lizzy said solemnly. "I promise."

She hesitated. "What is he meant for?"

"Our people," Xel replied. "It is something we have worked toward for a very long time—to heal the many rifts between them and create a home where they may finally belong." She met Lizzy's gaze. "One day, he must become King."

Lizzy nodded. King Leonydas felt inevitable now, as solid as the ground beneath her feet.

"I will take care of him for you," she said quietly.

"I should not tell you this," Xel said, pausing as if weighing the cost. "But I see now that il'Thren is intertwined between the two of you. If you both choose it, you share a future of great consequence."

"Oh," Lizzy said softly.

"I do not tell you this for either of you alone," Xel continued. "I tell you because together, you will touch the lives of many."

Lizzy nodded, the serenity she had felt beginning to give way beneath the weight of what was being placed in her hands.

"I know it feels heavy, little one," Xel said gently. "But you are stronger than you know."

"Not as strong as you," Lizzy said, looking up at her.

Xel smiled. "Your heart makes you stronger. That is your gift." Her voice softened further. "When you need physical strength, look to those around you. That is theirs to give."

Lizzy nodded again, and the peace returned, settling into her bones. Xel leaned down and placed a long, gentle kiss on her forehead. It was warm and gave Lizzy strength.

"I am sorry," Xel said as she straightened. "But it is time for us to part—for now."

"No," Lizzy said, sudden and desperate. She stepped forward and wrapped her arms around Xel, holding on as tightly as she could. "Please."

But Xel's form was already drifting, unraveling like fabric caught by a rising wind—light, luminous, impossible to keep. She no longer belonged to the physical realms.

"Do something for me," Xel said. Her upper body remained in place, though the rest was drifting and fading. "I need you to give something to Leonydas later. When the time is right."

"Of course," Lizzy sobbed. Xel touched her forehead lightly, and Lizzy felt a piece of her drift into her body.

"Thank you….Lizzy."

"Goodbye, Xel."

Xel's form drifted away, caught in a rising breeze that carried her across the plain and into the great, glowing city. As she reached it, the lights flared, livelier, as if the city itself were welcoming her home.

Then, slowly, Evnwyn faded. The light dimmed, and the

horizon emptied.

Lizzy was alone in the Borderlands.

She sank to her knees and wept, the sound small against the vastness around her. A cool wind swept steadily over the plain, drying the tears on her cheeks even as more followed. She hugged herself, breathing through the ache.

Then she heard voices. Faint at first. Familiar. Lizzy lifted her head. The air shifted, carrying the sound more clearly now, still muffled, but close enough to stir something deep in her chest. She stood and turned slowly, listening, then began to walk toward them.

As she moved, the plain seemed to change. The grass rolled gently, rising and falling beneath her steps, or perhaps it had always been that way, and she was only noticing now. She crested a small rise. Below her, the land dipped into a small wooded hollow.

Between the trees, a couple walked side by side, shoulders bumping as they laughed. Lizzy's breath caught. She hurried down the slope and slipped behind a tree, peering out through the leaves. Her mouth fell open.

Ahead, perched on a thick branch that dipped low enough to sit on, was herself. Standing in front of her was Vic.

Lizzy stepped closer, hardly daring to breathe. She caught her foot on a root and hissed softly at the pain, glancing up in alarm, but neither of them reacted. Even when she walked openly toward them, they did not see her. She stood only a few feet away.

"You'll never guess who I heard from the other day," Vic said.

"Who?" the other Lizzy asked, smiling.

Lizzy gasped. Understanding struck her all at once. This was the past. This was the morning everything broke.

"Ashley. She texted me. Wanted to see how I was doing."

"Huh, that's strange. I haven't even heard from her in a while."

"Well, yeah, I'm a lot cooler than you are," Vic grinned. "Of course she'd text me."

"*I'm a lot cooler than you are,*" Lizzy mimicked him. "What are you, ten years old? Besides, I'm obviously cooler." Lizzy wrinkled her nose at him, and they laughed.

"Uh-huh, well, maybe she still thinks I'm hot, and wants to hook up again."

"Eww…gross, Victor! I do not need that picture in my head. I still have that time you two were making out in the back of my car while I was driving seared into my brain."

"Gross?" Vic said, feigning offense.

Lizzy nodded quickly. "Yep."

Vic grinned at her. He knew what he was doing. She struggled not to smile and then punched his arm. "Stop that," Lizzy said, before changing the subject. "So, how are things going at work. Still running circles around the other residents?"

"Of course," Vic said, still grinning. "I really love it there, Lizzy. And I have *you* to thank for it."

"Me?"

"Yeah, if you hadn't decided to 'save the world' that day on the beach, I'd probably ended up working in a grocery store or something, like my brothers."

"You put in all the work," Lizzy said. "Not me. You earned it."

"Sure, but still, thank you. You'll never know how much I appreciate it. I love you, Lizzy."

"I love you too," Lizzy said, beaming at him.

"No, I really do love you."

"Uh, yeah. Just like I really do love you," the other Lizzy said, shaking her head. She wrapped her arms around him and hugged him tightly.

Lizzy watched from only a few feet away, her chest aching with a longing so sharp it stole her breath. She wished she were the one in his arms. Wished desperately that she could step in, change a word, a glance, anything.

If only she had reacted differently.

"No…" Vic murmured, his voice low as he leaned closer. "I'm in love with you, Elizabeth Luna."

Lizzy recoiled as if struck.

"Stop," she whispered, though she knew they could not hear her.

Her other self pulled back, uncertainty flickering across her face. For a moment, doubt held, but then she saw it. The way Vic looked at her. Completely undone by love. Lizzy felt it then, too, crushing and undeniable.

"Vic—" the other Lizzy began.

Vic reached for her, slow and careful. His fingers traced up her arm before cupping her cheek. He smiled softly and leaned in.

Lizzy's breath caught. She knew this moment. Knew what fear would do to her. She almost ran over and stopped herself, but the slap echoed through the trees.

Vic staggered back as the other Lizzy shoved him away.

"What are you doing?" she said, raising her voice sharply.

"I'm sorry, but I had to tell you. I couldn't keep it from you anymore."

"No, you didn't. You didn't have to do this to me…to us. We are friends. Best friends."

"But we could be more," Vic said evenly. He was sure of his words, his feelings, and it frightened Lizzy even more.

"No. Absolutely not," Lizzy said firmly. Angrily. "Just put that right out of your head. You are not in love with me. You're just confused. Lonely." Lizzy panicked and searched for a way to hurt him. She scoffed. "Just horny probably. You probably *should* hook up with my sister and get it out of your system. She never could stop talking about how good you were in bed."

Vic paused. Blinking.

"Lizzy, come on," Vic pleaded with her. "Please don't do this. I'm sorry, I really am. It's just been building up inside of me...for years. You've had to have known. Everything I've done?"

"I thought that was because we were best friends. Because you loved me."

"Exactly. We are best friends, we do love each other, that's why we should be more. I want to live the rest of my life with you."

"What the—are you proposing now, too?" Lizzy said, her anger edged with confusion. She held his gaze, waiting for the moment to pass. It never did. His eyes were full of love unrequited, unrelenting, and impossibly sincere. "No, Victor. Stop this right now. I understand you are feeling something for me now, but you just need to let it go because I don't feel the same way. I don't love you, Vic. Not that way."

Vic's face collapsed. Tears flooded his eyes, though he fought them, blinking hard as if sheer will might force them back. He turned away from the other Lizzy and scrubbed at his face with the heel of his hand, quick and ashamed.

That morning, he had stared off into the distance like that just for a moment. Now, he was staring straight at her, the Lizzy standing unseen in the Borderlands, watching herself break his heart.

She had felt it then. The pain within him. Now she could see it. The fear in his eyes that he had ruined what they were. The pain of being rejected by the person he loved more than anyone else. The quiet devastation of realizing he had reached too far... and lost her.

Lizzy's chest caved in. She sobbed, pressing a hand to her mouth as grief tore through her anew. And then, like sunlight breaking through the long dark of a nightmare, it dawned on her.

She remembered.

Vic turned back to her, clearing his voice.

"It's all your fault."

The other scoffed. "What are you talking about?"

He smiled. Not his usual boyish grin but the smile of a man who knew his heart. "It's your fault that I fell in love with you."

"Vic, please don't—

"Wait, let me finish, and then I'll drop it. We'll go back to normal, like it never happened."

She swallowed. "Go on."

He drew a breath, steadying himself.

"It's your fault because you are... everything to me." His voice wavered, but he pressed on. "You make me laugh. We make each other laugh. You listen to all of it. You give advice I actually trust. You care about me in a way no one ever has. Except maybe my mom."

He smiled faintly, then lost it.

"You believe in me. Completely. You trust me without question." His eyes shone. "And the way you care for people, really care, it's not just your job. It's who you are. All heart."

He hesitated, then added softly, "And if all of that wasn't enough... you're beautiful. That silly little nose. Those freckles that look like they were painted just for me. The way your eyes don't just look at someone, they see them. See me."

He met her gaze fully.

"I love you, Elizabeth. I always will. And if you're not ready, if you can't love me like that right now—I'll wait."

Lizzy, both of them, stood frozen, her mouth slightly open, her heart pounding.

For one reckless moment, she had let herself imagine it, saying yes, kissing him, choosing the life unfolding right in front of her. It would be perfect. Warm. Safe. A future she could almost touch. But what if things went wrong? She would risk losing what they had, and she needed him in her life always. She couldn't lose him.

"Ok, Vic," Lizzy had finally responded, coldly. "I'm sorry, but just let it go."

"Got it, Liz-ard," he said, clearing his throat and forcing a grin. "It's still all your fault, though."

The other Lizzy had almost broken. Right there. So close. But she quickly turned her back on him and walked towards the park exit. Ahead, they spotted something. A man collapsed as he clawed at his chest.

"Goodbye," Lizzy said, as she watched them run to the man's side. She turned away; she knew what would come next. "Thank you, Vic," Lizzy whispered as she walked away.

She stepped out of the park's trees and back into the waving grassy plains of the Borderlands. She closed her eyes and sighed. She understood now.

She stood there for a long time, long enough that the world felt thin around her.

Then suddenly, she was falling. Wind tore past her, violent and endless. She squeezed her eyes shut as if that could stop it—and then there was nothing.

Silence. Darkness. And then weight. Xel's body lay heavy in her arms. Lizzy gasped and opened her eyes.

Xel was dead.

Around them, the battlefield still churned with blood, fire, and cries of pain. Her friends were still moments from dying. With shaking fingers, Lizzy reached into her pocket and pulled out the necklace. It glittered. Lovely flowers blooming in the middle of desolate ruin.

Lizzy lifted the chain and slipped it over her head. It settled against her skin, light. Her mind settled—it was as if something that had been missing her entire life had finally clicked into place.

She looked up and met Ashley's eyes. For a heartbeat, Lizzy thought her sister would stop her madness. Ashley's face relaxed into some sort of acceptance. But Lizzy understood it wasn't acceptance of her—it was that she realized she had lost. Ashley's face hardened. She removed a feather from her pocket and threw it up in the air, calling the Tar Gulls.

Lizzy bowed her head. She closed her fingers around the necklace and lifted her other hand high, palm open to the sky. This time, she didn't have to think. The healing had a life of its own. The Aetherwilde.

The air sharpened, alive with a clean, electric hum. Then the light came— not from the tattoo, not from the necklace, but from Lizzy.

It burst outward in a radiant wave, rolling across the battlefield like dawn breaking through storm clouds. As it touched each person, she felt them. She shared their wounds and their sorrow.

The Aetherwilde didn't control her; it partnered with her—letting her choose. She healed the living. Even two of the Nyrdin. She left the dead to their fate. She could feel the Aetherwilde within her, vast but not endless, and she portioned it carefully, restoring just enough to keep the wounded standing. Enough to keep them alive.

Fresita gasped as pain fled her body. Ruby staggered, then steadied, staring at her own unbroken hands. Mykayla sucked in a breath and laughed once, breathless and disbelieving. Leonydas only glanced at Lizzy before turning his attention to Xel's body. Tears ran down his face as he crawled to her.

Lizzy's skin glowed. Her hair lifted and stirred, brushed by invisible currents as the Aetherwilde flowed through her and into the world. It was not power, it was right.

As the wave of light stretched toward Ashley and the two remaining Nyrdin, Ashley lifted her hand. She stepped forward—smiling. At last.

Lizzy felt it then, the hunger in her sister's eyes. The certainty that this power was hers by right. Lizzy drew the light back. The wave recoiled like a breath sucked in too fast. She let the necklace slip from her fingers, and the glow vanished.

Ashley screamed.

Only then did the others see Xel. Mykayla was the first to reach her. She dropped to her knees beside the body and broke, sobs tearing out of her chest.

Ruby turned, and the world seemed to collapse in on her face. Grief crushed down hard, sudden and absolute. Rage surged up through her arms until they shook.

"No," Ruby whispered—and then screamed it.

She spun toward Ashley. Above them, two Tar Gulls swept low, already lifting the last of the Nyrdin away. Another angled toward Ashley, talons ready.

Ruby planted her feet and thrust both hands towards the sand.

Her voice slipped into a guttural grunt as she spat a word that tasted like blood and fire.

"Brandwrath."

A vast surge of sand tore free from the earth as if scooped up by an unseen hand. It hurled itself forward and ignited.

Not gold or orange. A furious crimson blaze erupted, veined with black and violet, burning inward on itself. The fire did not flicker or dance; it raged, compressing heat and fury into a screaming mass that turned sand to glass and memory to ash.

Ruby held her arms outstretched, trembling, as if her body were the maw of a dragon vomiting its wrath upon the world. The ground shook beneath the force of it.

Ashley barely had time to react. She threw up a shield, sand hardened into shimmering energy, but the inferno slammed into it before it could fully form. Flame curled around her, searing her skin, devouring her clothes. Her hair caught fire as she screamed and fell to one knee, clawing desperately at the blaze.

The shield cracked. Shuddered. But the Tar Gull arrived. Its talons closed around Ashley and wrenched her free, hauling her screaming into the air just as the flames tore through the space she had occupied.

Ruby let the fire die.

She screamed not in triumph, not in victory, but in raw, broken fury as she watched Ashley vanish into the storm-dark sky.

Lizzy and the others held on to Xel.

"I'm so sorry, Leonydas," Lizzy sputtered. "I wanted to save her, I really did. But she was already dying."

"I know," Leonydas said, wiping blood away from Xel's face. "I understand."

Lizzy sighed, and a great tiredness fell over her. She didn't think she had ever felt so tired. Her eyes fluttered shut, and she collapsed.

CHAPTER 18

There were no dreams this time, only rest. Good rest. The kind you never want to end.

Lizzy didn't wake once for fourteen hours. When she finally did, she wanted nothing more than to fall back asleep. Wherever she lay was the most comfortable bed she had ever known. Her head rested on a fluffy pillow, a soft, full comforter tucked around her. Warmth radiated over her—somewhere nearby, a fireplace roared.

Her mind was still wrapped in the comfort of sleep. It was one of those rare moments when everything felt perfect, like the embrace of someone you love.

It almost felt like the comfort of the Borderlands. But as the memory of them returned, it immediately began to slip away. The more she tried to hold on, the faster it faded. Only Vic remained.

It had been her fault. He had been right—but it had been his fault too. She had always known that, and she had always loved him just as deeply. The time they had shared would remain dear to her forever. The loss was still there, still aching, but it was different now. Pain, not poison. An accident that was not her fault.

But Tita, that was someone else's fault.

Ashley.

Lizzy sobbed, her fragile peace crushed beneath the weight of Ashley's betrayal. She had loved her sister so much. But Ashley had hated her enough to try to destroy her.

Lizzy curled into a ball, dug her fingers into the pillow, and screamed as silently as she could. Every muscle tensed painfully, her body trembling. She relaxed for a moment, then screamed again.

Eventually, her body sagged, exhausted. Lizzy whimpered—and froze when someone nearby made a sympathetic coo.

She turned her head.

Flo sat beside the bed.

"It's okay, cupcake," Flo said gently, resting a hand on Lizzy's forehead. "It will pass. It always does."

"I don't want it to," Lizzy said. The thought of what her sister had done no longer felt like sadness. It was changing into something else. Lizzy pushed herself up onto her elbows, her fists shaking. "I want to remember it. I want her to pay for what she's done."

"Liz, be careful," Flo said, her voice slipping into something more serious. "That is exactly what happened to her. Instead of facing her pain, she let it consume her. Like an infection she chose not to fight. It became a weapon she used against you."

Guilt crossed Lizzy's face. She refused to be that way. She refused to let her sister win by succumbing to the same fate.

She fell back onto the pillow, drained once more. She could have cried again, but she was tired of it.

Lizzy stared at the ceiling.

"So... what do I do now?"

"Continue your journey to Lady Betela," Flo said, smiling as her voice returned to its gentle lilt. "Your friends are waiting to go with you."

"Is everyone okay?"

"Yes," Flo said softly. "Thanks to you."

Lizzy knew it was true. She remembered feeling them, touching them through the Aetherwilde. Even after she had passed out, she'd sensed them nearby. Protecting her. Caring for her.

"I was with Xel in the Borderlands," Lizzy said, thinking of the one person who had not survived the ordeal.

"I know," Flo replied matter-of-factly. "She told me."

Lizzy turned her head sharply. "What do you mean—she told you?"

"She came to me earlier. She wanted to be sure you made it back safely."

Lizzy shook her head, giving Flo a baffled look.

Flo smiled. "Forgive me. I forget sometimes. The Fae realm and the Borderlands lie very close to one another. In my kingdom, there is a place, a thinning of the veil, that separates this world from the next."

"And you saw her? Spoke to her?"

"Eh... from a certain point of view," Flo said with a chuckle.

Lizzy laughed softly with her. She understood that in this new reality, she would never understand everything. And maybe that was okay. Maybe not everything needed an explanation. It was enough that it had happened.

Lizzy sat up and wondered if she had been taken to a log cabin. The room was small, barely wide enough to hold the twin-sized bed she had recovered in. Large, dark logs formed the walls, and thick planks stretched across the floor. Paintings of distant forests covered the walls, making up for the lack of windows. Yellow firelight flickered from dozens of candles scattered about, though they were overpowered by a small fireplace that crackled steadily. Across from the bed sat a narrow desk cluttered with paperwork and old books.

"Where are we?" Lizzy asked.

"Café Calacoayan."

Lizzy nodded. It must be the room Ruby had mentioned.

"I found the necklace," Lizzy said, touching the blossoms resting against her chest. It felt warm against her skin.

Flo beamed. "I knew you would. *She* knew you would."

"What happened to Tita and the Blossoms?" Lizzy asked. "She didn't become Lady Betela?"

"No," Flo said, sadness softening her expression. "It was a responsibility she did not wish to carry—one she felt was never meant for her. Truth be told, it was by chance that she found the sword. I believe the necklace now belongs to its rightful bearer."

"And now I have to find the sword."

"Yes," Flo agreed gently, "but not this very moment."

Lizzy nodded. "I still have a journey ahead of me."

"Yes."

Lizzy's thoughts drifted back to her sister and to what she had done.

"My sister got away," Lizzy said quietly. "She'll be back."

"She did," Flo replied. "You are right, you will need to be very careful of her in the future. I fear her pain runs too deep to be reconciled... or healed."

Lizzy frowned. That pain ran deep in her as well, still threatening to become something else.

"Do not fret," Flo said as she stood. She gently caressed Lizzy's cheek. "Your journey toward healing has only just begun. But you have already made significant progress. I do not doubt the future holds many tests, but also joy and peace."

Flo left the room, humming softly to herself.

Lizzy immediately removed the necklace and cupped it in her hands, staring at it for a long moment. It was beautiful and appeared delicate, though its weight suggested otherwise. The fine lines that shaped the flower's petals were darkened with age, touched by a soft patina. Yet every so often, they brightened, pulsing with a faint, humming glow. She hoped it would call her name louder now, but it remained silent.

Lizzy closed her eyes and relaxed. She could feel the necklace resting in her palm—not its physical form, but its energy. Its presence. It was diminished from before, drained by the healing she had poured into everyone on the beach, yet there was still much left. She would have to be careful with it until she found the sword.

A chorus of distant laughter pulled her from her thoughts. Lizzy glanced longingly at the pillow. It was tempting, but a hot cup of coffee from Calacoayan was even more so.

She washed up and soon headed downstairs into the familiar atmosphere of the coffee shop. She had barely stepped off the stairs when Mykayla rushed to greet her. Grinning, she wrapped her arms around Lizzy and squeezed so tightly she lifted her clear off the floor.

"Ack!" Lizzy grunted, then laughed.

"Are you okay?" Lizzy signed, looking Mykayla over carefully.

"Of course," Mykayla replied, giving her an indignant look. Then she rolled her eyes and touched her back. "Just a little sore. Thank you for healing me."

"Anytime," Lizzy grinned back.

Fresita suddenly pounced onto the counter beside them.

"Lizzy!" Fresita said, pacing back and forth. "You rested well?"

"Yes," Lizzy said, then paused, giving her a quizzical look. "But I thought you would be a fairy again."

"Not yet," Fresita replied, sitting down to groom her face. "Not until you recover the sworrrd."

Lizzy gave an apologetic shake of her head. "I'm sorry."

"It is fine," Fresita said, flicking her tail dismissively. "I will surrrvive. I am Maeve."

Lizzy happened to glance past Fresita. Ruby leaned against the counter beside Sean, who was busy taking someone's order. Ruby's eyes met Lizzy's—nervous, guilty.

"Give me a second," Lizzy said. "I need to talk to Ruby." She gave Fresita an unsolicited but clearly appreciated scratch under the chin.

Ruby straightened as Lizzy approached. Tears welled in her eyes, spilling free as her gaze dropped to the floor.

"Lizzy, I'm so sorry," Ruby said through her tears. "I was so angry about what she did to Xel. I wanted her to pay."

"Ruby," Lizzy said softly, opening her arms.

Ruby rushed into them, holding Lizzy as tightly as she could.

"It's okay," Lizzy said, returning the embrace. "I would have done the same."

"But she's your sister."

Lizzy exhaled slowly. "I don't even know if I can call her that anymore. What she's done… I don't know her now. Maybe I haven't for a long time. I think I was only holding on to a memory of who she used to be."

"Still," Ruby said, pulling back slightly. "I shouldn't have lost control like that. I'm so sorry."

"It's okay," Lizzy said, lifting Ruby's face so their eyes met. She held her gaze, meeting guilt with love. "There's nothing to forgive. But if it helps you—then yes. I forgive you."

"Thank you," Ruby whispered, then fell back into Lizzy's embrace. They held each other for a long moment before Lizzy kissed her cheek. Ruby pulled back, and Lizzy gently wiped the remaining tears from her face.

"So," Lizzy said with a soft smile, "you look like you could use a cup of coffee—stat."

Ruby sniffled, then grinned and nodded. She reached for a pair of mugs. She already had them ready.

"Are you off today?" Lizzy asked, glancing at her. Ruby wasn't wearing her apron.

"Uh… no," Ruby said, her smile flickering. "I've been temporarily suspended."

Lizzy blinked. "What for?"

"For engaging the Gateway for personal use," Ruby explained. "It's carefully controlled and monitored. If things don't happen according to schedule, they tend to get upset."

"For helping me."

"Yes." Ruby nodded. Lizzy's face fell.

"No, it's okay," Ruby added quickly. "I did what was right. I think that matters more than sticking to a schedule. I'd do it again in a heartbeat."

"But you love your job."

"It's okay," Ruby said with a shrug. Her knowing smile returned. "I needed a break anyway. Besides, this just means I can go with you on your journey."

Lizzy smiled and took a sip of her coffee. It was just as good as the first time she'd tasted it. She let herself settle into the warmth and familiarity.

Ruby joined her, and together they walked over to Mykayla and Fresita. Mykayla nodded toward the fireplace. Leonydas sat nearby, staring into the dancing flames. The two elves Lizzy had touched through the Aetherwilde sat close to him.

"Give me a moment," Lizzy said, setting her coffee on the bar.

She approached the elves, who immediately stood and bowed deeply.

"Lady Betela," they said almost in unison.

They looked different now—more like Leonydas. Their faces were fuller, ruddier, and stronger. One stepped forward and bowed again.

"We cannot thank you enough for freeing us," he said, his companion nodding behind him. "We were foolish to join with Cendryn."

Cendryn, Lizzy thought.

Ashley is gone.

"Once we allowed her to brand us," the elf continued, "we were lost to her control. When you healed our wounds, you freed our minds as well. We are in your debt. We are here to serve you."

Lizzy nodded, uncertain how to respond. She glanced toward Leonydas. The elves understood and quietly withdrew.

Lizzy went to stand beside Leonydas's chair.

"Leonydas," she said softly, touching his hand, "I'm so sorry about Xel."

He twitched, as if to pull away, but stayed still. Lizzy withdrew her hand instead. Leonydas finally broke his stare from the fire and looked up at her, as though noticing her for the first time.

"Liz… thank you," he said, blinking back tears. "I'm relieved she was there to save you. I'm very proud of her. She was—"

His voice broke, and he turned away.

Lizzy blinked back her own tears and leaned forward, wrapping her arms around him. He stiffened at first, long enough that she almost pulled away, but then he returned the embrace.

She wanted to linger there longer.

But after a moment, he gently let go.

"I promise her sacrifice will never be in vain," Lizzy said, touching his hand again.

This time, Leonydas covered her hand with his own and gave it a gentle squeeze.

"I will be the best Lady Betela…" Lizzy paused, awkwardly searching for a better way to finish. "…ever."

Leonydas chuckled, and Lizzy rolled her eyes at herself.

"I know you will," Leonydas said as he rose from his chair. Then, to her surprise, he knelt before her on one knee. Lizzy gasped.

"I promise to protect and accompany you on your journey," Leonydas said solemnly, "as you become the best Lady Betela… ever."

"We all do," voices chimed in from behind them.

Lizzy turned, taking in their faces—Mykayla, Fresita, Ruby, and the two elves standing together. Beyond them, a handful of café patrons lifted their coffee mugs in quiet solidarity.

"To Lady Betela," the group declared.

Lizzy spent hours with them afterward, asking questions about their world and marveling at their answers. It felt like sitting with Tita again—listening to her stories, then discovering an illustration in her sketchbook that brought them to life.

Eventually, Lizzy glanced at her phone. Galloway had messaged her, asking whether she was coming to the hospital to be with Vic's family. She exhaled slowly.

It had been hours since they had said goodbye to him. Hours since she had, too.

Now it was time to continue her journey.

"Okay," Lizzy said, clearing her throat as she slipped her phone away. She leaned forward, meeting each of their gazes in turn.

"So… where do we go from here?"

The End.

Lizzy's Journey Continues…

Acknowledgments

As I mentioned in the dedication, thank you to my parents. Thank you for exposing me to so much art. Thank you for reading the Hobbit to me and everything else. Thank you for giving me a foundation from which to grow.

Thank you to writer, illustrator, and concept artist Amelie Butkus for her beautiful and wonderfully imaginative illustrations. They bring Tita's sketchbook to life.

Thank you to the editors and readers who read early versions of *A Realm Of Healing*. Your advice and thoughts on the story were immensely helpful.

Above all, thank you to Maria, my beautiful wife. Without you, I would have never finished this book. Your love, caring, and cheerleading kept me writing. I cannot thank you enough for everything you have done for me. I'm so glad we have the rest of our lives for me to love and support you back. I love you so much!

Finally, thank you to the readers. I hope you enjoyed this story and that it connects with you in some way.

About the Author

Chris was raised in a small town north of Houston, surrounded by woods that felt like the edge of a forgotten magical realm. Certain that magic lingered between the trees, he has been searching for it ever since—now in the spaces between skyscrapers.

He lives in the Dallas–Fort Worth area with his wife, Maria, and four mischievous, possibly magical, cats.

Be sure to sign up for my newsletter to stay updated about the next story in Lizzy's journey!

cacampbellbooks.com

www.ingramcontent.com/pod-product-compliance
Lightning Source LLC
LaVergne TN
LVHW091658070526
838199LV00050B/2201